TAKEOVER

EDIE BAYLIS

Boldwood

First published in Great Britain in 2022 by Boldwood Books Ltd.

Copyright © Edie Baylis, 2022

Cover Photography: Shutterstock

A CIP catalogue record for this book is available from the British Library.

Paperback ISBN 978-1-80280-158-3

Large Print ISBN 978-1-80280-154-5

Hardback ISBN 978-1-80280-153-8

Ebook ISBN 978-1-80280-151-4

Kindle ISBN 978-1-80280-152-1

Audio CD ISBN 978-1-80280-159-0

MP3 CD ISBN 978-1-80280-156-9

Digital audio download ISBN 978-1-80280-150-7

Boldwood Books Ltd
23 Bowerdean Street
London SW6 3TN
www.boldwoodbooks.com

To Zach: my son, my world, my right-hand man and best friend
I love you more than all the stars

xx

PROLOGUE

1965

Ted Matthews stared at his wife, sitting sullenly in the floral patterned armchair. He understood Barbara's disappointment, but what else could they do, being as their daughter had been so lax as to get herself in the family way by a good-for-nothing layabout?

Ted smoothed his hand over his thinning Brylcreemed hair – a habit he'd always been prone to when tense or nervous. And, right now, he was both. Plus he was angry. *Really* angry.

They hadn't raised Linda to behave like this. She knew the rules, yet she'd broken them in the worst way. At fifteen, she couldn't even marry that piece of scum to save her reputation, either – not that he'd have sanctioned that in a month of Sundays.

Sighing, he glanced up at the ceiling of his sitting room and although the sound was muffled, he could still make out his daughter sobbing from the bedroom upstairs. Linda had been like that ever since the man had arrived to take the baby, yet she'd known it had to happen and that it was happening today. That's why Barbara had carefully spelt out to her time and time again not to get attached to the child.

Ted shrugged. It was the best thing all round. *For everyone.*

He yanked at the ring-pull of his can of Special Brew. It might only be 4 p.m., but he'd be in the pub by now for a well-deserved clocking-off pint if he hadn't had to take unpaid leave to sort this out. Still, at least it was done now.

He glanced at the thick envelope on the coffee table. *That* would go some way towards putting this right. Shame a part of it had to go to that scumbag, but if that's what it took to remove the fool from Linda's life for good, then so be it.

Ted's eyes tracked over to the carriage clock perched on the mantlepiece. That *thing* would be here any minute. Or he'd better be. He made it very clear in the message he'd sent what time Bedworth should be here, and the piece of dirt best not be late.

Grabbing the envelope, Ted counted out the amount he'd decided on and stuffed it into another envelope. He placed the smaller envelope on top of the sideboard, making sure he stuffed the larger one into a drawer.

Barbara's eyes burned into him the whole time and Ted bit back the urge to shout at her. She knew as well as he did there was nothing else they could have done. They weren't in the position to bring up another young 'un. Despite him being a hard-working man, they barely had enough to keep things together as it was, but everything they did have, *he'd* supplied – no handouts for Ted Matthews and his family, thank you!

Well, that bastard, Bedworth, wouldn't screw up his daughter's life any more and at least now Linda could carry on. There was no way she'd have been able to do that had she kept the child. It might be the 1960s, but women were still ostracised about this sort of thing and he wasn't having that. Not to his Linda. Nor to any of his other kids by association, either.

The sharp tap of the door jolted Ted from his thoughts and he quickly got to his feet. 'Right, let's get this filth out of our lives, shall we?'

Barbara wrung her hands, her heart already sinking with the prospect. She hoped Ted wouldn't lose his temper. She knew he was cross – they *all* were – but it didn't achieve anything.

She bristled as the figure of Thomas Bedworth sauntered into her small living room, his faded shirt looking scruffier than usual underneath his moth-eaten leather jacket.

'All right, Mrs M?' Tom drawled, a cockeyed smile plastered across his face. 'Linda okay, is she?'

'Don't you *dare* ask how Linda is, you prick!' Ted spat. 'You know why I summoned you here this afternoon, so don't start getting fly!'

'All right, keep your hair on!' Thomas smirked, sitting down uninvited in one of the armchairs. *Who did Ted Matthews think he was? Bloody royalty?*

'The child has now gone, so being as this business is over, I want you out of my daughter's life,' Ted barked. Despite promising himself not to give away any outward signs of rage, he knew his hands were visibly shaking, which irritated him further. 'I should have stopped this from the start, rather than give you the benefit of the doubt. I might have known you had no respect for my daughter.'

Barbara's hands twisted tighter in her lap. 'Ted, don't make a scene...'

'Make a *scene*? This waste of space gets our daughter pregnant, buggers off and then strolls in months later thinking he's the bee's knees! I'll give him the bee's knees! He's not fit for anything, let alone our Linda!' Ted spat, eyeing Thomas Bedworth malevolently.

'Your daughter didn't have a problem opening her legs for me, Mr Matthews,' Tom sneered. 'It takes two to tango, you know?'

Ted lurched across the room. 'You fucking little sh...'

'TED!' Barbara screeched. 'Stop this! This is supposed to resolve the situation, not worsen it!'

Breathing heavily, Ted stuck his finger in his collar to loosen it and rolled his shoulders. Red-faced, he stared at the sneering mug of Thomas Bedworth. 'I want you out of my house and out of my daughter's life, but firstly I want assurance that you'll never darken my door again. You will have *nothing* to do with this family in the future. Is that understood?'

Tom bit down on his bottom lip in false consideration. That was perfectly fine by him. He had no intention of seeing Linda again and certainly never planned to see the brat now she'd finally popped it out. As it was, it had taken him far too long to get in her knickers, and even then the event was a major let down – like shagging a corpse. And then after that once, the stupid bitch had gone all frigid on him. That once was all it took, yet *he* was the one being treated like a prize twat?

'Bear in mind that child is mine too and you have offered me no say about what has been arranged.' Tom eyed Ted carefully. 'I could take umbrage to that.'

Ted grabbed the smaller envelope from the sideboard. 'That's why I said you'd get plenty of reason to stay the hell away!' He chucked the envelope into Thomas's lap, not trusting himself to get close enough to hand it to the man. 'There's three grand in there. More than enough to make you fuck the hell off away from here, I presume?'

Tom blew through his teeth in appreciation. He knew a pay-out was on the cards. It was the only reason he'd shown up, but he hadn't expected *this* kind of brass. He could do a lot with this. *A hell of a lot.* What an absolute bonus.

'Take the money and promise me that you'll keep clear of my daughter.'

Tom got to his feet, grinned at Barbara and then at Ted. 'You have my word. I won't be going near Linda, trust me.'

'Your word, like you, means nothing, but I hope for all our sakes that you honour it. Now get out of my house,' Ted spat.

1

'And you think this is the best timing?' Gary Stoker looked at his father, then between each of his three brothers. His thick eyebrows furrowed. 'They won't appreciate being disturbed. Not today. It's a bit inconsiderate.'

Seb Stoker rolled his eyes. He wasn't in the best of moods, having been disturbed from a rare evening off, but after being called in for this impromptu meeting, all they were doing was procrastinating.

If anyone could find an issue with something – anything – it was Gary. Out of all of his brothers, Gary was always the one to flap, looking for problems that most of the time weren't there. The bloke should have been born a woman with his penchant for over-thinking.

He fixed his father with the same look the older man was giving all of his sons. 'Personally, I don't give a rat's arse if it's some bird's birthday. If something needs doing, then it needs doing. What I'm more bothered about is why we're giving Reynold the heads-up?'

'It's called mutual respect.' Mal Stoker pursed his lips and frowned. Still attractive even in his mid-fifties, his face was an older version of his eldest son's; hard lines, strong jaw and cheekbones. By a long shot, Sebastian was the most able of all his offspring, but then Seb had been raised to take over the reins of the business and inherit it in its entirety one day. However, if there was one thing he would change about his first-born, it was that hot temper and streak of impetuousness, which, if not kept in check, was detrimental.

'But if it wasn't for the Reynolds, we'd be numero uno around here rather than sharing that title, so why should we help them?' Neil griped.

Mal sighed. 'You're being short-sighted, all of you. Think about it. If what I've heard is correct, then whoever's running the Aurora is treading on thin ice.'

Mal didn't know anything for definite, but he got the distinct gist that these people at the Aurora were of a completely different mentality. He'd heard bad things about their recently opened hotch-potch of a club encompassing a dubious gambling den with fixed odds, along with a strip club and brothel. And the word had it their girls were treated unfairly, too – underpaid and not looked after. No one liked gaffs that treated birds like shit. Where he came from, that sort of thing wasn't the ticket.

Mal might, along with thousands of others, have come from a basic working-class background in a less salubrious part of the city, he might have had his fingers in several pies and lived on the other side of the law, but he had his morals and didn't take kindly to anyone who possessed none – especially when it came to women or kids.

Seb sighed loudly. Pulling his cigarettes from his pocket, he lit one, slowly exhaling a curl of smoke. 'The Aurora is a bag of shit and could never be a threat to any of us on the strip.' He cracked his knuckles absentmindedly. 'From what I've gathered, it's a bunch of no-hoper Northern gypwacks trying their luck, that's all. They'll amount to fuck all.'

Mal smiled coldly and folded his arms across his still well-built, muscular chest. 'Very probably, but what none of you are taking on board is that any interference, however fruitless, is still interference and interference upsets the equilibrium.'

In fact, Len Reynold was the person Mal had aspired to be, and it had been mainly down to close watching of how Len had achieved his station that had prompted him to follow suit. He'd watched from the wings as Len had risen from a mere runner in one of the city firms, to running his very own firm and owning his own gaff by the age of twenty-eight.

Len's firm had quickly gained pace and trampled all but a handful of the other firms in the city. Mal had seen enough to know this was what he wanted too and he'd achieved it, but he'd always made sure he stayed to his own territory and didn't encroach on Len Reynold's patches. That way they co-existed with little hassle and no bad feeling.

Being seven years younger, he'd missed the gravy train of the flourishing black market at the end of the war, which Len had used as a means of a stepping-stone to the city firms, but by keeping in the shadows, he'd learnt a lot regardless.

Mal looked around his nicely equipped office at the back of the Royal Peacock – *his* casino – and nodded to himself in silent acknowledgement. Both he *and* Len had done all right for them-selves. 'As I've said, I have a mutual understanding with Reynold where the Orchid and its subsidiaries are concerned. We don't tread on each other's toes and we get the same respect in return.'

Seb tapped his ash into the large crystal ashtray in the centre of the round table. 'That's as maybe, but I...'

'It's prudent to act on small hints rather than assume they

belong to the seventy-five per cent of stuff which never amounts to anything,' Mal interrupted.

'But to go out of our way to pal up with the Orchid?' Seb countered, not ecstatic that his father believed his logical processes so inept that he should need extra tuition like some backward kid.

Mal knew his boys would find speaking to Reynold about those clowns from the Aurora an issue, but they didn't understand. The new generation was a different ilk to those of his and Len Reynold's day. The Stokers and Len Reynold might well be rivals on the casino strip and were far from the best of friends, but they went back a long way. 'It's called manners,' he said sharply.

'Seb hasn't got many of those,' Andrew laughed, his mischievous green eyes, which all the Stoker men apart from Gary possessed, sparkling.

Mal placed his hands on the table. 'Reynold must be told what I've heard and I want him told tonight. If it were me, *I'd* want to know and I'm pretty certain he would do me the same courtesy. We may be rivals in business, but we're not fucking enemies!' He looked at each of his sons in turn once again. 'I'm not suggesting you drag him away from his daughter's celebrations. Speak to John Maynard. He'll inform Reynold, but our part will be done in a timely fashion.'

Seb sighed. 'Okay, you're the boss!'

Mal grinned. 'Yes, I am, so go to the Orchid. Tell Maynard what I've told you and that I want a meet with Reynold.'

Seb nodded and pushed his chair away from the table. 'I'd best go and get myself changed then.' He was still not convinced Reynold would be happy about him turning up to his daughter's birthday bash to say there was a bunch of saddos trapping off about muscling in on their jointly split patches, but there could be a silver lining... There would be lots of pretty women in the Violet Orchid and being as his evening off had been scuppered, he may as well see if he could make up for it.

* * *

Samantha Reynold picked up the new clip-in flower – the type she religiously wore every year on her birthday and one of many similar ones her father had bought for her over the years.

She studied the exquisite, hand-embroidered silk, its details exactly replicating the intricate pattern and form of the flower. The perfectly shaped, lighter coloured petals and sepals positioned behind the darker central lip and throat showcased the splash of yellow stigma in the centre beautifully. Green leaves surrounded the flower, framing the rich violets and purples of the orchid.

Clipping the flower into her hair, Sam smiled at her reflection in her bedroom mirror. It had been a good day so far. A lot of people would prefer to not have spent their birthday at work, but she loved her job. A graphic designer for a small but on-trend design shop in the centre of the city, she enjoyed the creative and varied work.

She'd relished the recent fact-finding trip down to London for her latest project – a store front and rebranding for an eclectic interior design company on the King's Road in Chelsea. The meeting with the company's creative directors had gone well and the best part was that they'd loved her ideas.

She hoped to open her own design company eventually and, the way things were going with her work portfolio, that day might not be too far off. Plus, the money she would earn from this latest commission would put her just where she needed to move forward with that.

Of course, Sam's father would fund her business quicker than she could snap her fingers at. He'd been offering it ever since she'd first qualified, but Sam wanted to achieve it herself. And much as it would be easier to let her father bankroll the whole thing, it was important she was the one to make it happen. Her father had already done so much for her.

Like this place...

Sam gazed around the expanse of her balconied bedroom and beamed widely.

Although it had been sad moving from her small house on the outskirts of town, which in her early twenties she'd worked hard to secure a mortgage for, this place... well, in addition to being beautiful, it was perfectly located, so she'd reluctantly but gratefully accepted the offer of living in the sought after, newly developed regeneration around Gas Street Basin. Her father had purchased the gorgeous apartment in the Symphony Court shortly after its completion earlier in the year and it afforded her the luxury of city centre living, plus it was within walking distance to work. It was also on the doorstep of a plethora of restaurants, bars and entertainment venues. She even had her own balcony overlooking the canal waterway.

Yes, it was all good: her new apartment was amazing and work was getting busier and better every day, but tonight she wouldn't think about work. She would put her all into the party waiting for her at the casino – the party that was so important to both of her parents.

It was a bit of a long-standing family joke. Every year since she could remember – from a toddler, right up to now at thirty years old – she had been 'surprised' by a party in her honour. When Liam had phoned, suggesting drinks before dinner, she'd had a good inkling they wouldn't be going to dinner or drinks at all, but to her father's casino like she did every single year.

Sam clearly remembered all the parties her father had thrown for her – like the one for her thirteenth birthday. All her friends from school were invited and they'd all been allowed a *proper* drink from the bar for the first time. It might have only been a purpose-fully watered-down half-filled flute of champagne, but how grown-up had she felt, dolled up in her best clothes, sipping from the crystal-clear glass?

That party was the talk of the school for *months* afterwards. How lucky she was to have a father who owned a casino and how cool her family was.

But the party she remembered most was her eighteenth. That was the night her uncle was killed. Not that she was aware of that until the next day.

As well as the sadness of Uncle Jimmy's death, it had broken her heart to think her parents had managed to go the whole night of her party hiding their pain – her mother from losing her brother and her father from losing his best friend – purely not to spoil her evening. Her parents were the best and she felt blessed to have been so lucky, but she wasn't stupid. She had a good idea what her father did behind the scenes of his shiny casino. Not everything, but a lot more than her mother did. There was more going on there than a bunch of shiny roulette tables and immaculately dressed croupiers. But did it bother her? Of course not. Her father was her father and always had been. He'd been the one to give her piggy backs; the one to dry her eyes and make her feel like the most special person in the world. He'd been the one to cheer her up when she'd been sad, given her something to aim for, and he'd also given her the greatest gift of all – the ability to believe in herself. Sam hoped now she'd reached the big milestone of being thirty that she'd achieved that well and once she'd fulfilled her dream of owning her very own design business, her life would be perfect.

Hearing the intercom buzz, Sam glanced up. *That must be Liam.* Taking one last glimpse in the mirror, she grabbed her clutch bag and rushed through the door.

Getting into Liam's Audi, Sam smiled. 'It would be quicker to walk, you know? The Orchid's only round the corner.'

Liam grinned, his eyes sparkling. 'Yeah, but your father insisted. You haven't forgotten this is supposed to be a surprise?'

Sam laughed with delight. 'Of course I haven't!' It was so silly. Everyone knew that she knew, but who cared? It never stopped it being any less special.

It was less than a minute before Liam pulled up outside the Violet Orchid. He reached across and squeezed Sam's hand. 'You look stunning.'

'Thank you,' Sam said, hastily moving to open the passenger door.

Liam was another story. She knew her father was hoping they'd become more than good friends because he liked the man. *She* liked Liam too, but there was something missing. Okay, so they'd shared the odd night together in the past and Liam had made no secret that he'd like their relationship to move that way on a permanent basis, but Sam was happy enough on her own and wanted it to stay like that.

Throwing his keys to the parking attendant, Liam placed Sam's arm through his as they walked up the steps to the entrance.

'Evening, Miss Reynold, Mr Taylor,' the doorman nodded as he held open the large doors to the reception area.

Smiling, Sam walked across the plush carpet to deposit her jacket with the cloakroom attendant and glanced at her reflection in the mirrored panels of the casino reception.

Not bad for thirty, she thought with an impish smile.

The slinky cream satin dress she'd chosen for the evening accentuated the shape of her slender figure and set off the dark waves of her hair perfectly, the long glossy tresses cascading halfway down the criss-cross strap detail of her backless gown. She gently touched the large three-carat centrepiece diamond of the necklace resting perfectly against the hollow of her neck – another of the presents her parents had handed her this morning.

'Ready?' Liam grinned, his hazel eyes twinkling as he nodded towards the double doors, the usual hustle and bustle of the casino unusually quiet. 'Remember to look suitably surprised.'

Sam arched one eyebrow. 'As if I wouldn't...' She readied herself as Liam pushed the heavy double doors open.

2

Standing to the side of her husband, Gloria Reynold smoothed down the dark pink skirt of her tailored suit and fidgeted. She eyed the array of perfectly dressed, young and beautiful women surrounding them and hoped she didn't look like mutton dressed as lamb.

Never one for the limelight, over the years she'd made a consistent effort to take a back seat where her involvement in Len's casino was concerned, only ever venturing into the glitzy world her husband frequented when she really had to or when it was important for *him*. She'd been there when he'd first opened the Violet Orchid, and although it had been a huge source of pride that Len had progressed so well with his business to warrant purchasing a casino by the age of twenty-eight, this world of fancy clothes, big spenders and over-confidence was as far removed from what she found comfortable as it could be.

However, even Gloria's crippling nervousness of being surrounded by all these people so vastly different to herself could never do anything to dilute the love and pride in the man she'd married.

She studied Len's side profile as he towered above her; his concentration honed on when their daughter would burst through the doors. Devilishly handsome, even at sixty-eight, he cut an impressive figure in his tailor-made tuxedo, his physique still remarkably good.

Gloria had never dreamt a man such as Len would have been interested in her. Growing up in Erdington, they'd lived in the same road of back-to-back terraces. Len was good pals with her older brother Jimmy and a frequent visitor to their little family home.

It was only when she reached twelve that she'd developed a private fascination for the dapper, confident and grown-up seventeen-year-old Len had by then become. At twelve, the difference between her and someone of seventeen or eighteen was immense. Plus, after working odd jobs for local firms, both Len and her brother had progressed into something called 'runners'. *Proper* jobs, not errand boys for the local butcher or anything like that.

Gloria never knew exactly what runners were because both Jimmy and Len always stopped talking whenever she was in earshot, but whatever it was, her parents hadn't been too happy about it. She remembered the many earbashings Jimmy received from their mother about his line of work.

Her mother had changed her tune somewhat when Jimmy began bringing home more money in a week than their father earnt in a month and, soon after that, Gloria noticed her parents found themselves more accepting of her brother's trade.

Throughout all of this, Gloria successfully managed to keep her fascination for Len to herself. This was probably best, being as her brother and Len attracted a constant stream of older girls – girls a lot prettier and more grown-up than her.

Gloria smiled to herself as Len placed his arm around her and gestured towards the waiting photographer. She hated photos and had never been particularly photogenic – so her mother had always liked to say – but turning, she reluctantly smiled for the press.

No, her fascination for Leonard Reynold had started over half a century ago and hadn't waned since. She'd been unable to believe it when, after she turned sixteen, Len had suddenly asked her to the pictures. Gloria had been convinced it was a wind-up. Flushing crimson, she'd looked around for a bunch of Len's mates, including her brother, to jump from their hiding places and laugh hysterically at her gullibility for thinking it could ever be a remote possibility that someone like *Len Reynold* would be interested in a shrew-like boring person, such as *her* – Gloria Maynard.

But Len *was* very much interested and within the year they were married. Not only were they married, but with Len's fantastic earnings, they'd even bought a house – only a tiny one around the corner from her parents, but they'd bought it all the same. Everyone else she knew – every single person – rented, yet they *owned* theirs.

On top of this, Len was progressing fast in the firm he worked for. He'd done well, as had her brother.

Gloria never asked too much about what they did – that was men's business. All she knew was, as well as being gorgeous, kind and funny, Len loved her and treated her like a princess.

After ten years, Len had his own company – his very own business, with her brother Jimmy as his right-hand man. He'd even risked every penny they had buying a building in the city centre. It was a rundown dump of a place, but within a year and a lot of hard graft, it was a fully-functioning, sparkling casino – the very one she was standing in right now.

Len's firm and casino had gone from strength to strength and his business empire had expanded fourfold. Len had been one of the youngest men ever to own such a fabulous club and had set the precedent for the area, spawning several other casinos and clubs to spring up around him. But the Violet Orchid was by far the most glamorous, popular and successful one in the city.

Of course, they'd bought a bigger house, the first of three, and with money being no object, Gloria used her time organising the decoration and furnishing, which she enjoyed immensely. But this day was the most important. It was this day thirty years ago when her life had become complete – the day that marked when her darling daughter had arrived.

A flicker of sadness passed over Gloria's face. It was also the twelfth anniversary of the day that her rock of a brother had died.

Suddenly hearing hushed whispers, Gloria knew Samantha was about to appear. Clutching onto Len's arm, she stood in readiness.

'SURPRISE!' the chorus echoed, along with a cacophony of exploding party poppers, flashbulbs and the sudden thumping of music.

Gloria smiled, watching Sam making her way over the thickly carpeted floor of the casino towards her. Tears pricked her eyes. Sam was wearing the flower – the orchid – those flowers that marked her birthday and the club's namesake.

'I can't believe you've done all this!' Sam smiled, enclosing both her parents in a hug, her beautiful face lighting up with a wide smile. 'It's perfect. Thank you!'

'Happy birthday, sweetheart,' Len said, planting a kiss on his daughter's forehead. 'How does it feel to be thirty?'

'Old!' Sam laughed.

'A photo of all three of you, please?' a photographer asked, gesturing in Sam's direction.

Len, Gloria and Sam turned towards the camera, flashbulbs exploding as other photographers bustled into place to catch the moment.

Len kissed Gloria on the cheek. 'I'll be back shortly.'

'Where are you going?' Gloria asked, her fingers itching to keep hold of his tuxedo sleeve. 'It's Sam's birthday.'

'John needs a quick word, but I won't be long, I promise.'

Gloria watched Len stride towards John Maynard standing at the brightly illuminated bar before turning her attention back to her daughter.

* * *

Tom Bedworth shoved the remains of a microwaved burger into his mouth as he left the late-night café. He could have really done with something more substantial, like his usual egg and chips. This place wasn't skimpy on the chips and they always chucked in some bread and butter as well, but tonight he had a thirst on, so he'd just grabbed something to go.

Skirting around a couple arguing on the pavement, he haphazardly crossed the road at the Horsefair roundabout, narrowly avoiding getting clipped by the back end of a double-decker.

Reaching the other side of the road, he hesitated, contemplating whether to return to the Aurora first. Shrugging, he continued to the Gun Barrels. *The Aurora could wait.*

Yanking open the stiff door of the pub, Tom walked into the tap room, his ears immediately assaulted by the raucous chatter and tinny music blasting from the jukebox.

Grinning, he sauntered up to the bar. 'Evening, Dave. The usual, please.'

Dave pulled a pint glass from a shelf under the wooden bar and held it under the Carling tap. 'Back again?' he laughed. 'Thought you'd called it a night when you buggered off nigh on half hour ago.'

'Nah,' Tom winked. 'Just needed some grub. I'm only having a couple more and meeting Jock. Is he in yet?'

'Jock? No, not yet,' Dave replied, placing Tom's pint on the brass drip tray.

Picking up the pint, Tom scowled as he leant in a pool of lager on the sticky bar top. He pulled his cigarettes from his pocket and glanced around. It never hurt to keep his eyes open for suitable contenders. He needed a good range of women for the punters to choose from. They couldn't all be oriental birds and that was all Jock had managed to get on the books so far. They might be as cheap as chips, but he wanted variety – *choice*. Classy birds, too. He wanted to provide just as much eye candy as the places he would shortly be wiping off the map.

But wasn't that what, amongst other things, he paid Jock for? To sort the wheat from the chaff and make sure that side of the business ticked over nicely? That had been the point of looking the man up again, hadn't it? To help put his plan into motion?

But on the whole, everything was going well. Despite being off the scene for three decades, Tom found his native accent flowed without having to try too hard and it had been pleasantly straightforward digging out the word on the street.

It had been a bit of a gamble after all this time. Birmingham was a big place, but picking this side of town was purposeful. His flutter had paid off and it hadn't taken long to locate people he knew of old who were still in the business. Some he'd been able to accost for favours and others he'd pulled in to work on his behalf – like Jock Sawyer, which enabled him to quickly step back into the game. It was amazing what flashing the cash did around these parts, and he had enough of that – at least at the moment.

Now he'd established a good supplier, he could encroach on some of the better-known dealing patches. That part was most important because it was a vital stage of his game plan, which was already well underway.

Tom's eyes glistened with excitement. After all this time – all this bloody time of sitting on his hands waiting for enough time to pass since the first fuck up, it had finally arrived. *This* time he was not ballsing up. *This* time there would be no mistakes and he would get a *proper* pay-out. He would not be ripped off again. Furthermore, he would recoup every single penny of interest he would have accrued had he been given his proper dues in the bloody first place.

This time he would take *everything*.

3

John Maynard tried really hard not to let the resentment seep out of his brain onto his face. He didn't know why he was even bothering passing the message on because Len wouldn't be interested. Not today, anyway. Nothing could *ever* take precedence over his cousin Samantha's birthday. It never had done and never would. Even if the world was on fire, it would have to wait until her birthday was over.

He looked at Len and scowled inwardly, seeing his concentration fixed through the one-way glass panel of the office overlooking the main casino area below, no doubt on his daughter. 'I thought I should let you know straight away, even if you decide it's not worth considering.'

Len reluctantly pulled his eyes away from Samantha and slapped John on the shoulder. 'No, you were right to tell me. I was just thinking...'

John pursed his lips. *Thinking about whether Samantha's champagne was chilled enough?* That would be the first thing he would do when he finally got the reins to this place. No more birthday bashes for Samantha Reynold. *Ever.*

Len eyed John sadly. 'I'm also aware that as well as Sam's birthday, it's the anniversary of the day your father was taken. I don't know whether I've ever told you, or whether you'd guessed, but that's partly the reason I keep these birthday bashes going.'

John swallowed hard. He hadn't expected that, and an unexpected lump formed in his throat. 'I...'

'Let's have a toast!' Len walked to the drinks cabinet and poured out two shots of whisky, handing one to John. 'Here's to Jimmy's memory – my best pal – and to my girl, Sam.'

'Cheers,' John muttered, chucking the whisky down his throat.

Len placed his now empty glass on his desk. 'Now, tell me more about this message from Stoker.'

'There wasn't a lot said. The eldest son came in,' John sniffed. 'The aloof bastard – you know the one? He said Mal wants a meet ASAP. Something to do with the Aurora?'

Len frowned. 'The what?'

'That casino, doss house – whatever it is that's opened down the arse end of the Hagley Road.'

Len raised his eyebrows. 'Oh, I heard something about that. What the hell have they got to do with anything? They're hardly encroaching on our doorstep, and from what I've heard, aren't likely to either.' He grinned. 'I don't think we need to worry that any of our customers will favour there instead of here, do you?'

John shrugged. 'No, I don't, but it seems they're getting fly by sending out scouts to tout their business on our patches, as well as on the Stokers'. Word is they've been threatening runners.'

Len's eyes narrowed. '*Our* runners?' No one threatened people on his payroll apart from *him* and then only with good reason. His staff from the bottom to the top were equally important to him and always had been.

John shook his head. 'Not as far as I know, but I'm planning on finding out.'

Len nodded. 'I'll put in a call to arrange the meet with Stoker.' He glanced back down over the casino. 'We'll keep this to ourselves for now. I don't want anything spoiling Sam's night.'

John nodded resentfully. Of course, *nothing* could be allowed to spoil anything for Samantha... Besides, it was hardly likely anything would be mentioned to her anyway. She had fuck all to do with this place and never would.

Still looking down over the main casino, Len frowned. 'Is that him? The Stoker boy?'

John walked over to the glass and peered down, seeing Sebastian Stoker leaning against the bar like he owned it. 'Yeah, that's him. Arrogant bastard. I told him to take a drink, though. Thought it only right.'

Len nodded. 'Yes, good. It never hurts to have manners and he had the decency to bring the message. Right, I'd best get back down there before Gloria strings me up for disappearing on Sam's birthday.'

* * *

Tom laughed loudly, Jock's joke about the monkey tickling him no end. He slugged down most of his latest pint in one go, some escaping his mouth and spraying over his open packet of pork scratchings.

Finally catching his breath, he wiped his eyes with the back of his hand. 'Fuck me, Jock. That's a good one. I'll have to remember that.'

Jock Sawyer grinned. The joke wasn't even funny, but it didn't take much to make Tom laugh – not when he was in this state. But then Tom's unexpected return to Birmingham was a bit of good luck. After recently having his hours cut from the Rover factory in Longbridge, it had been a godsend when Tom offered to recoup his diminished wages with a few nice little earners.

It was just like the old days, except this time around Tom had gone up in the world with his gaff on the Hagley Road. All Jock had to do, apart from test-ride women – which was never a hardship – was filch some business from the pushers in certain patches.

He'd been surprised at the cut Tom was offering – it was a decent wedge. *Easy money.* That was until he'd cottoned on to *whose* patches were required. But it made little difference to him as long as he didn't get dragged into it.

Jock eyed Tom, unsure how much of this the man would remember. 'Getting back to business, we've made headway with two of the patches you wanted.'

Tom signalled to the barman for another pint, then, closing one eye to reduce the three copies of the ashtray swimming around his blurred vision, stubbed his cigarette out. He smiled, pleased to hit the target. 'That's good to hear, Jock, good to hear. Keep on with it and ramp up the pressure. This is just the start.'

Jock's face grew concerned. 'The firms know we're treading on their toes. Word is they're putting the feelers out. Their runners must have reported back our threats.'

Tom flapped his hand. 'You mean, *your* threats? Ah, but I know you won't let any of that old bollocks bother you.' He made to slap Jock on the shoulder, but his drunkenness caused him to miss and instead whack Jock in the chest. 'Hard as nails you are, Jocky boy!'

Jock grinned. *That much was true.* He wasn't a soft touch and doubly good with his fists and, come to mention it, any other weapon that came to hand, but there was a limit. 'You're stepping on the Reynolds' and Stokers' toes here, Tom,' he said cautiously, his voice guarded.

'Fuck Stoker and Reynold!' Tom yelled, his hand veering his pint in the air, lager slopping on both the table as well as Jock's arm.

Jock glanced around uncomfortably. *Was Tom trying to get them both killed?* 'Keep your voice down, mate,' he hissed. 'We don't want any undue attention.'

'They're not all that, you know,' Tom slurred, his voice still full volume. 'I could tell you a few things about them fuckers that would make your hair curl.'

Jock tried to smile, but failed. There weren't many people around here that didn't know exactly what either of those firms would dish out when needed. 'Shall we make tracks?' he suggested. 'We can discuss this another time.'

'Nah, I wanna stay here. I've got a new pint on the way.' Tom swung his head around to face the bar. 'Come the fuck on, Dave! Where's my bloody drink?' He groped around the table for his cigarette packet. With fumbling fingers, he took out another cigarette and lit it. 'Yeah, them lot... Fucking phonies, that's what they are.'

Jock stiffened. 'Tom, I really don't think y...'

'Cuckoos!' Tom roared, grinning widely as his fresh pint was deposited on the table.

'What are you talking about?' Jock frowned.

Finally Tom found the sense to lower his voice. 'One of them lot isn't one of them lot, if you get my drift?'

Jock sighed, getting frustrated. 'Tom, I haven't got a clue what you're going on about.'

Tom grabbed Jock's shirt. 'Mention that next time you put the pressure on the runners. Their bosses won't want folk to know that one of their kids isn't their own.'

Jock sat back astounded. 'Which? Who?'

Tom grinned, a trail of dribble hanging from his mouth. 'Never you mind, but just let it be known that everyone will learn of it if we don't get what we need.'

Jock sat back. *Tom really was far too pissed.* 'How the fuck do you know this?'

Tom cocked one eyebrow and smiled slowly. 'Because, my man, one of those fuckers bought my kid and a shit price they paid for it too.'

4

Seb leant casually against the shiny, black, marble countertop of the bar. He didn't need to check that he hadn't inadvertently placed his arm in a pool of spilt beer or champagne because the attentive bar staff ensured any spillage was immediately wiped up. The place was spotless!

He had to take his hat off to Reynold – this place was the dog's danglers. Although it was years since he'd ventured inside the doors of this rival casino, it was the business since its most recent overhaul.

That wasn't to say his father's place wasn't both sumptuous and glamourous – it was, but everyone knew Len Reynold refreshed his décor on a five-year cycle, making sure all the fixtures, fittings and upholstery were top notch, up-to-date and displayed no signs of wear or tear. And it showed. Never having diverted from the original colour scheme of purple, black, silver and white, the place oozed class on every level. It looked good. *Really* good.

Seb raised his bottle of beer to his lips and assessed the admiring glances he was receiving from a healthy number of women around the large room. The talent here was hot, too – no one could argue with that. He grinned at a slender woman with the deepest auburn hair. It was refreshing to see new faces instead of the familiar selection at the Peacock. Not that anything was wrong with the women at the Peacock, he might add. Both his father's and Reynold's clubs had a reputation across the whole city for their beauties, but the ones in the Orchid were a most welcome change of scenery.

Seb was now glad he'd been the one to deliver the message. That part had been straightforward enough. With his morose face, it hadn't been difficult to spot John Maynard. Admittedly, in the handful of times Seb had met him, he'd never had much time for the man, but despite the bloke being miserable beyond words with the added impediment of abruptness, at least he'd had the good grace to offer a drink on the house, so credit to him and Reynold for that.

Aside from his reticence to give Reynold and his firm a heads-up with the word on the street, Seb also knew it was prudent to stay on cordial terms. Which included Maynard. It was common knowledge Maynard would eventually take over the running of the Orchid from Reynold and, being as his own line for taking over the Peacock was assured, it would be *him* dealing with Maynard at some point in the future.

Signalling to the barman for a refill, Seb continued scanning the room, his eyes stopping suddenly on a brunette. This one was *stunning*. A real show-stopper.

Feeling his throat tighten with the vision of the woman's figure-hugging cream dress slithering to the floor, his teeth pulling at her lacy underwear, Seb took a lazy swig of his beer. *Nice. Very nice...*

Seb grinned as the woman turned, her eyes meeting his across the expanse of people. *She'd seen him.* She must be able to sense his interest and she wasn't looking away either. *Game on...*

Placing his bottle on the bar, Seb tugged at his cuffs, making sure they protruded from his jacket just enough, and was about to make his way over when another man approached the stunner and placed an arm around her shoulders.

That was Reynold.

Seb frowned. It wasn't like Reynold to flaunt a bit on the side. The man was well known for being true to his wife, everyone knew that.

Wait. Holy fuck! That wasn't Reynold's bit on the side, that was his daughter!

Seb's heart geared up a notch. Samantha Reynold had clearly changed a hell of a lot since he'd last seen her. Although it must be over ten years, if not longer, since he'd last seen the girl, he didn't remember her being so drop-dead gorgeous.

He watched Sam listening to whatever her father was saying and decided he'd make his way over to wish the girl a pleasant birthday regardless. After all, it was only polite and he was nothing if not polite. At least, when it suited him.

Seb's plans were cut short when the music suddenly dropped and the voice of Len Reynold boomed through the vast array of speakers.

'Good evening, ladies and gents. It gives me great pleasure to welcome you to the Violet Orchid in celebration of my daughter Samantha's birthday. I also have an announcement to make…'

Seb leant against the bar and picked his beer back up, intrigued to hear what Reynold was going to say. Then, after the man had said his bit, he'd resume the plan to re-introduce himself to that damn fine-looking daughter of his.

* * *

Sam inwardly cringed with embarrassment as her father spoke into the microphone. She glanced at her mother and raised her eyebrows, only to get a confused shrug in return.

Taking his place by Sam's side, Liam whispered into her ear, 'What's all this about?'

'No idea,' Sam replied. It was unusual. In all the birthdays she'd had here, her father had never taken the mic. And there was a surprise too?

Excitement bubbled. Trust her father to do something on top of the party. He never ceased to amaze her.

'Hey, maybe he's got you a cake with a hunky, six-foot, male stripper inside?' Liam laughed. 'Although why would you want that when you've got me?'

Sam was glad she couldn't respond to Liam's comment as her father's voice continued, the volume drowning out further ability for conversation. Would she need to have *that talk* with Liam again? The one about being better off as friends?

Suddenly, she felt horribly nervous. *Oh God, this wasn't anything to do with Liam, was it?* He hadn't arranged with her father to propose or something equally dreadful? Nerves fluttered and gained pace, causing a sudden urge to run from the room.

Stiffening, she watched Liam from the corner of her eye for an indication he was about to be handed the microphone, then drop to one knee... Oh, he wouldn't do that to her, would he? Not in front of all of these people? *Please don't let him do this*, she chanted silently.

Feeling an intense stare burning into her, Sam glanced back across the room, seeing the man leaning against the bar. She'd noticed him a few minutes ago and although too far away to see clearly, it distinctly felt like she knew him from somewhere. Try as she might, she couldn't put her finger on where or how she recognised him. There was something very striking and unusual about him – unnervingly so – and he was *still* staring at her. Almost peeling away her layers.

Unnerved and slightly uncomfortable, Sam turned back to Liam, fleetingly wondering whether she should ask if he knew who the distinctive stranger was. Thinking better of it, she instead smiled up at her father and joined the rest of the crowd eagerly waiting in anticipation for his words. As long as her father wasn't in cahoots with Liam for an ad hoc and awkward marriage proposal, then any announcement or surprise would be acceptable.

Seeing her father beckoning for her to join him, Sam frowned.

'Come on, Samantha. Come up here a moment,' Len's voice boomed through the microphone.

Sam reluctantly climbed the steps up the raised dais to join her father and stared at the sea of people in front of her. She blushed, her legs becoming shaky, her comfort in the limelight only slightly better than her mother's. *What was her father going to do?* At least Liam wasn't rummaging in his pocket for an engagement ring, so thankfully it looked like that theory was unlikely.

'I think most of you here tonight know how special my gorgeous daughter is to me,' Len said, looking first at Sam and then at the crowd. 'It's a family tradition to host these parties for Sam's birthday – the most important day of mine and my dear wife Gloria's lives,' he continued. 'But tonight I'm breaking tradition by doing some-thing that isn't usually done in my line of work...'

Sam frowned, utterly confused. *Break tradition?*

Len smiled widely and turned to Sam. 'I'm so very proud of you, my darling. You've proved yourself more than capable of everything you set your mind to do and so...' He turned to Gloria. 'Even my wife doesn't know about this, but I know she'll agree... I've made the decision that when I retire, Samantha will take over the business.'

At this, a collective gasp went up, followed by a round of loud applause. Sam blinked several times in succession. *What had he just said?*

'Congratulations, Sam, my dearest!' Len continued. 'But don't get too excited. I've got no plans to step down and don my pipe and slippers for a long time yet!'

A good-natured laugh resounded from the crowd, then turned into another round of rapt applause and cheering, along with flashes from every corner of the room as the press captured the moment.

Len hugged Sam and kissed her on both cheeks. 'I wanted to give you something extra special as a surprise for your thirtieth, sweetheart. I hope it pleases you.'

'Thank you so much, Dad,' Sam muttered, not knowing what else to say.

'Champagne on the house for everyone!' Len boomed, garnering another wild cheer and round of applause.

Unable to stand it any longer, Sam hurried from the dais and made her way back to Liam, who greeted her with a glass of champagne. Taking the drink, panic set in.

How could she inherit this casino and her father's business? She didn't want it! She had her own business planned. No, no, NO! Why would he do this? She knew nothing about this sort of thing.

'Wow, Sam,' Liam cried, making sure he took the opportunity to slip his arm around Sam's waist. 'That's amazing! You must be so pleased!'

'I never expected it, that's for sure,' Sam replied, hoping the smile on her face looked genuine.

Such was Sam's shock, she failed to notice the expression on John Maynard's face or that the tall stranger who had been intently staring at her over by the bar had disappeared.

5

Leaning back in his leather desk chair, Mal inhaled deeply and stretched his back to relieve the tight pain in his chest, the ache spreading up into his neck.

He massaged the back of his neck with his thick fingers in a bid to reduce the discomfort, but it was to no avail. This horrible suffocating pain was occurring more and more frequently, no doubt triggered by the recent stress.

Mal frowned. He didn't want a two-bit outfit such as the Aurora attempting to step on his toes and interfering with anything to do with his casino. Not that he knew much about the place, short of, by all accounts, it was one of those seedy, shitty places with few morals and even less organisation.

'Are you all right, Dad?' Gary asked, his face awash with concern, watching his father's face twist with pain.

'What? Oh yes, yes, I'm fine,' Mal replied, relaxing a little as the discomfort started to ebb away. 'Just tense, that's all.'

'You should see a doctor if you're having problems,' Gary continued, ignoring the warning looks from Andrew and Neil.

'Since when does anyone need to see a quack because of a bit of fucking stress?' Mal barked, knowing he was getting on the defensive, but he couldn't and *wouldn't* let on to any of his sons that he was worried over the increasing amount of breathlessness and pain. He didn't have time to be ill – not while random scrotes were digging around his patches. 'And where's Sebastian?' he snapped. 'I wanted the lowdown on what happened at the Orchid. Did he call any of you last night?' He frowned at the general shake of heads around the room.

'Seb probably pulled and is still otherwise engaged!' Neil winked in Andrew's direction. 'I know I would have!'

'I think you'll find that wasn't the reason for my attendance,' Seb said bluntly as he walked into his father's office, shutting the door loudly behind him. 'Although there were many delectable ladies present, I was distracted by what I heard...'

Mal folded his arms. 'I'm not interested in idle gossip. All I want to know is whether you got my message to Reynold. Are we having a meet or what?'

Seb eyed his father carefully. 'Yes, message delivered to Maynard. He said he would pass it on.'

'I take it you didn't see Reynold yourself?' Mal asked.

'I saw Reynold, but not to speak to. He was too busy...' Seb continued, amused.

Mal sighed. 'If you've got a point to make then just bloody make it, will you?' he snapped, rubbing at his neck once more.

Seb grinned. 'This "idle gossip", as you so succinctly put it, is that Reynold has broken with tradition by making his daughter heir of his business.'

A heavy silence fell in the room, the men exchanging surprised glances.

Mal rolled his eyes. 'Where did you hear this pearl of wisdom?'

'Reynold himself.' Seb raised one eyebrow cockily.

Mal sat back in his chair and rubbed his hand across his chin in confusion. 'Reynold has handed his business to his *daughter*? Are you sure?'

'That's what he said and, being as he announced it over the mic, it was pretty clear. A birthday surprise for Samantha, apparently.'

Mal shook his head in bemusement, then his eyebrows knitted together. Reynold only having the one kid, the girl, wasn't much use where firms like theirs came to pass, so it was always assumed Maynard would inherit the reins when it was time. 'Reynold is retiring?'

Seb shook his head. 'Not any time soon. He made that clear.'

Andrew blew through his teeth. 'Well, that will be a turn-up for the books, if it ever comes to pass that is. I wonder what Maynard thinks about this?'

'From what I saw, he wasn't best pleased, but it's no skin off our nose,' Seb grinned. 'In fact, the sooner Reynold retires, the better. If a woman with no experience of the industry is holding the reins, we're bound to increase our sway. For us it will be a win-win situation.'

The shrill bell of Mal's desk phone punctuated the general mumblings. Picking the receiver up, he motioned his sons to silence. 'Malcolm Stoker. Oh, hello Len...' He glanced up, all four pairs of his sons' eyes now watching intently. 'Yes, that's right... of course – that's fine with me... Yep, sure... Okay, I'll see you then.'

Replacing the receiver, Mal smiled. 'That's the meet arranged. The day after tomorrow at eight.'

Seb nodded. Standing up, he moved to the door. 'Unless there's anything else, I'm off to get news on our latest shipment.'

Mal watched his eldest son leave the office and ignored the background chatter as the lively debate about how Reynold's decision was doomed to failure continued. Although Len Reynold must have his reasons for wanting his daughter in charge, Mal didn't know what they were. And to announce it yesterday, of all days?

As well as being Samantha's birthday, yesterday was also the anniversary of the drive-by that had killed Len's business partner, Jimmy Maynard – shot through the head at the traffic lights near the Five Ways roundabout. He'd been driving Len's car to pick up Samantha to bring her to the casino for her eighteenth birthday. No one *ever* drove Len's Daimler, apart from Len.

Nobody claimed the shooting and nothing else followed either. There seemed to be no connection to Jimmy, Len or the casino and the general word was that it was a mistake, but Mal wasn't so sure.

Although feared, the Reynolds were respected and well-liked. The only person to gain from Jimmy's removal was his son and John Maynard had quickly stepped into his father's shoes, becoming Len Reynold's new right-hand man. It became clear to all that he would inherit the spoils when it was time, but now had that changed?

* * *

Sam stared out of the window along Corporation Street. Even though the window of her office was on the first floor, the angle of her desk allowed her a decent vista all the way up towards the junction with New Street and she absentmindedly watched executives, shop workers and shoppers making up the steady throng of people milling about, going about their business.

Approaching midday, it was getting busy, and with a jolt Sam realised she had achieved very little today, despite having arrived at work early. Her attention kept diverting from the job in hand to something – *anything* – that needed no questions and no answers.

Forcing herself to turn back to her large screen, she stared at the graphic she'd been working on, confident it had been perfect, yet now there was something not right with it. *A bit like several other things...*

Grabbing her mouse, Sam selected the background image of her graphic and played with the opacity levels. *Still not right...*

Shoving her mouse to one side in frustration, she fought against the urge to drag her fingers through her carefully styled hair. How could she concentrate with what had happened?

If her father announcing she was to inherit his business was supposed to be a surprise, it certainly had been. And not a good one. What was the point in working on anything if the dreams of her design business were futile? Her father's gift of passing his business to her was a death knell for her hopes.

Sam sighed, hoping last night her face hadn't given away her true feelings. She thought she'd concealed it well enough, but how long could she keep that up? She'd never been anything but honest with her father, but now she was being forced to pretend this change in circumstances pleased her?

It was no good. She would have to break the news to him. As much as she appreciated the sentiment, not to mention the honour that he thought her capable of running his business, the plain truth was, she didn't want it.

Sam's heart was and always had been set on reaching the top of her game in the graphic design industry and she was very nearly there.

Her face fell. She didn't want to hurt her father or appear ungrateful. Both her parents were fantastic, but whether she liked it or not, she just *couldn't* take up this offer. Aside from her heart not being in it, she knew nothing about that side of things and furthermore, didn't particularly want to...

But her father would be upset – his gesture was meant as an honour. Sam knew enough about his business to know that handing the reins to a woman was not the done thing – that's why she'd never spent a second's thought thinking it would ever be something put on her. And that had always been a relief.

Sam reached for her mouse and was about to attempt further manipulation of the graphic when her phone rang. She irritably snatched up the receiver. 'Sam Reynold.'

'Hello, beautiful!' Liam said brightly. 'Fancy a spot of lunch? We can go to that nice deli place you like up Temple Row? I'll meet you at...'

'I can't do lunch today,' Sam interrupted, her tone sharp. As much as she wanted some fresh air, she couldn't cope with Liam gushing about her good fortune.

'Oh...' Liam's voice was thick with disappointment. 'Are you busy with meetings?'

'Just busy!' Sam snapped. Now she had to explain why she couldn't do lunch? Liam was not her keeper and never would be. Belatedly realising she was being unfair, she softened the blow. 'I'm running behind on a work deadline.'

'Ah, okay. I understand,' Liam said, placated. 'How about after work then? Dinner?'

Sam inwardly sighed. It wasn't like she could tell him of her concerns regarding her father's expectations. He wouldn't understand. Liam would probably love to be in her shoes, but sadly that wasn't an option. 'I'm sorry, but I really haven't time at the moment. I've got things I need to sort out,' she said, trying desperately to keep the irritation out of her voice.

'What could be more important than having dinner with me?' Liam pushed, a mischievous note to his voice.

'Like I said, not tonight. Look, I've got to go. We'll catch up soon, okay?' Quickly replacing the receiver before Liam could continue, Sam frowned, her skin tingling with annoyance.

Liam was getting full on with his attentions again and she could do without the hassle – especially now.

Reaching for her bag, Sam slipped on her jacket and left her office, locking the door behind her. Since she'd been promoted, she'd moved from the open-plan layout to a separate office. At first, she'd missed the chat and bouncing ideas off her colleagues, but now she welcomed the silence and lack of distraction. Well, she *had* until this latest incident or when the phone rang with Liam on the other end...

Pursing her lips, she slipped down the corridor to take the stairs to the reception area and the street outside; for now, all she wanted was fresh air.

6

Tom lay face down in his bed, his head thumping with a vengeance. He groped around on the bedside cabinet, happy to find a half-full can of Tennent's Super. *That would do nicely.*

Gingerly propping himself up against the headboard, he winced at the warm, flat beer. Tom dragged the back of his hand across his mouth and sparked up a cigarette, balancing the overflowing ashtray on the duvet.

He glanced at the clock. Almost midday already, although that was hardly surprising, considering he'd had very little sleep last night.

Tom's forehead creased like a concertina. Unfortunately, the reason for his lack of sleep wasn't down to anything interesting, such as a woman. By rights, with the amount of beer he'd put away last night, he should have been in a coma, but that hadn't happened either.

Which way next to move with his plan was the thing that had kept him tossing and turning. Now he'd set the wheels in motion with Jock putting about the rumours, he needed to progress that, but who should he start with?

Tom took another long swig of warm beer. It was a genius idea bringing both Stoker *and* Reynold into the conundrum. He knew how prats like that worked – full of ego and kudos. Both men would rather saw their own legs off than have unsavoury rumours circulate about them.

Tom grinned. Yes, he could pull in double the wedge doing it this way, rather than twisting the blade in just one of them.

If he'd only been paid a fairer price in the first place, then there would be no need for this. Neither would he have spent the last thirty years simmering about being turned over.

Three grand? Three piffling grand was all he'd got. Three grand in exchange for such a prize? Not that he'd wanted it, but that wasn't the point. It was the *principle*.

Okay, so that three grand had enabled him to carve out a life for himself up north. It had been enough to get nicely set up with his little business enterprises, but had he known at the time exactly who he was dealing with, then he'd have insisted on a payment of at least ten times that amount.

Tom grabbed the letter he'd painstakingly typed yesterday and reread it once again.

Yep, that would do nicely for a start. All he needed to do was to locate the correct address, and then once he'd got it, this would go straight in the post box.

This time, without fail, he would get what was owed.

The bustle, smell and atmosphere of the market momentarily freed Sam's mind from her present worries. At least once a week, more if time allowed, she loved spending her lunchbreak mooching around the colourful market.

Even the walk from her office did her the world of good. Passing along New Street, past the Odeon then turning right at the Pallasades, it was then down through the subway to St Martin's Church and the bustling market.

The smell from a small donut shop above the open-air market always made Sam's mouth water, delighting her with memories of when her father took her to the funfair as a child. She loved everything about the stalls full of fresh fruit and vegetables, rolls of brightly coloured material and vast arrays of clothes, along with every type of goods known to man and the market stall holders all clamouring for business.

Perusing a stall stacked high with sumptuous-looking fruit and veg, Sam eyed the large trays of strawberries.

'They're 30p a punnet, love,' the man smiled, busy bagging up oranges for another customer.

'Go on then, I'll have two please,' Sam said. 'And chuck in a banana and a couple of apples to make it up to a quid.'

'Making a fruit salad?' The voice came from behind.

Sam turned in the direction of the voice, stopping dead seeing it belonged to the stranger staring at her at the Orchid last night.

'Doesn't seem much of a celebratory dinner for someone set to inherit one of the city's most prestigious clubs – aside from my father's, of course,' Seb grinned.

Sam moved to one side, aware the stranger's lips almost brushed against her ear as he spoke; the sensation of his breath against the delicate skin of her earlobe creating an inward shiver rippling along the length of her spine.

She reached into her bag for her purse, praying the burning of her cheeks wasn't colouring them. As her fingers fumbled with her purse, Seb handed money to the stallholder and took the white carrier bag of fruit.

'You didn't need to do that,' Sam cried, flustered.

'Relax! It's only a quid. It's not like you're beholden to me!

Besides, you were holding the queue up.' Seb's manner was easy, but his aim was not. At some point in time, this woman would be his rival on the casino scene, so he needed to weigh her up and see how the land lay.

He bit back a smile, pleased his initial assumption looked correct. Having Samantha Reynold at the helm of the Orchid would make bringing the Peacock into pole position a lot easier. There would be no more sharing first place once she took the reins. It would be a breeze. She might be beautiful, but she didn't have a clue – that much was crystal.

Sam held out her hand to take the bag of fruit, refusing to allow herself to get defensive. Instead, she smiled sweetly. 'Thank you. That's very kind, Mr...?'

Seb raised an eyebrow. Was she playing him or was she so green she genuinely didn't know who he was? Didn't she know who her father's rivals were? Did she know anything at all? *This would be fun...*

'Stoker. Sebastian Stoker.' Seb gestured to move from the market stall away from the crowds eager to buy their fruit and veg. 'Shall we get out of the way?'

Reluctantly, Sam followed the man still conveniently holding her shopping and eyed his powerful frame as he approached a less crowded area away from the hubbub of the stalls. *Sebastian Stoker?* Was she supposed to know who he was?

Frustration simmered. The name rang a vague bell, but this was a perfect example. How could her father expect her to take over when she didn't have the first clue about who or what anything was in this business?

Regaining her momentum, Sam took a deep breath, refusing to show embarrassment over her lack of knowledge.

Just pretend he's a client, she told herself. She dealt with all manner of people in *her* line of work both competently and efficiently, so she would look at this the same way. She would not let this self-assured man make her feel stupid. *No way!*

'What brings you to the market today, Mr Stoker?' Sam asked, a smirk playing in the corner of her mouth. 'Thinking of moving into the fruit and veg trade?'

Seb laughed, but his green eyes remained remarkably cold. 'No, I don't think so... Not yet, at least. I'm on my way to see someone. By the way, did you have a nice birthday? We met a long time ago and I would have re-introduced myself properly last night, but you were busy...'

'Yes, thank you. It was a good night,' Sam lied. *Did he say they'd met before? When? Who on earth was he?*

'When do you think we will be seeing more of each other?' Seb drawled, a lazy smile forming as his gaze moved purposefully slowly over Sam's body. 'Will you be present tomorrow night?'

Sam faltered. *What was that supposed to mean? He wasn't making a play for her, was he?* 'Tomorrow night?'

Trying not to snigger at Sam's clear awkwardness, Seb grinned, his eyes twinkling with amusement. 'Were you not aware myself and my father have a meet planned tomorrow night with your father?'

Sam inwardly cringed. *Meeting? What meeting? No one had said anything to her. Whatever was it for?* 'I... erm...'

'I take it the answer is no,' Seb laughed. 'No worries, but I'm guessing that when your father retires, our paths will cross more frequently, being as we'll be in the same *industry*.'

The emphasis on the word 'industry' rapidly gave Sam the realisation she needed. *How had she been so stupid?* Stoker – Malcolm Stoker – she remembered now; the Stokers owned the Royal Peacock! Her father had mentioned this rival casino several times and she'd met all the Stoker boys a couple of times many years back.

Irritation bubbled at her ability of making herself out to be vacuous – just as, by the looks of it, this man presumed too.

Refusing to allow her mistake to colour the moment, Sam smiled graciously and reached to take the carrier bag from Seb's hand. 'My father's retirement will be aeons away, Mr Stoker. He's no intention of going anywhere for the foreseeable future, if ever! Knowing him, I think he'll still be working until the cows come home.'

Her fingers brushed Seb's hand as she took the bag and she ignored the tingle it left on her skin. 'Thanks again for the fruit, but I must dash. I've only popped out on my lunch break and I've got a meeting with an important client shortly. It's been nice to see you.'

'Likewise,' Seb said, admiring Samantha Reynold's pert backside as she hurried off into the crowd. She was a tasty piece all right, yet that made little difference. It wasn't like he couldn't have his pick of beautiful women. The only thing of importance here was Samantha Reynold's involvement in the business.

A grin formed across Seb's face. Yes, he'd have no worries making the Peacock's standing more prominent once old man Reynold was spending his time tending his garden. The only pressing concern now, along with the scrubbers from the Aurora, was how to hurry Reynold along in the direction of his dotage.

Checking his watch, Seb moved towards the subway, keen to see if his delivery was present, correct and ready to go.

7

Returning to the office, Sam placed the bag of fruit in the corner out of the glare of the sun streaming through the window. She slipped her jacket off and sat down, quickly bringing her computer back to life.

The break to the market had refreshed her ideas on the design she'd been working on, even if bumping into Sebastian Stoker has caused other problems to flutter within her mind.

It was a strange one. That man's closeness in the market, his breath on her ear... He exuded magnetism, power and supreme confidence, yet he'd been *laughing* at her.

Oh, she'd clocked his veiled, patronising remarks over her lack of knowledge, and it was both infuriating and unsettling.

Frowning, Sam dug her teeth into her bottom lip and found her gaze drifting through the window before shaking away the conflicting thoughts crowding her mind. Whatever that man thought made little difference.

That settled it. Once she'd spoken to her father and explained her position and reluctance to become involved with the business, he'd understand. Then there would no longer be any need to be in

Sebastian Stoker's presence in the future, nor would she need to put up with his mocking arrogance either.

With renewed enthusiasm, Sam set her desk phone to divert, then played with the graphic on her screen, her mouse expertly manipulating the image.

Leaning back in her chair, she studied the new version of the graphic and smiled. *Perfect!*

Her lips curled into a satisfied smile. She might know nothing about the type of business her father ran, but she knew *everything* about graphics and design.

It was only then that Sam noticed the letter placed on the side of her desk. She glanced at it then her hand on the mouse froze.

Chamberlains Estate Agents?

With a frantically beating heart, she ripped open the envelope and scanned the contents.

The letter was short and to the point and contained the words she'd been longing to hear. The property – a building she'd had her eye on for years and one she'd made many enquiries about on and off – had just come onto the market. As well as having the most wonderful gothic architecture, it was in a prime location – perfect for her own design shop. And they were inviting offers...

This was what she'd been waiting for. Any other time she'd be overjoyed to have received this news, but now... now it made everything worse and underlined why it was imperative to be honest with her father.

And the sooner she did that, the better.

With shaking fingers, Sam unscrewed the top of a bottle of water, biting the inside of her cheek with annoyance when her phone began ringing. *It was supposed to be on goddamn divert!*

She snatched up the receiver. 'Yes?'

'Hello, baby!' Len said. 'Don't blame the receptionist, I told her it was important and couldn't wait.'

'Dad!' Sam cried. 'Is everything all right?'

Len laughed. 'Of course! Why wouldn't it be? I'm just checking you're still on for dinner tonight?'

Sam paused, her mind whirring. *Shit! How could she have forgotten?* Every year, the day after her birthday, her parents took her for dinner. But she *had* forgotten. 'Erm, yes, of course.'

'Great!' Len cried. 'The usual place, okay? Me and your mother will see you there at eight. Bye love.'

Sam stared at the receiver long after the line had disconnected. Finally replacing it, she closed her eyes and inhaled deeply. It was no use. She would speak to her father tonight about his offer and just hoped he understood.

* * *

Walking across the canal bridge then over the busy square, Sam wished she wasn't wearing this pair of Jimmy Choos. They pinched her left heel something chronic, but as another birthday present from her parents, she felt obliged to put them on tonight.

The early evening sun shone brightly and people were taking advantage of the outside seating in the restaurants around the canal basin. Music played from speakers outside the eateries and although it was a Tuesday, it was busy with a holiday-like atmosphere.

Even with the nice temperatures and surroundings, Sam didn't feel in the least bit celebratory. She subconsciously put her hand on her red shoulder bag, the letter from Chamberlains steadily burning an imaginary hole into the leather.

Approaching the Italian restaurant, Sam spotted her parents immediately. She picked her way through the tables, glad they had chosen to eat outside, rather than in. The dread of the conversation she needed to have sat suffocatingly around her neck like a fuzzy winter scarf and being confined inside would make it even harder.

Reaching the table, Sam plastered on a smile as her parents got up. 'Hi Mum, Dad,' she said brightly.

'Samantha!' Gloria beamed, pulling Sam towards her for a hug.

'How's my beautiful daughter today?' Len kissed Sam on the cheek. 'Sorry for bothering you at work earlier. You know what I'm like. Always double-checking things.'

Sam laughed, despite her impending worry. Yes, she knew what her father was like – a stickler for details. 'It's fine, really.' It was only then did she notice John Maynard also seated at the table. 'John! It's nice to see you.'

Not exactly true, Sam thought, seeing John's frosty smile. Her older cousin had never been overly friendly and the concept of explaining her reticence about the business in front of him was hardly ideal, but what could she do?

Ever since she could remember, he'd treated her with thinly veiled contempt; looking at her in a way that made her feel like she shouldn't be there.

John obviously had never liked her for whatever reason, but why, she was unsure...

'Are you ready to order?' the waiter asked, pouring Sam a glass of her favourite white wine.

'We'll have drinks first,' Len said, flapping the waiter away. He waited until the man retreated before continuing. 'So, Samantha. How do you feel about my announcement? Has it sunk in yet?'

Sam swallowed nervously. *Now was the time...* 'I must admit, I hadn't expected anything like that, Dad. Not ever. I didn't think that would ever be on the cards.'

Len grinned. 'Ah-ha! Well, I believe in doing what I think will be for the best in the long run.' He grabbed both of Sam's hands. 'And this, I believe, is it.'

Sam's heart plummeted further. She stared at her father's face –
the one she'd relied on her entire life. 'I'm honoured, I really am,
but I don't know the first thing about your business. I don't think I'd
be any good at that sort of thing.'

Len's frown deepened. 'You're my daughter, aren't you? You can
do anything you set your mind to. Haven't I always told you that?'

Sam squirmed in the chair. 'Yes, but...'

'Len...' Gloria said sternly, her eyes firmly on her husband.

'Have you got any further with that design shop plan of yours?'
Len asked.

Sam hesitated, unsure why he was changing the subject, but
decided she had to tell him about her dream building. It was the
perfect inroad to broach letting him down. 'Well, I heard today
that th...'

'That the place you've had your eye on for years has unexpect-
edly come on the market?'

Sam blinked. 'Yes! How did you know?'

Len laughed. 'Because it's no longer available.' His face broke
into the trademark grin reserved only for his daughter. 'It's been
sold... Sold to me...'

'*You've* bought it?' Sam looked at her mother in confusion, only
to see her smiling widely too.

Gloria nudged Len in the ribs. 'Oh Len, tell her the whole story,
for God's sake!'

'I know how long you've had your eye on that place and also
know, from what your mother told me, it will be another few
months before you raise enough capital to purchase it. By then it
would be too late, so I've bought it for you!' Len said.

Sam couldn't conceal her shock. *He'd bought that building for her?
The one she'd always wanted?* 'But that doesn't make sense! How can
I run a design shop if you're expecting me to take over your busi-
ness? Look, I need to discuss th...'

Len laughed once more and tipped the remains of his wine into his mouth. 'Your mother has berated me all day for allowing you to think that's what I meant.' He signalled the waiter for another bottle. 'As I said, I've no intention of retiring. Certainly not while there's breath left in my body, but as well as showing the world how much I trust you, I wanted to get something down on paper for legal purposes.'

Sam smiled, her eyes filling with tears. 'Oh, Dad...'

'It's important the business remains in the Reynold name, but Sam, darling, it will be in name only, so you don't need to worry.'

Sam looked at her mother and then back to her father. 'But what does that mean for me?'

Len grinned. 'It means you won't have to do a thing! Once I retire, you'll have final sign off, but John here will oversee and actually run the place. He knows everything there is to know, don't you, John?'

John's forced smile failed to reach his eyes. 'I'd like to think so, being as I stepped into my father's shoes when the need arose and have been involved in the firm since I can remember.'

Sam tried her best to bypass the malice dripping from John's face. *Was her father saying what she thought he was saying?* 'You mean...?'

'You really think I'd want you to ditch what you've always dreamed of? All I want is to make sure the business remains under the Reynold name so that eventually, when I'm no longer here, you and your mother will benefit from what I've built.'

Relief poured through Sam like a sieve. She jumped to her feet and pulled her father in for a hug. 'Oh, Dad, thank you! That's wonderful, but as soon as I get the money through for that contract, you must let me pay you back for the building.'

Len held up his hand. 'I'll hear none of that! Call it another birthday present! You're my daughter, my only child, and I want to ensure you have everything you want. You wouldn't upset an old man, would you?'

Sam tutted, tears of happiness burning the back of her eyes. 'Dad, you really are incorrigible! What will I do with you?'

Len grabbed Sam's hand. 'Carrying on making me the proudest father in the world, like you always have, will do nicely!'

'Ah look, here's Liam. I was worrying he wasn't going to make it,' Gloria cried.

'Liam?' Sam glanced around, spotting Liam making his way towards their table.

'I thought I'd ask him to join us,' Len winked. 'That's my next plan... That you'll produce some grandchildren for me to spoil very soon!'

8

John Maynard pulled up in the Aurora's car park, his face screwing up with a mixture of contempt and amusement. His eyes tracked across the façade of the dilapidated building, which was in dire need of emergency repointing work. It looked like the bricks were held together by gravity alone.

His gazed moved to the large garish neon sign:

THE AURORA

That would have undoubtedly cost a few quid, even though it was bloody hideous. Whoever was trying their luck with this shit-hole should have prioritised that the building stayed upright before ploughing money into a sign.

Despite his bad mood, a chuckle escaped John's mouth. By God, this place really was a dump. If it was as bad inside as it was out, then he didn't need to go in to draw an opinion of it.

He reluctantly got out of the car. He'd promised Len he'd check the place out – covertly, of course. Even though the Orchid had no worries about losing its clientele to this place, they still needed to confirm if this was the gaff behind the attempts to muscle in on their patches.

When *he* took over the reins of the Reynold's firm, he wouldn't pussy-foot around with stuff like this. He'd simply raze any competition, relevant or not, to the ground. And as for Samantha... she would be having sod all to do with it. No say, no *nothing*.

His irritation at being dragged into dining with the Reynolds to yet again pander over Samantha's sensitivities gradually subsided. Christ, his whole life he'd put up with Len Reynold's devout dedication to that idiotic girl as well as the equally simpleton wife, plus he'd kept what he knew under wraps all this time... And that hadn't been for nothing...

Had Len not immediately made it known to him after Samantha's birthday announcement the other night that his intentions were still set to follow what he'd always promised, then he certainly wouldn't be entertaining any of this crap. He'd have just made the decision to do things his way instead. Thankfully, Len had enough sense to know Samantha wouldn't cope overseeing the firm. Even so, having to do this was another example of needless time-wasting.

It was bad enough he had to take it up the backside that the Orchid and the Reynold empire would, on the surface, be under Samantha's control, but that wouldn't last long. All he had to do was keep Len on side for now.

John smiled. After all the work he and his father had put into the firm, it was *his* right to inherit the lot. Darling Samantha and his bloody thick as shit Aunt Gloria would never see a penny. That would be taken care of at the first given opportunity.

He walked across the car park, cursing under his breath as his foot went in a large pothole, painfully bending his ankle. Outside lighting and a new surface for the car park was another recommendation.

Nearing what he presumed to be the entrance, although the

wooden door was shut, John stared at a propped-up bicycle and two young men, wearing dark hooded tops and ripped jeans, huddled against the side wall.

He squinted against the gloom of the night. *Mmm, classy... Not even attempting to hide their drug deals.*

Clearing his throat, John walked up the stone steps to the door and looked about him. How did anyone get into this dump? Was it even open? He glanced at one of the many front windows. It was impossible to tell if there were any lights on behind the thick curtains and wooden shutters.

'You have to bang the door, mate,' one of the hooded men shouted.

Nodding his thanks, John banged on the wooden door, surprised it didn't fall off. Receiving no response, he was about to turn on his heels and retreat to his car when the door was opened by a large man wearing an over-tight shirt and a leather jacket.

'Yeah?' The man looked John over with interest. 'You here for the women or the casino?'

Another laugh bubbled at the back of John's throat. *They were marketing this gaff as a casino? Were these people insane?* 'Not sure,' he muttered. 'I thought I'd see what's on offer.'

The man jerked his oversized head, which John took to mean he'd been granted admission and stepped over the threshold, the door closing loudly behind him.

'Sign in, will ya? The guest book is over there.' The man pointed to a blue camping table in the dark hallway.

John quickly scrawled a random name in the spiral-bound note-book with the BIC biro attached to it with a piece of string. *Like someone was going to nick that?*

Did he really have to do this? Surely he'd seen enough?

Morbid curiosity getting the better of him, he followed the hallway down to where he could hear music, loud talking and swearing. Approaching a large room at the rear, as dimly lit as the rest of the place, John stood in the doorway and stared.

Several tables overlaid with horrible green tablecloths housed a collection of unmatching chairs around them. Cards were being played on the tables, the men clearly the worse for wear, no doubt aided by the scantily clad women leaning over in what he presumed was meant to be a tantalising fashion to top up the drinks with whatever cheap but potent spirit was contained inside the large bottles they clutched.

Feeling an arm snake around his waist, John spun around, finding a young, rather tired-looking Chinese woman.

'You want play cards, sir, or want girls first?'

'Cards, I think,' John muttered, extracting himself from the woman draping over him like a cheap suit. 'Any particular table I should join?'

The woman stared at him vacantly with a fixed smile. English was clearly not her strong point, but looking at her, John wasn't sure whether she had any strong points whatsoever. 'I'll join this one,' he said, moving towards the nearest table.

'No, sir, you need deposit first,' the woman cried, pointing to the corner of the room.

Squinting into the gloom, John could just about make out a man sitting alone at a table with his back to the room. All that was visible was a steady stream of cigarette smoke coming from his direction.

Ah, it was one of *those* set-odds sit-downs. A minimum cost of fifty or a hundred quid, along with the classic rigged tables trick, he didn't doubt.

Making his way over, John shoved his hand in his pocket, pulling out a roll of notes. He'd have one sit-down, watch for contenders for who might be infiltrating the Orchid's patches and then get the fuck out of this dump.

'What's the price to join a table?' he growled to the back of the man's head.

Tom Bedworth took his time before turning around to deal with the new punter. It looked better not to jump to attention – he'd learnt that a long time ago. It made him look more upmarket and important.

'The minimum stake for poker is fifty quid, mate,' he mumbled, taking a big mouthful of house vodka before making the effort to look at this latest loser. Loser or not, he *would* be losing. Everyone did, apart from *him*, otherwise there would be no point running the tables.

Everyone knew gambling was a mug's game, yet they still all believed they had a chance. Silly fuckers. He smiled smugly. Yeah, he'd make a killing from this set-up.

John clenched his teeth watching the man pretend to be engrossed in his odds book and felt like chucking him off his chair. Whatever he'd promised Len, this place was full of fuckwits and this dipshit here was taking the piss. 'You the owner?'

Tom loved it when people asked that. Nothing was more bolstering than being able to say he was a 'club owner'. All of these years and it was finally true. He might have made a name for himself up north with his dealing and brothels, but now he'd finally got his club. And it had only just started. Soon, once he had done what was needed, he'd be well on the way to being the *only* person in this city worth bothering with. He'd finally get his dues in the place of his birth.

Puffing out his chest, Tom sipped slowly from his tumbler of vodka, then turned around. 'Yeah, I'm the owner of the Aurora. First visit here I presume, Mr...?'

John had to blink several times as the man's face became half-illuminated in the dim glow of the overhead lighting. *It couldn't be, could it?*

No. He'd left years ago and was never coming back.

Andrew watched from the doorway of the warehouse as the van was unloaded. Keeping one eye on the gates to the compound, he made sure Gary directed the runners to stack the boxes in the correct place. Seb would go tits if the gear wasn't put exactly where he'd specified.

He didn't know why he was bothering wasting a second thought on something so trivial, but Seb had been in such a foul mood when he'd returned earlier, he didn't want anything else setting him off. Why was it such a big deal if the other half of this order wasn't arriving until the day after tomorrow? Personally, he'd rather that than risk the authorities sniffing around. The Irish weren't due to collect it until after the weekend anyway, so it wasn't like it made any difference, but then this was Seb.

Seb always had to be in control. Over *everything*.

Andrew's forehead creased as he stared at his younger brother. Gary was an odd one – always moaning and on edge. It was a standing joke between the rest of them that Gary should have been a bird. The way he flapped about and worried about everything, anyone would think he *was* a woman. Not to mention that he'd always got an easy ride and special treatment from their parents – like he needed to be protected.

Andrew scowled. And then there was Neil... Why couldn't Neil do stuff like this? Neil got roped into hardly anything, so why was *he* sent here with Gary today, leaving Neil to lounge around the Peacock, chatting up the birds as usual?

And while he was at it, Andrew didn't like that Seb was meeting Reynold with their father tomorrow either. Okay, so as the eldest, Seb had more clout, but surely *he* deserved more inclusion with the stuff that went on? He did more collar than Neil or Gary put together, yet never got allotted any important jobs like Seb did, and he was getting fed up with the imbalance.

Andrew had even suggested going to the meeting too, but his father was adamant only two of the Stoker men were present. Why? Because Reynold didn't want to feel outnumbered? He doubted it. Reynold would probably have half of his lot present. That miserable sod, Maynard would be there, and perhaps the latest surprising addition to the Reynold fleet – the daughter?

As the final box was unloaded, Andrew watched the two runners clamber back into the Transit. Nodding to the driver, he waited as the van exited the compound, then stepped back into the warehouse, pulling the heavy sliding doors closed behind him.

He walked across to where Gary fiddled around with the last remaining box and sighed. 'What are you doing now?'

Gary glanced over his shoulder. 'Just making sure all the labels are facing out.'

Andrew rolled his eyes. 'Have you got OCD?' Pulling one of the boxes from the shelf, he placed it on a worktop and yanked the lid off, humming appreciatively. 'Decent ammo. Where did you say these came in from?'

Gary shrugged. 'I didn't. Seb didn't mention it either. Put that back now, we need to get going.'

Andrew felt the familiar rush of irritation and glared at the back of his brother's sandy-haired head, watching him fuss with the box on the racking.

Leaving Gary to double-check the warehouse doors were locked, Andrew made his way back to his car. Starting the Rover SD1, he revved the V6 engine impatiently. 'Come on!' he muttered under his breath. He wanted to get back and have a few beers.

Finally climbing into the passenger seat, Gary fumbled with the seat belt. 'Are you and Neil going to the Aurora tomorrow night or it is just you?'

Andrew pursed his lips as he roared off up the road. That was another thing. He didn't want to dig about on a load of low-life scouts. 'Depends on what comes off from the meeting with Reynold tomorrow. They may already have insights into who this two-bit firm trying their luck are.'

Gary nodded. 'But would they tell us if they did?'

Andrew's concentration fixed on navigating the Queensway at record speed, the trippy blue-tiled walls rushing past. 'Dad seems to think working together on this will be in all of our interests, so I'm presuming the point of the meeting is to share information and tactics?'

Not that *he'd* bother doing that if it was up to him. None of them apart from his father felt it relevant to aid the Reynolds. It was more lucrative to point whoever was causing the issues *towards* the Reynolds and let them get the flack.

Taking the right lane from the Queensway tunnel, Andrew scraped through the changing traffic lights and shot up the road, turning into Broad Street, glad to be back amongst the comfortable chaos of upmarket nightlife, the gold sign of the Peacock in view up ahead.

'I'm worried about Dad,' Gary said suddenly.

Andrew felt like slamming Gary's head into the window just to shut him up. 'What do you mean?'

'He doesn't look well. I think he should see a doctor.'

'He's fine,' Andrew scoffed. 'Extra stress makes him like that, you know what he's like. He'll be back to normal as soon as all this is sorted.'

'I'd prefer it if he got checked out,' Gary pushed.

'I wouldn't keep saying that in front of him if I were you. You know he can't bear fussing.' *And you're the worst fusspot of them all, Gary,* Andrew thought.

Pulling into the underground carpark of the Royal Peacock, Andrew nodded at the security guard and impatiently drummed his fingers on the steering wheel, waiting for the barrier to raise, then backed the SD1 into one of the designated spaces reserved for the Stokers.

Getting out of his motor, Andrew hurried towards the Peacock's staff entrance, making no attempt to wait for his brother.

* * *

John eyed Tom Bedworth malevolently. 'What have you fucked up this time?'

Tom clenched his jaw. 'I've fucked up nothing.' *Apart from everything.* But the first part of that recovery started *here.*

'I don't know what you think gives you the right to come in here trapping off, Maynard?' Tom spat. 'Let's not forget why I left Birmingham in the first place.' He stood up. 'I'll remind you, shall I? Shit information. *Purposefully* shit information. And we both know why that was, don't we?' he spat, bolstered at the flash of fear or shock – he couldn't decide which, in Maynard's eyes. *Maynard wasn't expecting that, was he?*

And that's why he was back. More than enough time had passed and if nothing had come back from Jimmy Maynard's death in twelve years, then it was unlikely to now. Furthermore, he had the trump card up his sleeve and because of that, John Maynard couldn't drop him in it without dropping *himself* further.

This fucker had done him up like a kipper in the hope of upping his own game, but it had backfired. *But not any more.*

Tom's face cracked into a smile. If Maynard wanted to quit being such an egotistical prick, then things could work out for both of them.

He slowly poured Maynard a glass of vodka – making sure he gave him the chipped glass with something nasty that no one seemed able to get rid of, stuck in the bottom.

Tom watched John Maynard peer suspiciously into the glass of vodka. 'Instead of acting like the big "I am", why don't you start by putting your cards on the table?' An easy smile slithered across his face. Whether Maynard liked it or not, he wasn't in a position to argue and the sooner he admitted that to himself, the better. 'You as well as I know what the score is. You can't afford for it to be known what you tried to engineer back in the day.'

He could almost see the rage bubbling along Maynard's veins and the urge to laugh out loud was so strong that for a moment he didn't think he'd be able to control himself. He took a long swig of his vodka. 'I know what you want – it's what you've *always* wanted, but I want *my* dues too, so I suggest we work together.'

John's face contorted, making a gargoyle look attractive. 'And why the fuck would I want to do that?' he spat.

Tom laughed – this time, loudly. 'Because, Maynard, you haven't got any choice and you bloody know it! But I suggest *this* time you work with me properly. I have a lot of things planned and if you play the game, then we both stand a chance of getting exactly what we both want.'

Tipping the vodka into his mouth, John slammed the glass onto the table and sighed loudly, knowing that unfortunately Bedworth was right. And that was worse than the creature at the bottom of the glass he'd just emptied. 'Get me another drink then,' he muttered. 'And a fucking fresh glass while you're at it an' all.'

9

Seb looked around Len Reynold's office, the large room beautifully furnished with antique pieces, a striking contrast to the huge modern window spanning the entire back wall, offering an unparalleled vista of Broad Street, its hotels, clubs and bars.

His father's office was top notch, but Reynold's window made this place something else. He'd like an office like this. *Maybe one day.*

Seb nodded his thanks as a sullen-faced John Maynard handed him a glass of finest whisky poured from a large crystal decanter. He glanced at his father and frowned, noticing him surreptitiously insert a finger in his collar to loosen it.

'Thank you for coming, gentlemen,' Len said, his steely eyes scanning the two Stoker men. 'Shall we get started?'

Mal took a sip of whisky. 'Yes, I think it's wise to work together over the reports we've had about attempts to encroach on our patches.'

He looked between Len and John Maynard. Not ever being a fan of Maynard, Mal would prefer dealing directly with Reynold, but the man had the right to have his second-in-command present. The very reason why he himself had brought Seb along to the meet.

'Where did you hear these people, whoever they are, are trying to muscle in?' Len asked.

Mal shrugged. 'Some of our runners have been threatened. I presume you've experienced likewise? Word has it that it's stemming from a recently opened place up the Hagley Road.'

Len nodded. 'After we got your message, we put the feelers out ourselves and yes, it seems we've had similar issues. I can't say I'm happy about it.'

'You and me both!' Mal agreed. 'I'm planning to send two of my boys to visit this Aurora place to see if we can discover anything further. It's imperative we nip this in the bud.' Feeling another sudden rush of searing heat to his chest, he loosened his collar once more, realising his brow was beading with sweat. Annoyance crept in. He didn't want to come over as nervous.

Len tapped his gold pen on the green leather inlay of his desk. 'I had John visit the Aurora last night. A veritable shit-hole by all accounts. Do you want to take over from here, John?'

Folding his arms, John looked directly at Seb. *If the guy thought he could intimidate him with his stares, well think again.* 'The place is a Grade A dosshouse, full of cheap whores and losers. Whatever their game is, they don't have a chance of infringing on either of our businesses.'

'That's as maybe,' Seb countered. 'But I don't think attempts to infringe the way they've been doing can be ignored.' He moved his attention to Len. 'We both have reputations to uphold and we, for one, will not stand by while these gypwacks take the piss.'

'I can assure you we allow *no one* to take the piss, Mr Stoker,' Len said curtly. 'Measures will be placed to ensure these jokers get the message. That's if this *is* something to do with them? We can't be entirely sure at the moment.'

'Do we know who owns the place?' Mal asked, sweat building on his back. He placed his glass on the desk, spotting his fingers tremoring. He glanced at Len Reynold, glad to see that if he had noticed, he wasn't showing it.

John shook his head. 'There wasn't anyone of importance there last night and I did a fair bit of digging. I got the gist that the owner doesn't come to site,' he lied.

Seb frowned, watching Maynard closely. More likely the miserable sod had spent his time being serviced by one of the crack-ridden whores he'd mentioned and even that hadn't put a smile on his bloody face. 'Then who's in charge?'

John returned to the drinks cabinet and picked up the decanter. 'Seems like a hotch-potch of wasters.' He held up the decanter, offering everyone a top-up. Seeing the shaking of heads, he continued. 'It could be the place is merely a front for other activities and the main man will emerge once things are in place.'

'Or it could just be a low-end punk trying his luck and not connected at all,' Len added.

'Well, there's not a lot to see, so I wouldn't waste your time going. There isn't anyone or anything there of interest,' John said firmly. He'd reiterated the same story to Len first thing this morning. It wasn't like he was going to tell him the truth because he was still processing it himself.

Thomas Bedworth should not be back within the city limits. Furthermore, he *couldn't* be. The prick returning after all this time was bad enough, but to be so ridiculously stupid to stir shit up with territories? Bedworth knew damn well who governed those areas, so what the hell was he playing at?

The man had to go and he had to go quickly before he got the chance to drop him in it and cause untold bloody damage.

John scowled. He could not afford for his place to be jeopardised. Certainly not now and certainly not by that loser – that loose cannon. He had to get rid of Bedworth before the truth came out. If he didn't leave of his own accord, then *he* would have to make sure that it was orchestrated so that Bedworth disappeared in a way that offered no link back to him.

Seb studied John Maynard with interest. The man knew he was being scrutinised, yet didn't hold back his obvious dislike for both him and his father. *Well, Maynard, the feeling is mutual, mate. Not that you figure.*

'I'm presuming you'll continue putting tabs out on whoever is bankrolling the place?' Seb questioned, his clear green eyes now on Len. 'Especially as you're planning on stepping down.' He purposefully moved his gaze to John, glad to see his words caused a nerve to twitch underneath the man's eye. 'I mean, it's not the best timing to hand the reins to a woman if shit is about to hit the fan.'

Irritation rankled at the base of Len's spine. He studied Sebastian Stoker. The man was clearly a force to be reckoned with – Mal Stoker had done well with this son of his, but the self-assured arrogance of the man needed to go if they were to join forces on this latest development.

He fixed his eyes on Seb. 'Firstly, Mr Stoker, I have no plans to retire any time soon, of which I'm sure you're aware, being as you were privy to my announcement. Secondly, my daughter is more than capable of handling things should the need arise.' *Not that Sam would have to, but that wasn't the point.*

Seb held his hands up in submission. 'I meant no offence, Mr Reynold, and I'm very glad to hear that you have no plans to retire. My father has always maintained that we've enjoyed a cordial arrangement between our businesses.'

Mal shot his son a glare, wanting to wipe the smirk Seb wore clean off his face. Why did Sebastian always have to rock the boat? They were joining together on this latest infiltration of their territories, weren't they? He wanted things to remain amicable between the two firms. Just because Seb didn't agree with, as he put it, being 'pally' with the Reynolds, it didn't give him the excuse to chuck pointless digs around.

Another burst of heat and a fresh wave of perspiration broke out on Mal's forehead. It was no good. Sweat would run down his face any minute. *This was so embarrassing.* He pulled a handkerchief from his pocket and mopped his brow with a shaking hand.

'Are you all right?' Seb whispered.

'Yes, yes, I'm...'

'He's far from all right.' Len watched Mal closely, then reached for the telephone. 'I'm calling an ambulance.'

* * *

Gloria placed Len's plate on the table, then put her hand on his shoulder. 'Hunter's chicken – your favourite.'

'Thanks, sweetheart.' Len squeezed Gloria's hand, then watched her move around the other side of the large oval dining table to sit down.

He was a lucky man. He'd fallen in love with Gloria from the off and now, all these years later, he was still fortunate enough to have her at his side. To him, she was the most beautiful creature. Even in her sixties, she had a huge helping of timeless beauty and he thanked his lucky stars that he'd been so blessed. Most people couldn't say they'd been so lucky.

Shoving a forkful of chicken in his mouth, the delicious cheese topping melting on his tongue, Len frowned at the sadness on Gloria's face. 'What's the matter, love?'

Gloria looked up, her blue eyes misty. 'I was just thinking about Malcolm Stoker. I'm worried, Len. I mean, you're older than him and...'

'Mal Stoker will be fine,' Len soothed. 'People of our generation are tough nuts, Gloria.'

Admittedly, he'd thought Stoker was having a heart attack when he'd first seen him go that funny colour and clutch at his chest. And he'd done the decent thing by vacating his own office when the ambulance arrived to give Stoker some privacy, but as they'd carted Mal out, the younger Stoker said the paramedics suspected it was angina.

Gloria smiled weakly. 'It's all getting too close to home. First you talk about retirement and then doing that thing with your will, putting our Sam in charge... And that bit you said about when you're no longer here...' Faltering, she put her fork down and swallowed the fast-forming lump in her throat. 'I can't begin to think of that being a reality, but when something happens like it has done today to Malcolm Stoker, it puts things into perspective...'

Len grinned. 'Now don't you be worrying your lovely head about any of that old bollocks. Mal is different to me in as much that he worries too much. The man is stress on legs – always has been. By rights he should have developed angina by thirty, rather than sixty!'

Gloria laughed sadly. 'Maybe, but none of us are getting any younger.'

'Correct, but it changes nothing. You're stuck with me for a lot longer yet, Glor, that I'm sure of.' Len reached across the table to take his wife's hand. 'Talking of which, I must finalise Samantha's building purchase sometime this week too. I want her to move ahead with that as soon as possible.'

The other thing he needed to do was get his solicitor to draw up the documentation to ensure John had the legal clout to run things after he'd dropped off the twig, otherwise Sam really would be lumbered and she'd never forgive him. Not that he would mention any of that to Gloria.

The other thing he wouldn't mention was this business today with Stoker had brought it home to him a lot more that he'd care to admit. Although he still felt thirty, both physically and mentally, nothing changed the fact that he was sixty-eight – sixty-nine this year, so it really was important he got everything in place, just to be fully covered when the time came.

10

'What's that supposed to mean?' Seb barked. *Hadn't he got enough on his plate?*

Neil shrugged. 'Just telling you what was reported back like you asked.'

Seb wiped his hand across his forehead and stared at the ceiling with exasperation. Yes, he had asked to be immediately informed should there be any further infiltration attempts, but he'd expected elbowing around in respect of supplies, not *this*.

'What do you make of it?' Neil watched his brother intently.

Learning forward, Seb slapped his hands down on the desk. 'I make nothing of it, short of someone pulling a fast one.' His jaw clenched. 'And a dangerous fast one at that! Tell me who said this.'

Neil could see the anger in his brother's eyes. He'd toyed with the idea of 'forgetting' to mention this part, knowing it would put the cat amongst the pigeons and in all truth, he didn't want the hassle. 'Oh, come on, Seb. Surely you can't be taking this seriously? It's got to be bullshit.'

'Part is,' Seb roared, 'but I want to know *exactly* what was said and by whom.'

Neil sighed. 'Phil Blunt – the runner with the tat of a spider on his neck, you know the one?'

'Yes, yes, go on,' Seb snapped.

'Well, he took a right kicking. He was about to drop the usual order in for that club we supply on Hurst Street, when some fucker told him the order had already been dropped. By *them*.'

Seb's jaw ached as it clenched harder. *So these fuckers had over-taken one of their deals?* 'That coke order's been filched?'

Neil nodded. 'I've spoken to the club and they were offered two quid less a gram, so to be fair, you can see why they changed supplier.'

'To be fair?' Seb raged. 'You're okay with all of this?'

'Well, no, but...'

'Carry on, then,' Seb flapped his hand dismissively. He wasn't here for spiel.

'The bloke giving Phil a kicking said we either accept losing a percentage of our trade, or it would become public knowledge that one of us isn't a Stoker.'

Seb raked his fingers through his hair. 'And was this cunt one of these cheap wankers from the Aurora?'

Neil shrugged once more. 'No idea. A big bloke, red hair. That's all I know.' He folded his arms. 'You're taking this very seriously. You... you don't think there's any truth in what he said about us?'

Eyes narrowing to slits, Seb backhanded Neil. 'Don't you fucking dare! Don't you *ever* insinuate that about our mother, do you hear me?'

Neil stumbled backwards, his hand raised to his face in shock. 'I didn't mean that, I...'

'I want to speak to this runner. Bring him in immediately!' Seb snarled.

'What will you say to Dad?' Neil asked, eyeing Seb warily.

Seb stared at his brother in amazement. 'Are you stupid? Our father's lying in hospital with angina, most likely caused from stress, and you're expecting me to just casually mention that as well as losing one of our clients today, some ginger-haired fuck is trapping off that our mother's been unfaithful at some point and his sons are actually questioning the validity of it? Have a day off, Neil!'

Neil bit his bottom lip. *Putting it like that, it didn't seem the best idea he'd had all day.*

'Don't say anything about this to the others either. The less people who know about what's been insinuated, the better. Get me this Phil bloke in pronto. I need to find which toe-rag will be paying for this crap.'

Nodding, Neil got up. 'Are me and Andrew still heading to the Aurora tonight?'

Seb slammed his fist on the desk. 'I don't know. I can't fucking think with all these questions. I'll let you know later.'

After Neil left the office, Seb leant back in his chair and took a deep breath. He'd promised to take his mum up the hospital at visiting time. She was worried sick, but although he was now happy his father wasn't in any immediate danger with his health, that could change if he knew this sort of stuff was being bandied around and he wouldn't have his mother being tarnished with tales of infidelity. *No way!*

His eyes narrowed. The only person at risk here was the ginger bloke. One for filching one of their coke deals and two, for spouting shit. The guy was a dead man walking.

* * *

Happiness radiated from Sam. Thanks to her father's collateral, Chamberlains were happy for her to take the keys in order to measure up the premises for fixtures and fittings in lieu of the pending completion of the sale. She ran her hand along the stone overmantle of the large back room in the building, scarcely able to comprehend this place would soon be hers.

'What?' she laughed, looking at Liam. She realised she must look like a kid in a sweet shop, but she was too happy to be self-conscious over whether she looked silly or not.

Liam grinned, taking pleasure at Sam's excitement. Beautiful to start with, today she was positively stunning with radiance – the smile on her face so wide, so genuine. How he longed to take her into his arms and press his lips upon hers. To promise her that he would make her the happiest woman in the world *every* day if only she'd allow him to.

Liam had wanted Sam since the moment he'd first met her. Working for the Reynold firm, he had of course been invited to her customary birthday bashes and her twentieth had been the first time he'd laid eyes on her. That was now ten years ago and although, after spending a couple of nights together in the past, he'd thought perhaps something more was on the cards, she'd never wanted to make things more permanent, but *he* did.

She'd always insisted she wouldn't jeopardise their friendship by moving into a relationship. And they *were* good friends, but it was frustrating.

But now things were on the up, Liam was sure of it. After being promoted several times within the business, he was doing well for himself. Manager of the gaming tables at the Orchid, he knew he was well thought of by Len, but the best moment was when Len had taken him to one side a few months ago to say, in no uncertain terms, that if Liam wanted to make things 'official' with his daughter, there would be no opposition from him. Plus, there had been the remark at the meal last night about grandchildren.

Liam grinned. He couldn't think of anything he wanted more. Partly because Sam was a top looker, but also because being properly involved with her would ensure his position. As well as the promise of a never-ending stream of cash on tap, when Sam inherited the profits from the business, he'd be sorted for life.

If that wasn't worth pursuing, then nothing was. Yep, all he had to do was marry Sam or even just get her pregnant to forge an everlasting tie. Now it was a just a case of convincing *her*.

'This room will be my office,' Sam said, almost dancing over to the large sash window.

Liam stared at Sam, framed by the sunlight through the window behind her, and soundlessly moved from the other side of the room towards her.

'What are you staring at me like that for?' Sam asked. 'Don't you like the place? I know that I've been going on and on about it and driving you mad, but can't you see how beautiful it is? How *perfect* it will be for what I want to do with it?'

Shaking his head to gain semblance from what he actually wanted to do, Liam smiled. 'No, I love it. I think it's perfect too... Just like you...'

Sam's smile faltered. *Don't spoil things, Liam, please...* Turning away, she made a point of looking up at the window. 'Do you have that tape measure I asked you to bring? I need the dimensions of this window for blinds. I saw some that would be perfect and...'

'Sam...' Liam moved closer, his hand brushing a lock of her hair from her face.

Sam hastily moved away from Liam to the other window. Anything to break the awkward situation. Her father's blatant hint about grandchildren was bad enough, but whatever had been said was sufficient to give Liam a second wind in convincing her he was the one and she couldn't be doing with that. 'What's your opinion of the Stokers?'

'The Stokers?' Liam studied Sam's face suspiciously. 'What have *they* got to do with anything?'

'Nothing.' *Why had she mentioned them? It was the first name that had popped into her head.* Sam pulled a small notebook from her bag and made a rough sketch of the room. 'I just wondered what you thought of them. I bumped into Sebastian Stoker at the market the other day, that's all.'

Liam's hackles rose. He'd seen Stoker staring at Sam on her birthday and now the man just happened to 'bump' into her in the market? 'Did he bother you?' he snapped.

Sam frowned. 'No, why would he bother me?' Truth was, Seb Stoker *had* bothered her. She couldn't read the man and *that* bothered her.

'Seb's bad news. I've heard things about him,' Liam hissed. 'I presume you're aware the Stokers are your father's rivals?'

Sam bristled. Yes, she'd finally remembered that, but also knew her father and Malcolm Stoker went back years. 'Rivals perhaps, but enemies, no,' she said curtly.

'Don't trust them. Old school tactics are all very chivalrous, but even so...'

Sam's irritation mounted. 'I think my father can make his own judgement with how he operates. It's set him in good enough stead in this game for the past forty years. Casting aspersions on a family with their father in hospital isn't very becoming either.'

'Sam, I didn't mean...'

'I need to get back to work.' Sam shoved her notebook back into her bag, the enjoyment of the day deflating.

Liam's heart sank. He should have kept his opinions to himself. Mal Stoker was decent enough, but Seb was a different kettle of fish and he didn't like the man one bit. He certainly didn't like the thought of Seb bothering Sam. Not when it was important she kept her full attention on *him*.

Walking out the door of the big old building and watching as Sam locked up, Liam leant against the wall. 'I'll drop those keys back if you like? Save you some time?'

Sam's irritation faded. She always found it difficult being cross with Liam for long. 'Okay, thanks.' She chucked him the keys and stood back, admiring her new building, a smile creeping back onto her face.

'Let me take you for dinner tonight.' Liam wore his best lopsided grin that he knew Sam found endearing. 'Let me make up for annoying you...'

'Well, I...'

'Come on. You promised we'd go to dinner soon. Just you and me.' Liam raised his eyebrows. 'I'll even let you talk about blinds, curtains and cushion covers all night if you want?'

Sam laughed, all annoyance gone. 'Go on then, but I'll hold you to that. I'll make you carry all the paint I'm planning on ordering too!'

Liam smiled to himself, watching Sam wrapped in her tailored suit walk back to the office. He'd carry anything she liked. He'd paint the whole place pink with a toothbrush if it made her happy and guaranteed him a percentage of her coming money.

11

'Not now, you silly tart!' Tom barked, brushing the woman away. 'Can't you see I'm bloody busy?' And even if he wasn't busy, he wouldn't want a go with *her*.

He glanced contemptuously at the woman's veined, saggy breasts half-hanging out of her light pink top and cringed. For fuck's sake, surely they could do better than this lot? Good job the punters were all so wasted by the time they moved on to the women, they didn't notice quite how bashed with the ugly stick they all were.

Shrugging, Tom swigged from his vodka and continued flicking through his notebook, gratified by last weeks' takings. *Very nice...*

And Jock had the audacity to initially doubt whether the gambling side of things would be a goer? Well, he could eat his words now because out of the three sides of this venture, the gambling was the most lucrative at this time.

Pulling out his cigarettes, Tom sparked one up. But that would soon be changing. Jock's earlier visit had proved as much. Another successful infiltration of a patch. Okay, so on this occasion it was necessary for the runner to be roughed up, but shit happens.

Now they'd got control of that particular patch, it was one up the nose for the Stoker firm because it was one of *their* patches.

Tom glanced around his tiny office on the first floor of the Aurora. A few more weeks and he'd be able to kit out this place a lot better. At the very least, he'd make his office more fitting for his station. He eyed the cheapo desk in front of him with disdain. That could go for a start. He'd get himself one of those posh, solid wood ones, like the ones in old films.

Leaning back on his chair, he stopped abruptly, feeling the plastic bending under his weight. A proper desk chair was in order too.

Tom pulled out a wrap of cling film from his pocket and carefully cut a line of cocaine on his desk. Chopping at it with his switch card, he fashioned it into a nice thick line, then hoovered it up his nose through a rolled-up fiver. Now there would be a lot more of *this* for his own consumption at no extra cost, too.

Feeling the burn at the back of his nose and the rush building in his head, Tom grinned, his heart pounding as the cocaine took effect. Today was a good day and it would be even better by later on.

He yanked at the stiff desk drawer and pulled out the piece of paper where he'd scribbled down the address he'd found. Now he could post that letter.

Tom's face split into a grin. Or he could nail it to the front door along with a mouldy chicken? At least that would save a stamp... Tempting as it was, realistically that was a no-go unfortunately.

He'd get to the post box and then, after that, the first port of call was to check out the address and make a decision when to start the blackmail. It didn't matter whether he started with Reynold or Stoker. It was irrelevant which of them had purchased that slag Linda's kid. Rumours stuck better than the truth and if he played his cards right, he'd get a *proper* pay-out for keeping schtum. Now Maynard knew he was back, *he* would come in useful too.

Tom's eyes glistened with excitement. Maynard would not want anything mentioned that could cause him problems. And he could cause Maynard plenty of problems. *Big* problems.

* * *

Judith stared at her husband and felt like bursting into tears all over again. She'd been crying since it happened, including the best part of last night and most of the day. She glanced at Seb, standing at her side in the doorway of Mal's private room off the coronary ward, and smiled weakly.

'He's okay, Ma. Just asleep. I tell you what, you sit with him and I'll leave you to it for a while. Give you some time to chat when he wakes up.' Seb kissed his mother on the cheek and left the room.

He didn't like seeing his mother upset like this and neither did he like seeing his big, strapping father reduced to lying in a hospital bed, surrounded by wires and bleeping machines. He liked it even less that someone should cast doubts about his mother's reputation. Doubts that one of his own brothers thought to question?

Seb's anger simmered. The bastard who thought they could steam in and cause problems with his family would be dealt with sooner rather than later and, if things went to plan, that would happen tonight.

As Seb left the room, the shutting of the door caused Mal to stir. Blinking, he adjusted his eyes to the bright overhead strip lights. Seeing his wife, he smiled. 'Hello, love.'

'Oh, Mal!' Judith cried, rushing towards the bed. Bending down, she planted a kiss on his cheek. 'You gave me a right scare. You gave *all* of us a scare!'

Mal motioned for Judith to sit on the plastic chair at the head of his bed, dismayed to see her hands trembling and her eyes red and swollen from crying.

He loved his Judith to bits. There wasn't a thing he wouldn't do for her. His resolve strengthened. The last thing he wanted was to inadvertently put his darling wife through pain and worry.

Okay, so it had cost him a bloody small fortune over the years keeping her in posh frocks and the latest household gadgets. Christ, he'd even bought her a brand-new video recorder at the first opportunity, betting at the time even the Queen was getting hers on the tick from Radio Rentals. And none of that included the house Judith insisted he bought. Or the holidays...

But he wouldn't change her for the world. She'd stuck faithfully by his side whilst he'd built the business up; she'd turned a blind eye to all the comings and goings that she knew were far from legit, but best of all, she'd given him four strapping sons. For that alone, he couldn't have been more grateful.

The day Sebastian was born, Mal had thought all of his boats had come in. He'd been the proudest father ever. With Seb's dark hair and green eyes, he was a chip off the old block – a heir for the nicely growing business. Then along came the twins, Andrew and Neil, and finally Gary – the one they'd never expected, nor planned for. The runt of the litter, with a different constitution to the other three, but it hadn't mattered. He loved them all.

And, Mal thought with a smug smile, his sons were the one thing he'd always have over Len Reynold... Although that rivalry wasn't quite as acute after the man's decency when he'd collapsed at the meeting yesterday.

He glanced at the cuff monitoring his blood pressure with growing annoyance. As much as he hated to admit it, having a turn like this had put the fear of God into him. He'd thought for a moment that his time was up, which further underlined how much he dreaded leaving Judith. He also knew what it meant.

Judith took Mal's hand, snapping him from his thoughts. 'Mal, I...'

'You don't need to say anything, love. I know...' Mal said, squeezing her hand gently.

'You know? Know what?' Judith said, panic audible. Had the doctors diagnosed something she wasn't aware of? Something worse?

'I know what you're going to say,' Mal continued. 'But you don't need to. You're right – it's time.'

Seeing Judith's confusion, Mal smiled. 'I'm retiring, love. I'm too old for this game now.' He gestured to the electrodes covering his chest. 'Someone's trying to tell me something and I think it's about time I listened, don't you?'

Judith's hand flew to her mouth, her eyes brimming with tears of relief. 'Oh, Mal! You don't know how long I've waited to hear you say that! I was going to beg you again, but I never thought you'd hear of it.'

Mal grinned. 'I'm not driving myself into the ground any longer. Especially not whilst I have you.'

'Do you really mean it this time?' Judith asked, her eyes wide. 'You're not just saying it only to change your mind once you're out of here? I know what you're like, Malcolm Stoker.'

Mal chuckled. He had indeed promised this very same thing several times, but this time he meant it. 'I promise. The boys are more than capable and Seb can take his rightful place.'

'Have you said anything to him yet?' Judith asked, happiness bubbling.

'Not yet, but I'll tell Seb soon.'

'Tell me what?' Seb said, entering the room, a cup of coffee in each hand.

'That from now on you're in charge of running the Peacock and official head of the Stoker firm,' Mal grinned. 'Your time has come, son, because I'm bowing out. Me and your mother are going to spend some long overdue quality time together. Perhaps starting with a cruise.'

12

Seb seethed with pent-up rage as he stared at the sorry-looking, smashed-up face of the runner. It was clear the man would rather be anywhere else but here with him, but *he* ran this place now and so things would be done his way. Especially on this subject – the one thing that he would not allow, under any circumstances, for his father to get wind of. At least, not until he was fully recovered. And by that time, he would have dealt with it, eradicating any more instances of runners getting jumped or repetitions of burgeoning blackmail.

Having just left his father's bedside, *he* was now in charge. Blackmail was not going to happen. Neither was this fucking rumour going to gain pace.

Seb's eyes ran over the man in front of him, his eyes narrowing at the inflicted damage. The man's nose was broken – anyone could see that, a couple of teeth had gone and one eye was completely swollen shut. And that was just the damage he could *see*.

Seb chewed his bottom lip. This guy had taken a right pasting and he wouldn't put him through any more grief by asking him yet again to repeat the exact words the toe-rag had used.

Seb got the gist. It was exactly what Neil had reiterated earlier. *That one of them wasn't a true Stoker.*

He eyed the runner carefully. 'Phil? It is Phil, isn't it? I hope I don't need to point out that what this prick said is untrue.' His eyes narrowed. 'But we all know how rumours can fly out of control if they are repeated...'

'I – I won't repeat a word, Mr Stoker,' Phil muttered, his voice muffled from his swollen, cut mouth. 'I didn't even want to repeat it to Neil, let alone you, but I felt it my responsibility to do so.'

'You did right,' Seb said. 'I appreciate it.' He slapped Phil on the back, trying not to laugh as the man winced. 'But I do want the bloke that jumped you.'

Phil blinked several times, panic rising. He didn't want to get involved. He'd only get more shit. The bloke who'd jumped him last night fought like a rabid tiger and he didn't want a repeat of that.

'You did a sterling job last night. It took a hell of a lot before the twat got the better of you,' Seb said, getting close as he looked Phil up and down. 'You defended the Stoker firm honourably.'

Pulling a roll of notes from an inside pocket of his suit jacket, he placed it in Phil's hand. 'This is for your inconvenience. Something to make up for the pain and of course your *loyalty*.'

Phil stared at the wad of notes, unease snowballing at what this meant.

'So,' Seb smiled. 'Tell me more about the man behind this.'

Sweat soaked into Phil's stained T-shirt. 'I don't know his name and that's gospel.' He faltered, inwardly wishing he was on a different planet. 'But I do know where he drinks. It's... it's the Gun Barrels.'

Seb grinned. 'Then that's where we'll head right now.'

* * *

Phil sat stiffly in the back of Andrew Stoker's SD1, part of him feeling privileged to be chauffeured around by a member of the firm he'd worked for over the past five years, the other part wishing he was at the bottom of a large crater on the moon.

In all of those five years, he didn't think anyone apart from Neil Stoker had even glanced in his direction, let alone given him the time of day. In fact, he could count on one hand how many times he'd actually been in the same vicinity with members of the inner circle.

It was the same for all the runners – the lowest of the firm's hierarchy. The only one any of them ever saw was Neil and that was only during the weekly meetings. But now, here he was with not one, but *two* of the firm's top men. And from what he'd just learned, old Mal Stoker had retired with immediate effect, so *Seb* was now the boss.

Although Phil itched to ask how this sudden decision had come about, he knew better. Besides, he wasn't sure whether his voice box worked any longer, convinced he must have been struck dumb from uttering the information about the tosser who given him this bloody kicking.

His T-shirt clung to his back under his jacket. He was drenched in sweat all over and could only hope he hadn't left a wet patch on the car's leather seat. He glanced out of the window, realising with dread they'd already reached the Gun Barrels. Christ, he didn't know what would happen, but whatever it was, it was likely to leave him with the unfavourable reputation of being a grass. And he didn't want to think what the bloke who had jumped him would do next time he caught up with him.

Phil's hand brushed against the roll of notes Seb had handed him, now safely tucked in his breast pocket. He knew what the wad of cash meant. He was *owned*. The money was a burning reminder of that, so what choice did he have but to talk?

Seb turned around in the passenger seat, a ghost of a smile on his face seeing the man in the back flinch. 'Look sharpish, Phil. You're coming in with me to point this tosser out.'

Phil swallowed painfully. Even blinking and moving hurt. 'Y-you want me to go in there? With *you*?' He looked from Seb to the front door of the Gun Barrels, two men outside the pub already covertly peering at the car in an attempt to work out who was behind the blacked-out windows. *Shit. No one said anything about going in there with Seb Stoker!*

'How am I supposed to know which one of these fuckers is the right one?' Seb snapped, glancing at the shoddy façade of the pub. 'Jesus, I haven't been in here for donkey's years! I bet it's still a total shit-hole! But a shit-hole that still pays for our protection.' He turned to Andrew. 'Won't be long. Keep the engine running.'

'What's all this about, anyway?' Andrew hissed. *Something else he was being kept in the dark about?*

'Something I need to deal with,' Seb mumbled. 'Nothing to concern yourself with.' Opening the passenger door, he jerked his head in Phil's direction. 'Come on! I haven't got all day.'

Already feeling his adrenaline pumping, Seb barged through the heavy front door of the Gun Barrels, the loud chatter and raucous laughter immediately fading to heavy silence.

He scanned the room, noticing all eyes averting their gaze as his stare passed over them. Okay, so he stood out like a sore thumb with his tailor-made suit, but he suspected every single person in here knew exactly who he was. And *he* certainly did, Seb thought, looking at the man behind the bar.

If he remembered rightly, he'd personally collected protection money from this publican many moons ago when that was still part of his job. Now many others under him had that role. *How things change*, he thought as he sauntered across the room, wincing at the tinny rendition of the Prodigy blasting from the jukebox – the music appearing even louder with the lack of background noise.

As Seb approached the bar with Phil in tow, Dave smiled amicably, yet his nerves were clear. 'Mr Stoker!' he said loudly. 'It's been a long time.' He nodded towards the row of brass beer pumps. 'What can I get you?'

Seb shook his head. 'Nothing for me, thanks. I'm looking for someone.'

Dave's gaze flicked to Phil and winced. 'Taken a bit of a hiding, Phil?'

'That's why we're here,' Seb growled. He turned to Phil. 'Is he here?'

Phil shook his head. The bloke wasn't here, so could they go now? There might just be a chance he could get away with his reputation intact.

'The man I'd like to talk to drinks here.' Seb stared at Dave. 'I'd appreciate it if you could tell me who he is and where I can find him.' He leant on the bar, his eyes conveying that wasn't a question, but an *instruction*. 'A big fucker with ginger hair?'

Dave faltered, risking a glance at Phil. That poor bastard had already taken a hiding and would no doubt receive another after this – as would *he* if he wasn't careful, but he knew which man he'd least likely want on his back and it wasn't *this* one. 'The only bloke I can think of fitting that description is Jock,' he said. 'Jock Sawyer.'

'A fucking Scots bastard?' Seb spat. 'I might have known.'

'I don't know whether he's Scottish. All I know is that everyone calls him Jock.'

'Where is he?' Seb growled.

Dave shuffled uncomfortably. 'That I don't know either. He was in earlier, but then left.'

'Where does this fucker live?' Seb asked, frustration rising.

'I haven't a clue where he lives,' Dave added, 'but he works at the Rover.'

Turning to face the busy tap room, Seb pulled a roll of notes from his pocket. Peeling off a fifty, he slapped it on the bar. If he hadn't got an attentive enough audience before, then he had now. 'Anyone know where I can find Jock Sawyer? Just a business chat, you understand?'

People looked at the floor, fidgeting uncomfortably, some shaking their heads amongst mutters of 'I don't know' and 'not sure'.

Seb scowled and scanned the room once more. Either they were protecting this Jock person or they genuinely didn't know. He hoped for their sake it was the latter. Would he really have to stake out the factory tomorrow and wait until the dipshit clocked off?

'I think I know where he is.' A woman with badly bleached hair sitting at the bar ran her gaze over Seb, her eyes twinkling with appreciation.

Seb gave the woman one of his trademark smiles. 'And where might that be, love?'

'I heard him boasting he'd got a freebie owed at the Aurora tonight,' she shrugged. 'I'd never heard of it, but it's a new place up the Hagley Road.'

Seb grinned. *The Aurora indeed. How convenient...* Picking up the fifty-pound note, he pressed it into the woman's grubby hand, resisting the urge to thoroughly wash his hands. 'Much obliged. Buy yourself a drink, sweetheart.'

Turning back around, all pleasantries dropping from his face, Seb looked at Phil, then jerked his head towards the door. 'Let's go.'

13

Jock rolled off the small Chinese woman, then pulled his jeans back up from around his ankles. He reached over to the bedside table and grabbed his cigarettes, making sure to double-check the tart hadn't half-inched his wallet whilst he'd been concentrating on shooting his load.

He knew what these foreign types were like – always got their eye on an opening to swipe an extra few quid when they could, but he'd chop her hands off before that happened. This one wouldn't get very far if that was her game.

Lighting up a cigarette, he dragged himself to the edge of the mattress that had long seen better days and noisily sniffed up the thick phlegm in his throat.

'So? What do you think?' the woman asked, winding a spindly arm around Jock's waist. 'Have I got the job or not?'

Pushing her away, Jock glanced at the girl as she petulantly folded her arms across a virtually flat chest, his lip curling in derision. She was hardly a stunner. More of a fucking moose to be honest and nothing he'd normally bother going for. Good job this was a freebie because there was no way he'd pay for the privilege.

Jock knew Tom's insistence of taking a freebie as a bonus for how he'd moved the plan forward had an additional motive. The 'freebie' consisted of trying out the women wanting a job at the Aurora. Not that any of the ones *already* working here were any better, but it was true they needed more girls. The ones they'd got on the books wouldn't spread very far, but it wasn't like the cream of the crop would queue up to work in a joint like this, was it?

Jock's face screwed up further. Although he'd lived here most of his life, he'd never been a big fan of Birmingham. He didn't like the Brummies – found them a hard-nosed bunch, as well as being thick as pigshit. And it really had been a surprise when Tom Bedworth had shown up again after all this time. From what he'd heard, the man was doing well for himself up north; a couple of places with girls and a good percentage of dealing. He'd been pulling in a tidy wedge, so it was odd that he'd bother coming back.

And when Tom first told him he'd purchased a building – this one, now known as the Aurora – the place was far removed from the vision Jock had animatedly envisioned. The scene where the big money was pulled in was nowhere near this dismal dump. Tom may have had a decent amount of clout in Macclesfield, but Macclesfield was hardly Soho. Neither was it Birmingham and Jock worried that Tom hadn't weighed this up as carefully as he should have.

He frowned. He'd broached it once. Or at least, he'd *tried* to, but all Tom said was this was the way to do it.

Despite Jock's loyalty, he didn't buy that theory. The longer he spent with Tom since his return, the more it became clear there was a big part of the plan he'd failed to share. And Jock didn't much like it. In fact, it bothered him tremendously, but he wasn't in a position where he could afford to turn down the wedge Tom was paying. The prospect of the colour of money had twisted his arm and Tom had a habit of being very convincing – especially after a few sherbets.

But the way he'd trapped off in the pub the other night wasn't good. Tom's drinking and personal coke intake was worse than in the old days – and that was saying something! Tom should be careful about getting lairy and big-mouthed. Anyone could be listening and this was *his* earner too.

Jock ground his cigarette out in the ashtray, then shrugged his jacket on.

'Well?' the woman pushed, eyeing Jock suspiciously.

'Well, what?' Jock spat. 'Oh, you mean, have you got the job?' This Chinese bird was pissing him off. Bloody nagging already and he wasn't having that. His face cracked into a sneer. 'No disrespect, love, but you were shite.' He looked her up and down, 'And you fucking stink. We have standards here, you know?' *Standards? That was a joke! They needed some.*

'You bastard!' the woman spat, grabbing her clothes before flouncing out of the room.

Hearing the door open once more a few moments later, Jock rolled his eyes. If the cheeky bitch even thought about asking for any money, then she'd lose a few teeth. He swung around. 'What now?'

'Jock Sawyer?' Lurching forward, Seb wrapped his hand tightly around the man's throat.

Scrabbling at the thick fingers around his windpipe, Jock's initial shock turned to abject fear. This was one of the Stoker men. *This was because of what he'd been told to say. This was Tom's fault.*

* * *

Sitting in a layby in the hire car, Tom shoved the last remaining chicken nugget into his mouth and absentmindedly glanced at *The*

Sun's page three offering of the day. *Why couldn't Jock get birds like this into the Aurora?* They needed to up their game on that score. However, not everything was performing under par.

Tom grinned. Jock had done exactly what was asked with putting the word about and now he had two patches under his belt – one of them a Stoker patch, the other a Reynold one, so it was going well so far. Jock had done and said what was needed – many others wouldn't have had the balls, no matter how much cash was offered.

Scowling as a glob of tomato sauce flopped onto his jacket, Tom scrubbed at the mess with the single paper napkin accompanying the food and internally chided himself for being so clumsy.

Unscrewing the top of his vodka bottle, he gulped down a few more mouthfuls, scowling to see the bottle already half empty. He probably shouldn't have had all those drinks earlier either, but it wasn't like he couldn't handle it, otherwise he'd never have coped driving to this stake out and that would have meant a wasted night.

All things aside, he needed to move quickly on Stoker and Reynold. He had to make it clear that once he received acceptable pay-outs the rumours would stop, but this had to be timed right before they took it upon themselves to think about ill-conceived ideas of retaliation.

And then there was John Maynard...

His appearance out of the blue had knocked Tom off kilter. Oh, he'd done his digging and knew the guy was still around these parts, but what he hadn't expected was for him to turn up – and certainly not to turn up at the Aurora.

From what he could gather by the fleeting expression he'd caught on Maynard's ugly mug, the man hadn't a clue of *his* return to Birmingham. Well, now he did and could report that back to Reynold with bells on, because it would have no leverage. It could only work in his favour.

Maynard could say shag all without exposing himself to all and sundry and if his involvement was known, then at best he'd be run out of the city and be even more of a nobody than he already was. At worst, the man would cease to exist.

A wide smile broke across Tom's face. In fact, if he wanted to, he could add that to his plan.

He drummed his fingers on the steering wheel, his mind ticking. All things considered, that wasn't a bad idea. Should he work that into his master scheme before pulling off the pièce de résistance or use it alone?

Which would be more lucrative?

Tom snatched the piece of paper from the passenger seat and stared at the scrawled address. Frowning, he fired the engine, his nose wrinkling in distaste as the overpowering pine air freshener hanging from the rear-view mirror delivered another full assault to his nostrils. Why did hire cars always have those bloody things? Did everyone who rented cars fucking stink or something?

Shaking his head, Tom drove up the road, keeping a look out for the required turn. He'd already studied the map, so knew roughly where he was going, but never having had much call to frequent the upmarket side of the Edgbaston suburb, he couldn't say he was au fait with the area. All he knew was that he resented the leafy avenues and posh palatial houses.

He turned into the road he wanted, inwardly snarling at the widely spaced trees lining the street. Slowing the car to a crawl, he glanced left and right until he spotted the house he was looking for.

Bingo!

Oh, very nice. Very nice indeed.

Tom enviously eyed the large, white, detached building set back from the road behind high, ornate, wrought-iron gates and his resentment simmered.

That bastard Reynold got this, whilst *he'd* lived in a poky flat in Macclesfield?

Crunching the gearstick into first, the sound making his teeth on edge, Tom stamped on the accelerator. He wasn't hanging around here. There was no car on the drive, so even if he'd wanted to start the blackmail tonight, he couldn't. Besides, he was too half-cut to think straight, plus it would make sense to wait for the letter to arrive. Give that a couple of days to play on their minds before he ramped things up. And he had the Stokers to continue with in the meantime.

Yeah, this was coming together nicely.

Accelerating harder, Tom sped along the road. The quicker he got back to the Aurora and had some coke to straighten his head out, the better.

Shoving a cigarette in his mouth, he glanced down to grab his lighter, panic flaring when blinding headlights appeared from out of nowhere.

Yanking the wheel to the left, Tom could barely breathe as he watched in slow motion as another car ploughed headlong into a tree in his rear-view mirror.

Shit!

Heart pounding, he changed down gear and continued along the road. He had to get out of here fast. He couldn't afford to get breathalysed.

14

Sam spooned another mouthful of lemon sorbet into her mouth and murmured appreciatively, 'This is absolutely gorgeous, Liam.'

Liam's eyes ran over Sam's bare shoulders in the lilac strapless dress she'd chosen to wear. 'Not regretting me twisting your arm about coming for dinner now?'

Sam laughed. 'That reminds me! I haven't discussed blinds or curtains yet. We must get on with that conversation so I can make sure I haven't wasted the evening.'

Despite her earlier irritation, she was glad she'd agreed to come for dinner. It had taken her mind off how to broach letting down the design company she worked for. They had been really good to her the past couple of years and had opened up huge possibilities, as well as lots of doors. There was a big part of her that felt she was betraying them by branching out on her own, but it was all she'd ever wanted to do and so it would have to happen. Thanks to her father, it was happening sooner than expected.

As for Liam, he was great company when he wasn't putting pressure on about the possibility of a relationship. To anyone else, Liam might seem like the perfect choice – they got on well together;

he'd do anything for her; he was handsome and she was comfortable with him.

But that was the point... He was *comfortable*. There was no spark. And as much as she wanted there to be one, there just wasn't. There was no frisson of electricity when he was near – not like there was with the Stoker man.

'Fancy a club after this? What about the Dome?' Liam suggested.

'The *Dome*?' Sam shrieked, glad for the diversion from her mind traitorously returning to thinking of Seb Stoker. 'You're seriously suggesting we go to the Dome?' She'd frequented that nightclub on Horsefair regularly in the past, but now felt far too old compared to the rest in there. 'I don't know whether you've forgotten, but I'm thirty now, not twenty! We'd look like OAPs!'

'You'd still look better than most people in there...' Liam winked.

Sam inwardly hoped Liam wouldn't start pushing again – not when she was having such a nice evening. 'How come you're not working tonight? You have a lot of evenings off.'

'Now I'm the Tables Manager, I have the bonus of not needing to be there late nights like I used to be,' Liam replied, hiding his disappointment that it looked unlikely he'd succeed in eking out an extended evening with Sam. She had to see sense and give in to him soon. He was *counting* on it. 'Besides, they know where I am if anything drastic crops up.'

Finishing her sorbet, Sam placed the long-handled dessert spoon in the dish and pushed it to one side. Picking up her wine, it struck her that perhaps her father was behind Liam's frequent evenings off in a bid to spend more time with her. That was probably also why Liam had received the last few promotions. Not that he wasn't good at his job – he was, but she suspected his rapid rise up the ladder in the casino was part of her father's plan.

Sam knew her father didn't want her getting involved with anyone from the 'other' side of the firm, he'd never made any bones about that, but the casino side was a different matter. That side was completely legit and above board, so a decent man from *that* side of the business was something her father very much wanted for her. *Someone like Liam.*

Sam frowned. As much as she loved her dad, she would have to have words with him about that. He'd be busy at the Orchid tonight, so she'd call him in the morning for a chat.

'Okay, if you class yourself as too derelict for the Dome, then how about Ronnie Scott's?'

Sam raised her eyebrows. 'But we've just eaten?'

'We can still go for a drink,' Liam pushed.

Sam smiled. The well-known jazz club on Broad Street was one of her favourites. It offered some great musicians and a fantastic atmosphere, so it was tempting. Plus, it was only around the corner from her apartment. 'Well, maybe...'

'Ah ha! I knew I'd talk you into it!' Liam signalled the waiter for the bill. 'I'll just get this and then we'll make a move.'

Sam was reaching for her handbag, when the waiter approached. 'Sorry sir, but there's an urgent phone call for you.'

'For me?' Liam frowned, then glanced at Sam. 'Maybe I spoke too soon about having a stress-free evening.' He stood up, seeing the waiter indicate to the phone on the reception desk the other side of the restaurant. 'I won't be a moment. It's bound to be something and nothing.'

Pulling her compact mirror from her handbag, Sam checked her lipstick was intact and began shrugging her lightweight jacket on. If something had come up at the Orchid, maybe they should give Ronnie Scott's a miss? The meeting she had planned with her director to break the news about her plans was booked first thing and it wasn't the best idea in the world to attempt that after a late one. Her head had to be clear to ensure what she said came across the right way.

Closing her compact and placing it back into her handbag, Sam spotted Liam making his way back across the restaurant. Concern glimmered at his expression. 'What's happened?' she asked tensely as he approached the table.

Liam raked his fingers through his hair, his eyes searching Sam's. 'Shit, Sam, I'm sorry. It's your Dad. Len, he's... he's been in an accident.'

* * *

Tom's legs shook involuntarily. They were shaking so much that he could barely keep his feet on the pedals enough to drive.

Repeatedly glancing in the rear-view mirror for police on his tail, he gulped in large breaths of air. *Breathe, Tom, breathe! Stop panicking!* he repeated, hoping by some miracle this mantra would stop him escalating into full-blown panic.

Be realistic, he told himself. There was no reason why the cops would be after him. He hadn't done anything! That silly fucker in the other car had come out of nowhere, so it was his own bloody fault.

No one had seen him over at Reynold's place. The street had been deserted. And it was only a prang. That other bloke had probably driven off by now.

Tom fumbled for another cigarette as he continued through Quinton. Why he'd decided to take the long way from Edgbaston was beyond him, although going the back way seemed a good idea, giving less chance of running into a cop car. But the longer he remained on the road, the more likely he was to be pulled too.

Tom turned the radio up in a bid to stay alert. He knew that he was well over the limit and the car reeked of vodka. *Stupid, stupid!*

He stared at the bottle on the passenger seat and considered chucking it out of the window just in case, then thought better of it. He'd be glad of that once he got back and Jock had dealt with getting rid of this motor.

Stabbing at the electric window, the fag smoke choking him out, Tom drove up the Hagley Road. Nearing the Aurora, his brain scrolled through the best way of offloading the hire car. He'd have to think up a decent excuse to the rental company. The tosser who had pranged that tree had better not have clipped this bloody thing. He'd only get stiffed for the rip-off insurance excess on this bloody heap of shit otherwise.

Should he pretend it had been nicked or what? Jock would think of something. He'd always been good with things like this.

Just get back, get back... Nearly there now...

Chucking his fag end out of the window, Tom pulled into the Aurora's car park, backing the motor into a space in the shadows, right over in the far corner.

Grabbing his bottle of vodka, Tom turned the engine off and breathed a long sigh of relief. He didn't much fancy the noise in the Aurora, but what choice did he have? He was just relieved Jock was on site to deal with this. He'd have been fucked if he'd had to locate him at this time of night.

Tom stumbled across the pot-holed car park, yanking the key to the front door from his pocket. He wouldn't stoop to banging on the door like a punter, thank you!

Shoving his way through the stiff door, Tom frowned at the distinct lack of noise. Where was that monkey he paid to stand here and vet the customers? And furthermore, why was it so quiet?

Shaking his head, he walked down the hall. It was impossible they could have suddenly had a night with absolutely zero punters. That wasn't likely, was it? They were doing all right and word was spreading about the benefits of the place.

Panic intensified. Had the police been here? *Shit*. Had they shut it down? Had those clowns been busy openly dealing again? He'd already had words to keep it under wraps, not in full fucking view of every passing motorist and the neighbours. Or were the police looking for *him* because of that crash?

Sweat pooled, his shirt sticky. 'Jock?' Tom yelled. 'JOCK!' He didn't have time to fuck about, he needed that motor sorting and it needed to go pronto.

Barging into the gaming room, the one usually packed full with drunks and women, Tom stopped dead. The room was empty, short of the women huddled together in the dim light at the far end. *Where was everyone?*

'What the fuck is going on?' Tom roared. 'Where's that idiot on the door and where's Jock?' He stomped into the room. 'Furthermore, where the bloody hell are all the punters?'

He glared at the collection of frightened faces. 'You!' he spat, marching across to a grubby-looking woman. Grabbing a handful of her hair, he yanked her head back. 'Answer my question.'

If Jock had fucked off and left him in the lurch, he'd go tits. What if the cunt had run off with the takings? 'I'll ask again... Where is Jock?' Tom twisted harder at the bunch of hair in his fist.

'H-he's upstairs,' the woman yelped.

Releasing his grip, Tom scowled, then passed his glare along the other women before stomping up to the rooms used for paying customers. He'd sort that bunch downstairs out later, but for now he had to deal with the car. That took priority.

'Jock?' Tom stomped along the bare floorboards of the first-floor landing. Pushing open the first bedroom door he came to, it was empty, save an unmade bed.

He grimaced. The cheap whores. Had he not told them to sort the rooms out each time they finished so it was presentable for the next customer? He'd get *nowhere* at this rate.

Shaking his head in irritation, Tom moved to the next bedroom. Jock better not be off his head and passed out.

Shoving the door open, he immediately gagged at the sight. 'Fuck!' he cried, temporarily rendered motionless.

Tom's eyes locked on the body of Jock crumpled on the floor, a wide gash across his throat, dark arterial blood pooling around him; his face locked in a panicked grimace and his wide-eyed sightless gaze fixed onto the mildew-coated ceiling.

Tom's attention flicked around the room, clocking the blood splattered liberally over the wall and bedclothes. His head cranking into gear, he feverishly searched for whoever had done this. They could be still lurking about.

Satisfied he was alone, Tom forced his unwilling legs to move further into the room towards the man on the floor. He could see at a distance Jock was long gone, but still felt the need to check. Against his better judgement, he focused on the body and felt the night's worth of vodka making its rapid ascent up from his stomach.

'Christ!' he muttered, turning away, his hand quickly covering his mouth. Hadn't Jock been testing out a couple of new possibilities tonight? Had one of those slags done this, thinking they could turn him over?

Fury cascading over him, Tom stumbled from the room and somehow made it back down the stairs without his legs folding from under him. What the hell was he going to do about that motor now? And what in God's name was he going to do about Jock?

He barged back into the gaming room, all women jumping nervously at his entrance. 'What the fuck has gone on?' he screamed. 'Was this one of you? Where's that cunt on the door? Was it him?'

'Baz left,' one of the women muttered. 'He legged it as soon as that man turned up.'

Tom frowned, a trickle of ice cold running the length of his spine. 'Man? What man?' *This was the work of a punter?* He must have been a big fucker to take Jock Sawyer out. Jock was a prize fighter – or would have been under different circumstances.

He stomped over to the woman, who flinched at his close proximity. 'What. Fucking. Man?'

The woman looked up with terrified eyes. 'I – I don't know... We didn't see him. All we know is we heard a man's voice. He raced upstairs and Baz said he wasn't hanging around with a Stoker on the premises and then he left...' She began sobbing. 'Then we heard the screaming. It was horrible.'

Tom's stomach slithered down to the bottom of his legs, nausea rising quicker and more violently than on seeing Jock's slashed throat. The realisation that he may have misjudged the way of dealing with his blackmail plans seeped into his brain.

He dug his fingernails into the palms of his hands to keep himself from screaming. He had to think. *Think!*

Firstly, he needed to sort this out. His eyes narrowed. 'None of you have called the cops, have you?'

Watching the group of heads shake, Tom breathed a sigh of relief – at least on *that* score. 'No one is to repeat anything about this, do you understand? Not a fucking word!'

The women nodded nervously, every pair of eyes fixed to the floor.

'I mean it! If one fucking word of this gets out, I'll hunt you and all of your families down. That's a promise!' Turning on his heels as one of the women began to sob pitifully, Tom pulled his shirt sleeves up. 'Well, don't just sit there! Someone get the bin bags.'

He'd have to dispose of Jock and once he'd got the body out, this lot could clear the mess up in that bedroom. Only after that had happened could he work out where he went from here.

15

It took all of John's power not to not punch the air and skip down the stairs to the Orchid's entrance. How he'd managed to look quite so desolate and heartbroken when taking the call from a hysterical Gloria and then dutifully informing the staff of Len's sudden demise, he wasn't sure, but he'd achieved it somehow. But if he didn't get out of here quickly, then he'd be unable to stop the fast bubbling avalanche of glee from exploding.

He knew that he'd have to force the act back into place by the time he reached Gloria's house, but at least the drive there would enable him to release some of his pent-up exhilaration at this unexpected turn of events.

He nodded to the sombre-looking doorman as he reached the bottom of the stairs. 'Start closing up immediately, Terry,' he muttered. 'We're closing early tonight for obvious reasons. I'll update everyone as soon as I know more.'

Taking the steps leading to the casino's underground car park, John finally felt able to release a much-needed grin. It didn't matter what the details were. All he knew was that Len had face-planted into a tree and had, according to Gloria, died instantly. That was all he needed to know for now.

Yep, he would update everyone as soon as he found out how Len Reynold had happened to be no more, but by that time, the news would have already spread across the city like wildfire. It was probably already halfway across it by now as it was. And the details hardly mattered. Not to him, anyway.

Bloody finally! After all this time – after all the painstakingly long, dragged-out years, he was now in his rightful position. He could barely believe his good fortune. Len Reynold was dead and he would step into his place. *What a hardship...*

Pulling his car keys from his pocket, John pressed the central locking, seeing his indicators double-flash in the parking bay over in the corner.

He couldn't say he was looking forward to putting up with Gloria's incessant bleating for the next however many hours, but in reality, it was a small price to pay for his sudden change in status.

John Maynard – head of the Violet Orchid. John Maynard – head of the top Birmingham firm...

Change was afoot and he couldn't wait.

Striding towards his car, John froze as a figure stepped out from behind one of the many concrete upright pillars. His hand immediately reached for his knife, inwardly cursing himself for not having his gun to hand.

'At last! I've been waiting ages!'

Half-recognising the voice, John peered at the face under the hooded jacket in the dim lighting, realising with a jolt that he knew exactly who it was. 'What the fuck are you doing here?' he hissed, grabbing Tom Bedworth by the arm and dragging him roughly along the side of his car into the shadows. 'Are you mad?'

'Forget about that,' Tom said, opening the car door. 'You've got to help me. I'm in the shit.'

John put his hand on the car door. 'You're not getting in my car.'

'Oh, yes I am,' Tom spat. 'You owe me, so damn well come on. There's no time to lose before they find the car.'

'Car?' A sudden dread of realisation washed over John as he stared into the wild-looking eyes of Bedworth, realising exactly what he'd done. 'Oh my God,' he whispered. 'It was you, wasn't it? You stupid fuck! You took Reynold out? I *told* you not to pull a stunt like that. I said th...'

'It was an accident,' Tom hissed, jerking his head towards the driver's seat. 'Hurry up!'

Head spinning, John clambered into the car and started the engine. 'I don't believe this,' he muttered.

'It's worse than that. As well as needing you to help me offload the car involved, I also need you to put the dead guy who's been butchered at the Aurora by one of the Stokers at some point this evening, in it too,' Tom spat, his wide eyes white in the gloom. 'I disappeared for years because of my involvement in your fuck up, so I'm calling that in,' he continued. 'Otherwise, everyone will find out what you did.'

John gritted his teeth. *Well, this screwed his good mood somewhat.*

Shoving the car into gear, he screeched towards the barrier, knowing he had no choice but to help this arsehole. Gloria would have to wait. He wasn't losing his place by Bedworth dragging ancient welly up from the depths. The cheeky twat felt he could threaten to expose him, did he? Well, he'd deal with that oversight later, but first things first – he had to make sure nothing ballsed up his plan to take control. Then he'd make Bedworth pay for his insolence.

John stared at Tom, pure venom in his eyes. 'Get your fucking head down then until we get out of here and back to yours.'

* * *

Replacing the phone on the wheeled trolley, Mal flopped back against the pillows and sighed, not knowing what to think. He stared at the plain wall opposite, bare save for the loudly ticking hospital clock.

Shit. He'd been the one who'd thought his time was up, yet – bam! Len Reynold had been wiped out in an instant! He'd only seen him the other day – fit as a fiddle.

Mal had thought about not bothering taking the call and telling the nurse who had brought in the phone trolley to take a message instead. Despite doing nothing for the past couple of days, apart from lie in this hospital bed, he was knackered. Doing nothing always did that to him. It was like what he'd said to Judith earlier – just because he was retiring didn't mean he could bear sitting around or pottering about the house looking for things to do.

But although it was almost midnight, something compelled him to take the call. His initial dread was that something had happened to Judith. Thankfully, it wasn't that, but it still was far from good.

Mal had listened with a mixture of shock and sadness learning how Len Reynold's car had ploughed headlong into a tree. Only yards from his home as well. Killed him instantly it had, the poor sod.

Mal had listened to all the details the caller knew, which wasn't much, considering it hadn't long happened, and he'd found his mind wandering, thinking what a damn shame it was. A rotten piece of luck. That was until his senses sprang to attention hearing the words, *'the other driver fled the scene...'*

Mal grabbed his glass of water from the over-bed table, wishing it were whisky.

He'd initially presumed there was a problem with the car. He couldn't imagine it being Len's driving – the man had been driving for donkey's years, so he'd assumed a tyre blow-out or an engine fault had caused the car to career off-road. But to learn that *another* car had been involved? And that car hadn't stopped?

His pulse increasing, the glimmer of unease grew in Mal's stomach. Was this an unrelated hit-and-run type of smash here or was it more than that? Was it somehow linked to the threats to both his and Reynold's firms?

It couldn't be, could it? Surely no one would be that stupid?

'Mr Stoker,' a nurse cried as she bustled into Mal's room. 'An alert has just gone off at our station regarding your blood pressure. What are you doing to get yourself het up like this?' She glanced suspiciously at the telephone and moved towards it. 'I'll take this out of the way. There's no phone calls at this time of night. Only emergencies.'

Mal leant forward, putting his hand on the trolley. 'Get off it, woman. This *is* an emergency. I need to speak to my son.'

Picking up the receiver, Mal stabbed out Seb's telephone number and directed the nurse out of the room with a wave of his hand.

* * *

Standing in the bathroom of the self-contained apartment above the Royal Peacock, Seb stared at his reflection in the mirror. He looked into the hard green eyes glaring back at him and willed his adrenalin to subside.

This two-bedroom apartment was maintained to an excellent standard, yet was used infrequently by any of the Stokers, but now it was his. Now he was in charge of everything it was more convenient being on site here than anywhere else. Being as he was now the boss, he could choose to live in it if he wished. And he did wish.

It had been a godsend tonight anyway and that was what

mattered. It would have been a huge risk driving the whole way across the city to get home.

Seb's nose wrinkled at the blood splattered over his white shirt and suit jacket. These would have to be burnt. He'd have put old kit on if he'd thought a messy job was on the cards. *Bloody typical. One of his favourite suits as well.*

Turning on the tap, Seb held his hunting knife under the fast-flowing water, watching with detachment as the water, now red, sluiced away forever down the plug hole.

He stared back at his reflection. *Damn his temper.* It hadn't been his plan to kill that man. Well, he'd wanted to and might have ended up doing so, but not like that. That kind of thing left too many traces for his liking, but he'd had minimal choice in the way it panned out.

Seb's rugged face creased. He'd wanted answers as to where the source of the shit that was being spread had come from before he put the tosser down, but he hadn't counted on the man's brute strength. Jock Sawyer had the strength of an ox and before he'd been able to ask any questions, Seb had been left with only one choice. Finish him or be finished himself.

There weren't many people who he would say were a physical match for him, but to give the bloke his dues, this one had been, so he'd had no option but to get in first.

Now he was left with no answers and no means of getting them, either. Not unless he could ascertain where it had all originated from.

Quickly taking his suit jacket off and unbuttoning his shirt, Seb shrugged. At least what had happened tonight would put a stop to the rumours. It would no doubt get back to whoever the organ grinder was that it was a bad idea to tread on the Stokers' toes.

Hearing a knock on the door, Seb stiffened. Kicking his blood-stained shirt and jacket under the sink, he quickly sluiced off his hands and forearms, listening as the door continued banging incessantly. *Who knew he was in this apartment?*

Shoving the hunting knife back in his ankle holster, Seb moved from the bathroom towards the front door. 'Who is it?' he called, his senses on fire.

'Seb? It's Andrew.'

Rolling his eyes, Seb unlocked the door to find his brother. 'For God's sake, Andrew. Can I get no peace? It's gone one in the morning!'

Andrew looked at his bare-chested brother, dark patches on his suit trousers, and frowned. 'I've been trying to get hold of you. Dad's been ringing you at home, but no one could locate you. Eventually, I thought of here and...'

'What's happened?' Seb cried, fear for his father escalating. 'You said something's happened to Dad? Wha...'

'Nothing's happened to Dad.' Andrew shut the door behind him and walked into the large open-plan lounge of the apartment. 'I said Dad's been trying to get hold of you.'

'What's gone on?' Seb snapped. The momentary relief that his father was okay was replaced with annoyance at his brother dragging things out.

Andrew stared at Seb, his expression grave. 'It's Reynold. He's been done.'

'Done?' Seb frowned. 'What? As in...?'

'Yep. Dead.' Andrew helped himself to a glass of Scotch from a bottle in the cabinet. 'Run off the road.'

Seb sat down heavily and blew through his teeth. 'You're saying this wasn't an accident?'

Andrew shrugged. 'Not sure. It only happened a couple of hours ago, so we haven't much detail yet. All we know is that someone drove at him, ran him off the road, then left the scene.' He drank heavily from his whisky. 'It could be a hit-and-run but, being as it happened pretty much outside Reynold's own house, that seems unlikely.'

Seb bit his lip. 'And more likely to be linked to these recent threats?' Now was not the time to mention he'd just quietened at least one source of those harmful rumours.

'That's what Dad thinks, yes,' Andrew continued. 'He wants to see you first thing in the morning. He wants you to offer your assistance with immediate effect to the Reynold girl, being as she'll have to step into Len's shoes.'

Seb stared at Andrew incredulously. 'He wants *me* to go and help our firm's rivals? To help a woman with no clue whatsoever about the business? He has to be joking?' There was no way he had time to waste on that crap, especially when there was more than enough to sort out here.

'That was my reaction too, I must admit,' Andrew said, finishing his drink. 'But Dad's adamant. He wants you and you alone at nine tomorrow.' He did his best to hide his irritation that yet again he was being sidelined. That only Seb was ever party to important decisions – to *everything*.

Seb nodded. 'Okay, I'll be there.' Not that he had any intention of actually helping the Reynolds. With them being wide open it gave their own firm an advantage, so why would he want to dilute that?

Sure, it was unfortunate Len Reynold had karked it, but the only thing that bothered him more than anything else was whether this hit-and-run *was* connected to the threats. If it was, that in turn could mean something was on the cards for *them* next. They would need to be vigilant. *Very vigilant.*

'Where have you been, anyway?' Andrew's eyes hovered on a missed bloodstain on Seb's right forearm. 'I haven't seen you since you took back off again after we got back from the Gun Barrels.'

'Like I told you before, just a bit of business I had to take care of,' Seb shrugged. 'Nothing to worry about.'

Raising his eyebrows, Andrew stood up. 'Right, I'll leave you to it.' He nodded towards the stain knowingly. 'I suggest you get yourself a shower, though...'

16

Gloria's red-rimmed eyes were so sore from crying she felt like scratching them out, but even if she'd wanted to, she didn't have the energy.

Today was the first time in the three days since Len's death that she'd felt able to face taking a shower, but even that seemed pointless. *What was she without Len?*

Len had been her entire world for so long and she couldn't imagine life without him. Now she had to because he was dead and the pain was more raw than anything she'd ever experienced.

Her Len – the most wonderful man – was no more and she couldn't get her head around it. She *wouldn't* get her head around it.

Gloria looked across at Samantha, her darling daughter, the apple of her father's eye, and her heart broke further seeing the vivid desolation on her daughter's beautiful face. She'd do anything – *everything*, to remove her daughter's pain if she could, but there was nothing, absolutely nothing she or anyone could do.

'You really should eat something, Mum,' Sam said, her voice hoarse. Her suggestion was hypocritical. She'd been unable to stomach a mouthful of anything herself since it had happened, but she could at least try to ensure her mother kept her strength up. She would need it.

Uttering the words out loud that her father was dead when she'd called work to say she wouldn't be in for the planned meeting had been like a knife through her heart. They'd been great, telling her to take as long as she needed, but how long was *long*?

This wasn't something that would ever be okay. Her father was dead and no amount of time off would change that.

Sam closed her eyes and inhaled deeply to keep the fast-rising panic at bay. Three days now she'd relived the night of the accident – it flashed into her brain every time she stopped. Or breathed. Or *moved*.

In fact, Sam recollected very little after hearing the words coming out of Liam's mouth in the restaurant that night. She vaguely remembered screaming – the sound coming from her mouth like a wounded animal. She'd crumpled to the floor, not caring a jot that the entire restaurant was staring at her. All that had clanged around her head were the poisonous, agonising words that her father was dead.

Sam shuddered. She'd also tried to block out the scene that greeted her when she'd allowed Liam to bundle her into his car and race to her parents' home. Unfortunately, it was still stuck at the forefront of her mind...

Her father's treasured car was mangled at the foot of one of the big trees standing like sentinels along the road. She vividly recalled there being minimal damage to the tree, a piece of bark sheared off, yet the whole front of the car had been crumpled up like a concertina, the windscreen smashed.

Two fire engines were on site busy tidying up the mess, having cut her father out of the car. Her father's body had already been taken away by ambulance and her mother was being comforted by a female police officer and several neighbours – the sort who had never spoken before, but at the commotion, the street had been packed with people wanting to see what had happened, like ghouls.

Sam had wanted to scream at all of them to go away. She didn't want them there, witnessing her family's pain. *Her* pain.

She hadn't even been able to say goodbye.

Her father had been killed outright, the policeman told her. It was a 'godsend', apparently, because he hadn't suffered.

Well, it wasn't a godsend. It should never have happened.

She'd blindly watched the policeman's mouth moving: *A terrible accident... It looked like the other driver had failed to stop... No witnesses... No impact between the two cars, just the tree... It may not even have been a hit-and-run... The skid marks from the other vehicle may not be related... They would know more in due course after the investigations concluded...*

Sam's mouth formed a tight line. They could do and say anything they wanted, but it didn't matter. It wouldn't bring her father back, would it?

She stared at the telephone, the red light of the answer machine blinking from incessant well-wishers and people offering assistance. Her father had been well-loved by many people, but she'd been unable to face returning any of the calls. She had to at some point. Someone had to do something.

And it would be *her*.

Sam glanced at her mother once more. Her dad would want her to look after her mother, so she had to get a grip, *now*.

She took a deep breath. There was a lot to do and a lot to sort and she needed to get on with it.

As the doorbell rang, Sam tensed. No doubt that would be Liam again. He'd been over countless times, but she couldn't face spending time with him. His presence wasn't a comfort, it was the opposite.

Because she'd valued his steady friendship, she'd put up with his hints and constant pushing for her to enter into a full-blown relationship with him for far too long. Although the chance had been unlikely before, now it was zero. Liam's presence made her blood run cold.

The words that her father was dead had come from *his* mouth and had she not been having that stupid dinner he'd nagged her into, then she might have instead decided to go to the Orchid to talk with her father. If she'd done that, then her father might not have left at the time he had and might have missed meeting the car which had caused him to lose control.

She might have been able to stop any of it from happening.

Whether it was fair or not, right now Sam couldn't forget that Liam had been the one to shatter her life; to utter the words she'd never, *ever* wanted to hear.

When the doorbell sounded for the second time, Sam pushed herself up from the chair. 'I'll get it,' she muttered, noticing her mother wasn't listening, her eyes focused far away, staring at something – nothing.

She moved into the hallway and, seeing a silhouette of a big man behind the frosted glass, moved towards the front door, her heart sinking further. It had to be Liam – far too tall to be John.

Sam scowled. John had only been around once. The night it happened, her mother had phoned him immediately and he'd said he'd be round straight away, yet he hadn't bothered showing up until the next day. Even then it was only to gruffly state everything was in hand at the Orchid.

Personally, she didn't mind. The less she saw of her miserable cousin, the better, but he'd behaved like he wasn't even bothered, let alone devastated over what had occurred.

Unlocking the door, Sam pulled it open. 'Liam, I... Oh!'

'I hope I'm not intruding.' Seb's voice was low. 'There isn't a right time to do this, but I didn't want to leave it too long.'

Sam blinked, unsure how to react. She hadn't expected to see Sebastian Stoker. *What did he want?*

'Mind if I come in?' Seb asked, purposefully pulling his gaze from lingering on Samantha Reynold's full and very inviting mouth. She may look like she'd been dragged through a hedge, but she was still mighty fuckable. 'There are things, important things, we need to discuss.'

Completely taken off guard with Seb's unexpected appearance on the doorstop, Sam faltered. Although she was showered and dressed, she knew she looked a state, but what did it matter? Why the hell should she care what she looked like at the moment? It was hardly relevant. The only thing that mattered had gone for ever, leaving a hole in her heart the size of the Albert Hall.

Opening the door fully, Sam watched as Seb Stoker walked into the house.

* * *

Seb smiled at Gloria but received nothing in response. Sitting motionless in an armchair, she stared out into the large back garden as if he wasn't there.

He cleared his throat. 'I and all of the Stokers would like to offer our sincere condolences, Mrs Reynold, and, of course, to you as well, Samantha,' Seb said. 'My father especially. He'd have come himself, but he's only just been discharged from hospital.'

Still receiving no response, Seb glanced at Sam, the slight shake of her head telling him not to push it. He sighed inwardly. He was no good at stuff like this. He would make a shocking bereavement counsellor, but what exactly was he supposed to say? He'd come here for one thing and one thing only – to offer his help like his father insisted, and then get the hell out of here. But he wasn't completely heartless. He could see this pair of women were heartbroken and could only compare it to the rush of panic he'd experienced in Reynold's office when his own father had keeled over.

He'd also witnessed the worry and fear his mother had gone through. The difference here was that Reynold wasn't coming back and there was no happy ending.

Seb's frown increased. His father had gone to great pains to explain that had it been a heart attack, rather than angina the other day, then Reynold's quick reaction would have saved his life, therefore it was time to put all rivalry to one side. The least they could do under the circumstances was to help the man's daughter. But Seb still remained unconvinced. That was over and above the call of duty. But heartless or not, he still had to do what he'd come to do.

He pulled at the cuffs of his shirt, playing for time whilst thinking how to word this, and glanced around the luxurious sitting room. Without a doubt, Len Reynold had done extremely well for himself, but everyone knew that. It was what happened from here that counted now.

There had been no word and certainly no comeback from his removing that lying tosser at the Aurora shit-hole. There were no further rumours and thankfully Neil had said no more about the ridiculous situation, but regardless of anything, Seb had to move forward with this farce as his father wished.

He cleared his throat again. 'As I said when I arrived, there's never a good time to visit in situations like this, but there are things we need to discuss.'

Against her better judgement, Sam gestured for Seb to take a seat in one of the many armchairs. 'Can I get you a drink?'

'No, thank you. I won't take up much of your time.'

Sam moved to an armchair opposite and sank into it. 'What is it you need to speak to us about, Mr Stoker?'

'Please call me Seb.' Sitting forward, Seb clasped his hands. 'My father wants to offer you our assistance at this sad time. He and Len went back a long way and he wants to make sure you're not left in the lurch with the business side of things.'

A spark of indignation fluttered inside Sam. She stared at Seb coldly. She didn't need sympathy or special treatment – especially from someone who didn't mean a word coming from his mouth. 'Your father's sentiment is not shared by *you*, I presume, Mr Stoker?' she said, purposefully bypassing his request to be less formal. She didn't want to be less formal. She wanted Sebastian Stoker and his false niceties to leave this house.

Taken off guard by Sam's spot-on assumption, Seb smiled. 'That's as maybe, *Samantha*, but as my father requested it, here I am. He wants to ensure that now you have control of the business, we should assist you in any way we can.'

Sam's eyes ran over Seb's self-assured, easy smile that only accentuated the deep shadow of stubble under the surface of his cleanly shaven face. The dangerous coldness in his eyes, combined with handsome arrogance, was both intriguing and irritating.

The last thing she wanted was Seb Stoker's begrudgingly given assistance with *anything*, and it made the noticeable increase in her pulse rate even more unexplainable. 'Thank you for your concern, but that won't be necessary,' she said tersely.

Seb frowned, his anger bristling. *Was she really that much up her own arse? The Ice Queen above anyone's help?* It spoke volumes as to how the Orchid would survive if she took the threats to their shared territories so glibly. Or hadn't she yet worked out that her father's death might not have been an accident?

His immediate reaction was to wish Sam good luck and let her get on with it, being as she was so confident she could handle this alone. Let the Reynold's firm get trodden in the dust! Fine by him! All he cared about was making the Peacock a success, not the bloody Orchid.

Instead, Seb leant back in the armchair, resting his ankle over his opposite knee. 'I appreciate this is difficult, especially at the moment, but regardless of your or my feelings about this situation, I have to respect my father's wishes. And I'd like to think you'd want to respect your father's wishes too.'

He focused his gaze on Sam, still staring at him frostily. 'I presume you're aware that our fathers agreed to work together to thrash out the issues that recently arose and so I suggest we remain in partnership until that is sorted.'

Sam sighed. 'John Maynard deals with the business, Mr Stoker. He'll have everything in hand, but if you wish to confirm any of these things, please make an appointment with him.'

Seb continued to stare at Sam long after she looked away. She really was a snooty one with a chip on her shoulder. Despising that he had to remain civil to her, despite her cold defence heating his blood and pulling him into her orbit against his will, he forced a sympathetic smile. 'As I said, I understand that you've just lost your father, Samantha, but John Maynard isn't the one in ultimate charge of the business.'

Sam sighed loudly, no longer attempting to mask her annoyance. *What was it this man didn't understand?* 'As I keep saying, whatever you presume, it is John you need to discuss business matters with. I'm in charge of my father's business in name only. John has real-life control of the Orchid and I have my own business to run.'

Heat burnt Sam's cheeks. Although it was true, it felt like she'd just outlined her lack of knowledge of the industry as well as her inability to deal with it and that stung sharply.

Seb studied the emotions on Sam's face. *Poor Samantha... Boo hoo...* He bit back a smile at the fire he could see glimmering behind her eyes. So, she did have spirit underneath her usually perfectly styled exterior of fragile beauty. Or did she only come to life on days she hadn't bothered brushing her hair?

For someone to challenge anything he said, was unusual – mainly *unheard* of. And he liked it...

Seb felt a sudden and unexpected twinge of disappointment. If Samantha Reynold was in control of the firm in name only, like she said, then it looked like he was stuck with that shifty bastard, Maynard, after all. And he would rather be looking at her any day than *him*.

He reined in his meandering thoughts, remembering why he was here in the Reynolds' house. The important thing now was putting an end to anyone infiltrating their businesses, not who he dealt with to ensure that happened.

Just because the one person he'd already removed had been partaking of the Aurora's offerings, it didn't mean the orders were definitely originating from there. He had to know for sure where they were coming from before he blew the whole place into oblivion – and the more people they had working on that, the better. Even if that meant Maynard and his cronies.

'Okay, so just to get this straight – you're saying I need to discuss the next steps about these threats with Maynard? I mean, *Mr* Maynard...'

Suspicion glimmered in Sam's mind. 'I'm not aware of any threats, Mr Stoker. I think you must be mistaken.'

Seb watched Sam closely. *She knew nothing about any of this?* Part of him wanted to laugh, the other part felt almost embarrassed on her behalf. 'Forgive me for speaking out of turn, but if I were you, I would insist on regular updates from Maynard about what's going on.'

Alarm bells jangled in the back of Sam's head. 'What exactly are you referring to, Mr Stoker?' she asked curtly. Was Sebastian Stoker hinting that her cousin was keeping things from her that she needed to know?

Gloria was still staring transfixed out of the window when the realisation suddenly hit her around the face, like a plank of wood. She didn't want to say anything, especially in front of Sebastian Stoker, but as it stood, he may be all they had. Or rather, all *Sam* had. Her nephew John Maynard had always been a strange boy and, not that she felt good admitting it, she'd never much liked him.

When Jimmy died, she'd never dreamt Len would pick John to take her brother's place as his new right-hand man, but he'd insisted it was the right thing to do. 'He's Jimmy's boy, Glor,' he'd said. 'The very least I can do for my best mate is to make sure his son's on a decent earn.'

And John had settled into the role well enough. Gloria frowned. She'd never said anything to Len – it wasn't her business to, but she'd never trusted John and still didn't.

'It's not quite that simple,' she said suddenly, as both Sam and Seb turned in her direction having almost forgotten her presence. 'John doesn't have control over the business. *You* do, Samantha.'

Sam's eyes widened. 'But Dad said th...'

'I know what he said,' Gloria interjected. 'But that was never finalised. He was due to get the paperwork and legalities drawn up by the solicitor later this week...' Her red eyes fixed on her daughter. 'I spoke to the solicitor only yesterday – not that I particularly wanted to.'

Her voice faltered. 'He informed me the paperwork concerning John's legal standing over the business hadn't been signed. In light of that, you're the only one in charge of the Orchid and all of the underlying businesses. John has no say whatsoever. I'm sorry, Samantha.'

Sam slumped back in the chair and forced herself not to let the tears at the back of her eyes escape. The last thing she wanted to do was cry in front of Sebastian Stoker.

17

Ignoring that just about everyone present in the Gun Barrels was staring at him, Tom continued to the bar. Although conversation was at a normal level, the silent scrutiny of his presence was clear. A big part of him would have preferred to stay put, but after three days of being holed up in the Aurora ignoring that he was losing money hand over fist, enough was enough.

'The usual, please, Dave.' He leant against the bar, pulling a copy of last night's *Birmingham Evening Mail* towards him.

Flicking through the paper, he stopped, a wave of fresh panic ripping through him as his eyes scanned the words:

WITNESS APPEAL FOR CASINO OWNER'S DEATH

Police are urging members of the public to come forward after a road traffic incident caused the death of a motorist in Edgbaston on Tuesday night.

Len Reynold, 68, the well-known founder and owner of the Violet Orchid casino on Broad Street, was found dead at the scene after a head-on collision with a tree, yards from his home.

Investigations have uncovered that Mr Reynold swerved to

avoid an oncoming vehicle travelling on the wrong side of the road, but the other driver, along with the vehicle, have so far failed to be identified. Anyone with any knowledge or who was in the area around 11 p.m. that night is asked to come forward as soon as possible.

A small trail of sweat trickled between Tom's shoulder blades, still hardly able to comprehend that out of everyone to run off the road and kill, he'd managed to pick Len Reynold... At least there was no link to him or that bloody hire car though. And neither would there be.

But whichever way he looked at it, this had seriously ballsed his blackmail plan up and he needed to get things moving again before of all his hard work went down the shitter.

A ghost of a smile crept onto Tom's face. Now Maynard had agreed to play ball, things would be a lot more plain sailing. Yeah, that twat knew what side his bread was buttered on and was now well aware that, thanks to extenuating circumstances, it was the only way the miserable bastard could attain what he'd been angling for all along.

Tom frowned, knowing he'd have to watch the muppet like a hawk. Regardless of what he had on Maynard from the past, he didn't trust the arsehole as far as he could throw him. But roping Maynard into disposing of Jock Sawyer's body had also given him another means of leverage to add to what he'd already got, so theoretically the man could say fuck all. *Still, one step at a time.*

'Haven't seen you for a few days, Tom,' Dave said cautiously. 'Everything all right?'

Tom snatched the pint out of Dave's hand. 'Why wouldn't it be?' *Act normal*, he reminded himself. The most important thing was to keep suspicion as far away from him as possible. Acting jumpy only accentuated everything.

'Actually, if I'm honest, I'm having a bit of a nightmare,' Tom added, slurping greedily from his pint. He'd already worked through how he was going to play it in here because it was invariable someone would ask. *Always best to get in first.* 'There was me, thinking everything was going well, but now I've got bloody staffing issues.'

He tipped the rest of his pint in his mouth and handed the empty glass back to Dave, nodding towards the Carling pump for a refill. 'My security bloke had some kind of meltdown and buggered off. Left me right in the lurch, he has.'

Dave nodded, pretending to agree. 'What happened to him?'

Tom shrugged. 'No bloody idea. I got back from seeing a mate the other night, only for the girls to tell me Baz had disappeared,' he lied. 'They reckoned something to do with family issues, but it isn't on, is it? I've had to temporarily close the Aurora. How can I run a place without anyone on the door?'

Dave nodded again, not believing a word. As if anywhere worth its salt would close up because one poxy doorman walked off the job? 'What about Jock...? Can't he do it?' He paused, watching Tom's reaction. Many people in here were speculating over Jock, knowing who'd wanted to 'speak' with him the other night – especially as no one had seen him since. And no one more than *him*, being as he'd helped give the poor bastard's name up to Stoker.

'Jock?' Tom said, his face somehow remaining neutral. 'He's another one! He's fucked off too! If you must know, I'm hurt about it. Me and Jock went back years.'

Dave raised his eyebrows. 'What? He just upped and left?'

'Yeah,' Tom muttered. 'Left town apparently.'

'What about his job at the Rover? Jock worked his arse off there to pay for his kids. The job at yours was a bonus.'

Tom glanced over his shoulder. Leaning forward, he dropped his voice, but not so much so that the people next to him couldn't overhear. 'I think he got himself in a bit of shit last week. He confided in me that he'd got pissed and said things he shouldn't have said about someone and...' He dropped his voice lower. 'I think he might have done a bunk before it caught up with him.'

'That wasn't a Stoker was it, by any chance?' a man next to Tom at the bar asked loudly. 'Only there was one of them in here the other night looking for Jock...'

'They came in *here*?' Tom parroted. *Shit!* He knew one of the Stokers had been to the Aurora and offloaded Jock, but he didn't know they'd come here too. This was not good and made things even bloody worse. Did this mean they'd linked it to him? If they'd come here, then they could come back. *For him...* But they couldn't know *he* was anything to do with it – not unless Jock had blathered it out before he dropped off the twig.

'Are you all right, mate?' the man asked. 'You've gone a funny colour.'

'Oh, yeah I'm fine,' Tom muttered. 'Ate something dodgy last night. Still feel a bit rough...'

Fuck, fuck, FUCK. Damage limitation time...

With slightly shaking hands, Tom pulled a wrap of coke out of his pocket and scooped up a small amount on the end of his key, snorting it quickly.

'Hey, you can't do that here!' Dave yelled.

Tom raised his hands in submission. 'Sorry, sorry. I wasn't think-ing.' Inhaling deeply, grateful for the slight rush, he shoved the wrap back into his pocket and turned back to the man next to him. 'Out of interest, which Stoker was it that came in here?'

The man shrugged. 'The psycho-looking older one. He didn't know Jock's name, though. It was *Dave* who gave him that. I don't blame Jock for legging it! I wouldn't want that lot on my back!'

'Yeah,' Tom agreed, his eyes darting to Dave. *Dave had opened his mouth and given Jock up?* And if Dave could give Jock up, then he could easily give *him* up. It sounded like Seb Stoker as well. So *he'd* been the one who'd been to the Aurora... 'Did... erm... did anyone happen to mention anything about me the other night?'

The man shook his head. 'You? No, I don't think so. All I heard mentioned was Jock and that he was at the Aurora.'

Tom's heart lurched, a headache forming. 'Who said he was at the Aurora?' He glared at Dave accusingly. 'Was that you and all?'

'It wasn't Dave,' the man continued. 'It was that silly tart with the bad hair. You know, that craggy old brass. Melanie, is it? Stoker offered her money for the info.'

Tom nodded. 'I know who you mean. Oh well, you can't blame her for saying stuff if the cash was being flashed about.' But *he* could blame her, the stupid bitch. And Dave. This was half his fault too.

The man nodded for a refill and then grinned at Tom. 'I'm surprised she hasn't asked for a job at your new gaff.'

Tom nodded absently. 'I think she might already have done,' he lied, an idea suddenly forming. 'I'll have to check. My main issue is that I need a couple more men now I've lost Jock and Baz.' He eyed the man. 'You don't happen to know of anyone do you?'

'I know loads of fellas wanting jobs, mate, however I don't know whether they'd want to work at a place that's been marked by the Stoker firm!' the man laughed. 'Good luck with that!'

Tom scowled. *Fuck.* He hadn't thought of that. Still, at least this lot thought Jock had legged it and not that he was reduced to cinders in a burnt out hire car over in Ladywood. The rest he would have to sort. And quickly.

* * *

Sitting on the edge of the bed in the room that used to be hers, Sam stared at the wall, noticing lighter patches where Blue-Tac used for attaching multiple posters had once been. The days of the Bay City Rollers and Adam Ant were long gone.

Sam remembered being pleased to have left all the trials and tribulations of adolescence behind her at the time, but now that comparatively stress-free world seemed a lot more preferable.

A few days ago, she'd had a bright future and the prize of her very own graphic design business – the pot of gold at the end of the rainbow, inches from her grasp. Now it was dust – splintered fragments floating in the air.

Without any shadow of a doubt, she would have to have the planned conversation with her work about leaving – only now the reasons for her leaving were different. She wouldn't be leaving to branch out on our own, she'd be leaving to take over her father's business.

Since Seb Stoker had left the house after his impromptu visit, combined with the bombshell her mother had dropped, there was only one decision she could make. Well, the only one that was the right and proper, under the circumstances.

'Can I come in?' Gloria tapped the door, then pushed it ajar.

Sam moved along the edge of the bed so her mother could sit down.

Gloria looked at Sam's sad face. 'Samantha, darling, I've been thinking. Your father wouldn't want you to take any of this on. You heard what he said. The last thing he wanted was for you to give up your dreams.'

Sam nodded. 'But that was before. The additional paperwork was never drawn up putting John in charge, so I have to step up.'

'Perhaps I shouldn't have told you about the solicitor's findings earlier,' Gloria cried. 'It is sortable though, love. Now you're legally head of the company, there's nothing to stop *you* signing everything over to John.'

Sam bit her bottom lip. No, there wasn't, but she couldn't shake off the nagging feeling that, in addition to what Seb Stoker had told her, there was something in the back of her mind telling her not to.

Although she'd never particularly warmed to her cousin, something alerted her not to take up the idea her mother suggested.

Sam shivered involuntarily. She couldn't say what that something was – probably because there wasn't a set reason – not one she could name, but a *feeling*. And a feeling that however much she didn't want it to be there, it was – and it was strong.

As well as that, and although Seb hadn't said so in as many words, she'd got the distinct impression that what he'd said contained a hidden warning. A warning about John Maynard.

Of course, if she went ahead and signed things over to John it would be the answer to everything, but she just could not shake off the doubt that if she did that, she'd be doing her father a grave injustice. And that she would *not* do.

'Your father would be horrified to have left you in this position, Samantha, he really would,' Gloria continued. 'I urge you to seriously consider what I've said. You know he didn't want you to be involved with what goes on behind the scenes either. Remember how adamant he was that you didn't get involved with a boy from the other side of the business?'

Sam raised her eyebrows. 'A *boy*?'

Gloria flapped her hand. 'All right, but you know what I mean.'

Sam smiled, relieved to change the subject, even temporarily. 'It's good to see you smile again, Mum. Forget about me for a moment. How about you?'

Gloria patted her daughter's hand. 'I'm still taking everything in, darling. I – I don't know what to do or how to feel and I've no idea how to go on without Len.' Her eyes brimmed with tears. 'But one thing I *do* know and that is he wouldn't want us drowning in misery. I can see his face reprimanding us now!'

Sam laughed through her own tears and pulled her mother into a hug. 'I can't quite believe it myself either, but I'll make sure everything is all right.' She held her mother at arm's length and looked into her eyes. 'You both looked after me all my life and now it's my turn to look after you and everything else. I've made my decision – I'm going to make Dad proud and run his business – warts and all. John will help.'

And he *would* help. She and John may have a mutual dislike for each other, but they were family and this was about the family business. Yes, this was the best way – she would keep overall control, which would quell this unnamed flicker of concern, yet she'd still be able to rely on John to bring her up to speed and assist her with learning the ropes – even if it was just in the short term until they all worked out what to do for the best moving forward.

Gloria nodded, secretly relieved over Sam's decision. She'd dreaded the prospect of her nephew taking full control of the firm Len had worked so hard to build up from scratch, but didn't want to foist those concerns on Samantha, thereby influencing her choice. But her main concern first and foremost now was how John would react when he learnt he wouldn't have the role he'd expected. She suspected he would be nowhere near as amenable and helpful to Samantha as she hoped. The second concern was how Samantha would deal with the ins and outs of Len's firm. Although Gloria knew little of it herself, she knew enough to know the prospect worried her greatly.

18

Roaring along the Hagley Road, John chewed the inside of his cheek. Gripping the steering wheel, his hands trembled with pure rage.

How he'd kept his rag when that spoilt bitch informed him *she* would be actively running the Orchid and all the underlying enterprises after all, he didn't know, but somehow he'd managed it. And then for her to have the audacity to ask why he hadn't appraised her of all of this 'trouble' surrounding the Orchid's territories?

Since when was she aware of territories? Len had always made it crystal-clear that his darling Samantha and the dippy mother should be told nothing about *that* side of the business.

John's nostrils flared as he sucked in a huge lungful of air.

Somehow Sam knew, meaning *someone* had told her. But who?

Christ, after years of arse-crawling and putting up with the sickeningly fair and decent ways of Uncle Len, how had it come to this? To end up as a poxy right-hand man to his bloody cousin was one step beyond. And for it to be *Samantha* – the girl who fiddled with photos on a screen all day for a bloody living?

The stupid cow really thought he would assist in gaining her footing and telling her the ins and outs of everything?

Dream on, darling!

John scraped his hand through his hair. It was all very well Len being six feet under, but what use was that if he was still regaled to second fiddle? This should have been sorted years ago and would have been had it not all gone tits up.

He'd be helping Samantha out well enough. Just not in the way she expected. Before long, she'd be begging him to take the whole fucking place off her hands.

Tom-fucking-Bedworth might have got him over a barrel and he'd hoped to never see the loser again, but he was here and thanks to the man's idiocy, he'd now been roped into more shit – like disposing of that body, which he could have done without.

John scowled. Regardless of the threats Bedworth held over him, this time the man's return would work in his favour.

Screeching into the carpark, John stomped out of the car and wasted no time hammering on the front door of the Aurora. Being as this bloody idiot was shoving his big hooter in and causing problems around Brum, then he'd get some use out of him before he got rid of the fucker.

Where John came from, things worked two ways, but would make sure *he* got the lion's share.

Tom wasn't pleased to be disturbed so early. Jesus Christ, it wasn't even eleven in the goddamn morning and he'd already had Maynard on his back laying down the law. Now he'd got this stupid slag to deal with?

He knew it wouldn't take this greedy bitch long to come digging once she'd got the message an earner was on the cards. *Still, no time like the present.*

'Morning, Tom.' Melanie's bright voice contradicted that she looked like she hadn't slept for the best part of a week. 'You wanted to see me?'

She made a big show of looking around the Aurora's large room. 'Nice place you've got here,' she lied. 'Luce said you've got some work for me?' Moving towards Tom, her hand ran down the front of his stained T-shirt. 'You know I'm always up for regular work.'

'Come upstairs and we'll discuss it there,' Tom muttered.

'Oh, I get it! You want a freebie before you make anything permanent?' Melanie laughed, following Tom up the stairs, her feet clumping loudly on the bare steps. 'You hardly need to test me out, Tommy. I mean, it's not like you haven't sampled my wares more than a few times already, so you know I'm good.'

Tom jerked his head towards one of the empty rooms. 'Business is business,' he grinned. To be fair, Melanie was bloody good in the sack. It was just a shame about her face.

Shutting the door, he turned to find her already half-undressed. He frowned. He hadn't planned on bothering with a sampler, but being as she was offering...

He glanced at his watch. Half an hour before Lee and Steve were due to turn up. *More than enough time.*

Pushing Melanie onto the bed, Tom unzipped his flies and, without further ceremony, plunged straight into her.

'Fucking hell,' Melanie yelped. 'Haven't you ever heard of working a girl up to it?'

'You don't need working up to nothing,' he grunted. Fixing his eyes on Melanie's breasts rather than looking at her face, he continued thrusting. Despite being in her fifties, she still had a decent body on her. This would be her parting gift.

Raising her hips, Melanie grasped Tom's buttocks, knowing that would be all it took to push him over the edge, and grinned as he groaned loudly. *He'd always been a two-stroke.* 'So when can I start?' she asked, running her hand down his unshaven face.

'When you tell me why you told Stoker that Jock Sawyer was here the other night,' Tom growled.

Seeing the sudden change in Tom's countenance, Melanie stiffened, then attempted to unpin herself from under his weight. 'I – I never meant anything by it. It were just a passing comment, Tom. Trade's been slow the last few weeks and the guy offered a fifty for info.' Her eyes twinkled. 'Besides, he was a rare, nice looker, so what could I do?'

'Not opening your fat gob would have been a start!' Tom spat, closing both his hands tightly around Melanie's throat.

'Tom!' Melanie squawked, pulling at Tom's fingers. 'Don't be daft! There's no need to be...'

'Shut the fuck up!' Tom roared. 'You've caused no end of bastard problems, you whore. Jock's dead because of you!'

Melanie's eyes bulged as the grip around her windpipe tightened. 'I'm sorry. I didn't realise. I...'

'I *said* shut up!' Tom barked. 'You should have said nothing, you stupid slut! Nothing!'

Running out of oxygen, Melanie thrashed around under the weight of Tom's body, her face turning from red to purple, the whites of her eyes bloodshot as the blood vessels ruptured. 'Tom... I...'

'No point in begging now, you trash,' he smiled. Putting extra effort into his grip, Tom glanced at the pillow. If she didn't hurry up, then he'd use that.

* * *

Tom snorted a nice fat line from the bedside table and glanced contemptuously at the woman in the bed. *Fucking ugly pig.* Still, at least that was one down. People needed to start realising they couldn't fuck with Thomas Bedworth.

He inhaled sharply, enjoying the rush of the powder. All of these wastes of space needed to jump on a quick learning curve because they'd want to make sure they were in favour when he was cream of the city. When he was the one everybody wanted to know, everyone would wish they'd been more attentive when it mattered.

Tom wiped the back of his hand under his nose, making sure there was no trace of residue.

There was no point in them crawling up his arse once he was kingpin. It was *now* that counted. He would remember every person who stood by him, as well as more than remember every single fucker who didn't.

Hearing voices at the bottom of the stairs, Tom scowled. *It was like the M5 around here.* He quickly checked he was tucked back into his trousers and left the room, making sure he locked it behind him. He didn't want any silly tarts stumbling across Melanie before he'd sorted it. And sorting it was the first task.

He poked his head over the rickety banister. 'Thought I heard you,' Tom smiled. 'Come on up. We'll talk up here.'

Ushering the two men into another empty room, Tom was only grateful the girls were either downstairs catching up with their morning lager or still in their pits up in the attic. He didn't want any of the nosey cows overhearing.

Shutting the door behind him, he turned to face the two men, not bothering to offer them a seat. Not that there was anywhere to sit, short of the bed, but this wouldn't take long.

'Good to see you again fellas. Glad you're on board. I always appreciate loyal, long-standing *friends*.' Tom made sure he emphasised the word 'friends'. Not that they were friends –

just a couple of stoners he'd known from years back, but they were trustworthy and most importantly, not linked to the Stoker or Reynold firms. And that was, by far, the most important factor. 'Looking forward to earning yourself a good wedge, boys?'

Lee Baxter grinned widely, showcasing his missing front teeth. 'You betcha! Really appreciate this, Tommo! Couldn't believe it when we heard you were back, let alone that you've got yourself this gaff and all.'

Steve Maddox nodded enthusiastically. 'I've been wriggling since getting laid off from the Rover, so, got to ask, mate, what are we being paid and what exactly do you want us to do?'

Tom eyed Steve, noticing his brashness hadn't toned down in his absence. Neither had his looks improved, although he had gained an additional feature to his physical repulsiveness.

He peered closer at the man's cauliflower ear. 'What happened there?' Tom nodded at the mangled monstrosity on the side of the man's head.

Steve laughed, touching his deformed ear. 'Too many bare-knuckle stints in the gaff under the swimming baths in Northfield, mate.'

Tom grinned. *Still thick as fuck then?* But he had successfully deflected quite nicely from the question of money. He'd pay them handsomely for this first job, then pare it right down to basics after that. They'd swallow it because it was more than either of them were getting right now, which was diddly squat. This chunk would keep the situation primed and make them believe these pay-outs could be regular.

He folded his arms and leant casually against the door; partly to stop anyone coming in and the rest to help hold himself upright. 'I'll want you here most nights, but expect the occasional special job too.'

Lee glanced at Steve and then at Tom. 'What sort of special jobs?'

Tom shrugged. 'Could be anything.' He fished out two rolls of money and chucked them on the bed. 'That's for you once you've undertaken the first special job, which needs to happen either tonight or tomorrow.'

Steve's eyes locked on the fat wad of money. 'No problem,' he grinned, clapping his hands together enthusiastically. 'What do you need us to do?'

Tom smiled thinly. 'Firstly, I need your complete loyalty.'

'We'd never drop you in it, Tommo, you know that. Never!'

Tom nodded. 'Glad to hear it. What you do will not be forgotten in the future when I excel.'

'Got your sights set high, Tom? Steve grinned.

'I have,' Tom said, unsmiling. 'Now, this job... I need somewhere burned down.'

Lee blinked. 'Burned down? I didn't think th...'

'Whatever you need is not a problem,' Steve interrupted, nudging Lee sharply. Lee might be able to afford to pass this up, but he couldn't. 'Where? And how?'

'A pub. Do it whichever way you wish, but I want it done mid-evening when the place is packed,' Tom said bluntly. 'You know the drill. Make sure there's no cops lurking and that it looks like an accident.' He eyed both men slowly. 'If others get taken down as part of this, that's okay and more realistic, but the gaffer's got to go for definite. I want him finished.'

Watching the two men silently glance at each other, Tom turned to Lee. 'You're a sparky, aren't you?'

'Used to be,' Lee shrugged. 'Before all my work dried up.'

Tom grinned. 'Can you make it look like an electrical fault? A bad one? One that would cause fast damage? Anything but arson.'

Lee nodded. 'That's certainly doable.' He looked at Steve. 'You up for that?'

Steve rubbed his hands together. 'I'm up for anything, me. How much are we getting for this?' He jerked his head towards the money on the bed.

'Five grand a piece. You'll get it once the job's done.' And they'd better do it. This was the last chunk of his brass. A big gamble, but he couldn't risk those people hanging around. Not now he knew they'd squealed because they'd keep squealing.

'Which pub do you want done?' Lee asked.

'The Gun Barrels,' Tom muttered. 'The one just off Horsefair.'

'*The Gun Barrels?*' Steve gasped. 'You want us to off Dave? Why?'

Tom's eyes narrowed. 'That's none of your fucking business and keep your voice down. That's the job. Take it or leave it.'

Lee and Steve nodded, neither stupid enough not to realise they had no choice but to undertake the work. They would hardly be allowed to disappear now they knew the plan.

'Good. Make sure you do it well. I want no fuckups.' Shaking hands with the two men, Tom smiled. 'Remember, I need it done either tonight or tomorrow. Oh, and before you go, there's also a little something I want you to do for me now.'

Tom walked out the room towards the room where Melanie's body lay, knowing Lee and Steve would follow and, furthermore, do *exactly* what he asked.

19

Replacing the receiver, Seb got up from the desk that had once been his father's. Straightening his suit jacket, he made his way down to the Peacock's casino.

Nodding to one of the many security on the door, he smiled pleasantly at a group of customers depositing their coats in the cloakroom, before continuing into the gaming room.

He glanced around the busy tables, pleased to see the croupiers were, as usual, immaculately presented and doing exactly what they should be – making him money.

Things were ticking over nicely. Just the final handover with the Irish's ammo order tomorrow and then that was one more thing out of the way. However, Andrew would have to oversee that, being as he'd arranged for *his* evening to be spent with Samantha Reynold...

Seb's lips twitched into a smirk as he approached the table in the VIP section where two of his brothers sat. Tomorrow he would know for sure exactly how little idea Samantha had about anything in this game. He'd pretty much deduced that already, but it never hurt to make sure. Once that was done, he'd be in a better position to see how much his forced assistance to the Reynold clan would be of use to the Peacock. That's what all of this was about, after all.

Motioning to the barman to prepare a drink, Seb sauntered across to the table and stared at the two women sitting with Neil and Gary. The women's eyes lit up as he approached, their excitement short-lived when he spoke. 'Excuse my interruption, ladies, but I need to speak to my brothers.'

Crestfallen, the women hastily grabbed their clutch bags and reluctantly scuttled off to another table.

'Do you have to embarrass yourself by allowing them to drape all over you?' Seb snapped, plonking himself down in the vacated space on the crescent-shaped seating.

'I didn't invite them over,' Gary sniffed, looking at Neil pointedly.

Seb nodded his thanks as a waiter deposited a large whisky on the table. No, Gary wouldn't have approached the women. That was definitely Neil's talent. He certainly spent enough time practising it. 'I've just been on the phone bringing Dad up to speed,' he said, looking between his brothers. 'I'll be spending time with Samantha Reynold tomorrow night. It seems she's not aware of anything that's been going on.'

'Well, there's a surprise!' Neil rolled his eyes. 'I still can't believe you're wasting your time helping her!'

'Who said I am?' Seb raised his eyebrows. 'But Dad's right. We need to offer our assistance to some extent – at least until we find out exactly what is linked regarding Len Reynold.' He glanced at Neil, knowing his brother would understand that his look concerned the unsavoury rumours.

'I've heard nothing since,' Neil said, swigging from a bottle of Budweiser.

'What's this?' Gary frowned. 'Has something else happened?'

'No, nothing.' Seb smiled. And there should be no more

happening on that subject either since the one spreading the shit was no more. 'But we *do* need to deduce whether Reynold's accident was an accident.' The one thing he *did* know was that the 'accident' couldn't have been anything to do with that ginger-haired bloke because the man couldn't have been in two places at once.

Looking up, Neil raised his eyebrows. 'Oh, Christ, what's the matter with him?'

Following Neil's gaze, Seb watched Andrew rapidly approaching their table, his face like thunder.

'Who pissed on your chips?' Neil laughed.

'I'll tell you, shall I?' Andrew spat. Sitting down, he took a cigarette from his monogrammed silver case with shaking fingers. 'I've just been down to the private stock room to check how much coke we've got out the back and as I walked past the wine cellar, I happened to overhear a conversation...'

The back of Seb's neck prickled. 'Right? And...?'

Andrew drank greedily from the whisky that had just been placed on the table and waited until the barman retreated. 'The conversation was about which one of us isn't a true Stoker...'

He looked at Seb and then at Neil, his eyes narrowing at their exchanged glances. 'Wait a minute. You *knew* about this? You knew this shit was being bandied around and didn't mention it to me?'

Seb shrugged. 'It came up last week. Some shit-for-brains thought it would be a good idea to use as leverage.'

Andrew's fists clenched. 'I'll kill the fucker!'

'No need... That's been dealt with,' Seb muttered. 'But it seems the rumour is still rife...' He wouldn't mention Neil had almost thought about believing it. He wasn't having *that* start again.

Andrew stared at his brother, the penny dropping. 'So that's what all that business was about that night I finally found you at the apartment...?'

'What?' Neil said, watching Andrew and Seb exchange knowing glances. 'Now *I'm* missing something.'

'No one's missing *anything!*' Seb hissed, glancing around. He was *not* discussing Jock's removal here. 'And keep your fucking voices down.'

'If this rumour is still flying around, then we have to do something about it,' Neil pushed.

Gary slammed his glass on the table. 'Why have I not been told of this? Aren't we all supposed to be part of this business and this family? I'm sick of being treated as an afterthought! We are brothers, after all.'

Andrew looked at Gary, his sandy hair a stark contrast to the dark brown of his and the others. 'You sure about that, Gary?'

Blanching, Gary stiffened. 'What are you trying to say?'

Seb looked up quickly. 'You shouldn't have said that, Andrew.'

Andrew shrugged. 'Perhaps not, but don't tell me you haven't thought it!' He looked Gary up and down. 'I mean, he's never really been like us, has he? Even his fucking hair's the wrong colour!'

Neil nodded in agreement with his twin. 'He hasn't got the eyes, either. His are blue, not green.'

Gary trembled with a combination of hurt and rage. Ever since he could remember, he'd been the butt of his brothers' jibes. He knew as the youngest, his mother had babied him, cultivating a softer personality compared to that of his louder and competitive brothers, but he'd never *ever* thought any of them would throw something like *this* at him.

He felt his hands clenching into fists. 'You pair of cunts!' he roared, his eyes wild as he pushed himself up from the table, whisky and lager slopping onto the thick, plush carpet. He lurched across the table, his hands grasping for Andrew's suit lapels. 'I do everything I can for this fucking family and you say this sort of sh...'

'Enough!' Seb roared, jumping from his seat and ripping Gary's hand from Andrew's jacket. He glared between all three of his brothers. 'You're all making a fucking scene and I will not have it, do you understand?'

He nodded in the direction of the bar for replacement drinks and then swept his glare around anyone in the vicinity who may think it wise to stare at the commotion. 'We do *not* discuss this in public or anywhere ever again,' he hissed. 'It's not something *any* of us should or *will* think and I won't hear any more about it, understand?'

Seb jerked his head at Andrew and then towards the door. 'You – fuck off out of my sight.' He then turned to Neil. 'And not one more peep from you either!'

He stared contemptuously at the stain of whisky sloshed down the front of his own suit trousers. 'Now Gary, sit the fuck down and have another drink whilst I go and change my bloody suit.'

With that, Seb stormed from the casino, his temper blown.

* * *

Sam topped up her wine and waited for Liam to continue. He could say what he liked, but he didn't understand. It wasn't his fault – how *could* he understand?

The growing suffocation she felt around him had not diminished, her mind still associating him with the night of her father's death.

For once in her life, she wished she could confide in someone, but she couldn't. She couldn't talk to *anyone* about this. Not Liam, not her mother and *certainly* not John.

The back of Sam's eyes stung with the burn of forming tears. She wanted to pick up the phone and call her father – he'd know what to do. That was until, with the crushing sense of loss, she remembered that she couldn't and never would be able to again. And it bloody hurt.

She felt very much alone. More alone than ever. Being an only child, she'd always been comfortable with her own company, but *this* was different. Totally different. She was out of her depth in unfamiliar waters and it was not a pleasant feeling.

Liam moved to sit next to Sam on the sofa, ignoring her stiffen at his closeness. 'I really don't see how this can be a good idea,' he said. 'I've told you before that you shouldn't trust Seb Stoker.'

'Who said anything about trusting him?' Sam barked, drinking her wine far quicker than she should. 'All we'll be doing is going through what my father had planned.'

'And you have to spend the evening at the Royal Peacock for that? Why can't you do it over the phone?' Liam frowned, the thought of Sam being in the company of Sebastian Stoker of all people grating on every nerve ending in his body.

'Exactly what do you suppose I do then?' Sam snapped. 'If I'm to run this business, I need to at least know *something!*'

'But they're your rivals!' Liam cried. 'You really believe Stoker won't feed you false information for his own gains?'

'Like I said, this is regarding what was planned between my father and Mal Stoker. Seb was at the meeting when it was discussed,' Sam said. The fact that Seb could be doing this for his own ends had crossed her mind, but she couldn't allow Liam to know that. In fact, why was she justifying anything – to herself *or* Liam?

Liam folded his arms defensively. 'John Maynard should be dealing with this, not you. Leave it to him,' he said. 'That was what your father wanted.' He threw his hands in the air. 'And to give up your design business in the process? Len would've hated that!'

Sam reined in her escalating anger. Even though John had tried to mask his feelings when she'd told him she would be running things after all, she'd seen the hate and resentment deep behind his eyes. It had been too strong for him to hide and she'd sensed it loud and clear, regardless of the words spilling from his mouth about how 'he'd do everything to help her'. She didn't believe it. *Not one bit.*

Sam also knew her father would not want her shelving her design shop dream, but she wasn't allowing the business empire he'd spent his life creating to be slung down the toilet. Her mother had to be provided for and that wouldn't happen if she didn't step up. And she certainly couldn't leave it to John – someone she had unexplained reservations about.

She could continue with her dream at a later date – just not *now*.

Sam stood up, wine slopping down the front of her dress. 'If you don't agree with what I'm doing or how I'm going about it and how much my father would hate everything, as you keep telling me, then it's best you just bloody go!'

'Don't be like that. It's only because I'm worried about you.' Liam reached for Sam's hand. 'And because I love you...' He had to keep her on side. She'd begun to pull away from him – even more so since Len's death – and that was not how it was supposed to work. He had to show Sam she could rely on him. He couldn't lose his chance now – not when he was so close to securing his future.

'Just go, will you?' Sam shrieked, tugging her hand away from Liam's grasp. 'Please! I want to be on my own.'

When Liam finally slammed the door of her parents' home behind him, Sam flopped into a chair and put her head in her hands.

Composing herself, she poured another glass of wine, resenting the shaking of her hands. Tomorrow she'd move back to her own apartment. There was only so long she could cope being in the same house with her mother, knowing she would have to continually play down the brewing trouble occurring behind the scenes at the Orchid.

If she had to accept Sebastian Stoker's arrogant help to get to the bottom of what was going on, then she'd do it. She'd do it for her father.

She may not know much about his business, but now she was making it *her* business to learn and find out. And she'd be doing that quickly.

20

It wasn't anything out of the ordinary for John to call a couple of his men into his office; he did it frequently to discuss certain aspects of collections, so it wouldn't bring about any particular attention, but just to be sure, he kept an eye on who was passing in the corridor outside through the glass panel.

That stupid girl wandered around on a regular basis, no doubt trying to look important or to ingratiate herself with his staff. Yes, *his* staff – not hers. They would *never* be hers.

John frowned. At least enough of them weren't onside with her to matter. Not yet, at least, and that's all that counted at the moment.

Smiling coldly, he glanced at the three men in front of him. All of these boys had been with him for donkey's years and every single one of them had expressed their unhappiness about Samantha Reynold being involved with this side of the business, let alone thinking she could waltz in, expecting them to take orders from her.

'This is happening tonight, you reckon?' Sid asked, peering at John with beady eyes.

John nodded. 'Apparently. There's a chap on the Stoker side –

one of their runners, who has a runaway mouth when he's had a few sherbets. Hell knows why someone hasn't dispatched him yet, but I guess that just shows how little notice Old Man Stoker took of details what matter!' He folded his arms, his face forming a weird grimace that, to him, equalled pleasure. 'And this dickhead was overheard by someone I know who, in turn, told me.'

Tom was quite useful for digging the dirt, John had to give him that. Of course, he'd want his cut, but he'd be getting the bare minimum. And that was only if he was bloody right. Tom was such a drunk cokehead that he could have dreamt the whole thing up, but it was worth a punt.

John pulled his attention back to the three men. 'Not sure where the deal is happening yet, but I'm pretty sure it will be done by one of the Stokers themselves. That's why I want all three of you. I'll be watching the Peacock and I'll put a tail on whoever leaves around 9 p.m. Make sure one of you is in my office. I'll call and tell you where to come and what to do.'

John stood up from his desk and looked at each of the three men in turn. 'And boys, rest assured I'll make this worth your while.'

Sam could have walked to the Peacock. It was only a couple of hundred yards from the Orchid, but arriving by car looked more presentable, so a taxi it was.

It had been an extremely long day, which had passed at the speed of a dead snail. Although she had been busy moving her stuff from her mother's house back into her own apartment, for Sam, every minute, every *second*, dragged. And that was because all she'd been able to think of was what she was doing tonight.

She was dreading it. For *many* reasons.

'Having a bit of a flutter tonight, are you?' the driver said, his eyes meeting Sam's in the rear-view mirror.

'Something like that,' Sam smiled, quickly checking her makeup in her compact mirror. She glanced at the orchid clip in her hair – the latest, and last one her father would ever give her. *This one's for you, Dad.*

Wearing the flower was an easy decision. It was the rest that wasn't. She hadn't been sure whether to dress business-like or to go for the attire she'd usually wear to somewhere like this – or the Orchid, her *own* casino.

Her stomach somersaulted. How strange that sounded: her *own* casino.

But it was. The Violet Orchid was now hers and, despite what anyone else thought, she would do a good job of running it. She had to and would do whatever was necessary to make that happen.

As the taxi drew to a halt outside the Peacock, Sam fumbled with her purse. Pulling out a ten-pound note, she handed it to the driver. 'Keep the change.'

'Cheers, love,' the driver grinned. 'Hope you're lucky and win tonight.'

So do I, Sam thought, stepping out of the car. Shutting the door, she watched the cab drive off, before turning around and looking up at the Peacock.

A similar style building as the Orchid, the Peacock stood four storeys high, uplighters highlighting an illuminated vertical path between the windows on the first and second floors. The deep red of the 'Royal Peacock Casino' signage spanned the length of the building and 'Roulette, Slots, Blackjack, Late Bar and Restaurant' were signed above in smaller neon lettering.

Sam walked towards the entrance, where a doorman opened the double glass doors. Nodding her thanks, she continued up the red-carpeted staircase to the casino's reception, glad she'd gone for a black cocktail dress rather than a business suit.

'Good evening, madam,' the beautiful blonde receptionist gushed as Sam entered the lobby. 'Do you have your membership card?'

Sam faltered, realising she hadn't thought this meeting with Seb Stoker through very well. She didn't think she'd ever been inside the Peacock before. If she had, it was a very long time ago. 'Oh, erm... I... erm... I don't have a membership card. I'm here for a meeting with Mr Stoker.'

The blonde blinked, her false eyelashes casting spidery silhouettes across her flawless face. 'Mr Stoker?'

'Yes, Sebastian Stoker,' Sam added, belatedly remembering there were several of the Stoker men.

The receptionist picked up the telephone. 'Can I take your name please, madam?'

Feeling her clammy hands slip on her clutch bag, Sam hoped her smile remained in place. 'Samantha Reynold.' She watched the woman tap digits into the telephone, her long nails clicking as they hit the buttons.

'No need to page me, Serena. I'm expecting Ms Reynold.' Seb strode towards the reception desk, his hand outstretched towards Sam. His eyes ran appreciatively over her. 'You look lovely, Samantha.'

And she did. *More* than lovely. What needled him more and more each time he laid eyes on her was that even her overly privileged and defensive attitude wasn't enough to dilute the intrigue he felt about the woman.

Women usually threw themselves at him – hanging off his every word – and the fact that Sam didn't piqued his interest.

'Good evening, Mr Stoker.' Sam shook Seb's hand, horribly

aware her hand was sweaty to the touch, and tried not to stare too long at the man who had hold of it.

Seb Stoker looked even more handsome in a tuxedo than he had in the tailored suits she'd seen him wearing previously. The cut of the jacket emphasised his wide shoulders and slim waist and the expensive material showed the outline of muscular legs under the perfectly fitting trousers.

Slightly irritated with herself for being glad she'd decided on the cocktail dress over the business suit, she quickly pulled her eyes away before he caught her looking. She released her hand from his grip. It would be prudent to remember that what this man looked like had absolutely no bearing on why she was here.

Watching Sam pull from his grasp, Seb's fingers instead moved to touch the flower clip in her dark, glossy hair. 'How apt,' he remarked, meeting her brown eyes. 'You wear your casino's namesake?'

Seb's raw gravelly voice, his lips inches from Sam's ear, vibrated through her entire body, his proximity both intoxicating and off-putting in equal measures.

This man was dangerous and on top of that a rival of her father's business, yet his overpowering magnetism drew her like a moth to a flame. She had to get a grip. What was the matter with her?

Regaining her inner composure, she forced herself to smile. 'I always wear an orchid on special occasions, Mr Stoker,' Sam said, her voice clipped.

Seb stepped back, his hand dropping back to his side and his green eyes twinkled with amusement at Sam's sarcasm. An abrupt, bordering on rude manner would normally aggravate him, but with *her* it was invigorating.

Besides, two could play at that game...

'I'm honoured you warrant our meeting tonight as a special

occasion,' Seb smiled. 'Let me show you around.' He gestured proudly towards the main casino area.

Sam followed, her heels sinking into the plush deep-pile carpet, unable to deduce whether Seb's response was sardonic, or if he'd taken her scorn as a compliment. She could only hope it wasn't the latter.

She looked around the large gaming room, sporting the same deep burgundy carpet. There were plenty of well-spaced roulette tables in the centre and slot machines around the perimeter of the room, but the thing catching her eye the most was the unusual lighting, which formed a gold swirl across the ceiling in a moulded figure of eight. Not too bright, yet not too dim. The place looked good.

She chewed her lip, unsure why that should surprise her. It wasn't like anywhere rivalling her father's casino – *her* casino, would be shoddy, but it was clear Seb took great pride in the Royal Peacock and she admired his attitude.

Taking Sam's elbow, Seb smiled. 'I presume I don't need to explain what all of these areas are.' He nodded towards the roulette wheels and the blackjack tables.

'I don't think so, no,' Sam laughed, part of her not entirely sure whether he was being serious, but decided to give him the benefit of the doubt.

'We have a restaurant,' Seb continued, gesturing to a door at the far end of the room. 'Have you eaten or perhaps you'd just prefer a drink in the bar?' He pointed to a large, galleried overhang above. 'The bar is upstairs.'

This time Sam's smile was cool. He was treating this like a date and that it was definitely not. 'I think I'd prefer to just get on with our discussion.'

Seb shrugged. 'Okay, whatever you wish. In that case, we'll go straight to my office. I'll get some drinks sent there.'

Sensing a strange twinge of annoyance in Seb Stoker's face, Sam forced a smile, realising she'd come over far too sharp to class as polite. Regardless of her dislike of the nervous uncomfortableness this man spawned in her, she still needed his help. 'How is your father, Mr Stoker?'

Seb turned and looked at Sam quizzically before speaking. 'He's a lot better now he's out of the hospital. He's not a big fan of those places, but thank you for asking.'

Sam followed Seb through another door and walked down a corridor towards his office. It would be tempting to have more than a few glasses of wine before getting publicly humiliated over her lack of knowledge, but she didn't dare do anything to cause her guard to slip. It was bad enough accepting this man's help without acting like an imbecile in the process.

'Are you sure it was wise sending Gary to do the deal with the Irish?' Neil asked, his concentration firmly on a new blonde waitress.

Andrew shrugged. 'Gary wanted more responsibility, didn't he? You heard him. And being as Seb's busy chasing the Reynold skirt tonight and you do sod all, apart from lounge around here every night, I thought for once I'd join you.' He motioned to the waitress for fresh drinks. 'Besides, Gary can't exactly fuck this up because all the hard work has already been done. It's literally a case of taking the final payment once the drivers have swapped trailers. Even *he* should be able to manage that.'

Neil pursed his lips. 'I'm surprised he hasn't chucked himself off a cliff after what you said the other night.'

'Oh, come on,' Andrew scoffed. 'I was only joking.'

'Except you weren't,' Neil countered, raising an eyebrow. 'Admit it!'

Andrew scowled. Okay, so he *wasn't* joking and if any of his other brothers were honest, neither were they. Gary had always been different to the rest of them. Aside from his different colouring – his sandy blonde hair and blue eyes, compared to their dark, almost black hair and green eyes – he also was as far removed as possible in sharing their mentality.

Whilst they'd all enjoyed daring adventures, Gary was quiet and reserved – preferring to look for frogs and newts in ponds than have a scrap or play football. Now, as adults, Gary was the worrier – over-discussing things and procrastinating, rather than getting his hands dirty.

Andrew wasn't stupid. There *could* be some truth in what had been said and if there was, didn't that mean that their mother had...? Did their father know about any of this? Was that why their father always let Gary get away with stuff? Not because Gary was the baby of the family, but because of an entirely different reason?

Neil watched his twin brother carefully. 'You think it's a possibility, don't you?'

Andrew turned his drink around in circles on the table. 'I don't know,' he said quietly, looking into the same green eyes as his own. 'But if it *is* true, then what does that mean?'

'It means he's not a fucking Stoker, that's what,' Neil spat. 'And that would explain everything.'

'What do you reckon Seb thinks?' Andrew asked, worry beginning to snowball. It bothered him more every time he thought about it. Had Gary always irritated him because deep down he'd always known the man wasn't his true brother?

'You know what Seb thinks about it. He doesn't want us to entertain the thought!' Neil barked, recollection of his brother's sharp backhand the other day still vivid. 'But then, Seb never levels with us on anything. And that will only get worse now he's head honcho. It's started already, or haven't you noticed?'

'All I noticed was that hot chick he ushered in earlier,' Andrew laughed, eager to get off the subject. 'Seb's punching above his weight with that one. What happened to the evening with Samantha Reynold? Got a better offer, it seems, thank fuck. Don't know why Dad wants us involved with the Reynolds anyway.'

Neil laughed, despite himself. 'That *was* Samantha Reynold.'

'What?' Andrew choked. 'I don't remember her looking like that! No wonder Seb agreed to help out. Bloody typical. I wish I'd volunteered now.'

Both men continued their drinks, but no matter how much they skirted around the topic, the subject of Gary played on both of their minds.

21

Staring at the map Seb spread over on the desk, Sam focused on the areas outlined in red. They ranged across a wider area than she'd expected. The same applied to the green areas.

'So, just to recap, these green areas are Stoker territories, the red are mine, and these,' Sam pointed to the blue areas, 'these are ones we share?'

Seb sipped from his thick crystal tumbler of whisky, before tapping the blue areas with a pen. 'That's correct. This, this, and this. All of these are ones we both supply and deal in – within allotted areas, of course.'

Sam frowned, wanting to ask what that meant. *God, why was she in this position?* She knew absolutely nothing and it was mortifying. As much as she resented it, she'd had to bite the bullet and ask this man to go through everything bit by bit. John should be doing this, not forcing her to humiliate herself in front of their rivals.

And that was just it. The Stokers *were* rivals. Shared patches or not, what happened if Seb hadn't agreed to take her through everything from scratch? After all, he didn't have to. The less she knew, the more he stood to gain. Liam's words repeated in her mind: *'Don't trust him. He could feed you lies...'*

Yes, Seb Stoker could feed her lies, but what choice did she have but to risk it? She was doing this for her father, remember? To ensure the business remained in good hands.

She'd listened to what Seb had said about the coke dealing and the runners and although she'd pretended to understand, she didn't. She was blind to the terminology and the jargon and, well, *all* of it. It was like a foreign language. And to hear out loud that her father's business – now hers, was part of shifting drugs around the city, although not entirely a shock, still came a little sharp.

However, all of this had at least temporarily diverted her from the all-consuming nearness of the man in front of her.

Against her will, Sam found her eyes tracking once more to one of Seb's hands splayed across the desk, noticing the size of his knuckles and wondered, not for the first time, what it would feel like for those hands to be on her... Those fingers against her skin...

Clearing her throat, she leant back over the map, taking extra care not to stand too close in case the urge to reach out and trace her finger along one of Seb's overwhelmed her enough to actually do it. 'You're saying there's a place all the way out here?' Sam tapped on a circle at the far end of the Hagley Road. 'This is the place where you think the issues are originating from? What are they threatening, exactly?'

Getting up, Seb moved around the desk. Standing next to Sam, his arm brushed hers. 'We can't be a hundred per cent sure. Not yet. The people, or person from the Aurora – we don't yet know who because there doesn't appear to be anyone in charge. At least, that was what Maynard reported back the other day after he was sent there to check it out by your father.' He watched for Sam's reaction. 'Again, I'm surprised Maynard hasn't brought you up to speed with any of this, but to be frank, I'm not sure if he's levelled with any of us.'

Sam bristled. 'John would never have kept anything from my father, if that's what you're insinuating? I don't think he's purposefully been withholding info from me either. It's just all of this has been a shock to him – to *all* of us.'

She held Seb's glare, but realised she was making excuses for John. He *had* kept this from her, but she wouldn't admit that in its entirety.

Seb shrugged. If Sam wanted to lie to herself, that was her prerogative. 'At the end of the day, all of the ins and outs of firms such as these can't be learnt overnight. There's a hell of a lot to know and that's something you'll have to get up to speed with, but for now, you must concentrate first and foremost on this. Whichever way you want to look at it, it seems like the Aurora, or something to do with that doss-hole, have been sending scouts out to threaten the runners in our patches. Both mine, yours and our shared ones.' His eyes narrowed. 'They're undercutting our prices. They took two patches last week – one of yours and one of mine. They lost me, and probably you too, a good earner.'

Seb studied Sam, his concentration wavering. She really was gorgeous, but aside from her distracting beauty, there was something else. Something he hadn't expected.

She'd actually had the balls to swallow her ego and come to his club, laying it on the line that she knew fuck all, rather than blag otherwise, like everyone else would have. She was also *interested* and willing to learn. Samantha Reynold clearly wasn't as stupid as he'd thought.

He pursed his lips. Despite his initial and vehement reluctance to help this woman and the Reynold firm, the acknowledgement she wasn't anywhere near as vacuous as he'd first thought garnered a small amount of grudging respect for the woman.

He'd tell her what she needed to know, but see what she did with it before making his final assessment.

Not noticing Seb studying her as she mulled over what had been said, Sam frowned. Things were beginning to make sense. *Apart from one thing.* 'And no one *really* knows who runs this Aurora place?'

'Do you think if I knew that for definite they'd still be standing?' Seb snarled, his concentration back in line.

Sam raised her eyebrows. *Is that what everything came down to? Violence?* 'Ever thought about tactics? Being one step ahead?'

'I think of little else,' Seb growled. 'But some people don't understand words.'

'Violence is one thing I'll never get used to,' Sam said, reaching for her wine.

'Well, sweetheart, if you're going to run your old man's joint, then I suggest you accept it's part and parcel.' Seb tipped whisky into his mouth, fleetingly wondering whether he'd been a tad hasty in his updated judgement of Sam's attitude. 'If you're above doing things the way they need to be done, then I'm wasting my breath helping you.'

Sam folded her arms defensively but swallowed the retort itching to escape. *Remember you need his help, Sam. It doesn't mean you have to do things his way.*

Seb watched Sam closely for a moment before continuing. If she was going to *really* understand, then she had to be aware of all possibilities. 'Perhaps you might not be quite so keen on being *nice* if you thought your father's accident wasn't an accident?'

Sam almost spat wine across Seb's desk. *Did he just say what she thought he had?* 'Are you that desperate to score points that you would throw in rubbish like that?'

Exhaling loudly, Seb sat back down. Knitting his fingers together, he looked at Sam, seeing a mixture of anger and hurt behind her eyes. 'I can see you think little of me, Samantha, but I have nothing to gain by chucking insults at you or making up lies.'

He topped up her wine glass before refilling his own whisky. 'I'll admit I'm not particularly happy about helping you – it's something my father wants. But...' He held his hands up, sensing Sam about to interrupt. 'That doesn't change that if my father is correct in his thinking, then what happened to your father could very well happen to one of my family and *that* I would very much like to avoid, as I'm sure you can appreciate.'

Creeping tendrils of fear moved along Sam's spine, up into the roots of her hair, and she found herself shakily sitting down and reaching for her glass. 'What makes you or your father suspect something like this?' she asked tentatively.

Glad Sam was finally taking the situation on board, Seb focused. 'I suspected something might be linked, but I'm well known for being cynical – just ask my brothers.' He smiled coldly. 'But when my father says the same thing, that means it's not just me thinking the worst and has to be taken into consideration.'

Sam shook her head to Seb's offer of a cigarette. Lighting one, he placed his gold lighter back on his desk. 'Do you not find it strange this happened to your father yards from his house? Directly after both firms received word that threats were being made to our runners?'

'Well, I...' Sam frowned. Contemplating that her father's death may have been purposeful was not something she wanted to consider. 'Just because it happened near my parents' house doesn't mean it was deliberate! A road is a road, is it not?'

Seb nodded. 'It could be coincidence and a genuine accident, but to me it stinks of being linked. My instincts tell me it's connected and that whoever it was down to was watching your father's house.'

Sam brushed her hair off her face in a bid to get more air to quell the fast-rising nausea. She hadn't contemplated this, but then she hadn't known about the threats to the firms until yesterday either.

'I don't want to make things worse for you, but you need to take this as a feasible option,' Seb added, seeing the expression on Sam's face.

'Are you saying we're all in danger?' Sam asked, her voice small.

Seb shrugged. 'I don't know one way or the other, but I can't ignore that possibility.' His hard green eyes met with Sam's. 'As you will no doubt quickly discover, firms such as these have a habit of gathering enemies, therefore complacency is not an option that can ever be considered.'

Sam's nausea was replaced with a ball of pure anger as the resolve in her mind strengthened. This put a totally different slant on things. Her eyes hardened. *Could it be true?* Was it plausible her father's death had not been an accident, like Seb Stoker said? If it was, then God help whoever was responsible. 'Patches aside, have you received anything untoward? Anything personal?'

Seb paused. 'There was one thing, but nothing on the same vein as this and that's now been dealt with...'

Sam frowned. 'What do you mean, *dealt* with?'

Seb flapped his hand dismissively. 'Not worth recounting. It was something and nothing.' He wasn't about to discuss that some fuckturd was bandying around his own and his brothers' parentage. Neither would he explain how he'd sorted it – especially not to *her*. She'd probably faint or call the Old Bill. She needed to wise up and fast.

He tapped his cigarette ash in the large crystal ashtray in the centre of his desk. 'As I said, I don't know if what happened to your father *is* linked, whether it centres on your firm, both our firms, or whether the Stokers are being dragged into this purely via association because of our shared patches.'

Sam frowned. 'What do you mean?'

'My father mentioned a possible link with what happened on your eighteenth. I know it was different, but was it?'

Sam blinked, her mind spinning. *Her eighteenth birthday?*

She remembered it clearly. How could she not? She had been waiting for Uncle Jimmy to take her to the casino for the usual surprise party, but the car hadn't arrived. After an hour, she'd begun to wonder whether because she'd turned eighteen, she was no longer having surprise parties after all. A car finally showed up – not Jimmy, but another member of her father's business. It was only the next day she'd discovered Jimmy had died. 'The night my Uncle Jimmy died? The car accident? What's that got to do with it?'

Seb frowned. 'Accident? It wasn't a bloody accident! It was a drive-by shooting. The only person who ever drove that very distinctive car of your father's was *him*. Apart from that night...'

Sam felt faint. *No one had ever told her this.* 'So it should have been my father who was shot?' She looked at Seb, her eyes wide. 'And now after all of this time, his death has been achieved, just in a different way? Is that what you're saying?'

Seb sighed inwardly. He'd had no clue these details had been kept from her. *Had she been shielded from everything?* 'No one knows, but we need to find out.'

He stubbed his cigarette out in the ashtray and studied her pale face, his decision made. His father was right. Sam needed their help and Seb knew he would be the one to do it. 'I know this is a lot to take in. You've been left in the lurch with just about everything and you haven't even buried your father yet! Let me get you another drink. You look like you could use one.'

* * *

At the Gun Barrels, Dave poured two more pints and laid them on the sodden beer towel. 'You found yourself some work yet, Lee?'

Lee greedily gulped at his fresh pint and grinned. 'Yeah, as it happens, I've got something on the cards. It couldn't have come at a better time neither, Dave, I can tell you that!'

Dave grinned. 'Glad to hear it. I know it's been hard for a lot of folk since they started cutting back at the Rover.'

'And what about you, mate? How's things going here?' Steve added.

'Now the beer taps aren't playing me up, a lot better!' Dave grinned. 'Thanks for having a look at that last night, mate. I didn't get chance to thank you for sorting it out.' He waved away the five-pound note Lee held out to pay for the drinks. 'Have those on me. There's a couple more in the bin for you both after you've finished those.'

'Cheers,' Lee grinned, chucking a sideways glance at Steve. Surely they'd get time to fit another few pints in before everything went up in flames?

He surreptitiously glanced at his watch. It had only just gone nine, so aiming for around ten would be good. Admittedly, he felt a bit bad because he liked Dave, but money was money. Tampering with the lights last night in order to get an excuse to 'fix' them, then set up what was needed had been the only way. No one could afford to be choosy these days.

'Hey fellas!' a man propping up the bar grinned. 'You seen Tom tonight?'

'Tom?' Steve said, trying to look neutral. 'Haven't seen him for a while. Why?'

The man shrugged. 'Ah, he seemed a bit edgy the other night, that's all. I think he's worried the Stokers are on his back. He wants to keep well out of that shit.'

'Then I suggest you do too, Mick,' Dave said sternly, getting rather fed up of Mick stirring things up. He didn't much like that he'd personally dropped Jock Sawyer in it and certainly didn't want the whole world to know, courtesy of Mick's huge gob.

'Don't the Stokers own this pub?' Mick pushed.

'They don't own it, no,' Dave sighed, pouring yet another pint for the two other men. He just paid the Stokers' security premium. That's what they liked to call it anyway. And it was because of that very reason he'd had no choice but to give Seb Stoker Jock's name. He just wished Mick would shut up about the whole thing.

Seeing the expression on Lee and Steve's faces, Dave frowned. 'You okay, lads?'

'Yeah, yeah, we're fine. Just tired,' Lee muttered, picking up his new pint and gesturing to Steve to move to a table away from the bar. He could see without even looking too closely that the man was thinking along the same lines as him.

Sitting down on a rickety stool, Steve leant forward. 'What the fuck have we got ourselves involved in?'

Lee shrugged. 'Dunno, but we're being paid, so ask no questions, eh?' Besides, it's not like we can ditch it now. Not without bringing unwanted attention, anyway.' He could hardly ask Dave if he could wander back down to the cellar and start replacing the wiring he'd already swapped out once. It had been dodgy enough last night. But either way, they could do without Motormouth Mick, his beady eyes and gob like the Dartford tunnel banging on.

He nodded towards the man still jawing away at the bar. 'Let's hope he's one of the ones who ends up as collateral damage in this, eh?'

Steve nodded. 'Tom never said this was to do with the Stokers?'

'Not our business, mate. We're here to do the job, not have an opinion. We'll just wait for it to get busier and then I'll drop the switch and then we get out of here fucking sharpish, okay?'

'Okay,' Steve nodded, his adrenaline pumping in readiness.

* * *

Sitting in his car, John Maynard had eaten chips, listened to the radio and done more than enough waiting for one evening.

The youngest of the Stoker boys wasn't the one he'd expected when he tailed the motor leaving the Peacock. He rarely saw this particular Stoker involved with anything, let alone dealing with a handover to the Irish.

He grinned. The man hadn't even attempted to cover his tracks and it had been ultra-simple to follow him straight to the drop. *Silly, very silly*. He could have been the Old Bill. No wonder this one did sod all if he played things this way.

Initially, John had been incensed finding himself shoehorned by the likes of Bedworth. That was until he'd looked at it rationally. Aside from being put in a position he couldn't be found to be in, it could work in his favour. And after he'd got what was rightfully his, then Bedworth could take a sharp exit stage left. But for now, this was the way he'd have to play it.

Besides, it wasn't all bad. Not only did he now have an extra stick to hit the Stokers with, but to get one so quickly was a lucky break. What was even better was because this particular Stoker had very little involvement, the man wouldn't have a clue as to his identity.

John's eyes tracked to the phone box opposite. The call he'd placed an hour ago meant that three of his best men would be arriving by kick-out time, but not before *he'd* gone into the pub to get friendly with this Stoker prick. And from the length of time the man had already been in the Hare and Hounds, he was no doubt a few sheets to the wind by now.

As much as John hated Bedworth, he had to give the man his dues for a decent plan. With the way everything was panning out it could just work, especially with the extra and unexpected piece of intel he'd gleaned, enabling him to pull this one off tonight.

He shrugged. It wasn't like he'd got a lot to lose and luckily, he had more loyal men at the firm than not. He couldn't see many of them ever changing allegiance to deal with Samantha.

The name 'Samantha' stabbed in John's head in staccato syllables. *The stupid bitch.* Why couldn't she have just let things be? It would have been so much easier and less detrimental to her in the long run.

Hearing breaking news coming through on BRMB about a pub ablaze in the city centre, John shrugged. *Tom's boys pulled that off all right, then?*

He flicked the radio off. More than enough time had now passed to allow Gary Stoker to drown whatever sorrows he had. Judging by the expression on his face when he'd arrived there were a fair few sorrows to drown too.

It was time to make a move.

John jumped out of the car and wandered over to the pub.

The Hare and Hounds wasn't anywhere Gary would normally go for a drink, even on the frequent occasions when he needed to escape from the claustrophobic and gung-ho world of his brothers and father, but there was a reason for that. Aside from Moseley only being down the road from where the Irish handover had taken place, no one knew him or his family around here. And that was just the way he liked it. Especially at the moment.

Frowning, Gary picked at the edge of his sodden beer mat, his brain still stinging from the recent revelations. So, his brothers thought he was a usurper in the family and that they didn't share true blood? Well, Andrew thought that, as did Neil by the looks of it, but did Seb?

His teeth dug into his bottom lip, the pain a distraction. Could any of it be true? Could he be the one who didn't belong? It would make sense with how he'd been treated by them all his life and he was sick of it. Sick of always being made to feel like the runt. And now they'd got this to vulture over, things could only get worse.

Maybe he should just up and leave them to it? His brothers clearly felt they'd be better off without him – not that he'd ever really been included in their tightly knit fold to start with.

Gary stared at the fresh pint on the table. Being Happy Hour, buying two Carlings each time he'd gone up the bar seemed a good idea, but it also meant he'd have to get a taxi back now. The last thing he wanted was a tug from the coppers. That would be bloody typical and give his brothers even more ammo. He could only imagine the endless round of jibes heading his way about not being able to hold his drink if he ended up losing his licence.

No mistake, he was fairly hammered, but that was good because he needed something to quieten his swirling thoughts with all this shit playing on his mind. At least no one could moan he hadn't done the business with the Irish.

Gary patted the twenty grand safely stashed in his inside pocket, then leant on the table, only to drunkenly miss, almost chinning himself.

Grinning sheepishly, he leant back in the wooden chair, happily listening to a guy strumming on his guitar in the corner. This pub had a good atmosphere - a *nice* atmosphere with no pressure, unlike the Peacock.

Gary found himself wondering, not for the first time, how much simpler things would be if he could come somewhere like this after an honest day's work at a normal job in one of the many factories in this city. It would make things less stressful. He wasn't cut out for this kind of life and he knew it, even when his brothers weren't constantly reminding him.

Turning to pick up his pint, he was surprised to see a stranger sitting in the spare seat at his little table.

'Hope you don't mind me sitting here?' John Maynard said. 'I've just finished work and my hooves are killing me. I couldn't face standing at the bar.'

'No problem,' Gary slurred.

'My name's Rob,' John lied. 'I haven't seen you before. You new around these parts?'

'Yeah, I moved last week,' Gary waffled, happy to become a different person, even if only for one night. It wasn't like he could say who he *really* was. Although it was unlikely people would recognise him, they'd certainly recognise the name 'Stoker'.

Tonight he would be anonymous.

'I've lived here all my life,' John continued. 'The only time I thought about moving was when my wife died earlier this year.' He stared at his pint sadly. 'Didn't think I could bear staying around with the memories, you know? But then, my family are good 'uns and I'd miss the boozers and me mates, so I decided to stay put.'

'I'm sorry to hear about your wife,' Gary said, feeling bad for the man. 'That must have been difficult.'

'Aye, it was,' John said. *Not that he'd know.* He'd rather hack his head off then get tied to a moaning bird, even if it guaranteed him a shag. And from what he'd heard, it wouldn't even do that half the time.

'I can only presume it must be important to have support from families and friends,' Gary said bitterly, suddenly overcome with self-pity. If he had a dead wife, no doubt his brothers would take the piss out of that as well.

'You got trouble?' John pressed. 'With your family, I mean?' *Come on, Gary – you can talk to Uncle John, you pointless piece of shit.* 'How about I shout you a beer, mate? I'm a good listener and you look like you've got the weight of the world on your shoulders.'

22

Bleary-eyed, Judith watched Mal replace the handset on the cradle. 'Who on earth was that ringing at this time?' she snapped. 'I'd hoped these sort of calls in the middle of the night would stop once you'd retired. Shouldn't people be calling Sebastian if there's a problem?'

'It wasn't business,' Mal said gruffly, picking the phone back up and keying in the number that he knew off by heart – the number for the phone on what had, up until recently, been *his* desk at the Peacock. 'It was the hospital.'

'The hospital?' Judith shrieked, scrambling to prop herself up on the pillows. 'What's happened?'

'I don't know exactly,' Mal muttered. *Come on Seb, pick up.*

'Who's in hospital?' Judith cried, pulling at Mal's pyjama top.

Mal flapped his wife's hand away, hearing his eldest son's voice answer. 'Sebastian? No, I'm fine.' He glanced at Judith. 'You need to get to the hospital, son. It's Gary.'

'Gary?' Judith cried. 'What's happened to him?'

'Shut up!' Mal hissed. 'It's all right, it's your mother. Yes, Gary's in the QE. He got clumped... I don't know, son... They've only just called...' He looked at Judith, tears now streaming down her face. 'Okay... yes, that's probably best. Call me as soon as you know, okay?'

Putting the receiver back down, Mal sighed, feeling the familiar throbbing of adrenaline pounding in his veins. *Was this it?* Was whatever going on with Reynold now dragging them into it by association? Was his family the next target?

'W-what's going on, Mal?' Judith sobbed. 'Are you not going to tell me what's happened to my baby?'

'Gary's hardly a baby! He's thirty years old!' Mal squeezed his wife's hand. 'Apparently, he was taken in via ambulance with a head injury.'

'Head injury? What sort of head injury?' Judith cried, launching herself out of bed and pulling her dressing gown on. 'Come on! We have to go up there!'

'Stop right there,' Mal barked. 'I know little myself, so there's no point in us all traipsing up there. Seb will see what's what. Stop panicking!' He wasn't about to tell Judith that her fear was very real and so would his be if he allowed her panic to infect him. And he couldn't do that. It would help no one.

'Why did they ring if it wasn't serious? Oh God, Mal, what if Gary's got brain damage or is in a coma? You hear all these things and...'

'Judith!' Mal yelled. 'Stop it, will you? We're down as Gary's next of kin, so it's standard procedure to call. Before you run around like a headless chicken, let Sebastian see what's going on and then we'll go from there, yes?'

He wanted to run around like a headless chicken himself, but if he did that he'd more than likely end up back in A&E, therefore he would sit it out and wait to see exactly what was reported back.

* * *

Even though it was 1 a.m. by the time Sam returned to her apartment, she didn't rush straight to bed. There was little point. Although it was more than nice being back in her own space, there was no way she would sleep – at least not for a good while. Her mind was too busy processing not only everything she'd learned tonight, but also what had happened just before she'd left.

Kicking her heels from her aching feet, Sam allowed the black cocktail dress to fall to the floor. She'd pick it up in the morning. Right now, she needed to think.

Slipping an oversized T-shirt over her head, she padded along the hall to the kitchen and opened the fridge. She eyed a bottle of wine, knowing she probably shouldn't have any more, but what did it matter? It was the only way she stood to get any sleep.

Pouring herself a large glass, she made to replace the remainder of the bottle back in the fridge, but thinking better of it, took it with her into the lounge. Flopping onto the sofa, she flicked the uplighter onto a low light position and sat back, gratefully sipping at the wine. *What a bloody night!*

Thanks to Seb Stoker, she now knew the extent of what her father had shielded her from. Although a lot of what she'd hadn't been altogether surprising, it was still an eye opener. *Her father supplied cocaine?*

Sam frowned, suspecting that was only the tip of the iceberg, but it didn't matter. Nothing mattered aside from sorting this out.

She swilled down most of her wine in one go, staring at the glass in the hope of an answer appearing. Of course, it was feasible Seb could have manufactured the whole thing to get a response from her that would work in his favour, but after everything tonight, she no longer thought that a credible option.

In contrast to what she'd expected, she believed him. Tonight had given her a glimpse of another facet to Seb's usual façade. In addition to his fierce attractiveness and the brash over-confidence she'd initially classed as patronising, he'd patiently explained how everything worked and, surprisingly, he'd done it without an air of arrogance and without making her feel stupid. She'd appreciated that.

It had also underlined just how much John was withholding. However miffed he was about her being in charge, there had been ample opportunity for him to bring her up to speed, but he'd chosen not to and it was clear why.

Her cousin wanted her to fail. That's what it was all about and that hurt.

'Just like his father – loyal,' her father had said on many occasions. Well, John hadn't proved loyal to *her*.

Resentment simmered. They were family, for God's sake, yet John was jealous of her and must always have been. He was jealous because *she* was the daughter of Len Reynold.

Sam's unease grew. If she couldn't trust John, then who could she trust to make sure the business that meant everything to her father wasn't ruined by whatever was going on here?

As for the rest – why had her father not told her the truth about Uncle Jimmy? He may have wanted to protect her from the less than salubrious side of this world of his, but he should have told her. If not at the time, then at *some* point.

Did her mother know about what had really happened to Uncle Jimmy or was she in the dark too?

A knot formed in Sam's stomach as she reached for the bottle of wine.

Seb's theory that she'd first dismissed as ridiculous now held more validity. It was viable that the shot which killed Jimmy was meant for her father. Sam clearly remembered her dad's possessiveness over that motor and it was true he never allowed anyone to drive his Daimler. Her eighteenth birthday was the first and last time anyone else had got behind the wheel...

Her eyes narrowed. There were many things she was determined to get to the bottom of. Although the last thing she'd initially wanted was to be involved in the running of her father's business, now she was more determined than ever not to let it fail.

A steely determination throbbed in Sam's veins. If Seb was right and her father's death wasn't an accident, then she would be avenging that too.

She tipped the last of her wine into her mouth, finding her thoughts returning once more to Seb Stoker.

She'd seen his face when he took the call that came in about his brother at midnight... Seb had reined in his panic and played down the worry and anger, but she'd seen it etched across his rugged feature for a split second; heard it in the tone of his voice.

He was worried. *Very* worried. And Sam couldn't help but wonder whether the attack on Gary Stoker was linked to the threats or what had happened to her own father.

Had retaliation to Seb's family begun now too? And if so, who could be behind it? It all seemed absurd, but something was happening. There were too many coincidences and she didn't like it.

Dizzy from the incessant avalanche of unanswerable questions, Sam was glad to be interrupted by the phone ringing.

She snatched up the receiver. 'Hello?'

'Sam, it's Liam.'

'Why are you calling at this time of night?' Sam asked, disappointed at the sound of Liam's voice. She'd asked Seb to update her with news of his brother when he could, but it wasn't him...

'I just happened to be driving past and saw your lights on,' Liam lied. 'I thought I'd check you were okay.'

'I'm fine,' Sam frowned, anger simmering. Liam knew she was meeting Seb Stoker and he'd come to goddamn check on her. 'I'm tired,' she snapped. 'I'll call you tomorrow.'

23

Doing the standard morning walk around, Liam inspected the roulette wheel of the closest table, pleased to see it was free from fingerprints and polished and cleaned to the Orchid standards.

Although it wasn't yet 10 a.m., every trace of it being busy and profitable last night had been obliterated by the dedicated and conscientious cleaning staff – just as he insisted upon. No hint of anything, short of the lasting and healthy increase in the company bank balance.

His idea of monthly gaming incentives had gone down well, pulling in an increase of just over twenty-five per cent additional profit compared to an average Tuesday night. This was definitely something he would keep going with and, if only he could tell him, Len would be impressed with his business acumen.

Walking towards the corridor leading to his office, Liam's brow furrowed. He also wished he could tell Len he was worried about Sam. Was it not bad enough she'd dug her heels in and overridden the choice of handing over the reins to John, as was intended?

Even though Len had been unable to legally finalise the details, it wouldn't have been impossible for Sam to implement. To pull out of her dream business, as well as the property that had all but completed, was insane. Len would be turning in his grave. But not as much as Len would turn if he knew how quickly Seb Stoker had got his claws into his daughter. That she'd actually taken Stoker's advice over John Maynard's was unpalatable enough, but to spend so long at the Peacock with the man?

Liam's eyes narrowed. He'd admit he'd spent the majority of the evening driving past Sam's dark Symphony Court apartment. And then when he'd finally seen her light come on. *Relief...*

But phoning up had opened up another can of worms. Sam hadn't been able to get him off the phone quick enough and that stung. Had *he* been there with her? *Seb Stoker?*

Anger and jealousy slithered into Liam's veins. The thought of that man's hands on Samantha, taking the place he'd worked so hard for, made his skin crawl. He had to get it through to her, whatever happened, that Stoker couldn't be trusted.

Approaching his office, Liam spotted John Maynard coming from the opposite direction and a glimmer of hope sparked. 'John, could I have a word?'

Inwardly scowling, John forced a smile, his good mood over how seamlessly things had gone with jumping that Stoker muppet dwindling. *This Liam guy was a prick. Yet another one who thought Samantha Reynold was amazing, the bloody idiot.* 'What can I do for you?'

Liam gestured towards his office. 'If we could just pop in here?'

Nodding, John entered the room and waited whilst Liam sat down at his desk.

'Please take a seat.' Liam indicated to the chair opposite. 'It's a bit awkward... I wanted to run a few things past you that are bothering me.' He shuffled paperwork on his desk as he thought how to broach the subject. 'I presume you're aware Sam spent the evening last night at the Peacock with Seb Stoker?'

Tensing, John leant forward. *Seb Stoker interfering? Again?* 'I can't say I was, but it was so busy yesterday I hardly had two seconds to catch up with her at all,' he lied, unwilling to let someone such as Liam, who had nothing to do with his side of the business, be party to Sam not keeping him informed with the Orchid or its running.

Liam smiled uncomfortably. 'It's probably nothing, but Sam seems wary about coming to you. I keep telling her the Stokers can't be trusted, but she went ahead regardless of my opinion.'

John nodded. 'Seb Stoker isn't one of my favourite people, but that's no secret. What did he have to say?'

Not that it really mattered now because, after last night, Seb Stoker would be far too busy working out who burnt down one of his earners and jumped one of his own to bother with Samantha's troubles, but if this prick gave him a heads-up, it would save having to dig himself.

'Well, that's just the thing. Sam was gone hours. I drove past her place a couple of times. I was worried, you understand?' Liam said hastily, not wanting to sound like some kind of weirdo stalker. 'It was past midnight when she got back. I phoned, but she made it clear she didn't want to speak to me. Neither did she give me any information about what was discussed with Stoker, so I'm afraid I can't be much help.'

John's face remained neutral. What had Stoker been filling Sam's head with? No doubt trying to turn her against him? He sighed loudly. 'I'm surprised Stoker wasn't having a paddy that one of the pubs on his protection payroll went up in smoke last night.' It wasn't yet common knowledge that the younger Stoker had had his head bashed, so he'd keep that to himself.

Liam frowned. 'I heard something about that this morning. What happened?'

John shrugged. 'Haven't got a clue,' he lied. 'But getting back to Stoker, I don't feel anything he could say would be of benefit to

Sam, the Orchid or this firm. The man has an agenda and is using Sam's inexperience to cash in. As you can appreciate, that's not something I want to happen.'

He studied Liam. *He had to tread carefully.* 'Actually, I'm glad you've broached this. There's a lot of nasty stuff going around about the Stoker firm at the moment – not that that's anything new. Word has it that a man disappeared shortly after Seb Stoker was seen looking for him.' John raised his eyebrows. 'I'm not insinuating anything in particular, but it goes to show the general consensus around this city about the man and it will not do the Orchid any favours harbouring an association with these people.'

'What should I do?' Liam asked, his worry accelerating.

'I don't think it's a question of what *you* can do, Liam. It's more of a question of what *I* should do. We both know Len wanted me to run this firm, so I have to ensure I do everything so that it continues to run as well and as profitably as possible.' John stood up. 'Leave this with me.'

Liam smiled, glad to have got all of this off his chest. 'I hope we can put this right. Like you, I don't trust Seb Stoker either.'

* * *

Getting up in the morning to sit behind her father's desk, rather than the one at the design shop, was a strange feeling and one which would take getting used to, but get used to it she must.

Even with the additional wine last night, Sam had not slept, her mind churning. She stared at her hands, resisting the urge to chew her nails – something she hadn't done since she was a teenager. She looked around the office, having moved nothing since taking over. Everything was still exactly as her father left it. *Like a shrine.*

She pulled the first addition of the *Birmingham Mail* towards her, her eyes drawn to the headline on the front page:

LIVES LOST IN MYSTERY PUB BLAZE

The well-known pub the Gun Barrels, situated off Horsefair in Birmingham city centre, caught fire last night around 10 p.m., trapping many terrified customers inside.

Witnesses close by at the time recalled hearing a loud explosion, followed by fire that spread at record speed, ravaging the historic building. Although the emergency services were on the scene within minutes, several people perished in the mystery explosion including well-respected publican David Thrower, 59.

Mr Thrower had been licensee of the Gun Barrels for over thirty years and was thought to have been in the cellar at the time, where it is believed the explosion and fire originated.

Several other regulars also died, including Mick Fowler, 46. Others are yet to be identified. The injured have been taken to the specialist burns unit at Selly Oak Hospital, where they remain in a critical condition.

Further investigation is being undertaken by the West Midlands Fire Investigation Unit and the Police to determine the definite cause of this tragic event, but the initial findings point to the cause being an electrical fire.

Shaking her head in sadness, Sam took a long drink from a bottle of water in the hope it would slake the dryness of her mouth.

Her nerves fluttered. Talking of fires, the meeting she'd called with the Orchid staff later on this afternoon would be a baptism of fire. It would not be easy gaining the trust and support of the men who had worked underneath her father and more importantly, John, for so many years.

She wasn't stupid – her decision to take over this role would not be easily accepted. It was no secret the vast majority expected John to continue overseeing the business. More importantly, from the snippets of information she'd gleaned, they were not over the moon about her being in charge either. She couldn't say she blamed them – after all, on the face of it, she'd appeared from nowhere and had no history, but it was imperative she gained their trust and she had to do that quickly. She would not fail. She *couldn't.*

Her resolve strengthened once more.

The general consensus was a woman such as herself would not have the first clue how to run this place. That might be true, but she was learning. But there was also one thing fuelling her that they didn't have. Her father could have been murdered. Murdered by someone who wanted the Orchid off the map.

The question was – who? And why?

If Seb was correct and the removal of her father had previously been attempted twelve years ago, then someone had waited a very long time before attempting it again. That was a long grudge to hold over gaining possession of a club.

Sam focused on the framed photograph on her father's desk and a lump formed in her throat. Her parents were beaming widely and she sat in between them – a gappy-toothed twelve-year-old.

At a sudden tapping on the office door, Sam looked up. 'Yes?'

'Have you got a minute?' John asked, walking into the room.

Sam's stomach churned. The last thing she needed was John adding to her problems. 'Of course.' Pushing her mouth into a smile, she gestured for him to sit down, only to notice that he already had. 'Is everything all right?'

John cleared his throat. *Look at her sitting there, grinning inanely like the thick bitch she is*, he thought acidly. What he was about to do would leave a nasty taste. The prospect of uttering the words he knew he must say made him want to cut out his own tongue, but it was for the greater good and a necessary tactic.

Looking at Sam, he felt the sudden urge to laugh. She was so transparent it was scary, but at least her downfall would not be a drawn-out process. 'I see you've called a meeting this afternoon?'

Sam deflected her nerves by taking a sip of water. 'That's right. I felt it important to formally introduce myself. It's important that everyone's on side.'

John nodded. *Fat chance of that.* He stared his cousin straight in the eyes and cleared his throat. 'And that's why I'm here. I owe you an apology.'

* * *

Attracting plenty of admiring glances as he strutted down the hospital corridor, Seb glanced at his watch: 1.30, they'd said, so he'd best not be kept waiting. He hated bloody hospitals. That smell and the overpowering weight of misery and death hanging in the air made him want to chin someone.

Following the signs for the ward he'd been told to collect Gary from, Seb turned the corner, immediately spotting his brother sitting fully dressed on the end of a bed, with a doctor speaking to him. If Gary needed to wait around for medication or anything like that, then he'd just have to get a cab.

'Ready?' Seb asked, approaching Gary and nodding politely to the doctor.

'Ah, Mr Stoker.' The doctor extended his hand. 'I'm glad I've caught you. I'm Dr Fisher – lead consultant for the Head Injury Department. I wanted to personally thank you for the generous donation your business made last year.' He beamed. 'It funded the purchase of another CT scanner and I can't emphasise enough how vital that is wi...'

'You're welcome,' Seb interrupted, hastily shaking the doctor's hand. He hadn't even known his father had donated cash to the hospital. Still, it never hurt offloading chunks of profit here and there. Generous donations to good causes went down well in the press, plus it meant less Corporation Tax to pay. 'Is my brother fit, well and ready to leave?'

The doctor glanced at Gary. 'He's had a bad bout of concussion, but fortunately there's no lasting damage.'

That's your opinion, Seb thought, cutting Gary a sideways glare. Like he didn't have better things to do than collect people from hospital who had been stupid enough to get beat up. Had he taught his brother nothing?

Oh, he'd seen this morning's paper and read about the mysterious blaze at the Gun Barrels. His skin prickled. His immediate reaction was annoyance – another place to cross off their list for protection money.

An electrical fire, they reckoned? Seb chewed the inside of his cheek. He wasn't so sure. One of the people killed was the gaffer – the man who'd offered Jock's name up. Initially he thought he was reading too much into it, electrical fires happened, but that was until he'd seen the other article a few pages in – the missing person alert for a Melanie Briscoe, fifty-four.

Seb didn't recognise the name, but seeing the accompanying photo, he'd have recognised the woman's addled face a mile off. It was that old slapper he'd handed fifty quid to.

Fifty quid for the info on Jock's whereabouts and the fifty quid that had got her topped.

'Missing', it said, but could it really be coincidence?

The two people who had called Jock Sawyer out were now either burnt to a crisp or missing, presumed dead.

Whatever happened, it didn't sit well.

If it *was* connected – and it certainly looked like it might be – then it was only a matter of time before it became public that he'd been asking around in the Gun Barrels.

Everyone had seen the state of Phil's face and knew Seb had wanted retaliation for his runner. He hadn't needed to voice that.

Seb's brow furrowed. Phil would be pulled in for questioning next. And Phil worked for *him*.

Seb clenched his fists. He had to get to the bottom of this before anyone caught up with Phil. He couldn't have anyone, especially the Old Bill, sniffing around. The Stoker firm could not and *would* not be implicated.

Seb dragged his hand through his hair. *Shit, shit, SHIT!*

He knew what this meant. He didn't like it, but nevertheless, he would have to step in and break the connection, however much against the grain it went.

And now more shit because Gary had got himself clumped like a fucking loser?

Seb glared at his brother, still motionless on the end of the bed with the doctor, waiting for a response. What had the man even said again? Christ, he couldn't remember.

Rage pumped mercilessly in Seb's veins. Didn't he have enough to deal with? This meant undertaking yet another job of retaliation in addition to whatever had gone on with this fire and the rest of it. It wasn't like a member of the Stoker family could be set upon without reprisal. 'Thank you for sorting my brother out, Dr erm...'

'Fisher,' the doctor prompted. 'Gary must take it easy for a couple of weeks. Concussion can take a while to settle down.'

Seb jerked his head in Gary's direction. 'Come on, then.' Grabbing his brother's arm harder than necessary, he half-dragged him down the corridor, itching to get out of the place.

'Slow down!' Gary moaned, his head pounding.

Yanking his car keys from his pocket, Seb pulled Gary through the hospital entrance and pressed the button for his car's central locking.

'You've parked in the ambulance bay!' Gary cried.

'So what? I'm busy and haven't got time to stroll around car parks.' Seb yanked open the passenger door. 'Get in.'

Jumping in the driver's seat, Seb wasted no time firing the engine and screeching away from the hospital. 'Now do you want to tell me what the fuck really went on?' he growled.

Gary wished he'd remained in hospital longer. Well, he would, had it not been for the crazy loon who'd tried to piss on his bed three times last night. He knew questions would be asked and there was little point putting off the inevitable. 'I don't know what happened, Seb,' he said. 'All I know is I got jumped as I walked to get a cab.'

'What happened to your fucking car?' Seb growled.

'I'd had a few and decided to leave it,' Gary muttered.

'What were you doing in Moseley?'

'Just fancied a drink somewhere different,' Gary said. 'The handover went well, though.'

'I gathered that, otherwise I'd have had the Irish on the phone long before now,' Seb barked, negotiating the traffic lights at Selly Oak. 'You dropped the cash in the lock-up?'

'Erm... Not exactly...' Gary garbled, knowing the shit was about to hit the fan. 'The money's gone...'

'You *what*?' Seb roared.

24

John's apology was not something Sam had been expecting, but then again, not much that had happened lately had been expected either.

'I should have supported you immediately, rather than allow my disappointment over not taking the reins make things difficult,' John continued, the force needed to stop him from scowling making his face feel like it would crack. 'But I'm here now and I'll do everything in my power to make this work for you. For *all* of us. We're family, after all.' *More's the pity...*

Sam smiled, although she was not entirely convinced. Although appreciating John's apology, she couldn't help but question his genuineness.

John sensed Sam's mind ticking. He had to play this smart in order to turn it around. 'I should start by filling you in with how everything is run around here.' *The edited version – the one that will leave gaping holes in your ability to do anything competently.*

'Thank you. I'll jot down anything that might prove useful.' Flipping the top of a notepad over, Sam's pen poised over the paper. 'So, in addition to the shared patches with the Stokers and the ones we singularly hold, can you confirm which ones of ours have had runners threatened on?' She pulled out a small version of the map she'd recreated from the one Seb Stoker had shown her and laid it in front of John. 'I'd also like to know how much coke is shifted on average. Particularly in these two patches.' Her pen pointed to the areas on the map.

John almost choked. *How the fuck? Where had she got this information from?*

Instead of immediately punching Sam in the face for catching him off guard, John had to think and think fast. So, Liam was right with what he'd said earlier. Sam *had* run to the opposition and met with Seb Stoker last night?

Well, he'd nip that in the bud. Stoker was a major contender and a big fly in the ointment. He had to wreck any credibility the man had scraped together in Sam's eyes and he had to do it quickly.

He feigned interest in the areas Sam had outlined. 'Hmm, this isn't quite right.' John tapped his thick finger on the map. 'What patches did you say these are?'

Sam frowned. 'Our two areas here. Have we had threats to those?'

John shrugged. *This would be fun.* 'I wouldn't know because those patches are Stoker territory. Nothing to do with us.'

Sam peered at the map. Had she copied something incorrectly? She'd meticulously checked she'd outlined this map exactly as Seb's. 'Are you sure? I...'

'I've been doing this long enough to know which areas we own,' John laughed. Picking up a pen, he drew a shaky outline around the adjacent areas. '*These* are ours and it's *this* one in the middle that's a shared territory.'

Sam's heart pounded. Perspiration formed on the back of her neck as she berated herself for the wine she'd consumed before copying the map last night.

John ignored Sam's obvious discomfort. 'Where did you get this from?' *Like he didn't know...*

'I... erm...' Sam fidgeted. 'I was discussing the shared areas with Seb Stoker. I felt it important to continue the arrangement my father had with his father.' She looked at John pointedly. 'And I appreciated *someone* giving me the heads-up with how everything worked.'

John folded his arms and sighed dramatically. *Oh, he was enjoying this.* 'I suppose Stoker marked these areas out?' He paused for effect. 'God, Sam. That fucker is setting you up! His whole business depends on ours failing. He's a ruthless bastard.'

Fear ignited in the pit of Sam's stomach. 'That can't be right. Despite my initial reticence to deal with him, he was very helpful.'

'Yeah, I bet he was,' John sneered. 'Seriously, be careful. If you insist on dealing with him, then *please* double-check with me.' *Was the doubt creeping in yet?*

Sam faltered, stuck between defensiveness and panic. Liam had said similar. Had she ballsed up? Had she allowed herself to be set up with the oldest trick in the book? 'I don't understand how I could have copied it incorrectly.'

Because you're stupid? John thought. 'I don't expect you did. I suspect Stoker purposefully gave you the incorrect information.' He folded his arms. 'I expected him to try something, but he'd have never got away with this one with me. He knows damn well I know where our patches are!' He laughed, then pretended to look contrite. 'Sorry, I didn't mean that to come across as patronising.'

Irritation and disappointment ballooned inside Sam. Had her instincts to trust Seb Stoker been wrong after all? Was her unease with John down to personal annoyance, rather than genuine mistrust? After all, her father had trusted him.

Confusion swirled. *This was awful.* Sam fumbled with her glass of water, not knowing which way to turn. Sighing resignedly, she looked at John. 'Why would Seb go out of his way to mislead me?'

'It's simple! Had you been left believing those patches were ours, that would give *his* patches extra protection – until you found out, that is.' A trace of a sneer moved across John's face. 'But by then, it would just be passed off as incompetence on *your* part by everyone.'

Sam's heart plummeted. John was right. How could the firm take her seriously for glibly accepting Seb Stoker's words? *How could she have been so stupid?*

John smiled triumphantly. He could see he'd thrown a spanner in this stupid little girl's theory. She'd thought she was one up on him for a minute, but now her confidence was crumbling. *It was perfect.*

He glanced at the map in derision. By the time she worked out this map was actually correct, she'd have already given up and passed everything back to him.

John leant further back in his chair. 'No offence, but Stoker is aware you know fuck all. You also should know he's been arranging drops in our shared territories with the Irish.' He shrugged. 'I mean, I'm guessing you know Len refused any part of Irish deals. He refused to fund the IRA, as he put it. The further Stoker deflects you to concentrate on the wrong territories, the less you'll notice and the more they'll gain.'

Sam swallowed uncomfortably. She'd have been a laughing stock within the firm. She'd let her father down already.

Damn Seb Stoker. But could he really have lied to her? He'd seemed on the level last night and she found it difficult to believe that her instincts were wrong.

Her eyebrows knitted together. *Whereas John...*

Sam looked at her cousin, sure she'd just seen a glint of smug satisfaction behind his eyes, and quietly gritted her teeth.

She may be new to all of this, but she was learning and learning fast. Gone was the old Samantha Reynold. The new version was tired of all the cloak and dagger bollocks. It stopped here. She was not a sad little girl who could be messed about. She was Len Reynold's daughter and it was high time she acted like it.

'I have to take a certain amount of responsibility for this, Samantha,' John said, capitalising on Sam's confusion. 'Had I not reacted so badly to your decision to run the place, I could have saved you from this embarrassment, so I'm sorry.'

Sam smiled thinly, knowing if what John had just said was true, then she should be grateful to learn the score before it was too late, but mistrust still jangled and that could not easily be quashed.

'Leave Stoker to me,' John pressed. 'He obviously thinks he can manipulate you, so I'll deal with him from now on.'

Sam tensed. Something was still telling her not to be hasty. She momentarily thought about mentioning the theory about Jimmy to John, but again something stopped her. She'd work this out herself. 'I understand what you're saying, but I'll keep things as they are. If Stoker is trying to manipulate me, then instead of allowing him to realise I know, I suggest we let him believe I'm none the wiser. That could prove beneficial.'

John shrugged. *Damn, so she was digging her heels in?* Samantha wasn't going to be as easy to sideswipe as he'd presumed. Never mind. It would happen soon enough. 'As you wish. Just keep me updated with anything Stoker says from now on.'

'Of course.' Sam watched John rise from his seat. 'And thank you.'

'That's what family is for,' John said, his smile evading his eyes.

Closing the office door behind him, he continued walking down the corridor to the main reception area. Now he'd go and check in with the lads to see what drops were due tonight. That and pick up the money lifted last night, of course.

25

'You fucking prick!' Andrew roared, his eyes flashing. He didn't think he could get any more livid than finding out Gary had lost the entire second payment of the Irish cash. That was until he'd heard what one of the runners had to say.

Sitting despondently at the desk, Gary rested his throbbing head in his hands. He knew he'd fucked up and fucked up royally. This was the last thing he needed, what with all the shit that was already flying around. 'Give me a break,' he snapped. 'Do you not think I've already had all this from Seb?'

'But he doesn't know the latest yet!' Andrew roared. 'What's going on, Gary?'

Gary looked up wearily. 'Look, I still feel like total shit. I've only just got out of hospital. I shouldn't even be here, yet you're going on and on – talking in riddles.'

Andrew launched himself from the other side of the room and grabbed Gary around the throat. 'You sarcastic shit, with a bunch of poxy excuses! I'll...'

'What the hell is this?' Seb entered his office, seeing Andrew poised to smash his fist into Gary's face.

'Ask him!' Andrew hissed, reluctantly dropping his grip from around Gary's throat.

Gary rubbed at his neck. 'He's pissed off about the money. I've already said I'm sorry, but I've no idea what his problem is with everything else.'

And when his head was feeling less mangled, he'd take the first opportunity to put things right. He didn't know how or with what as yet, but whatever happened it would be something that would show his brothers that he was just as competent as them. Never again would there be any gum-flapping about him not being a true Stoker.

Seb glared from Gary to Andrew. 'Do you want to enlighten me with what you're referring to?'

'I've just been informed that *he*,' Andrew prodded his finger sharply into the side of Gary's head, 'spent the evening getting pissed with Maynard.'

Seb's eyes flashed. '*Maynard*?'

Gary looked up, his eyes panicked. 'What? I didn't!' The memory of the evening at the Hare and Hounds was a little fuzzy, but he'd had nothing to do with Maynard! 'A bloke sat down next to me and we chatted, that's all. I think he said his name was Rob...'

'You think?' Neil yelled. 'Do you think at all, Gary? For God's sake, a runner saw you! That man you were sitting with was Maynard.'

Gary stared at Seb, Neil and Andrew. *Had that bloke been Maynard? He didn't actually know what the man looked like.*

Seb's eyes narrowed. 'What did you say to him, Gary? I need to know everything.'

'I can't remember,' Gary mumbled, feeling sicker by the second. 'I was pissed. I didn't say much.' *But he had, hadn't he?* He'd been moaning. Moaning about *them* – his brothers, and the whole set-up. Exactly what he'd said though, he didn't know. *Shit, shit, SHIT.*

'Hold on a fucking minute!' Neil yelled, squaring up to Seb. 'Wasn't the jump a bit convenient to have happened after Gary has been secretly meeting up for drinks and chit-chat with our *friend*?'

Seb's green eyes flashed with menace. 'Exactly! I bet you any money Maynard is behind this. He set up the jump.' He paced around the office, anger flooding his veins. His mind churned over the situations that could possibly be derived from this. But then, if his stupid-arsed brother didn't know what he'd even said to the man, how long was a piece of string?

A muscle in Seb's neck twitched relentlessly. 'Christ, something else to deal with.' He wiped the back of his hand across his mouth in utter frustration. 'Have you not heard about that blaze at the Gun Barrels last night?' He glanced at Neil and Andrew, who shrugged dismissively, their wrath still centred on Gary. 'If we're not careful we'll be implicated with other stuff, too – stuff that needs sorting out. I need that Phil bloke brought to me again, but not here. Andrew? Can you sort that? ASAP?'

Seb stared at Andrew, seeing him still chomping at the bit, and knew he had to deal with this situation first. Jaw clenched, he swung around, pointing at Gary, his frustration at breaking point. 'And you! You fucking imbecile. What were you thinking? You moan and bleat like an old fucking woman, so God only knows what shit you've spouted about us.'

Gary turned to Seb wide-eyed. 'I wasn't meeting up with Maynard! I swear! I didn't even know wh...'

'I'll have to speak to Sam Reynold about this.' Seb raked his fingers through his thick hair. 'Maynard's a liability and there's no way I'm having that sidling piece of shit causing issues. Sam needs to know what her cunt of a cousin is up to.'

'Oh, listen to this,' Neil raged, poking Seb squarely in the chest. 'You're going to run to that conniving little bitch and tell her that we're on to them? Half of this is *your* fault. Let's not ignore that all of this shit also corresponds to *you* spending the evening holed up with the Reynold girl...'

Swinging around to face Andrew, Neil raised his arms theatrically. 'Isn't that a strange coincidence? Fancy that! You know, how Maynard just happened to know what was going on with our deal... Between them, Gary and Seb have ensured these people know everything.'

Seb's temper flared further. 'Hold it right there! I've said fuck all to Samantha about anyth...'

'Ah! *Samantha*, now is it? How cosy,' Andrew spat. 'You've got a point, Neil. Our Sebastian's too busy dipping his wick with that tart to notice the gen she's squeezing out of him whilst her hand's around his dick!'

Fury exploded within Seb for reasons he couldn't quite pinpoint. 'Sam Reynold is not a tart, she's...'

'Between you and dickhead here,' Andrew jerked his head in Gary's direction, 'you're selling us out to the Reynolds. For fuck's sake, Seb! Surely she can't be *that* good in the sack?'

Seb launched at his brother, grabbing him around the throat. 'How dare you accuse me of betraying this family! This firm is what matters to me and always has. You'd do well to remember that *I'm* in charge here, not you!'

Wrenching Seb's iron-like grip away from his throat, Andrew laughed. 'Are you stupid? It's all a plan! Maynard is that tart's right-hand man. She knows what's going on and that dumb act of hers is to reel you in.' He shook his head. 'Can't you see what she's doing? And he wo...'

'Stop calling her a tart! I've already told you once. If you weren't my brother, I'd give you the fucking kicking of your life,' Seb snarled, pushing himself into Andrew's face.

'What about him then?' Neil roared, pointing back to Gary. 'We all know he isn't our brother and half the city does too, by the sounds of it.' He stared at Gary, hatred burning brightly. 'You're probably related to Maynard and that bitch, hence why you've been feeding them all of our info.'

'*What?*' Gary screamed, jumping to his feet.

'I'll happily give him a kicking!' Andrew scrambled across the desk to reach Gary. 'Concussion will be a bonus once I've finished.'

'Stop this right *now!*' Seb roared, pulling Andrew back over the desk and smashing his fist squarely into his nose.

Blood spurting from his nostrils, Andrew launched himself back at Seb, his fist connecting with a satisfying crunch.

'What in God's name is going on?' Mal shouted, pushing open the office door so hard, it slammed into the wall.

As his four sons froze, Seb and Andrew's fists still raised and Neil's hand around Gary's throat, Mal shook his head in a combination of fury and disappointment. He eyed each one of them in turn. 'I come to the club for the first time since I got out of hospital to see how you're getting on and I find *this?*'

* * *

Tom thought driving all the way out to Northfield purely to meet Maynard was a bit excessive and, as well as that, he wanted to avoid bumping into anyone. Like Ted Matthews. Or worse, Linda.

He hadn't been down this neck of the woods since the day he'd left and had planned on keeping it that way.

Shoving his way through the heavy traffic on the Bristol Road, he was glad to pull into the front car park of the black and white timbered pub.

Avoiding sinking his front tyre into one of the many large potholes, Tom scowled. He could do without bodging up the suspension of this motor having only just bought it. Okay, it wasn't like he'd spent thousands – five hundred quid to be precise – but that was still five hundred quid he could do without losing, especially as he'd forked out all of that brass for Lee and Steve. But at least they'd done what he'd asked.

A wide smile replaced Tom's scowl. Oh, he knew they'd done it. They'd reported back to him quick smart – obviously to pick up the cash, but fair's fair, they'd done a cracking job.

And to get the clarification from today's paper that the Gun Barrels was fucked, and with it Dave, was perfect news. The fact that the divot motormouth, Mick, had copped it too was a bloody bonus. Plus, the report was that all investigations were pointing towards an electrical fire, which couldn't be better.

Tom rubbed his hands together as he strode across the car park. Yep, the boys had done an excellent job. Removing that old slapper was done and dusted as well. Another missing person never to be found.

The only fly in the ointment was having to deal with Maynard. Still, best get on with it.

Pulling open the side door of the Oak Apple, Tom winced at the stench of stale beer and ignored the fact that his feet stuck to the carpet.

He spotted John Maynard straight away, sitting underneath one of the large draughty windows. Walking over, Tom nodded towards the flat-looking spare pint on the table. 'That for me?'

'Evening, Tom,' John muttered sarcastically. 'Yes, that's yours.' He nodded at the stool opposite. 'I haven't got much time, so sit down and let's get straight on with it.'

Tom sat down, gratefully swigging at his pint. He was choking for a drink so badly that even the strong taste of line cleaner didn't put him off. He pulled his cigarettes from his pocket and tried his best not to look too self-satisfied with the recent outcome. 'Presume you've seen the papers? All done, dusted and perfectly executed, as promised,' he winked. 'How's it going from your side?'

'Yes, I saw the papers,' John said. He wouldn't give this muppet any inkling he was impressed the job had pulled off so well. He didn't want to give the twat any kudos. 'And everything's good from my side.' He wasn't going into specific details about anything with this piece of shit either. All Bedworth needed to know was that things were on track.

He wouldn't mention a dicky-bird about Gary Stoker being jumped and the nice wedge he'd pocketed. Even after paying the boys, he still had 11k in his back pocket and Tom would insist on a cut if he knew about it. And he'd rather drink bleach than give this tosser any more readies than necessary.

John grimaced at the spittle hanging from the side of Tom's mouth. 'As I said, things are on track and there will be plenty of ructions soon, believe me.'

'Good, good,' Tom said, his jaw clenching rhythmically.

John studied Tom suspiciously, noticing the man's pinhole pupils. 'You on gear?'

'Gear?' Tom continued slurping at his pint. 'No. Well, occasionally. Only for testing purposes, though,' he lied.

John's mouth flattened. He could do without Bedworth being coked up. Silly mistakes could be made and the man was pointless enough as it was. 'I want to check you fully understand there are to be no deviations from the plan.'

'The plan?' Tom frowned, his concentration diverted to a game of darts over the far side of the room.

'Yeah, the plan – the one we discussed the other night?' John followed Tom's eyes. 'Fucking concentrate, will you?'

'Oh yeah, the plan. Yeah, sure. Why would anything have changed?'

'Just nailing home the point.' John knew all about how Bedworth loved to add bits to previously agreed arrangements and they both knew how *that* had turned out...

He scowled. He wouldn't have ever had anything to do with the fucking idiot in the first place had there been another way around it. That first screw-up was down to Bedworth too, which they'd both paid for big time and it was not something he'd risk again. 'You grasp the Reynolds must be left out of this? At least until you hear otherwise. All efforts are to be concentrated on the Stokers for the time being.' John ground his cigarette out in the ashtray. 'After what happened to Reynold, you need to stay well clear.'

Tom sighed. 'Yes, I know. You said that the other night.' *But what Maynard didn't know wouldn't hurt him.* There was no way he'd ditch the chance of double money just because it might make things awkward for Maynard. 'There's no link between me and the car thing anyway, otherwise they'd have pulled me in by now.'

John nodded. 'That's as maybe, but you need to trust me on this.'

Tom flapped his hand. 'Yeah, yeah. No worries, I hear you.' He nodded to the bar. 'You shouting another one up?'

'I can't hang around. I've got a drop to make.' John's elbow brushed against the fat envelope in his inside pocket. 'I've also got to see Gloria tomorrow morning to finalise last minute arrangements for Reynold's funeral.' It was bad enough pretending to be nice to Samantha without sorting out fucking hymns and eulogies. *Christ, the whole thing made his head hurt.*

'When is that happening?' Tom asked casually, secretly wanting to tell Maynard what a tight bastard he was. He could at least buy him another pint.

'The funeral is in three days,' John muttered. 'Bloody thousands will be there, including the Stoker bunch and everyone who's anyone.'

'Hmm,' Tom shrugged. And it would be the perfect opening for his next move – the one he wouldn't mention. It was also tempting to go along himself and get a glimpse of his kid, but that would be downright stupid. Besides, there was plenty of time for that.

'You've got to be kidding?' Sam muttered, wrapping a towel in a turban around her wet hair. This was the final straw.

As her apartment intercom continued to buzz relentlessly, Sam dried her face on another towel and quickly pulled her dressing gown around her.

She'd had a dreadful day. As well as being made aware of Seb's attempts to set her up, there was now the added confusion over John.

The meeting this afternoon had gone down like a lead balloon too. Oh, she'd seen the scorn behind the eyes of virtually every single man in there. John had ended up chairing the rest of the meeting after she'd become flustered with the barrage of questions fired at her. It had been so embarrassing.

Sam glanced at her reflection in the steamed-up mirror, sure she'd aged ten years during the last week. She'd made such a pig's ear of things and was angry with herself for not handling things – *everything* – better. It seemed every possible decision she'd made since taking over had been the wrong one. And everyone knew it.

The intercom buzzing stopped, replaced with banging on her front door. What the hell was the point of security if people could just wander into the apartment block? Liam had no right to invade her space like this. His friendship was really testing the boundaries.

'I'm coming, for God's sake,' Sam hissed, padding along the hallway in bare feet. She yanked open the door. 'Liam, you really... Oh!'

Seb Stoker pushed past Sam into the hallway. 'I need to speak to you about Maynard.'

Momentarily taken aback, Sam closed the door, her surprise fast turning to annoyance. 'Mr Stoker, I...'

'Fuck this "Mr Stoker" shit, Samantha,' Seb barked, noticing for the first time that the woman whose home he'd just barged into was standing in a dressing gown with dripping wet hair. 'And who the fuck is Liam?'

'That's none of your business,' Sam snapped, following Seb as he marched down the hallway into her lounge like he owned the place. 'How did you know where I lived?'

'If you remember, you gave me your business card last night. Rule one – don't put a home address on it if you want your personal life to be a secret,' Seb said coldly. He hadn't time for game-playing. Sam could get as snotty as she liked, but he needed to know if his brothers were right and that it was *him* who had been played.

His eyes ran over Sam as she stared at him suspiciously. Was she in on this with Maynard? Well, he would see. As much as he'd previously reached the conclusion he would help her, if he'd been wrong in his assessment and she was playing shit like that, then he'd take her down too.

Feeling Seb's penetrating gaze burning into her through the fluffy white towelling robe, Sam shivered, feeling naked and exposed from the scrutiny. 'What is it you want, *Seb*?' she said frostily, overriding the disturbing sense of exhilaration at the imagined exposure. 'I'm kind of busy.'

'Busy?' Seb yelled. 'Swanning around in a fucking toga and lying in a bath or whatever, is busy is it? You should be concentrating on your firm! You know, the one I've been trying to help you with!'

'How dare you storm into my house and tell me what I'm supposed to be doing or not doing!' Sam countered. 'Are you going to get to the point?'

Seb perched on the arm of Sam's sofa and held her stare. 'How about you begin by telling me where Maynard was last night?'

Sam's gaze was drawn to the patch of dark hair under the two undone buttons of Seb's usually pristine white shirt. Her heart thundered wildly, questioning not for the first time how someone she did not particularly even *like* could engender raw attraction in every single one of her senses.

She forced her eyes to meet his and it was only then she noticed the darkening swelling around his left eye. 'What's happened to your face?' She found a small smile creeping onto her lips. 'Aren't you a bit old to get into playground scraps?'

Self-consciously raising his fingers to his fast blackening eye, Seb's jaw clenched. *Playground scraps? The cheeky bitch.* It was down to her that he and his brothers were at each other's throats and, thanks to wonderful timing, his father was now doubting his ability to run the family firm.

Anger seeped from his pores; anger at Gary's stupidity; anger for Neil and Andrew questioning his judgement; anger for his father's waning trust and anger with himself. Despite feasible justification making him suspect the woman in front of him could well be in with Maynard and a plan to sell the Stoker firm up the river, he was loath to believe it. Something wouldn't let him assume this woman was part of anything Maynard was up to.

He'd seen something in her last night – a determination; base honesty of her situation, yet a resolve to deal with whatever had been foisted on her plate. And he'd liked that. Liked it a lot. Liked it almost as much as what he was looking at right now...

His eyes fell onto Sam's cleavage, visible in the dressing gown, and watched a droplet of water run from under the towel turban, making a watery track between her breasts.

The need to trace his tongue along the route the water made caused a familiar twitch in his groin, and Seb hastily reminded himself why he was here. 'I asked you where Maynard was last night.'

Sam folded her arms, self-consciously pulling her robe tighter around her. 'At the Orchid, I presume? In case you have forgotten, I was with you at the Royal Peacock last night.'

'I haven't forgotten, Sam. I haven't forgotten at all.' Seb's face was hard, a nerve twitching under his eye as he fought to regain control of his senses – at complete conflict with his internal fury.

Getting up, he stormed over to the cabinet and snatched up a bottle of brandy. 'Thank fuck for that! I thought you might only have Cinzano or Advocaat!' He turned back to Sam. 'In fact, if I remember rightly, I spent a long time painstakingly explaining to you how things work. Like easing myself into a frightened virgin.'

Sam's cheeks coloured with his analogy, along with the sudden image in her mind's eye of how this man would behave between the sheets. She would do herself a favour remembering what John had said. Seb classed 'helping' her as giving her false information to make her seem a fool.

'You presume a lot of things!' she said curtly.

Seb downed half a glass of brandy, then wiped his mouth with the back of his hand. 'I presume nothing. Maynard has turned my firm over,' he said. 'I'm left trying to deduce whether, like the rest of my family believes, you're part of that or not. That's why I'm here.'

Sam rolled her eyes. 'I don't believe this! You're accusing *me* of being against you in some ridiculous association with John Maynard?'

'It's hardly a stupid accusation,' Seb spat. 'I'm ninety-nine per cent sure Maynard is behind what happened. Think about it – he was drinking with my brother last night, who then gets jumped. Whoever jumped him pocketed a large amount of *my* money. Meanwhile, I was conveniently out of the way...'

Sam's eyes narrowed. 'And so that means I concocted it? That's ludicrous. You know that isn't the case.'

Seb moved closer to Sam, wanting to pull the towel off her head to see her wet hair dripping down her, then licking it off her bare skin. 'As I said previously, I presume *nothing*. You may have made yourself out to be green where the business is concerned to set me up, enabling you and Maynard to lift the money from my deal.'

'Oh, you mean, the money from the *Irish* deal? One of the many you've arranged on our joint territories, knowing my father wanted nothing to do with them. Yes, I know all about those.'

Seb smirked, placing his finger against his mouth thoughtfully. 'But your father isn't here and, considering you allegedly know nothing, it's strange how you know about the Irish and where the deals take place, isn't it?'

Sam's anger grew. 'I will honour my father's decision and won't allow deals with the Irish on any of my patches, shared or not.'

Seb laughed, his green eyes sparkling. 'Allow it? But you didn't even know about it. Allegedly...'

Sam snatched the bottle of brandy from Seb's hand and poured herself one. 'You say *I'm* the one playing games, when you purposefully gave me wrong information to make me look a fool?'

Now it was Seb's turn to be surprised. '*What*?'

Sam squared up to Seb, pointing her finger into his face. 'Don't pretend you don't know. The territories? The map?'

A sarcastic smile suddenly spread across Seb's face. 'Ah, I see. Nice try, sweetheart, but no cigar.' He grabbed Sam's hand, pulling it from his face and holding it down against her hip. 'Don't bother with deflection tactics. Maynard has turned me over. He's taking the piss and when I prove that, I'm going to have him.'

He moved closer, his mouth inches away from Sam's. 'And if I find out you're involved, then you will also be paying for that.'

Sam's breath hitched, Seb's proximity and threat both aggravating and intoxicating; the combined scent of aftershave, anger and pure male, heady and overpowering. She pulled her concentration back into line. 'How dare you threaten me! Get out!'

Seb dropped his grasp of Sam's hand but held her eye contact. Slowly walking away, he reached the hallway before stopping. 'I've told you before Samantha, Maynard is not on your side. And for reasons unbeknown to me, I don't believe you're involved with whatever his plans are. If you ever work out that he's your enemy and if he's still breathing by then, come and see me. I might still deem you worth helping. Until that point, you're on your fucking own.'

It was only when the apartment door slammed, signifying Seb's departure, that Sam sank into the sofa and start to sob from a mixture of fear, disappointment, anger and the worst one of all – pure and abject *lust*.

John tried his best to act like he cared what Aunt Gloria was rattling on about, but he didn't give a jot. She could have been sat there starkers, banging on how she'd won the lottery, and it was unlikely he'd take any notice. There was too much going on and the last thing he needed was for his valuable time to be taken up with this miserable cow.

However, it was part of the bigger picture, so it was something he'd have to swallow – a bit like this over-sugared tea.

Trying not to pull a face, John tipped more of the revolting liquid into his mouth, feeling like smashing the oh-so-pretty floral china teacup into Gloria's nose. 'Sorry I haven't been around, Aunty,' he said. 'I thought you'd prefer the time to yourself.'

'I know you're busy,' Gloria said, thinking that although she was glad John hadn't visited more often, coming only once in the week since Len had died was a trifle lame. The only reason he was here now was because *she'd* requested he help with the funeral arrangements.

'How are you feeling now Samantha's moved back to her own

apartment?' John asked, deciding to use this time digging for snippets of information and planting a few seeds.

Gloria wrung her hands. 'I'm getting there.' Her bottom lip
trembled. 'I don't know what I would have done without her, especially over the first few days, but she needed to get back and get her
head around this business with the firm and her unexpected
change of career.'

She eyed John closely. 'I know you expected to be the one taking
over, so I hope you're not too disappointed with Sam's decision to
remain in charge?'

John smiled, silently thinking he deserved an Oscar for his
acting ability. 'All I'm bothered about is making sure Uncle Len's
hard work remains safe. We're family and I'm doing all I can to help
Sam.'

Gloria nodded. 'Yes, she said you've been helpful and I'm glad
about that.' She was surprised, though, she had to admit. She
thought John would have had a real issue with the change of plans.

John placed his dainty teacup on the coffee table, happy to get it
out of his hands, and looked at Gloria, his expression full of
concern. 'I must admit, it's unfortunate timing for Sam to be taking
over, what with all of these problems this other firm is causing.'

'I recall Sebastian Stoker mentioning something about that, but
Sam's taking it all in her stride. He's been helping her too, which is
good. It's not a time for rivalry, especially at the moment,' Gloria
smiled.

John bristled but kept his anger from unravelling. 'Like I said to
Sam, all is not what it seems. My personal feelings are that Stoker
has an agenda – several, if truth be known.'

Gloria looked up. *Sam hadn't mentioned this.* 'Anything I should
be concerned about?'

'I believe it's all in hand,' John lied. *And yes, you, more than most,
should be concerned, but I'll let you work that out.* The daft cow hadn't

twigged he knew her hidden secret and he wanted to keep it that way. At least for now. When the time was right, he'd pull it on her with a flourish, but until then... 'Most of the problems are from within the Stoker family themselves.'

'Oh!' Gloria exclaimed. 'I'm sorry to hear that. Each time I've ever met Judith and Malcolm I've always been impressed at what a tightly knit family they are. It's so rare these days.'

John nodded, desperate to laugh. 'It's never nice for anyone when rumours are going around saying that one of your children doesn't belong to you... It's all rubbish, of course.'

Gloria sat up, startled. 'What? What does that mean? Oh my gosh, poor Judith! She must be horrified! Why on earth would someone say something like that?'

John shrugged. 'People love scoring cheap points to cause trouble.' He looked at Gloria. 'I don't even know whether it's alleged one of them has a different father or that one of them isn't related at all, but I *do* know it's caused big ructions between the boys.'

Seeing Gloria's fast-paling face, John mentally chalked one up to him. 'Anyway, that's their problem. Now, shall we go through the final arrangements for the funeral? I want to make sure it all goes perfectly.'

And everything would go perfectly. It was just a question of how long it would take.

* * *

Judith clutched Mal's hand, her face etched with worry. 'Please tell me what's bothering you.'

Mal stared through the large French windows into his garden, disappointment raging. He didn't want to talk about it because he hadn't fully processed it himself. His sons being at each other's throats last night was something he'd never thought he'd ever witness.

'Mal?' Judith pressed, her heart racing, unable to remember the last time she'd seen her husband so distraught. Either something else was wrong with his health, or something was wrong with one of her boys. Panic threatened to overwhelm her. *Please, no.*

She clutched Mal's hand tighter. It had been horrific enough when she thought she'd lost him the other week, but something else had happened and she had to know what. She just *had* to.

'Mal?' she repeated. 'Are you going to tell me what's happened to upset you so much? You must stop getting involved in stressful situations.'

Mal turned his face away further. How could he tell her? Anger pulsed harder and his jaw clenched. What was the matter with him? It wasn't true, so why had it passed through his mind?

Shame covered him like a shroud, reluctantly admitting that although only for a nanosecond, he *had* contemplated it being something to question and that was enough to make him feel the worst person ever.

He wanted to kill whoever had started these rumours. And that was something else he'd learnt: Seb had taken care of that side of things too. That was a major risk in itself, but despite his son's rapid action, it had not been enough to stop the rumour mill. People were still talking and talking enough to make his own sons question the truth.

Judith watched the emotions passing over Mal's face with ever increasing concern. 'Either you tell me what's distressing you, Malcolm, or I'll get the boys around here for a family meeting.'

Taking a deep breath, Mal turned to his wife. 'Okay, but you're not going to like it any more than I do.' He sighed deeply. 'When I arrived at the Peacock last night, I found all of our sons about to lay into each other.'

'What?' Judith gasped, horrified. 'They've never fought with each other, apart from when they were playfighting as youngsters.'

Mal nodded. 'This was far from good-natured. Seb and Andrew had already landed blows by the time I got there and...'

'Oh, Mal, whatever for? They know better than to turn on each other. It's always been us against the world. Is it serious?'

Mal ran his tongue across his teeth, stalling for time. Judith never asked questions or pried into his business dealings, but where the boys were concerned it was an entirely different kettle of fish.

'Part of it is ill-feeling over Seb helping the Reynold girl,' Mal said. 'They don't trust her and think she's setting us up.'

Judith frowned. 'It's only right Sebastian helps Samantha. We're not the type of people not to help out a good man's family.'

Mal raised his hands. 'I know that, but it isn't going down very well.' It was a bit more complicated than that, but he wasn't about to tell Judith about the disaster with the Irish that also came to light last night. She'd have a fit about his age-old dealing with them.

Judith's brow furrowed. 'Wait! I know what this is all about. You're doubting Sebastian's ability to run the firm, aren't you?' She snatched her hand away from her husband's. 'For God's sake, Mal. You've got to give them chance to settle into their new roles. Sebastian is a born leader and more than capable, but there's bound to be envy from the other boys. It must be hard for them having their brother as head of the firm whilst they remain in the same position.'

She studied Mal suspiciously. 'Don't you dare even think about retracting your retirement.' Getting up, Judith paced around in agitation. 'You promised me. *Promised*. You'll kill yourself going back to that stress level. Let the boys iron out their differences and I'm sure th...'

'It's not just that... Someone's been spreading rumours. Horrible rumours...' Mal interrupted. *He had to tell her.* 'Someone's trying to destroy both our and the Reynold firms.'

Judith paused her pacing. 'You're not saying Len's death wasn't an accident are you? Is that what you're saying?' Her hands flew to her mouth once more. 'Oh my God! Even more reason for us to help the Reynolds. I'll speak to the boys. They can't leave that poor girl dealing with this alone. Who started these rumours about it not being an accident?'

'Actually, myself and Seb both believe Len's death wasn't an accident...' Mal muttered. 'But the rumours weren't about that.'

Judith frowned. 'Then what are you going on about? That Samantha engineered her own father's death? That's ridiculous! She loved that man. That reminds me – I must go and see Gloria before the funeral and...'

'It's being said one of the boys isn't ours... Or rather, isn't *mine*...' Mal said quietly.

Judith's glasses case fell from her hands onto the floor and she stared at her husband in shock. 'W-what?'

Mal shrugged. 'I know it's ridiculous, but...'

'But the boys are questioning it?' Judith interjected, sinking onto the armchair, her eyes filling with tears.

Seeing the abject pain on his wife's face, Mal instantly regretted being honest. He should have kept it from her. He shouldn't have said anything. 'Well, I...'

'And they're turning on each other because of it?' Judith whimpered, tears pouring down her face. She looked at Mal, seeing an expression she'd never thought she'd see. 'You don't believe it, do you?'

The slight hesitation before Mal's reply made Judith realise her husband *had* questioned it. Perhaps not for long, but he'd still questioned it nevertheless and her heart split in two.

27

Sam's attention focused on a narrowboat making its way along the canal at the Gas Basin. What it would be not to have a care in the world and drift along at a leisurely pace.

To think that if someone had said less than two weeks ago, when she thought she knew exactly which way her life was heading, that her whole existence would be flipped on its head in the most extreme way possible, she'd have laughed, believing the concept absurd.

But it wasn't absurd and neither was it funny. It was real and it was happening.

Liam picked at his Ploughman's and watched Sam's fingers on the stem of her wine glass, turning it around on the table. 'Are you all right?'

Sam jumped slightly. 'What? Oh, yes, just miles away.'

Liam studied her with concern. 'Anything I can help with?' He itched to ask whether her present mood was anything to do with Seb Stoker. It probably was. God knows what that man had done now to make her and everyone else's lives harder, but he must refrain. Sam had made it clear she did not appreciate his concern where that toe-rag was concerned, but it was difficult. 'I thought having a break from the Orchid and coming for lunch might cheer you up, but...'

'It's not you,' Sam interjected. 'I've just got loads on my mind.' She smiled wanly. 'It doesn't help that I got a call from Chamberlain's first thing this morning, asking me if I definitely wanted to pull out of the purchase of that building.'

'It's not too late to go ahead with your original plan. All you have to do is sign everything over to John and then you can get on with your life as if nothing has changed,' Liam pleaded.

Sam stared at Liam. But everything *had* changed. It had changed completely. She couldn't backtrack – not now. Not while there were so many things not sitting right.

She might have denied the possibility of John being behind any of what Seb suggested last night to him. She may have also dismissed the possibility of him being behind what had happened to Gary Stoker as ludicrous, but was it?

As much as she didn't want to think it possible that John – her own cousin – could betray and lie to her in this way, deep down she believed Seb Stoker could be right. And that crushing disappointment churned like a cement mixer in the bottom of her stomach.

'This is something I'm going to have to do, Liam,' Sam said flatly. 'Or rather, something I *need* to do.'

And it was. Her dreams of running her own design shop now seemed like a passing fancy from a thousand years ago compared with what lay in the balance now – even more so if a member of her own bloody family was trying to ruin everything.

Liam nodded, secretly gutted. He wanted her away from all of this. Before this happened, he'd been sure she'd been on the verge of giving things a go between them and yet now Sam seemed further away from him than *ever*. 'Then if that's the case, you'll be glad to know that the rewards night I set up brought a twenty-five per cent increase in profit. I was only telling John about it yesterday and...'

'You've been speaking to John?' Sam said, her concentration piqued. 'John has nothing to do with the casino side of the business.'

Liam shrugged dismissively. He could hardly say he'd spoken to John over his concern about her. 'I bumped into him in the corridor, that's all. Why? Is there a problem?'

Sam shook her head wearily. 'No. Sorry. I'm a bit edgy. Ignore me!'

Liam reached across the table and took Sam's hand. 'I could *never* ignore you, Sam.'

Smiling awkwardly, Sam pulled her hand away under the pretence of picking up her fork. She pushed her food around the plate, unable to eat. It would stick in her throat like broken glass.

Was John *really* betraying her? Was he really a threat to her father's empire? To her? To *all* of them? 'I'm having to rethink things about certain people,' she said quietly.

Liam bent his leg around the chair so he wouldn't start jigging around with glee. *Sam was doubting Seb Stoker.* It must be him she was referring to, which meant the man would be nicely out of the picture, leaving *him* free to continue his decade of rightful pursuit of this woman.

He waited to see if Sam would embellish further on the issue, but she didn't. 'What's happened to make you change your mind?'

Sam waved the question away. 'I don't want to go into it, but let's just say I should have listened.'

'You don't need Stoker. John will help you and he only said th...'

'So you *have* been discussing me with John?' Sam cried, outraged. 'Is everybody hell-bent on talking about me behind my back? Saying how stupid and gullible I am?' She felt both of those things, as well as being confused. More confused than she'd ever been. She didn't know who to trust. Was there anyone she *could* trust?

'It's not like that at all.' Liam internally castigated himself for blurting out something so stupid. 'We're just concerned, that's all. Being concerned and caring isn't the same as thinking you're stupid or gullible, Sam!'

Sam bit down on her bottom lip. She was being paranoid. How would anyone take her seriously – how could she take *herself* seriously if she acted like everyone was conspiring against her?

'I'm not going to lie,' Liam continued. 'Both myself and John are worried. Seb Stoker is dangerous. Only recently a man disappeared after Stoker was seen looking for him... I presume you've seen the papers today about that blaze at the pub? The Gun Barrels was on the Stoker payroll... Don't you find it strange the *exact* place Stoker was looking for the man who "mysteriously" disappeared was the very place razed to the ground?'

Sam paled. She'd heard about the blaze. Who hadn't? But she wasn't aware of the rest.

'Stoker's offer of help is for nothing other than his own gain, Sam!'

Sam's forehead creased. 'So you keep saying!' she snapped. On the outside she could see that clearly, but on the inside, things were telling her a completely different story. Quite the opposite, however little sense it made.

Liam raised his hands. 'Look, I didn't bring you to lunch to stress you out. I'm sorry.' *He'd promised himself he wouldn't mention Stoker. Why had he opened his gob?* 'Let's talk about something else.'

Sam pushed her chair back. 'I really should get back.'

Liam sat forward, disappointment flooding him. 'We've only been here half an hour. It's a beautiful day and you've barely touched your salad.'

Sam smiled stiffly as she stood up. 'That's as maybe, but I've got tons of things to do and I also need to see if there's anything else I need to do for my mother regarding the funeral.'

Liam got to his feet, beckoning the waiter for the bill. 'Surely that's something I can help with? I could go and see Gloria or take you to wherever you need to go?'

'It's fine, Liam, really, but thank you.' Fishing a twenty-pound note from her purse, Sam placed it on the table, desperation to get away surging. 'I'll get this.'

'But...' Liam realised Sam had already walked away. He flopped down into his chair, watching as she picked her way through the outdoor seating area. That had not quite gone to plan. If anything, he'd made things even worse.

* * *

Answering the front door for the second time that day, Gloria was surprised to see Judith Stoker.

'I'm sorry for descending unannounced,' Judith said. 'I've wanted to come around all week but didn't know when would be the right time.'

Gloria stepped to one side, ushering Judith into the large square hallway of her home. 'It's fine, Judith. It's nice to see you. Come out into the garden. I was just getting a bit of sunshine.'

Following Gloria through her large open-plan sitting room into the beautiful garden, Judith sat in one of the wicker patio chairs and gratefully accepted the proffered glass of white wine.

'I don't usually make a habit of drinking in the afternoon,' Gloria said, smiling weakly. 'But, well... with everything...'

'I think I'd be on my third bottle by now if it were me!' Judith laughed. If she could have got away with it, she would have already had twenty bottles by now.

The earlier conversation with Mal still stuck its barbs painfully into her heart and nothing could be said to make that better, but she didn't honestly know why she'd felt the urge to call on Gloria Reynold. All she knew was that she felt strongly that she should.

What she'd said on the doorstep was true. She'd wanted to offer her condolences before now, but as usual – like the rest of her life, she'd felt unable to take sides or step out of line with Mal and her sons' line of work.

No one had told her she shouldn't come here, but her reticence stemmed from years back, when she'd spent an evening chatting with Gloria Reynold. She'd thought they might become good friends. That was until Mal pointed out her new friend was married to his rival and it wasn't good business sense to become involved on a personal level.

Judith had always thought this stupid, but she'd done what was asked, because that's what good wives did – they listened to their husbands and looked after their children. Any friends she did have were the wives of Mal's associates. This had never bothered her before, but today it did. Today she'd felt like there was no one she could turn to. No one who understood.

Straightening up in the chair, she sipped at her wine and reminded herself why she'd come in the first place. 'I won't sit here uttering niceties or platitudes, I'll ask you straight. How are you, Gloria? Is there anything I can do to help?'

Gloria smiled sadly. 'What can you do? Len's gone and there's nothing I or anyone can do about it.'

Judith looked around the beautiful, landscaped garden and sighed. 'Sometimes I wonder whether the things men like ours do is worth it when it comes down to it.'

Gloria stiffened. 'You think Len's death was something to do with the firm? Part of some revenge campaign?'

Judith blinked. There was no way she would add to Gloria's grief by repeating that was exactly what Mal thought. 'What I meant was there seems to be an awful lot of people out to cause problems for people like us.'

Gloria nodded. 'Men!'

Judith laughed, despite her inward misery. 'How's Samantha coping?'

'What, with losing her dad or taking over the business?' Gloria topped up both of their glasses.

'Both, I guess? I hope Sebastian's been of help?'

Gloria sighed. She could see the turmoil on Judith's face. 'Yes, Sebastian has been helpful. It's been most appreciated.' Something else was bothering Judith and she could only presume it was those vindictive rumours John had told her about. She didn't want to make the poor woman feel worse, but felt compelled to offer solidarity. 'Don't pay attention to rumours, Judith,' she smiled. 'You as well as I know that men are strange creatures.'

Judith's eyes widened, a lone tear escaping. 'You've heard then? Heard about what's being insinuated?'

Gloria nodded. 'I've heard something – only today, actually. But don't let it bother you. No one in their right mind will believe it. It's ludicrous!'

'My sons are at each other's throats over it.' Judith sniffed. She pulled a tissue from her bag and dabbed at her face. 'I'm sorry. Listen to me! I shouldn't be moaning about my problems when you've just lost your husband.'

Gloria shook her head. 'It's fine, honestly. You're not seriously telling me your sons believe this rubbish?'

Judith dug her nails into her palms and nodded slowly. 'It seems that way. Mal walked into the Peacock last night to find they'd come to blows. It's awful, Gloria. I haven't brought my sons up to turn on each other like this.'

Nausea flooded Gloria. She hadn't for one minute thought it was that serious.

'It's all centring on Gary. They believe he's the one. They think he's either got a different father or isn't related to us at all,' Judith continued. 'It must be his colouring. He's so different from the others.' She looked at Gloria. 'Gary *is* Mal's son.'

Gloria squeezed Judith's hand. 'I never thought otherwise.'

'I think even Mal doubted it for a moment.' Judith burst into tears. 'I – I'm sorry. I really didn't come here to lump this on you. I'm terrified something is going to happen. My sons are good boys and fiercely protective, but they won't stand for people who turn on them and now they think Gary is one of those people.'

Gloria's heart raced. 'Where has this dreadful rumour come from?'

Judith shook her head in despair. 'I don't know. No one really tells me anything. Even Mal. All I can grasp is that it's come from someone trying to blackmail both our firms. I'm worried about what might happen. Gary isn't like my other sons. I'm scared they'll kill him. He's already been attacked once.'

'I heard he'd been in hospital. That was by one of your other sons?' Gloria gasped.

'I didn't think so, but now I'm beginning to wonder...'

28

Not much phased Seb. Even the most violent acts he'd been part of over the years, the torture he'd witnessed and the murder he'd either had a hand in or sanctioned, had not been enough to cause him to break into a sweat. He was a Stoker through and through. But this... *This was different.*

Shoving his finger into the neck of his collar, Seb rolled his shoulders to ease the fast-building tension and accompanying headache. *Come on Sebastian, get a bloody grip, man*, he chanted silently, whilst stealing a glance at his watch.

Andrew and Neil had better deliver on time because this waiting was doing zilch for his escalating blood pressure.

Hearing the wheels of a vehicle crunching along the gravel pathway leading to the lock-up, Seb gritted his teeth. Perspiration beaded between his shoulder blades and he resented the white cotton of his shirt sticking to his skin.

Standing motionless, he waited in the gloom, only one fluorescent strip light at the far end of the cavernous lock-up switched on.

Hearing the double doors of the van slam, Seb tensed, his hand hovering over the Beretta as security in his waistband.

Three sharp bangs on the metal door sounded, followed by a pause, then two more and he waited as the heavy doors opened.

'He's here,' Andrew muttered, pulling a man, wrists shackled, inside. Neil followed, steering the man in from behind.

The crash of metal on metal as the doors shut jolted Seb's head. He indicated to Andrew to remove the sacking covering the man's face.

Andrew none-too-gently pulled the sack from Phil's head, exposing the man's panicked face. 'Get that off him,' Seb barked, not happy to see the gaffer tape across the man's mouth.

Scowling, Neil ripped the tape from Phil's mouth, pulling with it the top layer of skin.

'Fucking hell!' Phil howled.

Seb groaned inwardly. 'Hello, Phil.'

Phil blinked as his eyes adjusted to the light after the darkness of the sack and the back of the van. He looked around, wide-eyed, panic intensifying. 'What's going on?'

Seb repositioned himself, spacing his legs on the concrete floor. He wouldn't drag this out. He wasn't in the habit of banishing one of his own – especially one who had always been loyal and done nothing to warrant such treatment. How he wished he didn't have to do this and that there was another way, but under the circumstances, he had little choice.

For the firm's sake and Phil's safety it had to be done, Seb knew that, but it would mean splitting up this man's family, at least in the short term, and that wasn't something he relished doing.

This poor bastard had done sod all and that's what made this so bloody wrong.

Wrong, but necessary.

Not having received an answer, but instinctively knowing something was horribly wrong, Phil's panic grew. He fidgeted from foot to foot, his eyes darting around looking for escape routes, of which, having been to this lock-up plenty of times to drop goods, he already knew there to be none.

His frightened eyes tracked back to Seb. 'What have I done?' he cried. 'I did everything you asked. I've always done what you asked Mr Stoker, I...'

'I'm sorry to have interrupted your evening, Phil,' Seb said, not wanting to hear the man's pitiful begging. It was making his ears hurt.

'I – I told you who that man was, didn't I? You said I was right to inform you of what he said. I haven't breathed a word about any of it! None of it! I've said nothing to no one! I wouldn't, I swear, you've got to believe me!' Phil gibbered, pulling against his wrist restraints.

'Do you want me to quieten him down?' Andrew looked to Seb, his fist poised.

Seb immediately waved his brother's suggestion away. 'Phil, I don't ever apologise, but on this occasion I will. You've done nothing wrong, but circumstances dictate that you can't remain around.'

'Wait!' Phil squawked. 'I didn't breathe a word about what you did to Jock Sawyer, did I? I said I wouldn't and I haven't. I don't know what this is all about, but I won't get you in the shit, Mr Stoker.'

Neil's eyes darted to Andrew. 'What's that about Jock Sawyer?'

Andrew shrugged, knowing full well what it was about. He glanced at Seb. Why wasn't he getting on with dispatching the man? They couldn't risk this bloke being dragged in for questioning by anyone and spilling under duress what he knew about Jock Sawyer's removal. No bloody way. And, okay, so it wasn't great offloading one of their own, but Seb had told him and Neil to bring the man here, so what was the hold-up?

'Phil, you need to make yourself scarce.' Seb pulled a fat envelope out of his pocket. 'There's enough money here to set you up and keep you afloat for the foreseeable. And there's also a ticket t...'

'But I ain't done anything. You said so yourself! I can't just up sticks and disappear!' Phil yelped, panic across his face. He backed away, only to be pulled back into position by Andrew and Neil's heavy hands. 'I've got a wife and kids. They'll...'

'You will do as I say,' Seb growled. 'Your family will be well looked after in your absence. I will keep the time as short as possible. Hopefully less than a year.'

'NO! *Please!*' Phil screamed, flailing against the strong grip of Andrew and Neil. 'I can't leave my missus and kiddies. Surely there's another way?'

Andrew stared at Seb in astonishment. What was this shit? He was putting Phil out of the country for a while? That was it? Jesus Christ, the man could still talk. How could they know for sure the bloke hadn't returned before it was safe to do so? They couldn't put tabs on *all* the airports. This was bollocks! It was too risky and he wasn't having it. Too many people were taking the piss here.

He glared at his elder brother. 'What are you doing, Seb? Has shagging that tart made you go soft in the head all of a sudden?' Andrew poked Phil in the back. 'And now *he's* refusing to take your over-generous and crazy offer?'

Seb stiffened, his anger mounting. 'Shut it, Andrew. Phil is one of our own,' he hissed between his teeth. He'd bypass the dig about 'soft' and the reference to Sam for now. This wasn't a soft decision – it was fucking decent and the right thing to do. Andrew was losing it lately and that he would *also* have to deal with. And that runaway mouth of his. But not now. Not in front of others.

Phil's eyes darted between Seb and Andrew, fear intensifying. The fast-rising antagonism between the brothers would spiral out of control if he didn't do something to placate the situation. There was an opportunity to walk out of here, which he hadn't thought available when entering the lock-up, so he'd best hurry up and take it. 'Okay, okay. I'll disappear! I – I'll go wherever you need. I'm sorry. It's just a shock. Just promise me you'll take care of my family.'

Seb smiled thinly, his cold eyes still half-fixed on Andrew. 'That goes without saying, Phil. You'll be contacted as soon as the route is clear for your return.' He put the envelope in Phil's hand. 'It's all in there – the ticket and details.'

He then turned to his brothers. 'Now fucking untie him. He shouldn't have been trussed up in the first place!' Pulling his cuffs straight, Seb glared at Andrew. 'Make sure he gets on the plane. I'll see you back at the club. I've got other things I need to sort out.'

Unshackled, Phil got to his feet, his shaking hands clasping tightly on to the envelope, his eyes suddenly darting to the Beretta pulled from Andrew's waistband. 'What th...'

Swinging around as the shot rang out loudly, the staccato noise amplified by the cavernous hulk of the warehouse, Seb watched with horror as Phil crumpled to the ground, a clean bullet hole through the centre of his forehead.

He stared at Andrew incredulously, rage pounding in his veins. 'What the fuck?' Seb screamed, his urge to bludgeon his brother held by a thin, fraying thread.

Shoving the Beretta back in his waistband, Andrew shrugged. 'It had to be done, bruv. You're not thinking straight.'

Shaking his head, Seb yanked open the heavy warehouse door and slipped out into the night, his body trembling with adrenaline. He had to leave. If he didn't, he knew for certain he would do something to his brother he would bitterly regret.

* * *

Grunting with satisfaction, Tom rolled off Amelia and wasted no time pushing himself to the edge of the bed to drag his jeans off the floor.

'While you're here, Tommy, I thought I'd mention I have a couple more girls interested in working here,' Amelia said, tracing her pudgy hand down Tom's back.

Tom glanced at Amelia and wiped his hand under his nose, scowling at the mess on the back of his hand. Bloody hay fever. His nose was running like a tap. He hated this time of year. It always interfered with snorting the powder. Right got on his nerves, it did.

'Did you hear me, Tom?' Amelia pressed, inspecting her face in a small mirror.

'Yeah, I heard,' Tom mumbled. 'Are these girls you know?'

'My daughters, actually,' Amelia said proudly. 'I think you'll like them and they're eager to meet you.'

Tom's ears pricked up and he glanced at Amelia. *Daughters? They'd be younger than her, then?* 'Sure. Bring them to meet me. Make it next week, though. I'm up to my neck for the time being.'

'I expect they'll have several mates interested too. Right lookers, they are,' Amelia enthused.

Standing up, Tom pulled up his jeans, then yanked his T-shirt over his head. Sparking up a cigarette, he glanced back at the woman lounging on the bed. 'Okay, but can you fuck off now? I've got things to do.'

Picking up Amelia's discarded clothes, he chucked the bundle at her, then jerked his head towards the door. 'Put your clobber on outside or somewhere else, woman,' he barked.

Quickly cottoning on that Tom was not in the mood to discuss this subject further, Amelia scuttled from the room.

Tapping his foot impatiently, Tom waited until the door had closed before unwrapping a fresh wrap of cocaine and expertly hoovered up a line. Flopping into the chair next to the bed, he pulled at the ring-pull of a can of beer.

Thank fuck for that. So now what?

Whatever happened, he needed to get a shift on. He was almost out of cash and he had people to pay. It was all very well getting the Gun Barrels razed to the ground, but apart from having to find somewhere else to drink, housing people with their ears to the ground for word on the street, he could do without going too far afield.

On top of that, Lee and Steve had got nowhere locating the Reynolds' runner who had caused him to lose Jock and he was pissed off about that. He'd hoped to add that muppet to the list to ramp more pressure on the situation, but by all accounts, he'd disappeared off the face of the fucking earth. *And what good was that? Sod all, that's what.*

Tom tipped warm beer into his mouth and brushed his hand over his stubbly chin. It had now been a week since that letter would have been received at the Reynolds' house and that was presuming anyone had looked at it, due to the unfortunate timing of Reynold's demise. But even if the wife had seen it, it meant nothing without proof.

He frowned. He needed proof – *that* was a definite. As for the Stokers – from what he'd heard they were well on their way to spontaneously combusting, so that part was going well, but it wasn't *them* he really wanted.

Tom needed his demands to be taken seriously. And he knew there must be proof – the question was *where*?

It would be unlikely to be within the house. He'd been told of the desperation to keep everything under wraps, so they wouldn't have risked the kid stumbling across any paperwork. It *had* to be at the casino. If only he could get in there...

Taking a long drag of his cigarette, Tom leant back in the chair and exhaled a thick cloud of smoke to gather at the mildewed ceiling.

Wait a minute. When was this funeral? Maynard said three days, didn't he?

Screwing his eyes shut as he calculated how long it was since he'd spoken to Maynard, Tom's brain hurt with the effort. He'd last seen Maynard yesterday, so that meant the funeral was two days from now...

Grabbing the newspaper from the floor, Tom brushed a clump of unsavoury-looking hair off it and flicked through the pages until he came to the obituary section. His eyes scanned the list of recently departed, his jaw clenching and unclenching as the cocaine pounded in his brain. *Ah-ha:*

REYNOLD, Leonard Paul. Passed away after a tragic accident on 20th June 1995, aged 68 years.

Beloved husband of Gloria, father to Samantha and much loved and respected local businessman and owner of the Violet Orchid casino, Birmingham.

On 29th June, the hearse will lead the drive-by procession along Broad Street at 1.15 p.m. so the public can pay their respects, followed by a private service for friends and family at St Francis of Assisi, Bourneville at 2 p.m.

The wake for friends, family and business associates will follow at the Violet Orchid, Broad Street.

All inquiries to Lamberts Funeral Directors, 01212429641

Tom's face cracked into a wide smile as he ground his fag out on the bare floorboards. *This was it. This was his opportunity.* He'd go to the wake. No one would notice him. There would be plenty of people who wouldn't be recognised that day – no one would question it. It wasn't like it was a normal night. They'd all be far too busy blathering over Reynold's death to take any notice if he had a bit of a wander around.

Maynard was the only person guaranteed to recognise him. The man had already lectured him about how he should have nothing to do with the Reynolds at this point in time, but Maynard could fuck right off if he thought this opportunity to grab the proof he needed for the shit to hit the fan would be missed.

The documents he knew to be in existence must be kept in there. No doubt in the old bastard's office – well away from prying eyes, so it was happening whether Maynard liked it or not.

This was the only way forward, so providing the man was out of the way when he sneaked into the wake, then it was job done.

Tom's eyes gleamed with excitement as he swigged the last of his lager down, before chucking the can on the floor. One of those tarts could clean this shit-hole up – he had better things to do. *Far better things...*

29

Gloria didn't think her hands would ever stop shaking. She glanced at herself in the mirror. At least her face was no longer swollen from crying. She just hoped she looked good enough to do Len proud.

Her eyes ran over her black skirt suit, the best and only black one she owned. Len had got this made for her for Jimmy's funeral. *Only the best for you, Glor, and for Jimmy* he'd said.

She'd worn it to several funerals since, but had hoped wearing it for her own dear Len's final service would have been a lot further off. Was it disrespectful to wear it again for her husband's? Maybe she should have bought a new one?

Fresh tears stung the back of her eyes and she willed herself not to break down. It was guaranteed she wouldn't make it through the service without shedding a tear, but she wanted to at least start off on the right foot.

Looking up at the ceiling to quell the forming tears, Gloria blinked, a lump lodged in her throat. The hearse would be here soon and then it would be non-stop all day until the final person had left the wake. Only then would she really cry.

The funeral was the final journey – the permanent end. Until

Len was in the ground, it wasn't completely over, and she dreaded the second it was.

There would be so many people present. Not that she didn't want Len's funeral to be well-turned out, but all those people would want to talk to her offering sympathy, whereas she just wanted to be left alone.

Gloria dabbed some perfume onto the pulse points of her wrist – Len's favourite perfume. Applying a touch more dusky pink lipstick, she blotted the excess away with a tissue.

Sam would be here shortly. She'd missed her daughter dreadfully since she'd returned to her apartment. Gloria sighed. She hadn't wanted Sam to have to take the reins of the club, but her headstrong daughter was adamant about doing so.

One thing was for certain – today would be hard enough to get through as it was and Samantha couldn't see *this*.

Gloria's fingers shook as she pulled the letter from the top drawer of her dressing table. She'd scarcely been able to believe it when it arrived last week. For a long while, she'd been half-waiting for something like this, but as the years passed, the chances of it happening lessened, and eventually it had all but disappeared from her mind. But for it to happen now couldn't have come at a worse time.

Even though she didn't want to, Gloria found herself pulling the letter from the envelope and slowly unfolding it. She closed her eyes momentarily before staring at the typed words.

She knew what they said – she'd reread them enough times in the hope that somehow they'd changed, but unfortunately they were still exactly the same.

Sam hurried into her mother's bedroom. 'Are you ready?'

Flustered, Gloria shoved the letter back in the dressing table drawer. 'I – I didn't hear you arrive.'

Sam glanced suspiciously at the dressing table. 'Everything okay?'

Gloria nodded. 'Yes, just a letter from someone saying they were sorry to hear about your father.' She smiled sadly. 'I see you're wearing one of your orchid hair clips?'

Sam nodded and smiled sadly. 'I couldn't not wear one today!'

Even though Sam wanted to, now was not the right time to question if her mother had been aware at the time whether her brother Jimmy's death had been purposeful, rather than an accident.

She desperately wanted to know, but what if her mother wasn't aware of the speculation? Knowing her father, she probably wasn't, so wouldn't that be opening up old wounds and giving her mother more things to worry over on top of losing her husband? Maybe she shouldn't ever ask? Either way, it wasn't a subject for today.

Bending down, Sam kissed her mother's cheek. 'Come on. It's time to go. The hearse has arrived.'

Paling, Gloria looked up at her daughter. 'Oh, Sam, I don't know whether I can do this.'

Sam squeezed Gloria's hand. 'Yes, you can. It will be hard, but we'll get through it together.'

* * *

Sam had been doing all right. *Sort of.* Although the hearse had arrived just after getting to her parents' house, nothing had seemed real until she was in the back of the limousine following the Daimler containing her beloved father.

The flowers surrounding the coffin on its final journey were perfect: 'Len' one side, 'Dad' the other, and a huge centrepiece on top of the casket. The big display of purple, white and silver orchids from the staff at the casino had done him proud.

They had done the expected drive-by of the casino, finding Broad Street packed on both sides with people paying their respects. Although it was touching to see how many people in the city respected her father, each minute was becoming harder – more final – and it was all getting on top of her.

Turning into the church gates, hundreds of people gathered outside where speakers were erected on poles to cast the service to those who couldn't fit inside. Sam's heart thudded. How would she get through this? She wanted to run away and pretend none of it was happening.

Liam squeezed Sam's hand and she fought her immediate reaction to pull away. She hadn't wanted him accompanying them in the limousine reserved for the family, but she'd felt unable to rock the boat today.

Stepping out of the car onto worryingly shaky legs, Sam helped her mother out, her own sadness increasing seeing the desolation on her mother's face.

Unable to stop herself from staring transfixed as her father's coffin was unloaded, Sam felt like her legs might buckle.

'I'm here,' Liam said softly, gently steadying Sam with his arm.

Sam forced herself to smile and then nodded to John, who was staring at her with eyes cold as ice. Throwing off a shiver, she reluctantly moved into the church.

Spotting the unmistakable figure of Seb Stoker sitting on the opposite side, Sam's stomach lurched. It took all of her power to continue up the aisle to the front.

Although she'd expected him to be here, she was reluctant to even be pleasant after the last time they had met. His barging into her apartment, making her feel two inches tall and accusing her of everything under the sun was not appreciated. Plus, he'd fired something within her which chose this very inopportune moment to reassert itself as the thundering of her heart at the mere sight of his wide-shouldered outline attested.

Keeping her eyes firmly fixed on the coffin, now safely resting on the wooden trestle at the head of the church, Sam walked past the Stoker family and took her place on the first row of pews with her mother.

Glad to be sitting down, Sam picked up an order of service, tears pricking to see the photo of her father printed on the front. Inhaling deeply, she prepared herself for what she knew would be the hardest day of her life so far.

30

'A lovely service, Mrs Reynold,' Mal said, gently taking Gloria's hand. 'Len will be sorely missed both personally and from within the industry.'

'Thank you,' Gloria sniffed, smiling weakly at Mal and Judith.

'I've Len to thank for giving me the incentive to open the Royal Peacock. Birmingham won't be the same without him,' Mal continued, smiling at Gloria and then at Sam. 'Thankfully, your daughter will continue his legacy.'

His eyes veered over to Seb standing some way off, his hand firmly around a bottle of beer. 'I hope Sebastian has given you all the assistance you need?'

Sam glanced at Seb. 'He's been very helpful.' *If purposely scuppering everything she was doing counted?* But she wouldn't voice that. Malcolm Stoker seemed a nice man – the same sort as her father. He wasn't to know his son was doing the opposite of what had been asked. That's if he actually *was*. 'And how are you now, after your stint in hospital, Mr Stoker? I hope you're feeling better?'

Mal thumped his fist against his chest. 'Everything seems to be settling down nicely, thank you.'

'Or it will when he fully retires,' Judith added, cutting her husband a sideways glance. 'Only the other night he took it upon himself to go over to the Peacock and came back more het up than usual.'

'Yes, thank you, Judith,' Mal hissed through a forced smile. 'I'm sure these ladies don't want to hear about that!' Pretending to shrug bashfully, he grinned. 'After all this time it's difficult switching off, but I'm learning. Or trying to, at least.'

Sam smiled, but she could see there was a bone of contention in the Stoker camp. Seeing the small, yet poignant glances exchanged between her mother and Judith only compounded that. Something was far from right, but she had no idea what. On top of that, she'd have to be blind not to notice the remnants of the black eye Seb still sported and, if she wasn't mistaken, one of the other Stoker brothers looked like he'd taken a whack too.

Swallowing down her irritation, she found herself glancing back in Seb's direction, his icy glare centred solely on one of his brothers. It looked like whatever was going on could be serious. Seb had made no effort to acknowledge her either. After his stinking attitude and the things he'd said, she felt the *least* he owed her was an apology, but clearly that was beneath him too.

Sam followed Seb's line of sight, finding his concentration now fixed on her cousin. What would he accuse John of this time? She frowned, unsure why she'd avoided informing John what Seb had said. Probably because John had gone out of his way to help her these last few days. Only yesterday, they'd spent almost the whole day together, going through the ins and outs of things she didn't even know existed.

Feeling dreadfully guilty, Sam frowned, knowing she shouldn't doubt John. Even less so since he'd made the effort. He was family, remember?

Her mind raced uncontrollably. No matter how many times she

told herself that family's word took precedence over anyone else's, the doubt still nagged, chafing away on the inner surface of her brain like an abrasive scourer. Christ, she felt awful that she'd *ever* doubted John, her own cousin. But the fact remained the same – regardless of how much she downplayed it, she *still* doubted him. And this prickling guilt picked away at her relentlessly.

Sam took a deep breath. All of this aside, she had to keep up the public pretence that a good relationship was maintained with her own family *and* the Stokers. She turned back to Mal and Judith. 'Thanks once again for coming. I'd better go and mingle.'

Squeezing her mother's hand before she moved away, Sam pushed her way through the crowd, walking hastily towards the staff corridor. She had to have a break for a few moments before facing any more condolences.

She wished the wake could have been held in a nice hotel – one with large patio doors leading to gardens so that she could get some fresh air and some space – but her mother was right. Where else but the Orchid was fitting?

Sam had almost reached the staff doors when she felt a hand on her arm.

'You haven't let that Stoker man collar you again, have you?' John said. 'He's bound to feed you more bullshit.'

'No, Seb hasn't said a word to me,' Sam muttered bitterly, Seb's public rebuff stinging.

John glanced around. 'There's been more trouble in the Stoker camp.'

Sam sighed. *That was painfully evident.* 'What problems the Stokers have between themselves aren't our concern.'

John's lips pursed. 'It *is* our concern and you need to seriously consider breaking the Orchid's connection with them.'

Sam frowned, worry glimmering. 'What, you mean like the shared territories? We have good deals on that front, do we not?'

John nodded. 'True, but by all accounts, they're turning on each other and we don't want to be involved with that.'

Sam blinked. She didn't want to talk about Sebastian-bloody-Stoker. She looked at John questioningly. 'And?'

'You saw the injuries?' John grinned. 'They've been fighting amongst themselves.'

Sam gasped. 'Are you serious? Whatever for?'

John leaned closer. 'Word has it that Seb attempted to kill the youngest brother when he found the money from a deal had been filched behind everyone's backs. Luckily for Gary, Seb only got as far as clumping him before the other brother, the one with the bust hooter, stopped him.'

Sam raised her eyebrows. *Seb had been the one to put his own brother in hospital the other day? He couldn't have...*

John lowered his voice further. 'And to make it worse, they've found out Gary isn't a true Stoker... He's not their real brother.'

Sam's head swung back to the mingling crowd, able to make out the Stokers standing united – playing the part as they always did.

'I mean, it's not like Gary looks like the rest of them, is it?' John added for good measure.

Sam had to agree that Gary certainly was the odd one out with his dirty blonde hair, compared to the striking dark hair of the rest of the Stokers, but to say *that*?

'I keep saying they can't be trusted. None of them! The shit will hit the fan, Samantha. You must cut all ties with them before it does.'

'I'm not discussing this at my father's funeral. We'll talk about it another day,' Sam snapped.

She watched John nod politely, then retreat back into the crowd, a rare smile across his face.

Sam's brow furrowed. Seb couldn't have attacked his brother – if Gary *was* his brother – because she'd been with him when the call came through. The only way that could be true was if he'd done it before she'd arrived at the Royal Peacock. And she didn't believe that was the case.

John was lying and if he was lying about that, then he could be lying about *everything*.

* * *

Liam had watched Sam talking to her mother, which had only fuelled his desperation. A funeral was hardly the best place to ramp up his play for the woman, but he couldn't help it. He'd do anything to be with her. *Anything.* Now she'd wandered off into the crowd, her face covered with grief and stress.

Of course, he knew Sam wasn't going to be overly happy – it was her father's funeral, after all, but there was something else. And whatever else had happened, it had made her unhappy and Liam didn't like that. Not one bit. It would deflect her from appreciating the attention he needed to give her in order to regain his fast-receding place in her life.

Spotting Seb Stoker leaning against the bar with a self-assured look on that mug of his, Liam's fists clenched. As much as he didn't want to think about it, uneasy thoughts slithered back into his mind – the same thoughts which had plagued him ever since the evening Sam had spent in the man's company. The nightmarish scene in his mind of Seb Stoker's hands all over Sam, his mouth on hers – or worse – forcing himself on her...

Liam scowled. Samantha should be *his*. She should always have been his.

For God's sake – even Len had all but promised that and he'd have had a fit if he'd thought one of the Stoker men was sniffing around.

Several times, Liam had seen Seb watching Sam like a hawk –

studying her like his prey. But it wasn't all bad. He'd also spotted Sam glaring at Seb. The only way he could describe what he saw in her eyes was something akin to malice.

Adrenaline flooded through Liam's veins. *If that bastard has touched her... Upset her...*

Worse, Sam had shut down on him too, making excuses not to take his calls. Although he'd accompanied her to the church, he believed that would not have happened had Gloria not arranged it.

His eyes tracked back to Seb Stoker. How he'd love to plant his fist in the man's chops.

Sensing someone approach, Liam turned. 'Oh, hello, John. It went okay today, didn't it?'

John's usual morose expression remained static. 'It went as well as could be expected.' He nodded towards Seb Stoker. 'I see he's still hanging around?'

Liam bristled. 'Yes, but there's been no contact between him and Sam today. Nothing at all.'

John smiled inwardly, glad to hear things were working. He'd just drop a few words in this shit-for-brains' ear to further the cause and then after that, with this lot busy, the coast was clear to nip out and see what Bedworth wanted. Why the man had asked to see him tonight was a mystery. Bedworth knew it was the goddamn funeral, but then again, being as it was important, he'd better go and see what was up.

He turned his attention back to Liam, who was hovering and waiting for him to respond. 'Samantha must have finally seen sense and is doubting Stoker. Besides, I've heard he's got other stuff on his mind too.'

Liam's ears picked up. 'Anything I should know about?'

John glanced around. 'I shouldn't really tell you this, but as Len held you in high regard, especially where his daughter was concerned, I will.'

Liam glowed. *Everyone knew him and Sam should be together. He knew it! He was on a fast-track to success!*

Despite wanting to break with habit and grin with a newly forming idea, John kept his face deadpan, adding a convincing hint of concern. 'Before I tell you the rest, I think it's only right to inform you Stoker is putting about his intention to make Sam one of his conquests in order to aid his mission. Apparently, he reckons it's a dead cert.'

He watched in silent satisfaction at the growing anger forming on Liam's face. Yep, he was bang on with that assumption too. This muppet's obsession with Samantha made him another person to add to the ever-growing list of happy helpers, unwittingly aiding his goal.

Primed, Liam moved to storm back into the casino and lay Stoker out flat on his back, the disrespect of delivering the man's comeuppance at Len Reynold's wake the only thing stopping him.

Seething, he turned back to John, jaw clenched. 'You'd best tell me what you know then, because I'm not having him use Sam as a notch for his filthy fucking bedpost,' Liam spat.

* * *

The minute Tom saw John Maynard's motor pull out from the car park, he made his move.

He grinned as he waved away the cloakroom attendant's offer to take his jacket. He wasn't leaving anything to chance or that could implicate him.

Appraising the sumptuous surroundings of the Orchid, Tom's smile grew wider. *Oh, very nice*, he thought, his eyes taking in the opulence dripping from the chandeliers in the high-ceilinged casino lobby.

Yeah, this was the business and only served to underline just how much he stood to gain.

Glancing to his right, he spotted a gents toilet. Quickly slipping inside, he made his way straight into one of the many cubicles. He didn't think he'd even been into a gents with more than one trap and they had at least eight in here. *The place was like the Ritz.*

As Tom shut the cubicle door, his eyes skimming over the gold taps, the line of basins and the spotless mirrors, he closed the thick wooden lid of the toilet and sat down, his fingers fumbling in his pocket.

Pulling out a small wrap of cocaine, he cut a thick line on the pristine enamelled cistern behind him. He needed a top-up before he lost his nerve.

Tom snorted the line through a rolled-up ten-pound note, sniffing the last bits deep into his nostrils. Licking his finger, he dabbed at the remaining bits of coke and shrugged. It was hardly like he'd get germs – the place was too bloody spotless.

Relaxing slightly, he allowed the cocaine to take effect. It was a hell of a risk being in the Orchid, but today was the chance of a lifetime and not one to waste. No one would notice him. There were so many people here, no one would be asked for membership cards. It was probably the one and only time in the Orchid's history that the casino was closed to the public. Besides, it was also the only viable chance to get a peek at all of these bastards – both firms together in the same place for once.

Maynard wouldn't want him here under any circumstances, but that wasn't his problem. Neither was he stupid because Maynard was, at this very moment, on his way to the Aurora.

Tom grinned. He'd made sure word had been sent, saying it was important they meet. *Clever, clever.*

He'd known Maynard would rush to see what he'd been called for. He'd be thinking about himself as usual, the sly, greedy bastard.

Well, Maynard could fuck right off. Tom was doing everything which had been agreed, but he wouldn't be stopped from doing his own thing in addition.

He'd already instructed that ugly slapper, Amelia, to keep Maynard entertained until he got back and this wouldn't take long. Costing him an extra fifty quid it was, so the stupid bitch best do her job properly, otherwise she'd find herself in the same place as Jock Sawyer.

Tom's yellowing teeth gleamed in the brightly lit cubicle as the rush of cocaine ramped up.

He grinned. There were plenty of ideas up his sleeve – all of which should bring a pretty pay-out. It was an unmissable opportunity and Maynard need never know he'd set foot in the place.

Tom's face suddenly morphed into a grimace. The notion that his own child was somewhere within these four walls crept back into his head and he shook it away in irritation. What did it matter? The plain fact was that it didn't. The only thing he wanted was payback and dues. Money plus some.

And that was what he would get. Thanks to Maynard, he'd now got an excellent opening.

Tom rose from the toilet seat, pocketed the remains of his wrap and grinned, the cocaine-induced confidence surrounding him like strong arms.

They were all here. *All of them*. Now all he had to do was get to the staff area. Once he'd done what was needed and got the required proof to continue his master plan, it wouldn't take long to get his arse back to the Aurora.

No one would be any the wiser until things went pear-shaped and if he played his cards right, he'd be long gone by then. He wasn't a gambler for nothing.

31

With a final glance from left to right, Tom could hardly believe his luck at finding the corridor deserted. Slamming the door, he leant back against it and froze, holding his breath, his senses finely tuned for any noise or movement. All he could hear was the muffled music and buzz of chatter from the main casino.

His heart pounded. He had to wait to see if anyone had spotted him slipping out here, but didn't think anyone had. The casino was packed with many unknown faces, so his wouldn't stand out. Any other night, yes, but not *this* night.

Tom's breath caught in his throat, the cocaine rush in full swing. Taking advantage of the wake was the best idea he'd had in ages – if not *ever*.

Although it was more than tempting to partake in the free bar, he had no time to waste. There would be ample opportunity to benefit from multiple bottles of the best champagne to his heart's content once he'd located the proof needed to back up his threats. It stood to reason he'd find it here. If not exactly what he was looking for, then *something* offering what he required, either way.

Tom's face split into a wide grin. Being as he was feeling lucky, he might even stumble across a few other things that would come in handy – like carelessly left around details of upcoming prosperous deals, perhaps? Or even wads of cash?

His eyes sparkled. *Now that would be nice.*

On the same vein, he couldn't make it obvious someone had been in here. The element of surprise was reduced if people had an inkling something was afoot.

No, he'd waited far too long to get compensation and, no matter how tempting it was, he must exhibit control.

Resentment festered further. He'd seen the casino – in fact, it had been difficult to drag his eyes away from that massive room, dripping in money. Money of which a fair chunk was owed to him. They *all* owed him. Even behind the scenes was bloody posh. And what had he got? Three grand?

Satisfied no one had detected him and the corridor was clear, Tom stealthily made his way along the thickly carpeted walkway.

He glanced through the panel of the first door he came to, the reflection of the sneer on his face mirrored back at him through the crystal-clear glass. This room wasn't posh enough to be the boss's office – or what *would* have been the boss's office.

Continuing, he passed three other rooms, stopping at the one at the far end. *This was it.* He pressed himself against the glass. Empty too. Not that he expected anything otherwise, but it always paid to be alert.

Trying the heavy silver door handle and finding it unlocked, Tom breathed a sigh of relief. He hadn't actually considered what he'd do in the event of it being locked, which was a bit short-sighted, but it wasn't, so no point in worrying about that.

He glanced at his watch, aware his window of time was narrow. Opening the door, Tom rushed into the office.

* * *

'Look at him,' Andrew hissed to Neil, contempt clear on his face as he nodded towards Gary. 'Are you telling me he looks comfortable in his own skin?'

Neil shook his head in exasperation. 'He looks about as comfortable as I would in a bird's fucking dress!' He raised his bottle of beer. 'As much as I hate to say it, I really do think he's behind all of the shit going on.'

Andrew's eyes narrowed as he continued staring at Gary. 'He can't even stand with us, the traitorous cunt.' He shoved another cigarette in his mouth. 'He knows we know – you can see it. Oh, he might have denied everything, but he knows.'

Neil nodded. 'And to think all these years we've been forced to accept him, when he's not even our proper brother?'

Andrew rolled his eyes. 'Or even related at all...'

Neil glanced at his father and then at Seb, who was eyeing both him and Andrew edgily. 'What are we going to do about it? Seb ain't convinced and won't hear a word of it.'

He turned back to Andrew. 'You haven't helped matters either by taking it upon yourself to off Phil. That wasn't what Seb wanted and he's bloody livid. You're lucky you're still walking!'

Andrew scowled. 'Seb doesn't know *what* he bloody wants at the moment. He's not thinking clearly. Someone had to do something rather than to allow the man to walk away with all the risk that brings.'

His fists clenched in his pocket, his nails digging into his palms. 'And no, he hasn't said a word about it yet. He's far too busy buried between Sam Reynold's legs, handing over our business, to lose any sleep over what *I* did,' Andrew spat.

'I wonder who Gary's shagging to help his cause?' Neil sniped. 'Most likely Maynard!'

Andrew laughed loudly at Neil's barb, then watched Gary suddenly slam his beer bottle down, whisper something to their mother and then storm off across the casino. 'See he's got his knickers in a twist again?'

'Probably off to look for his boyfriend to slag us off,' Neil grinned.

'Give it a fucking rest,' Seb hissed, moving closer to his brothers. Not trusting himself to contain his wrath for the stunt Andrew had pulled in overriding his decision the way he had, he'd purposefully maintained as much distance between them as possible.

Andrew was fast becoming a loose cannon and it was worrying. Increasingly so, but he could hardly smash his brother's brains back into place here – they had to maintain appearances. But he *would* be picking it up with Andrew before long. That was a definite.

Now he'd have to pay off Phil's wife and somehow justify how the death of her husband had occurred.

Seb's eyes narrowed. He didn't need all this extra crap. Hadn't he got enough to deal with?

It was frustrating enough that all day he'd had to force himself to be cordial to Samantha Reynold, when all he wanted to do was scrub the snotty attitude from her beautiful face. That and kiss her until she quit glaring at him. 'I know what you're doing. Just give this shit with Gary up now, please.'

Andrew frowned. 'Oh, come on! You're the only one who th...'

'I told you to fucking leave it!' Seb spat. 'And I meant it. You've done enough fucking damage as it is. You know *exactly* what I'm referring to.'

Putting his hand on Andrew's shoulder, he grinned. To anyone watching it would look like they were having a jovial conversation, but Seb's eyes portrayed to both of his brothers the exact opposite. 'Gary knows you're talking about him, as do I, and therefore, so will everyone else. I could even *hear* part of it. We do not broadcast our business, you know that.'

Seb lowered his voice to an almost inaudible level, using all his restraint not to wrap his hands around his brother's neck. 'You need to drop this shit before something stupid results from it.' He jerked his head in their parents' direction. 'Do you want to cause even more grief? You've already offloaded one of our own! Dad thinks we're a bunch of cunts because of the other night and I won't have our mother getting wind of this crap about Gary.' His eyes narrowed. 'Fucking sort it out now, do you hear me?'

'Oh, bollocks to this!' Andrew muttered, making sure the crowd-pleasing smile remained on his face. 'I'm out of here.'

'I'll join you,' Neil said and together they walked away, leaving Seb standing at the bar, his face thunderous.

* * *

Sweat pouring down his face, Tom was almost at the point of hyper-ventilating. *Where the fuck was everything?* He'd been through virtually every drawer he could get into. He'd even been through the filing cabinets, but had found nothing of any use, apart from that map, which had been stupidly left out on the desk.

He patted his pocket where he'd stuffed the piece of paper, knowing exactly what it represented.

Okay, so he had a pretty good idea of what patches to move on to next, but having this map removed a lot of the groundwork. It was useful, but not what he'd come for. *Not even close.*

'Fuck's sake,' he muttered under his breath. He'd spent more time making sure everything was put back the way it was than looking for what he needed. It was not going well.

The safe wasn't difficult to find, but he couldn't get into the bloody thing. He glared at the large black metal monstrosity in front of him. The tools he usually relied upon for picking locks had failed dismally on this particular occasion.

Tom's face screwed into a scowl. The one opportunity, and

possibly the *only* opportunity he'd ever get, and he'd put his neck on the line for jack shit.

Gritting his teeth, he glared at his watch. It was no good. He'd have to go. Maynard's alarm bells would ring if he failed to show up much longer, plus, the longer he hung around, the higher the chance became of somebody stumbling across him.

Slipping out of the office, Tom pulled the door shut. Despite the disappointing outcome, he breathed a sigh of relief. At least he'd got the map. Now he'd just got to get back through the casino unnoticed and then he was out of here. There would be another way to get the proof. There *had* to be.

'Who the fuck are you?' a voice suddenly growled.

Swinging around, Tom found a man standing a yard away, wearing a none-too-friendly look on his face. 'Oh, hi,' Tom stammered. 'I was just looking for...'

'This place is out of bounds! It's staff only,' the man growled, slamming Tom heavily up against the corridor wall, his head rebounding noisily. 'What the fuck are you doing here?'

Terror and panic convulsed through Tom's body. Getting caught would ruin everything. *Everything.* 'I must have taken the wrong turning when I was looking for the gents,' he blathered.

Before he could do anything else, Tom found himself pulled down by the hair, his head twisting at a painful angle.

'You're coming with me,' the voice barked.

Tom had little choice but to follow in the direction where his hair was being yanked. His heart pounded. He couldn't be discovered here. *No, no, NO!*

His hand fumbled to his waistband, his fingers closing around the handle of his knife. Pulling it from the holder, Tom lashed out, slashing a long slit down the front of the man's thigh.

Howling in surprise, the man released his grip of Tom's hair and barely had time to register the blade driving deep into his neck.

32

'Jesus H. Christ,' Neil muttered, glancing at his brother. 'Are you telling me this is the best on offer?'

'By the looks of it, it's *all* that's on offer,' Andrew replied, grimacing at the overpriced lager, wishing it was still in the can it had clearly just been tipped from. It tasted like out-of-date supermarket own-brand lager, probably why the horse-faced creature behind what constituted a bar had disappeared into another room to pour the drink.

He glanced around the dimly lit room – dimly lit for a very good reason – to hide the overall state. It would have to be pitch black for him to be blind to exactly how bloody ghastly the place and its collection of women actually was. On top of that, at least a couple of them didn't look anywhere near old enough to have left school, let alone anything else.

'This was your idea,' Neil hissed. 'In pursuit of information or not, there is no way I'm putting my dick in any of *those*.' He nodded towards the skimpily dressed women lounging across a sagging sofa in what he presumed were supposed to be alluring poses.

Andrew sighed. It had seemed a good idea to slide out of the wake to check out the Aurora whilst everyone else was otherwise occupied. Neither had he been prepared to stand there any longer getting an ear-bashing about Gary and everything else either. Things were moving far too slowly on all points and he wasn't having it. This was *his* chance to show why he should have more clout where the running of the firm was concerned.

He'd sorted out one possible liability in the name of Phil, and if he unearthed who was behind the shit originating from the Aurora, then maybe his father would realise he should be at level pegging with Seb, rather than still relegated to second fiddle.

Yes, they'd been told there was no point checking the Aurora out, but that was Maynard's opinion. Neil was supposed to be checking it out over a week ago and that had been put off. It was time they saw for themselves.

Andrew's mouth pursed in frustration. He'd make his *own* decisions, thank you!

Despite not wanting to look, Andrew felt his eyes traitorously move back towards the woman on the far end of the grubby sofa and inwardly shuddered. Rolls of fat hung over her leopard print lycra crop top, her breasts sagged down to her knees and her skirt left little to the imagination.

As much as he didn't want to be here, it was important to do some digging. Someone attached to this place must know something about their family and he wanted to know who that person was. 'Come on.' Andrew jerked his head in the direction of the sofa.

Neil followed Andrew's gaze. 'No. Fucking. Way!'

Andrew dragged Neil forward by his jacket sleeve. 'Fact-finding only,' he muttered. 'Evening, ladies,' he said brightly as he approached the sofa. 'Mind if we join you?'

Neil squashed himself between two women, inwardly gagging as they stroked his thigh in unison. *This had better be worth it.*

'What can we do for you fine gentlemen?' one of the women purred.

Andrew tried not to laugh at the expression on his brother's face. He hadn't expected Neil to be quite so squeamish. He wasn't usually choosy, although this lot were vastly at the highest end of the gross scale. 'What are you offering?' he drawled, trying not to stare at the hairy lump on the end of the woman's nose.

'It depends how much time you've got.' The woman's hand traced up the inside of Andrew's thigh, worryingly close to his nether regions. 'And money... Shall we go upstairs?'

Moving away from the woman's wandering hands, Andrew got up. 'I'll just pop to the gents and then I'll be with you,' he winked, looking around. 'Where is it?'

'The bog's just down there,' the woman smiled, grabbing her handbag in readiness.

Nodding his thanks, Andrew kept his smile fixed until he was out of view. *Jesus Christ.* He'd go upstairs with the moose, but there was no way he'd be getting his kit off. Or hers.

He'd use the time, with help of the wad of notes in his inside pocket, to tempt the skank into becoming loose-lipped over who ran this gaff. But there would be nothing else... Jeez!

Seeing a door that looked like it could be a toilet, Andrew walked along the long corridor, but hearing movement and voices from up the back stairs, he stiffened.

He recognised that voice.

Quickly slipping into what he presumed was the toilet, he waited. The voice had now stopped and boots tramped heavily down the stairs. Using the tip of his shoe to wedge a small crack in the door, Andrew flattened himself against the wall in the tiny dark room, sure without looking behind him that, due to the stench, he'd been correct in assuming this was the toilet.

He waited, one eye getting a good view along the corridor. Not daring to breathe as the figure moved past towards the main room, Andrew frowned, his eyes narrowing.

Fuck. He was right about that voice. Maynard. Why the bloody hell was he here again?

* * *

Racing up the bare wooden steps to the first floor of the Aurora, Andrew's eyes darted around the landing, hoping that Maynard had not spotted Neil downstairs or that he was on his way back up here.

It wasn't like he'd had time to check because he needed to speak to the woman Maynard had been with before she went back downstairs or another punter was sent up for her services.

His heart crashed in his chest as he scanned the doors leading off the landing. *Which room had they been in?*

Spotting a door slightly ajar, Andrew rushed towards it. Pushing it open, his nose wrinkled with the heavy scent of unwashed bodies and sex. A thick-set woman in her mid-forties with tangled hair and an over-tight, purple, see-through negligee sat on the edge of the unmade bed, dragging wet wipes down her cellulite-ridden thighs.

'I ain't ready yet,' the woman snapped. Glancing up and seeing Andrew's attractive face, her manner softened. 'I won't be a minute though, love. Give us a tick and I'll be with you. I'll just make sure I'm looking nice for you.'

Ignoring the woman's unsavoury promises, Andrew stormed into the room regardless.

'Hey! I said I...'

'Who's just been in here?' Andrew barked.

The woman scowled, the deep frown only accentuating her lack of looks. 'I'm not telling you that! That's breaching confidentiality, that is. We don't ev...'

'Oh, shut the fuck up!' Quickly moving forward, Andrew grabbed a fistful of the woman's hair. Twisting a large chunk, he ignored her howling. 'Now isn't the time to bother with confidentiality, woman. Just tell me who you've just had in here and I'll leave you alone.'

He shoved his free hand in his pocket. Pulling out a fifty-pound note, he waved it in the woman's face. 'Answer what I asked and you can have this too.'

With her beady eyes on the crisp note, the woman flapped her hand. 'Okay, okay. Get off my fucking hair and I'll tell you.'

Relaxing his grip, Andrew took a step back and folded his arms, knowing the woman was still focused on the money in his hand. 'Well?'

The woman flattened down her mussed, tangled hair and glared at Andrew. 'Why do you care?'

'Get. On. With. It.' Andrew's patience was on the brink of completely abandoning him.

The woman sighed. 'Maynard. John Maynard.' She picked up a makeup bag and pulled at the press-studs, fishing out a powder compact and brush. 'Happy now?'

'Not particularly. What was he doing here?'

The woman eyed Andrew incredulously. 'What do you think?'

Andrew stepped forward, his face an angry mask. 'Don't play fly with me, you stupid bitch. Answer the fucking questions without trying to be witty, okay?'

Contrite, the woman nodded and placed her powder brush down. 'I was told to keep Maynard entertained until the boss got back.'

The hackles rose on Andrew's neck. 'And who's the boss?'

The woman's eyes narrowed. 'I don't know. I've only been here a few days.' She didn't know this bloke, but she certainly wasn't dropping Tommy in it – not when he was about to employ her two girls.

Andrew frowned. 'Does Maynard come here a lot?'

The woman shrugged. 'How should I know? I was just told to keep the bloke busy for a while.'

'Do you know anything?' Andrew snarled. 'Who told you to keep Maynard busy?' Maybe that person was the one who called the shots? Furthermore, it could be *him* behind all the grief.

'Some bloke – a bloke called Lee,' the woman sniffed. She didn't mind giving *Lee's* name up. She'd heard the ugly bastard talking about her, saying she was a fat old cow, so he could fuck off as far as she was concerned.

Andrew stiffened. 'Lee? Where's this Lee bloke, then?'

'Dunno,' the woman sniffed. 'He's not here either. And before you ask, I don't know whether he'll be back tonight or what, but whatever happens, I'll be in the shit being as Maynard refused to hang around.'

Andrew pursed his lips. This silly tart knew sod all. *Shit.* He could go downstairs and grill some of the others, but hopefully Neil had already done that. Whatever happened, he wasn't going to get anything useful out of this one.

Hearing a loud buzzer, the woman leapt from the bed. 'Shit!'

Andrew's head jerked in the direction of the noise. 'What? What is it?'

'It's the alarm! It means the fucking cops are here!' the woman panted. 'I knew something like this would happen tonight. I could feel it in my bones.' She eyed Andrew nastily. 'Here, you aren't a cop, are you?'

'Am I fuck!' Andrew cried. 'Is there another way out of here?'

The woman nodded towards the window. 'If you're quick, you

can lower yourself out of there and drop onto the fire escape. There's another exit out of the car park too, behind the hedge.'

Throwing the fifty-pound note on the bed, Andrew eased himself out of the window, only hoping Neil had managed to get out too.

33

Watching with relief as her mother clambered into the taxi, Sam shut the door of the cab and waved it off. She moved back from the edge of the pavement and leant against the wall of the Orchid.

Sam had seen her mother starting to flag. The strain on her face was obvious and as she'd always struggled with crowds and people, let alone under these circumstances, she'd felt it only right her mother should be encouraged to go home.

Sam wished more than anything that she'd been able to escape too, but someone had to stay until the bitter end. It was only right and what her father would have expected.

Taking a deep breath, she resolutely walked back up the stairs to the casino, glancing at her diamond-encrusted Gucci bracelet watch and scowling as a man barged into her as he rounded the corner.

'Sorry, love,' the man muttered, continuing down the stairs.

Sam shook her head with irritation and weariness. *There could only be an hour or so of this left now, surely?*

'Oh, thank God!' Liam panted, appearing at the top of the stairs. 'I thought something had happened.'

Sam shrugged Liam's arm away, claustrophobia mounting. 'Like what?'

'I thought that Stoker bastard had collared you. I couldn't see him and I couldn't see you either, so I thought th...'

'Are you obsessed with that man? You seem to be very concerned about what he's doing!' Sam snapped.

'So would you be if you knew his plan was to bed you,' Liam said, his hand moving to Sam's cheek. 'I can't let him use you. I...'

'I was seeing my mother into a cab, Liam. How silly of me not to check with you first to make sure you approved. But then again, I should be grateful I've got you looking out for me being as I clearly can't make any kind of rational decision!'

Turning on her heel, Sam yanked open the door, ignoring Liam rushing up behind her.

'I'm sorry,' Liam begged. 'I didn't mean to make...'

'Just leave me be, please,' Sam said calmly. 'I need some space.' Striding through the casino, her eyes fixed firmly ahead, she passed straight into the staff corridor. Heart clamouring, she had to stop herself from breaking into a run to reach the sanctuary of her father's, or rather, *her* office.

She had to get away from Liam; from *everyone*, even if just for a moment. All the people, all the questions, all the assumptions... She felt like she might scream.

Barging into her office, Sam slammed the door and fell against it. Her eyes shut, she breathed slowly in a race to control her escalating panic. *Calm, Sam. Calm.*

'Looks like you had the same idea as me,' a deep voice growled.

Sam all but collapsed with shock at the unexpected voice. Her eyes shot open to see Seb Stoker sitting at her desk. 'What the fuck are you doing in here?' she screamed, her eyes wild.

'Oh, get off your high horse, Samantha,' Seb sighed. 'I needed some time away from the hordes, plus I thought I saw my brother heading this way. Clearly, I was wrong.'

Sam's eyes narrowed. 'That gives you the bloody right to trespass into private areas of my club, does it? I've heard you like looking for things you can use against me in your quest to gain control over everything!'

Seb stared in silence at Sam and continued casually drinking from his tumbler of whisky.

'You don't deny it, then?' Sam spat, her eyes darting around, seeing if she could spot anything that had been moved. 'The map! The one that was on my desk. It's gone!'

Seb rolled his eyes. 'If you're referring to the map you copied from mine – that, according to you, was full of fake information, then why would I want that?'

Sam scowled. Why did he have to be in here making her angrier? It was only then she noticed how tired Seb looked, weariness replacing the usual brash arrogance on his handsome face.

'Think what you like, Sam. I'm not in the mood for arguing with little girls,' Seb muttered, placing his glass on the desk.

Sam moved forward, the intensifying irritation driving her. Is that how Seb Stoker saw her? A silly little girl? An inexperienced, pointless woman, only good for ridicule and the recipient of patronising comments?

A flush of disappointment replaced her annoyance and anger. Even though this man didn't owe her anything – the opposite, in fact – she'd really thought, really *believed* by the end of the other night she had found an unexpected ally. To discover Seb might be working against her after all riled her more than it should. Plus, there was something about him that both excited and unnerved her. And that was heady.

Whether she wanted to admit it or not, she wanted him to see her as someone to take *seriously*. Someone who was capable.

And, squirming inwardly with embarrassment at her silent acknowledgement, she also wanted to know if he felt the same pull of attraction to her as she did for him... The one that grew in intensity each time she laid eyes on him.

Standing opposite, she glared at Seb; the strange desire to see how far she could push him glimmering stronger. 'Being as you're still sitting in my seat, I'll just stand, shall I?'

Seb got up and, with a flourish, bowed towards the now empty chair. 'My deepest apologies, Samantha.'

Pushing past, Sam sat down, the warmth from where Seb had been sitting seeping into the back of her thighs. She knew she was being pedantic, ridiculous even, but she felt unable to act rationally around this man who had the effect of jangling all her nerve endings at the same time. 'Now if you don't mind...?'

Shaking his head, Seb moved towards the door. 'You really are a spoilt little girl, aren't you, Samantha?'

Stinging tears burnt at the back of Sam's eyes with the collective pent-up emotion of the day. Every insult, no matter how small, was accentuated. 'Stop calling me a little girl! Save your insults for someone who cares,' she spat, staring Seb squarely in the eyes.

'Are you concerned that I might take Maynard out for setting up to filch my deal and attacking my brother?' Seb said, his arrogance returning. Placing his hands on the desk, he leant closer. 'Or have you worked out that I was right and you're hoping I save you the trouble of firing him?'

Sam jumped up from her seat. 'You're that much of a prick to have ridiculous digs at me during my father's funeral? Threatening to beat people up at a wake? Have you no shame?'

Seb shrugged. 'Shame? No, not really. When I get proof it was Maynard, then it's irrelevant where justice is done.'

Sam's heart pounded. 'Then that speaks volumes. I can see

through you, Mr Stoker. You're blaming John because you want no one to find out that your own brother nicked your bloody money.'

She laughed nastily. Giving this man the satisfaction of knowing she was leaning towards believing his words over those of her cousin was the *last* thing she wanted him to be aware of. 'Everyone knowing you can't trust your own must be embarrassing, but it won't wash with me.'

'I can't imagine who informed you of that,' Seb countered. *He wouldn't lose his temper. Not today. But he might kiss her to shut her up instead.*

Sam walked away from the desk, exhilaration flooding her at the veiled anger brooding on Seb's face. *Didn't like that, did he?*

She snatched up the decanter and poured herself a large whisky. Sebastian Stoker thought he could intimidate her and make her out to be a fool? There may be countless unsavoury threads weaved against her or both of them, but if it wasn't him all along, then he was still both the common denominator *and* the problem.

Let's see how he liked stuff thrown back at him, because she'd had enough of his games. Seb would not get away with his underhand ways tonight.

Sam brought the glass up to her lips, a smile creeping over her face. 'You're very sure about everything being John's fault, aren't you?'

Seb raked his fingers through his hair and sighed loudly. 'Believe what you want. I don't care. I'll leave you to it.'

Sam watched Seb move towards the door, obstinacy enveloping her. 'Don't tell me you're unaware everyone knows what you've done? I can only guess that's why you sloped off to hide like a coward, unless it was to go through my things? Possibly both...'

'I ain't no coward,' Seb spat, swinging around, his eyes flashing dangerously. 'I hide from no one.'

Bingo. Sam smiled. *That hit a nerve. Here's back at you, Sebastian Stoker.* 'If you say so...'

Backing Sam up against the desk, Seb tilted her face up to his. 'You should learn when to stop winding people up.'

Wanting to yank Seb's hand away from her face out of principle, Sam felt powerless to move under his strangely hypnotic and intense green gaze. Heart thundering, she felt like the world's biggest traitor as she found her eyes moving to his mouth, his lips only inches from hers.

As Seb's mouth crashed down onto hers, the indignant urge to push him away immediately dissolved as intense heat surged through Sam's body.

Finding her lips yielding to his, his tongue igniting raging fire as he explored her mouth, her arms wound around his neck. Moving to press closer against him, his hand at the base of her spine holding her tightly, her longing exploded at the hardness she could feel pressing against her stomach.

As Seb's other hand moved to her waist, his lips now tracing down the sensitive skin of her throat, Sam found her hand running down the lapel of his suit, her fingers tugging his shirt from his trousers.

Then she froze. *What the hell was she doing?*

Pulling away, Sam glared at Seb. 'How dare you!' she yelled, her face flushed with traitorous desire. 'Don't think I haven't heard about your pathetic plan!' She couldn't allow herself to fall for this oldest trick in the book, no matter how much she wanted to.

Hiding the disappointment at losing the wave of raw longing he'd felt like never before, Seb laughed. 'You want me as much as I want you, Samantha. Let's just get it out of our system and then we can concentrate on everything else.'

Seb's bright white smile made Sam burn even harder for him,

but she couldn't go back on what she'd said. She couldn't back down now. *No way.*

Her eyes glinted. 'I know your aim is to bed me and gain pillow-talk about my firm's secrets, but you'll have a long wait. I'd rather sleep with a corpse than jump in the sack with an arrogant, violent bastard like you!'

'Is that your latest crazy idea?' Seb said, his eyes dancing. 'Or is that yet another conspiracy theory Maynard has convinced you of?'

Sam scowled, refusing to give Seb the satisfaction of being right. *Again.* 'Not at all. It's just people who attempt to kill their own brother don't turn me on, that's all.'

'You what?' Seb cried, rage overtaking his lust.

Sam fought the urge to step back and instead kept the sneer plastered on her face. *Speak to me like shit, Stoker, and I'll treat you like shit.* 'People know you found out your brother turned you over and lifted the money from your oh-so-important Irish deal. Well, that's karma for you, isn't it?'

'You nasty lying piece of sh...'

'Oh, how silly of me!' Sam sniped, her eyes narrowing. 'I forgot that wouldn't count as killing family, being as Gary isn't your brother!'

Colour flooded Seb's face, a twitch under his eye evident. 'You bitch!' he spat. 'How dare you say that!'

Sam faltered, shame tearing her insides. She shouldn't have said that. It was out of order. She wasn't like this, she wasn't a bitch, yet she was behaving like a top-class one and she didn't like it. This man made her behave out of character and it was unsettling, but the need to hurt Seb – for reasons she couldn't quite justify to herself, was strong. And it still was. As well as the feel of his mouth on hers... Her fingers moved involuntarily to her lips, still swollen from his kisses.

She knew she was attacking him for having the power to make

her succumb to desire when she should be able to remain in control of herself. She should be stronger than to muddy the already treacherous waters with even more fraught confusion.

Unable to help the venom from flowing from her mouth, Sam faced Seb without hesitation as he backed her into the large cupboard at the rear of the office. 'Or is it you who's not the true Stoker...?'

Seb couldn't look more like a younger version of his father if he tried, but that wasn't the point. She was on a roll – a nasty one. And she couldn't get off it.

Sam raised her chin defiantly, looking Seb straight in the eyes as he loomed above her. She knew his fist was clenched and could almost hear the adrenaline pounding through his veins, the noise overshadowing the crashing of her own heart.

Was he going to kiss her again? Her breath hitched, wanting him to, despite what her brain was screaming.

Seb slammed Sam against the cupboard with a crash, his rage for this exquisite and dangerously beautiful woman at fever pitch. Despite her insolence, which he would usually take from no one, he still wanted to bury himself inside her, and it was suffocating. 'There was me thinking you had a brain in your head! Do not speak of things you know nothing about!'

'Get your hands off me!' Sam yelled, pushing Seb away with all the force she could muster.

Shaking her head in anger, now mainly at herself, she stepped away from the cupboard and went to close the door which had come slightly open, finding something sticking and preventing it from shutting. She didn't know what was kept in here, she hadn't got round to sorting through half of what was in her father's office, but if Seb had smashed or wrecked anything by what he'd done...

'I suggest you leave now,' she muttered, yanking open the door to free whatever was jamming it. 'OH MY GOD!' Shrieking, she jumped back in horror at the sight of a bloodied body wedged into the bottom of the cupboard.

Sam's heart pounded in her chest so strongly she felt it might burst from her rib cage and jump onto the floor. Waves of light-headedness and nausea poured over her like a waterfall.

The trembling started in her toes before rapidly spreading up her legs, through her stomach, past her chest, branching out along her arms to the end of her fingertips. A buzzing electrical sensation then moved at lightning speed up her neck, over her face and then along each of the long, dark brown hairs of her head.

Her eyes fixed on the vacant gaze of the crumpled man in the cupboard, a stab wound with congealed purple blood around the small but fatal slit on his neck clear. Her eyes then moved to the thick and growing pool of blood drenching a tarpaulin lining the floor of the cabinet.

Nausea rose again, this time faster, and her hand flew to her mouth as her brain struggled to process the scene. She crouched down, unwilling to get close to the man, but knew she must. He was dead. *Definitely* dead.

A strange combination of fear and rage thundered through Sam like a freight train.

Not only had a man been murdered, but whoever had committed such a crime had the disrespect to do it during her father's funeral. And what did it mean? This man had been dumped in her office. Was it a message?

Wait...

Gingerly peering further in order to see the man's face, Sam froze as the enormity of the situation sunk in.

This was a Stoker. Gary Stoker. This was Seb's brother...

Unable to make her brain function coherently, Sam's trembling increased as the world around her moved in slow motion. Time and space ground to a halt. It had only been a few moments since she'd opened the cupboard and discovered this... this nightmare.

She heard Seb's voice telling her to shut up. It sounded like it was underwater, yet he was moving back towards her...

Sam remained paralysed: unable to speak or react. He was almost behind her...

Seb Stoker had killed his brother and now he would kill her. *Was that correct? Was what everyone said about him the truth after all?*

Snapping herself back into action, Sam swung around as Seb loomed closer. 'You murdering bastard!' she screamed, launching herself towards him, her hands flailing towards his face. 'You animal! You despicable fucking bas...'

'Stop!' Seb roared. Fending off having his eyes scratched out with Sam's nails, he grabbed her arms and pinned them against her sides.

Holding her against the wall using his body, he glared into her wild eyes. 'Fuck's sake! What the hell's wrong with you? First of all you start yelling at me and then you launch yourself at me like a mad woman! Do you want me to kiss you again? Is that it?'

Because he'd more than happily oblige. The feel of her soft lips on his had been exquisite, triggering something he'd never felt before and he was more than up for a repeat.

Grinning at Sam's silence, he craned his neck to look into the cupboard. 'What is it? A fucking spider or something? Oh, FUCK!'

Releasing Sam, all thoughts of kissing her again now extinguished, Seb rushed towards the cupboard. Ripping his suit jacket off, he squatted down onto his haunches and pressed his fingers against his brother's neck, desperately feeling for a pulse. He tried to stem the bleeding until he realised it was pointless.

'Shit. Shit!' he hissed. 'NO! Come on. Gary! Don't do this to me!'

Flattening herself against the wall, Sam watched in detached fascination. 'Oh my God,' she muttered. 'You seriously expect me to believe you didn't know he was in there?' She would have laughed if the situation had not been so desperately grave.

Seb turned to Sam, his eyes filled with terror and pain. 'Help me help him, for fuck's sake! Don't just stand there!'

Sam paused as she took in the raw pain in Seb's face and realisation whacked her between the eyes. *No one was that good an actor...*

The combination of fear and rage reared up again, as well a bubbling guilt at her earlier accusatory words. *Seb hadn't done this – Seb hadn't killed his brother.*

'Fucking help me!' Seb roared, then turned back to his brother. 'Gary! Come on!'

'He's dead,' Sam said quietly, suddenly experiencing a crushing sadness for this big powerful man in front of her on his knees, disintegrating before her very eyes, and a steely resolve grew in her mind.

'NO' Seb roared. 'He can't be! I won't allow it!' Dragging Gary from the cupboard, he cradled him in his arms, the front of his white shirt thick with his brother's blood.

Sam moved towards Seb. 'I'll call the police,' she said softly, daring to lay a hand on his shoulder.

'No!' Seb grabbed Sam's hand, the pain in his eyes now replaced with manic rage. 'You can't!'

Startled, Sam frowned. 'But...'

'You need to help me sort this, Sam,' Seb said. 'And we need to sort it now! My parents must not find out about this just now. Christ! It will finish them! I need time to think about what to do.'

'You want me to help you conceal your brother's body?' Sam spluttered. *Was Seb insane?*

'That's exactly what I want you to do. I'd do anything for my parents, Samantha. As would you with yours, I don't doubt.' He looked back to the tarpaulin and what it contained. 'I don't want to hide it from them and I *will* tell them, but not yet. My father's just out of hospital and my mother's in enough of a state about everything as it is.' Seb's lips tightened. 'It won't be for long, but I really can't tell them that... that one of their sons has been murdered whilst they've been chatting on the floor above. I can't tell them that now. Not here. Not like this...'

Sam nodded mutely. *She understood that much.*

Seb's eyes locked onto Sam's. 'Then I'm going to find whoever's done this.'

And as much as he didn't want to admit it, he knew there could only be two rational choices: Maynard or one of his own brothers.

* * *

Seb watched Sam lift his brother's legs whilst he took the shoulders, betting lifting bodies onto tarpaulins wasn't anything she'd ever done before. In fact, he'd always imagined she hadn't even had cause to wash up a plate, but he'd take his hat off to her – she'd got on with what he'd asked and he was grateful for that. *Grateful and impressed.* And that alone helped divert from his pounding grief.

Keeping busy whilst they fetched another tarpaulin from the stores and scrubbed the inside of the cabinet had also helped. They'd cleaned the arc of blood from the corridor ceiling that he hadn't noticed until Sam insisted they looked for more traces. 'You can't get stabbed in the neck without it being messy,' she'd said bluntly. And she'd been right.

But it was strange there wasn't more blood. Whoever had done this had done it in the corridor, then rapidly dragged Gary through the office into the cupboard. They'd either cleaned the majority of the mess up themselves afterwards or laid a tarpaulin beforehand.

Seb's pulse rate increased. *When he got his hands on who had done this...*

Averting his eyes as best he could, he covered Gary's face with the rest of the tarpaulin. *Pretend it's someone else*, he told himself. *Anyone else. Just someone. It doesn't matter who. It's not your brother lying here...*

Flinching as fingers touched his, Seb's head snapped up, pulling him from his thoughts.

'I'll do that,' Sam said softly.

Nodding, Seb turned away and grabbed the cloth. Turning his back, he continued scrubbing at an already clean piece of floor so that Sam couldn't see the unfamiliar tears forming in his eyes. Clenching his teeth, he willed for self-control before he turned around. He couldn't have anyone seeing how gutted he was. Gary may have been an irritating twat and a bit of a wet lettuce, but Gary was his *brother*. He didn't care what anyone else said, this should not have happened.

Forcing the lump from his throat, a steely cold stare replaced the pain in his green eyes. This was Len Reynold's wake. There were no members of the public present tonight, and that meant Gary's killer was someone he knew. Or who *Sam* knew.

Try as he might, Seb couldn't shake his original suspicion. His gut was telling him this was Maynard's doing. The man had already organised Gary to get jumped so he could lift that money, but he lacked the proof. Now the bastard had killed his brother?

His fist clenched, crushing the floor cloth in his hand. Maynard was desperate to set the Stokers up. What better way to do that by knocking the family off kilter? By killing one of them? And picking the one least likely to offer resistance?

Seb risked a glance at Sam, seeing her head bowed over Gary's body, now completely wrapped in the tarpaulin, concentration on her face as she deftly stitched the sides with a large upholstery needle and thick twine, reserved for invisible repairs to the casino seating.

Admiration for the woman crushed his chest. She may not be used to dealing with this sort of thing, but she was doing a damn fine job and had shied away from nothing.

Sam Reynold was nothing to do with this. He'd seen her reaction. Seb's brow furrowed. He also knew that initially she'd thought it was him. She thought *he'd* done this. But then, guessing the sort of things Maynard had been cramming her head with recently, that wasn't too much of a surprise.

His jaw tightened. He may be a lot of things, but he wouldn't kill his own bloody brother.

Sweat beaded on Seb's brow as he slowly realised that if it turned out to be Andrew and Neil responsible for this and not Maynard, then he'd have no choice in breaking that cardinal rule. And that he dreaded.

It *had* to be Maynard.

But both Maynard and his brothers had motives. They were all here tonight and, furthermore, he didn't recall seeing any of them present at the wake when he'd come down here on the lookout for Gary.

'I think I'm done now,' Sam said, her voice unnaturally loud in the silent room. She got to her feet, using the table to pull herself upright, her knees stiff from the length of time kneeling on the hard wooden floor of her office. She saw Seb studying her. 'What?' she frowned.

Seb shook his head absentmindedly. 'Nothing. I was just thinking...'

Sam's face softened. 'Are you all right?'

Seb shrugged. 'You thought I'd done this, didn't you?'

Heat flooded Sam's cheeks at the truth of Seb's words. She had indeed initially thought that. What was wrong with her? *Would she ever get it right?* She smiled weakly. 'Okay, I admit it. I did and I'm sorry, I really am. I know from your reaction that you didn't, but either way, I should never have thought it, let alone said it.'

'How do you know I'm not just a good actor?'

Sam sighed. 'I'm not arguing about this again.'

'For the record, I didn't do it. But I think I know who did...'

Sam stiffened, guessing what Seb would say and she didn't want to hear it. 'I'm presuming you're blaming my cousin again?' She shook her head in frustration. 'For God's sake, Seb. John wouldn't do this.'

'Oh, yes, he would. He had the motive. If it wasn't by his own hands, then he was behind it. And he was here, but then...' Seb's eyes narrowed. 'So were my brothers...'

Sam gasped. 'You suspect your *brothers* could have done this?'

Seb raked his bloodstained fingers through his hair. 'Christ, I don't know! It has to be one of them.'

Andrew's actions over Phil Blunt paled into insignificance compared with the prospect of one or both of his brothers being linked to Gary's murder. And he silently prayed he was correct with the suspicion in the forefront of his mind about Maynard because he would need his brothers' help with keeping this from his parents. Even though it would only be for the short term, he couldn't do that alone.

But if Gary's death *had* been at the hands of Andrew, Neil or both of them, it would kill their father and their mother would never get over it. *Ever.*

And neither would *he.*

Sam placed her hands on the desk and stared at the tarpaulin-covered body. 'We haven't got time to analyse it now. They'll be missing us upstairs. Or me, at least. We've been gone ages. Do you know what you're going to do with... with...' She indicated at the tarpaulin.

Seb nodded. 'I know a place.' Not that he'd ever forgive himself for storing his brother's body in the only place he had quick access to. But he had to do something whilst getting things back on track.

Grabbing his suit jacket, Seb moved towards the door. 'I'd best get going. I'll need a van.' He glanced at Sam. 'And I need to know the best way out. A way that no one is likely to be hanging around. No bar staff – nothing. A fire escape?'

'You can't go like that!' Sam cried, staring at Seb's blood-soaked shirt.

Seb shrugged. 'What choice do I have? Don't know whether you've noticed, but it's not like I have a wardrobe here with plenty of choices!' He numbly began putting on his jacket. 'I'll have to take my chances.' He held out his hand. 'Keys? Van keys?'

Sam opened a drawer at her desk. Rummaging in a tray, she picked out several keys and checked the key fobs. 'Take this one. It's a white Transit. It's one of the pool vans used for the drops.' Although she still had a lot to learn, she was now glad she'd made it her business to find out how some of the other parts of the business went down, otherwise she'd be completely blind to everything.

Seb took the keys. 'I'll get it back to you as soon as, or if not, I'll replace it. Now, what's the best route out?'

'Wait!' Sam moved to another cupboard, only slightly hesitating before opening it. She pulled out a pair of dark green overalls. 'I noticed these the other day. Think they must have been my father's. Put them on.'

Seb shrugged off his suit jacket once more and began unbuttoning his shirt, his fingers fumbling over the buttons.

'We need to hurry.' Sam stepped forward. 'Come on, let me help.' She quickly unbuttoned Seb's shirt, her fingers surprisingly steady.

Seb found himself staring at the top of Sam's head as she made easy work of undoing his shirt, taking note of the glossiness of her hair and getting the urge to run his fingers through it. Feeling his groin throb with the beginnings of arousal, he berated himself for allowing his thoughts to wander at a time like this.

Sam knew she was transfixed by Seb's hard muscular chest as he shrugged off his undone shirt and heat rushed to her cheeks once more. Hoping he hadn't noticed, she stepped backwards. 'Give me your clothes,' she muttered. 'I'll get rid of them.'

The spell broken, Seb slipped off his trousers and stepped into the overalls, zipping them up. He handed his clothes to Sam. 'What you going to do with them? Burn them?'

Sam shrugged. 'Leave me to worry about that. Come on, you need to go.' She looked at the bulky tarpaulin on the floor. 'There's a trolley down the corridor,' she said. 'Put him on that. If we're quick we can...'

'I'll carry him,' Seb said coldly. Bending down, with a grunt he hoisted the heavy tarpaulin onto his shoulder. 'My brother ain't going in a trolley.'

Sam moved to unlock the door. 'The last door on the left is a fire escape. It's the nearest one.'

Her hand was on the handle when banging on the door made her jump back, both her and Seb freezing in their tracks. She looked at Seb and then back at the door. 'I won't be long,' she called.

'Is Seb in there with you?' a voice called. 'It's Andrew, his brother. It's important.'

Eyes narrowing, Seb threw Sam's arm off as she attempted to restrain him and he yanked the door open.

'Seb?' Andrew's eyes moved over the green overalls and then to the tarpaulin on his shoulder. He cast a disapproving stare at Sam before turning back to Seb questioningly.

Seb's eyes blazed. If Andrew had done this, he'd rip him limb from limb with his bare hands. 'Anything you need to say to me, you can say in front of her,' he growled.

Andrew scowled but decided he should placate the bad feeling between them. 'I'm not here to argue. Me and Neil have come from the Aurora. We thought it wise to form our own opinion about whether there was anything worth seeing and guess who we saw?'

Seb swallowed his rising impatience. *Gary's body was bloody heavy and Andrew wanted to play guessing games?* 'Get on with it!'

Andrew's eyes were stone cold. 'John-fucking-Maynard!'

Seb frowned, a sinking feeling growing.

'By the way, what the fuck is that?' Andrew asked, nodding at the large tarpaulin draped over Seb shoulder.

'You'd best come in,' Seb muttered, not noticing Liam peering from behind the jutting wall at the end of the corridor.

34

Watching a flock of greenfinches in the stone birdbath through the patio doors, Gloria sipped her tea and smiled.

Len loved watching the birds during the little spare time he had. How she would do anything for one more day sitting here with him. Even an hour. Just to remind him how much she loved him. How much she'd always loved him and that she'd love him until her last breath – and beyond.

But she couldn't. It was over. *Len was gone.*

She dabbed at the fresh tears on her cheeks. Her grief had shifted – moving from raw pain and utter shock at Len's unexpected death into the long, hollow void of the rest of time without him.

The funeral had been a closing point and in a way it was comforting because although hard, unbearably so, now she could begin reminiscing about the wonderful life they'd shared. The life Len had made better than she could ever have imagined.

The immense turnout at the service and wake showed there were huge numbers of people who felt he'd enriched their lives, too.

Taking solace from this, Gloria placed her cup of tea on the small table to the side of her armchair and smiled wistfully, watching the birds outside once more.

Startled by the sudden ringing of the telephone, she got up. It was probably Sam. She called a couple of times each day to check how things were.

Gloria picked up the receiver. 'Sam? Oh, hello, Judith.'

'I'm sorry to call, what with it being the day after Len's funeral, but I didn't know what else to do.'

Gloria frowned, the worry and strain in Judith's voice evident. 'It's not a problem. Whatever is the matter?' There was a pause. 'Judith?'

Judith's voice cracked. 'It might sound an odd question and I know you had countless other things on your mind, but you didn't happen to see Gary – my youngest – at all last night, did you?' She faltered. 'You didn't notice anything strange?'

'Strange?' Gloria frowned. 'No, I can't say I did. The only time I really saw him was when he was standing with you. I left before the end. I'm sorry, I should have come and said goodbye, but it was all getting a bit much.'

'No, no, I completely understand. It was silly of me to bother you,' Judith apologised. 'I'll let you get on. I'm sorry to have disturbed you.'

'Wait, Judith,' Gloria said hastily. 'Has something happened?'

'Well, that's just it. I don't know, but I've got this feeling. Gary didn't come back last night and no one can get in contact with him.'

'Is he with a girlfriend or a friend or...'

'No, Gary doesn't get involved,' Judith said. 'But this is out of character and you remember what I told you the other day about these... these rumours?'

Gloria's heart sank. 'That can't be anything to do with it, can it? How could it be?' She heard Judith sniff, obviously crying. The woman was clearly worried.

'Things have got even more strained between the boys. Andrew and Neil especially,' Judith said sadly. 'In front of me they pretend everything's fine, but I'm their mother and I can tell when things aren't right.' She paused. 'I can tell by their body language there's still a lot of bad feeling. They were even having digs at each other last night. Gary walked off in the end, as did Andrew and Neil. The whole lot of them dispersed and no one's seen Gary since.'

Gloria remained silent, choosing her words carefully. 'You think Gary's had enough of the accusations and gone off for a while? Is that what you're saying?'

Judith hesitated, scared to speak her worries out loud in case it made them come true. 'I – I don't know. Maybe. Or another fight? Or worse...'

'Worse?' Gloria cried. *What was Judith saying?* 'You don't think...'

'Gary's a sensitive boy – not like the others. I – I'm worried it's all got too much and that he might... might have ended it...'

Gloria gasped. 'Oh my God! You don't really think that could be a possibility, do you?' Perspiration formed between her breasts. 'He wouldn't... wouldn't... would he?'

Judith began sobbing. 'I just don't know...'

Gloria's guilt weighed heavily. If that young man was so distressed to kill himself because of those untrue rumours, then she'd never forgive herself. She could have put an end to this. She still could.

She needed to think. 'Try not to worry,' Gloria soothed, hoping her reassurance meant something. 'I'm sure he'll turn up. In the meantime, I'll call Samantha. She'd have been there until the last person left, so I'm sure she'd have noticed anything unusual, or perhaps saw where Gary went.'

'Thank you, Gloria,' Judith sniffed. 'Again, I'm sorry to have bothered you.'

'Don't even think about that. I'll call Sam now.'

Replacing the receiver, Gloria sank back into the armchair and put her head in her hands.

Sam's mind was still swirling from what had happened last night, not paying much attention to what her mother was saying down the end of the telephone line.

How could any of this be? She was a graphic designer, for God's sake, not... not *this*!

But she wasn't a graphic designer any more...

Last night had shown in screamingly fluorescent lettering flashing within her brain that she was well and truly involved in something utterly different to what she was used to. Something completely alien. And something she had to get used to *quickly* because there was no room for error.

And when Seb's mouth crashed onto hers, without ceremony – without *anything*, apart from him taking the opportunity to help himself to what he'd wanted at that precise moment, the utter confidence and power in the way he'd held her, the feel of his lips...

It might have only been short-lived before she'd pushed him away in anger at the sheer audacity, but her body had reacted otherwise. She'd wanted his mouth on hers... Wanted *him*...

Even after finding his brother's body, she'd felt it as she'd unbuttoned his shirt. *That raw attraction...*

Whether she liked it or not, it was there, screaming in her ear.

But Seb Stoker was an aggressive, over-confident, brash...

Sam's thoughts paused as her mother's voice filtered into her brain and her stomach lurched, listening to the question that had been asked. She bit her lip, glad her expression was not visible down the telephone line.

'No, I didn't see Gary Stoker. Although, after you left, I did go down to my office for a short while. I needed to take a breather.' Sam paused, concern bubbling at the worry detectable in her mother's voice. 'Why do you ask?'

Sam listened carefully as her mother explained why Judith had called. Apprehension churned. Why was Judith so worried? Had she known something was on the cards? Did she know what had happened? 'Sorry, Mum, I didn't notice, but Gary's a grown man. I'm sure he'll turn up.'

As her mother changed the subject, remarking how well yesterday had gone, Sam was relieved to finally put the phone down. She hated having to lie.

She rested her chin in her hands. As much as her mother had hidden it, she'd heard the worry, almost panic in her mother's voice and her nerves jangled. Why was her mother so concerned about Gary Stoker or Judith's worry? As far as she knew, her mother and Judith weren't good friends.

To anyone else, panicking over a grown man who couldn't be located a few hours later wouldn't overly be a cause for alarm and would be shrugged off, so why were they so worried? But they would be *very* worried if they knew what had happened. What *she* knew had happened and what she'd helped to conceal...

Icy tendrils prickled. Did Judith or her mother know something she didn't? Something Seb didn't?

Sam had said Gary would turn up eventually... Wasn't that the usual thing to say in such circumstances? But she hoped to hell he didn't, for everyone's sake. She didn't even know what Seb had done with the body or where it had been taken.

Sam fanned her face with a clammy hand. Well, that was it now, wasn't it? She was an accessory. She may not have had a hand in killing the man, but she *had* helped conceal the body, so had therefore assisted in concealing a major crime.

Sam stared at the phone, now silent in its cradle. The urge to ring Seb was strong. For all she knew, he might have been pulled over – the body of his brother found in the back of the van belonging to the Orchid – to *her*. He could even be locked up in a police cell at this very minute...

And then it was only a matter of time before the police came for her...

She couldn't call Seb. That would be stupid. She'd have to wait and hope he got in contact soon. *Very* soon.

If she was lying for him, and she was, then he needed to bring her up to speed.

Sam's lips set in a thin line. They *had* done the right thing though, which was one consolation. It would destroy Mal and Judith Stoker to discover at such a fraught time that their youngest had been murdered. Not that there would *ever* be a good time to discover that, but any time would be better than the present.

A mixture of butterflies and dread churned in her stomach, a heavy knot pushing against the constant fluttering. Could John *really* be behind this, like Seb believed?

Seeing Andrew Stoker's inconsolable reaction when learning what the tarpaulin contained had at least showed Seb that he could cross his brothers off the suspect list. And although nothing had been said, Sam knew he was mightily relieved about that.

She scraped her hair from her face. With less than an hour's sleep, she knew she looked dishevelled, but there were worse things that could happen: like her cousin being behind all of the things Seb believed. Those motives were things she didn't want to think about, let alone acknowledge.

In her opinion, Seb's reasoning verged on clutching at straws; more along the lines of laying the blame at someone's feet, rather than no one at all.

She shuddered. Aside from this, nothing changed that John was at the Aurora last night. Andrew and Neil had seen him with their own eyes. And if all of them had been there, then who had killed Gary?

She knew her father had previously sent John to the Aurora to dig on who was behind the place in relation to the threats, but he'd been adamant there was nothing of interest there. If that was the case, what had made him leave her father's wake to go back there again last night?

Sam frowned. It couldn't have been John who'd killed Gary, unless he'd done it before leaving the wake. But either way, Seb could be right. None of this meant that John wasn't *behind* it.

Sam gulped at the glass of water on her desk. She was going round in circles. None of it made sense. *None of it at all.*

Her nerves were shot. Even walking down the corridor to her office this morning, she'd felt ridiculously uncomfortable. She didn't think she'd feel comfortable walking down there ever again.

Fear churned. What if the murderer had been looking for her? That map had disappeared from her desk, so had Gary merely been in the way?

Blood pounded in Sam's veins. She had to stop this. She was a bag of nerves. She was being ridiculous and paranoid and there was no room for that.

Jumping with the sudden knock of her office door, Sam shivered. 'Who is it?'

Seeing the door handle being tried, she scrambled to her feet, her hand reaching for the letter opener on her desk.

'It's me. Liam!'

Putting the letter opener down, Sam hurried towards the door, unlocking it.

Liam stepped into the office and looked around. 'Why did you lock the door?'

Sam's initial relief at seeing Liam evaporated. 'Just habit,' she said, moving back to her desk.

Liam stared at Sam curiously. 'You don't usually lock the door.'

'I do now,' Sam snapped, eyeing him pointedly. 'I got sick of people deciding to keep walking in here. People wouldn't have dreamt of doing that to my father.' She sat back down and looked at Liam with impatience. 'What is it you want?'

Liam frowned. 'What is it I want? I came to see how you are! You bit my head off last night and then when I next saw you, you were in such a daze I couldn't get any sense out of you. I'm worried about you. Is that so bad?'

Sam inhaled slowly. She couldn't remember seeing Liam again after Seb and Andrew left last night. Her head had been all over the place. She had to keep control. 'Yesterday was hard, Liam. I'm sorry if I was out of sorts with you. It all got a bit much by the end. I was just glad when it was all over.'

Placated, Liam sat down opposite Sam and smiled. 'As long as you're okay.'

Sam nodded, but she wasn't okay. *Far from it.* And Liam scrutinising her made it a thousand times worse. She stared at the pile of waiting paperwork, hoping he'd take the hint. 'Is there anything else? I've got lots to do and...'

'You disappeared for ages last night.' Liam looked at Sam questioningly.

Sam glanced up. 'Disappeared?'

'Yes, after you bit my head off at the top of the stairs, you rushed off down this way and I didn't see you again until the end.' *Would she tell him the truth or not?*

Sam sighed, irritated. 'Like I said, I needed some space. I shouldn't have to justify every single thing I do!'

'No one's asked you to, it's just that I heard you were down here with Seb Stoker...'

Sam's heart lurched. 'Who told you that?' *Who had seen her go into the office? And who knew Seb was already in there? Had they seen Gary's body being removed?*

Her heart pounded. Had the person who'd killed Gary been lurking around watching? Was whoever the person who had told Liam this the murderer? 'I asked, who told you that?' she repeated, her voice high-pitched.

Liam raised his hands. 'Whoa! What's got into you?'

'I want to know who said that!' Sam cried, her pulse racing.

'Only the barman! I asked if he'd seen you and he said he thought you must be with Seb Stoker, being as he'd seen him go down that way earlier, that's all!' Liam lied.

Relief poured through Sam. She wiped her hand across her face, not caring if she smudged her lipstick.

Liam watched Sam's reaction carefully. He hadn't been entirely truthful. With his own eyes from his position at the end of the corridor last night, he'd seen Stoker answer this office door to another one of his brothers. Plus he'd heard Sam's voice too. She'd been in here with him.

If only he'd been closer, he'd have had a better view and been able to properly hear what they were discussing. They'd been discussing something – and something *major*, by the tone of their voices. He'd also been sure he'd heard the brother utter Maynard's name...

It was unfortunate he'd been unable to hang around, but he'd have been spotted. As much as he didn't like to admit it, he didn't know whether Sam's presence would have been enough to keep him safe.

After all these years, she was hiding things from him. And he didn't like it. 'Is something going on between you two?' Liam asked, his eyes accusing. 'Between you and Stoker?'

Sam sat bolt upright. 'What bloody right do you or anyone have to question where I am, who I'm with or what I do?' she yelled.

'Don't *ever* question me like that again. I'm in charge of this place. Not you!'

'Christ, Sam!' Liam shook his head. 'What's happened to you?'

'Just get out and leave me the fuck alone!' Sam yelled.

Liam stared silently at Sam. He knew what had happened to her. *Seb Stoker had happened to her.* And now it looked like not only was she turning against *him*, but also turning on her cousin. John was trying his upmost to help Sam run this place, yet she was scheming with the Stokers? And if he wasn't mistaken, scheming with them about *John*.

If something didn't happen very soon to change that, then both he *and* John would lose their place.

Standing up, Liam stormed towards the door, turning to Sam in disgust. 'You've changed, Sam. And I don't like it.'

After Liam stepped through the door, Sam slammed it behind him and leant up against the cool wood, her heart crashing in her chest.

Yes, she had changed. She realised that. But she had to look at things in a completely different perspective now – one that she'd never thought herself capable of, but she had no choice. Not now. Not if she wanted this business to work.

And she did want it to work. Both for her mother's sake as well as her father's.

She had to find out for definite who was behind her father's death. There was no room for reasonable excuses any longer. She had to find out what and who was behind all of these problems before she or another one of her family became a statistic – like Gary.

And she couldn't do that if she continued thinking the way she used to.

35

Seb couldn't say he was over-impressed at finding his father waiting for him when he arrived at the Peacock. Slipping his suit jacket off, he hung it on the brass coat stand in the corner of the office and walked to his desk, grateful his father had at least chosen to sit on the Chesterfield, rather than take the obligatory chair he'd been so used to.

He eyed his father, knowing why he was here, but it was imperative to act like he didn't. He glanced at Andrew and Neil, hoping they adhered to the plan. 'What brings you here? Can't stay away from the place? Mum won't be best pleased.' Seb's face broke into an easy smile – the polar opposite of how he felt.

Mal leant forward on the maroon leather sofa and looked at each of his sons in turn. 'Your mother's too busy worrying herself to death about your brother,' he said, his face grim. 'I'm taking it there still isn't any sign of Gary?'

Seb shook his head. 'No, we haven't seen him.'

The enormity of lying to his father was not something he took lightly and he very much wished he wasn't in this position, but it was the only position he could take – at least until he knew for definite who had done this. And that was something which, for once, he, Andrew and Neil all adamantly agreed on.

Once his father's health improved and they'd tied up all the loose ends behind the problems strangling the firm, then he'd break the news about Gary. And that wasn't something he was looking forward to. The longer it went on, the harder it would be when they discovered what had happened to their youngest son. The image of his mother's devastated face floated into his mind and he hastily shook it away.

'There's been no word at all?' Mal pressed suspiciously. 'I take it you've checked Gary's usual haunts and asked about?'

Seb sparked up a cigarette. He'd been chain-smoking like no one's business and was already halfway through his second pack of twenty and it wasn't even mid-morning. 'We've asked around – subtly... We can't make it obvious one of us has gone AWOL. We don't want anyone getting wind that our defences are down.'

Mal nodded. 'I agree, but Christ, your mother's doing her nut!'

'Gary will be somewhere taking stock of his life. You know what he's like. He hasn't been in the best place lately,' Andrew added, his face neutral. 'Especially since that disaster with the Irish.'

He hoped his father didn't question the redness or puffiness of his eyes. Gnawing guilt over the way he'd treated his little brother had plagued him all night, crushing his chest like a succubus, and he didn't think he'd *ever* have a proper night's rest again.

Mal cracked his knuckles, his fists still bearing the scars of the fighting days of his youth. 'You lot didn't exactly make that easy for him, did you? Determined to make him feel like a piece of shit over it.'

'Oh, come on, Dad,' Neil countered. 'Why should we have made it easy for him? You wouldn't have given *us* that leniency. You'd have ripped strips off if it had been one of us! It was a balls-up on Gary's part – a *big* one and he knew it. We all know that comes hand in hand if anyone screws up.'

'That's as maybe,' Mal said gravely, studying his sons closely. 'But what about the rest of what was said?'

Seb's eyes darted to Andrew and Neil. They'd had the roasting of their lives that day their father burst into the office and they'd assured him no more would be said about the rumours concerning Gary's heritage. But Andrew and Neil hadn't exactly stuck to that...

He had to play this down.

Sitting forward, Seb clasped his hands together. 'We all know that rumour was utter bullshit. Our heat of the moment stupidity got sorted out. What's that got to do with Gary not being here?'

Mal raised his eyebrows and said nothing for several seconds. 'Don't try to pull the wool over my eyes, son,' he snapped. 'I'm not blind and neither is your mother. We've both sensed the atmosphere between you boys and neither of us like it. I've never been more disappointed than seeing you lot at each other's throats.'

He also knew Judith still thought he disbelieved her and he hated that. *Hated* it. The last thing Mal ever wanted was for his wife to feel her faithfulness was being questioned. 'You were even having digs at each other last night. At a wake, no less!' Mal's voice grew louder, more incensed. 'Have you no respect?'

Andrew glanced at Neil. 'It wasn't about that.'

'Then what was it about?' Mal raged.

'There's a lot of pressure with things at the moment. Tempers are frayed.' Seb tried to remain calm. 'Sometimes it's felt,' he glanced at his brothers, 'that Gary doesn't pull his weight.'

He ignored the dislike of his own words, knowing it important to maintain normality. What he'd said may have been true but speaking of Gary like that now – now he wasn't here and never would be, bit hard.

'If you didn't treat him like a muppet constantly, then maybe you'd find him more accommodating!' Mal knew Gary had his shortcomings when it came to getting stuck in, but treating any of his sons differently was out of the question.

'He'll be back,' Neil said quickly. 'He's stropped off to lick his wounds and sulk in private.' He glanced at Seb, feeling a strong urge to punch the wall.

Blood pounded in Neil's veins. He wasn't sure how long he could sit here pretending everything was all right, whilst the cunt who'd murdered his brother was still out there.

Gary wouldn't be coming back. *Ever.* That his last words to his brother were unsavoury, stuck in his throat something chronic. He could still scarcely believe what had happened. Even if Gary *wasn't* his true brother, he shouldn't have said the things he'd said. And for Gary's resting place, temporary it may be, to be a chest freezer in one of their lock-ups was the worst fucking insult.

It seemed his brother had died trying to stop whoever was snooping around. Snooping around for what, no one knew, but they would find out. They would *have* to find out because the person who had done this was going to die too.

With growing dread, Neil realised that whatever happened, nothing could grant him any forgiveness for the way he'd treated his brother. Least of all *himself.*

'Like Neil said, Gary will be back,' Andrew repeated, seeing his twin's building distress.

Mal stood up. 'I hope for all of our sakes you're correct, otherwise the way your mother's fretting, she'll call the Old Bill before long and I'm not sure I'll be able to stop her.'

'Don't let her involve the Old Bill! Leave it with us. I'll put more scouts out, okay?' Seb said resolutely. *He had to come up with something fast.* 'Now get yourself back home. No stress, remember? This will all resolve itself fast, I'm sure.'

Seb kept his smile in place until his father had left the office and his footsteps were no longer audible along the corridor.

He turned to Andrew and Neil, his eyes narrowing. 'Although we think Maynard wasn't there at the time Gary was offed, I'm certain he has *something* to do with it. The same way I'm sure he was behind lifting the Irish money.' Seb ground out his cigarette in the ashtray. 'I also want to know what the cunt was doing at the Aurora last night.'

He stared at his brothers in turn. 'It's time to bring Maynard in. We may not have proof, but we're going to get the truth out of him as to what his fucking game is one way or the other. And whether you like it or not, we're bringing Sam in so she can hear what he's got to say about it as well.'

Neil stared at Seb, aghast. 'You want *her* to witness that? Jesus, Seb. Haven't we got enough shit to deal with?'

Andrew glanced at Seb, seeing the determination in his eyes, and had to admit he'd had a slight change of heart about the girl. 'She's all right, Neil. You didn't see how she dealt with things last night. I did, and she needs to be there. Maynard's her blood, after all.'

Seb nodded in acknowledgement and moved towards the door. 'The scouts being sent to look for Gary will tail Maynard instead. They'll let us know when there's a suitable jump point and unless there's a very good reason, this will happen tonight.'

* * *

Sam wasn't in the best frame of mind to deal with John, but it had to be done. Even though her nerves were still shredded and Liam's accusation had made things even worse, she could not afford to let that outwardly show.

Her initial suspicions about her cousin had returned with a

vengeance and on top of that, him sneaking around the Aurora without so much as a word was doing nothing to help. Now he would get the opportunity to tell her about it. *And if he didn't tell her...*

The knock on the door made her jump. Sam bit back her growing frustration. *Calm it down, Sam*, she mentally chanted. *Do not show you're afraid.*

But she *was* afraid. Afraid of what all of this meant and where it might end.

'Come in,' she called, thankful her voice held no trace of wavering. 'Ah, John. Come and sit down.' She gestured to the opposite chair. 'I thought we should have a catch up.'

John sat down heavily. *What was he? A fucking lapdog?* He didn't have time for this. Why she'd summoned him for a meeting, God only knew. She'd probably run out of mascara or something, the stupid bitch. Not only did he need to find Bedworth and give him a round of fucks for being nowhere to be seen last night, but he also wanted to throttle this cunt sitting in front of him.

What he'd just learned from Liam had boiled his piss more than he thought possible. And how he would keep his trap shut to this whore – this fucking slag, who had thieved his very livelihood from under his nose, he didn't know. Even more so now he knew for definite she was in cahoots with Stoker.

Oh, by Christ, he'd make sure the bitch got hers. How he'd enjoy seeing her face when her world crumbled from under her. He could barely wait.

So, it looked like she *was* shagging Stoker, plus they'd been talking about him? He might have known. Well, not for much fucking longer.

He'd felt like caning Liam when he told him what he'd seen last night. Wanted to rip his goatee clean off his stupid chin for the mere fact of being the messenger. The bloke was proving useful in unwittingly giving him info, but for how much longer that was uncertain, being as the stupid twat had told him he'd just rowed with the ungrateful bitch.

None of that mattered, anyway. Now he'd weighed up Samantha and exactly what her game was, it was easy enough. He knew how she felt about family, so anything he said over Stoker would take precedence.

John smirked as he met Sam's eyes, then leant back in the chair and stretched out. Was she going to say anything or just sit and stare at him like a dummy? *No clue, this bird – none whatsoever.*

Watching John, Sam knew her hands were clenching into fists in her lap below the table. She quickly moved them into view on the desk. He couldn't act more uninterested if he tried. 'Am I keeping you from something important?' she said sharply.

John slowly inspected his fingernails. 'I've got a fair bit on, yes, and being as you wanted to see me, I was wondering if you were going to actually say anything?'

Sam smiled pleasantly. She'd given John more than enough time to be upfront about the Aurora, yet he'd said nothing. *One last chance.*

'I wanted to ask whether you had any updates?' She knitted her slender fingers together on top of her notebook. 'You know, anything you need to bring me up to speed with? Anything you may have overlooked?'

John shrugged. 'Like what? I've already said everything from my side is running perfectly well. Not that it doesn't usually. If you're asking about the state of play with the casino, then you need to speak to Liam rather than me.'

'Oh, that's strange.' Sam raised an eyebrow. 'I thought during your regular chats with Liam, you'd know enough to relate that side of things too?'

A nerve fluttered in John's neck. 'Chat with Liam? He speaks to me in passing. Am I missing something?' *What was she getting at?*

Sam smiled sweetly. 'Missing something? I think you might be.' She leant back in her chair, mirroring John's relaxed stance. 'Like why you failed to mention you left my father's wake last night to go to the Aurora?'

A flush of cold washed across John. *How the Christ did she know he'd been there?* 'Liam told you I'd been to the Aurora? Why would he say that?' A glimmer of panic formed. Had she got a tail on him? No, she didn't have the nous for that. She trusted him – or at least she *had*.

'I didn't say Liam had said that, did I?' Sam said slyly.

'Then who did?' John snapped, before his face broke into a smile. 'Ah, wait! I can guess... Sebastian Stoker? Am I right?'

Sam's silence spoke volumes, but John wouldn't let on that he knew she'd been with Stoker last night. He'd let her admit it, because she would. *Any. Minute. Now...* 'How many times do I have to explain everything Stoker does is to cause unrest and make us doubt one another?'

He ran his hand through his hair and looked at the ceiling in pseudo-exasperation. 'I'm on your side, Samantha. The Stokers will say anything to turn you against me.'

Sam looked for a hint that John was lying. Although his words and actions were plausible, it was there – there in his eyes. But she'd let him believe she was falling for it. 'Are you telling me you *didn't* leave my father's wake to go to the Aurora?'

John shook his head. 'I left Len's wake, yes, but not to go to the Aurora.' *This would get her.* 'Whether or not you find this hard to believe, Samantha, yesterday reminded me of losing my own father. Do you remember the wake we had for him all those years ago? An almost identical set-up to yesterday? I needed a break and I apologise if you can't understand that.'

Sam almost faltered. A week ago she would have. She'd have accepted John's words without hesitation, feeling crushing guilt for even contemplating accusing him. *Not any more.* His words may be filled with sentiment, but his eyes were hollow.

Andrew and Neil were telling the truth. John had been to the Aurora.

John watched Sam closely. She said nothing, but he knew he'd scuppered her theory. *Ha ha, Samantha, you're so easy to fool.* 'I walked up Broad Street and thought about going into one of the other bars for a drink, but I didn't. I came back here. I wanted to see if you were all right, but you weren't anywhere to be seen.' He raised an eyebrow. 'Seems like you needed a break too?'

'So you didn't go to the Aurora?' Sam repeated for good measure.

'No, I did not,' John said, his voice stern. 'I went before under your father's orders, you know that. There's nothing to see there. We were wrong about that place, so why would I want to go there again?'

Sam nodded. She'd let John believe her to be stupid. She also wouldn't rise to the dig about her. He'd been to the Aurora but had returned. The question was when? Could he have returned in time to murder Gary Stoker? Or had he done it before leaving for the Aurora?

Had John watched her in the office with Seb? Had he killed Gary, shoved him in a cupboard and watched the body being discovered? Watched as Seb and his brother took the heavy tarpaulin out via the fire escape?

Watching Sam's mind ticking, John folded his arms. 'I think we've been set up.'

'What do you mean?'

'It's been the Stokers all along. They started with those threats and have been using the Aurora as a smokescreen,' John said, his eyes cold. 'It's them. No one else. Their plan to ruin this firm is working. They've worked you so well you're doubting me. I hate to think what Len would feel about this...'

Sam somehow forced herself to nod sadly, rather than smash John in the face for daring her bring her father into his lies. 'You're right.'

She needed to let John think she believed his crap. Seb was right and always had been. It was John behind this. That and that alone was now crystal-clear. She would try to get hold of Seb tonight and see exactly how they would deal with this.

36

Pulling into the alleyway around the back of Edgbaston Street usually reserved for deliveries, John drummed his fingers on the steering wheel.

If Bedworth didn't show his face soon, then he'd have to give this up as a bad lot and take his chances going to the Aurora again or, more sensibly, get word to meet somewhere else instead. He'd have to be even more careful now Samantha had somehow got wind he'd been there.

The net was closing in and he couldn't afford that.

He glanced at his dashboard clock. *For fuck's sake!* The stupid prick had told him in his usual big-gobbed way that he was planning on meeting two birds in the Whistling Pig this evening, that's if Bedworth remembered, the state the man was in half the time.

Gnashing his teeth, John jumped from his car. He wasn't hanging around any longer. Slamming the door, he glanced around for lurking traffic wardens. If he ended up with a fucking ticket, he'd go tits. Plus, he couldn't be long, the way darling Samantha was watching his every move.

His jaw clenched. How he hated doing that stupid little girl's bidding. He couldn't stand it any longer. Bedworth had better have some good news or he'd go berserk. Wasting his time by calling him to the Aurora last night, and then not even having the decency to show up?

His brows furrowed. He'd only just got out of there in the nick of time as well. After deciding he wasn't waiting any longer with that grizzled old hag Bedworth had asked to keep him company until he got back, John had only just pulled out onto the Hagley Road when the cops pulled in. It had been *far* too close.

Just the thought of being collared in that dump made John's teeth curl. If that had happened, he'd definitely be unable to deny being there.

Storming down the road, he cut through the dank, stinking confines of the bus station. The pervading, choking stench of the consistently pumping diesel engines clung to the back of his throat, making him feel sick.

Stepping over a tramp lying on the floor near one of the stops, he barged his way through the clumps of people waiting for their bus, ignoring the scowls and insults hurled in his direction.

'Fucking buy a car,' John muttered, glad to reach the doors leading from the bus station to the indoor market, pleased the place was still just about open, otherwise he'd have had to walk all the way around.

This relief was short-lived when the smell of exhaust fumes was replaced by the even worse smell of fish from the countless fishmonger stalls.

John felt like punching Bedworth repeatedly in the face for this when he finally caught up with him. Having to chase the fucking skank all over the city was not in any way, shape or form his idea of a good time.

Squinting against the daylight as he barged through the double doors onto the main road the other side of the market, John pushed past a man standing on a wooden box, ranting about everyone's perils coming back to haunt them on judgement day, and scowled even harder.

He shoved his way along to the Whistling Pig, the grotesque 1960s frontage all the worse for its horrible orange colour.

Bursting through the battered wooden doors, his eyes adjusted to the murky, smoke-laden atmosphere and scanned the room through the haze, ignoring the suspect-looking man playing a Bontempi organ in the corner and a group of old men staring suspiciously at him from under their trilbies, their snuff boxes on the sticky table next to their pints of Ansells bitter.

There he was. Bedworth...

John's eyes focused on Tom Bedworth, sitting at a table against the far wall with a pair of girls perched on his lap who looked no more than fourteen.

Scowling, he made his way over and banged on the table. 'A word?'

Tom's head swung up, his face breaking into a grin. 'Ah, Maynard!' he yelled. 'Pull up a stool and have a drink.'

John leant on the table, tipping it slightly and watched the girls scrabbling to save their Babychams before they hit the deck. 'I don't want a fucking drink. I want a word!'

He jerked his head towards the toilets. 'Either in there or outside. Your fucking choice.' He stared at Bedworth's face, seeing the man was clearly off his bonce. *Jesus Christ! How had he got saddled with this loser?* The sooner he could offload this moron, the better. It wouldn't be a minute too soon. The twat was a liability.

Not waiting for an answer, John grabbed Tom by the shoulder of his leather jacket and manhandled him into the gents. 'Fuck off!' he growled to the teenagers rolling joints next to the sink.

Taking one look at the expression on the stranger's face, the two lads hastily made their exit out of the toilets.

Turning back to Tom, seeing a stupid grin on his face, John felt like he might implode. He grabbed him around the scruff of the neck, slamming him into the cracked wall tiles. 'Where the fuck were you last night?'

'Take it easy, my old mate,' Tom slurred, still smiling like it was a normal day out. 'Chill, yeah?'

'Fuck that!' John raged. 'You sent an urgent message and so I risked my neck by coming to the Aurora only to find you were nowhere to be seen? Do you want to explain before I fucking hurt you? Do you think I've got time to piss about for shag all?'

Still smiling, Tom patted John's hand, indicating to release him from his grip. He reached into his pocket and pulled out a wrap of coke. 'Yeah, sorry about that. I got held up. You know what it's like.'

John watched with escalating ire as Tom cut a line on the filthy sink. *He'd had enough of this.* He smacked the wrap out of Tom's hand, then swiped the line of powder off the enamel to the floor.

'What the fuck are you doing?' Tom screeched. 'That's all I've got on me!'

'Stop pissing around,' John roared, screwing his heel into the wrap in case Bedworth had any bright ideas of retrieving it from the piss-soaked floor. 'Maybe if you weren't so off your fucking head then you might be some use! You're a bleeding liability!'

Tom grinned once more. Raising his hands in the air, he did a strange kind of jerky jig. 'Fear not, Maynard! All is good. I've upped the game. You worry too much. The pressure will cause them all to break very soon and then we'll both be where we want to be.'

John stared at Bedworth's gleeful dance with astounded detachment and building rage. 'So you keep saying!' he snarled. 'You absolute cretin!' This turd needed to be committed. And he certainly needed to stop snorting all of his deals. The man was living in a dreamworld. 'I sneaked out of a wake last night to see you. Something important, you said, and you weren't even there!'

Tom nodded. 'I came back but had to make a swift about turn. That old bitch opposite called the cops again. Four times she's done that now. They never find anything, of course.' He tapped the side of his bent nose. 'I'm cleverer than that.'

'What is it you wanted to tell me?' John spat. 'You know, the things that were *so* important?'

Tom flapped his hand and stared at the wasted, mashed-up wrap of cocaine on the floor. 'Can't believe you did that!' he muttered. 'Good job I've got loads more where that came from.'

John stepped forward, his teeth bared. If Bedworth didn't get to the point, he'd smash his face into the urinal and keep doing it until he knocked some sense into him.

'The Orchid's a nice place, ain't it?' Tom said casually, his eyes sparkling. 'Much nicer than I expected.' His face suddenly formed a scowl. 'Although it proves just how much I got ripped off.'

John tensed. 'You went to the Orchid?' *He couldn't believe this.* 'When? I told you stay away from there, you fucking moron!'

Through his coke-addled head, Tom knew he should think of a justifiable reason. Explaining that he'd got Maynard out of the way so he could mooch about in Reynold's office looking for proof to back up his threats wouldn't go down too well, he didn't expect.

But he did have some news which he could have used as a vague blag. The fundamental problem was, the afternoon of steady drinking and snorting powder had diluted his rationality. He was on a roll and nothing could stop him.

He grinned, his crooked teeth looking even worse in the sickly light from the bare bulb hanging from the ceiling. 'I came to the Orchid to find you.'

'Why?' John gasped. 'Do you listen to nothing I say?'

Tom flapped his hand. 'Yes, yes, I do, but this is great! Look!' He pulled a twist of foil from his other pocket and gleefully unwrapped it. 'Look at this. Fucking top notch gear this is! I have the contacts who can cook this up and if you supply me with a shed load of powder from the Orchid, th...'

'Crack?' John barked, staring at the three small rocks in the foil. 'You want to start cranking out crack? Using my cocaine? And you came to the Orchid to tell me that?' His face took on the colour of an over-ripe tomato, the urge to pummel Bedworth's head to a pulp overwhelming.

'Partly,' Tom grinned, shoving the foil back in his pocket. He spun around on the wet floor. 'Ta-da! Great idea, ain't it?' He leant against the wall for support. 'It's good shit and all.'

'For fuck's sake,' John muttered. 'I hope no one saw you.'

'Nah, they were all too busy. Besides...' Tom began twirling around. 'I'm invincible!' He then pulled a sad face. 'I didn't get what I was looking for, but I did up the ante.'

John felt like he might burst a blood vessel. The guy had been snooping around the Orchid? Christ! And look at him, he thought he was untouchable.

Tapping his foot on the floor in an irritating rhythm in line with the banging in his head, Tom grabbed John's jacket sleeve and pulled him close. 'Hey, have they found the dead guy in the cupboard yet?'

John blinked, partly because Tom's breath smelt of dog shit and partly because he was sure he couldn't have heard correctly. 'The what?'

'A guy accosted me outside Reynold's office. He grabbed me, so I had no choice.' Tom held his hands up, grinning maniacally. 'Oh, come on! What would you have done?' He mimicked drawing a blade across his neck. 'After that, I shoved him in the cupboard. Bloody classic, it was!'

John stared in disbelief. *Was Bedworth serious? He'd topped someone and shoved them in a cupboard?* His face morphed into a scowl. The man was wankered and spouting shit.

Shoving Tom hard in the chest, John watched with a small glimmer of satisfaction as he stumbled backwards, falling onto the drenched floor under the urinals. 'Sort yourself out, Bedworth, for God's sake, and then come and find me.'

'But it's true!' Tom cried, watching John stomp out of the gents.

* * *

'What's he doing up here?' Neil said, eyeing the surroundings with disdain.

'I've no idea, but this is where the scout said he was.' Seb kept his eyes trained on his wing mirrors. 'Maynard was watched leaving the Orchid earlier and tailed here.' His head jerked towards the blue Ford Mondeo further down the alleyway they'd backed the van into. 'From here, he went to the Whistling Pig and is still in there, but he'll be coming back for his car sooner or later. That's when we'll get him.'

Neil continued looking around the alleyway. Not a soul in sight, short of the delivery doors to shops which were now closed for the night. The only possible contender that could open a door and spot them was the Chinese takeaway, but then again they should be safe because that lot threw away nothing, and served whatever leftovers they had to the next load of unsuspecting customers.

Besides, grabbing Maynard wouldn't take long, although he couldn't say he was over-enamoured with Seb's plan for afterwards. He'd much rather get stuck in straight away, but if Seb insisted they wait for Samantha Reynold until they really put the pressure on, then that's what would happen.

'You'd best jump in the back. As soon as Maynard's within grabbing reach, I'll bang on the wall,' Seb instructed. *He'd* be the one apprehending Maynard. That was a definite.

He waited whilst his brothers leapt from the cab into the back of the van and then returned his concentration to the mirrors, hoping Maynard wasn't in the pub for the duration. It had already gone eight.

Sure, there were plenty of men who he could have ordered to do this, but for this particular instance, he wanted to be present. He'd waited too long and this bastard had caused too much shit for it to be otherwise.

Adrenaline ramped up in Seb's veins, the anticipation for getting his hands on the person he believed had offed Gary rising. No one else would own this pleasure. Maynard was *his*.

Spotting movement at the far end of the alleyway, Seb tensed and squinted through the twilight. *Was this him?*

The man continued walking towards the van and Seb slunk down in the driver's seat. *Yep, it was him. Maynard. Game on.*

With his heart pounding, Seb twitched with impatience whilst the man shiftily made his way closer, furtively looking around several times.

On the lookout, he should be, but however careful Maynard was, he wouldn't get out of this one. He would answer every single question. And he would take as long as was required to get every last thing out of him. Once he'd spouted the lot, then Maynard was done.

Seb would get his answers and Sam would get hers too. Never again would she have cause to question or doubt him and she could hardly have an issue with Maynard's removal once it was proved exactly what a traitor the bastard was.

Seb grinned. *And he would prove it. He could sense it.*

As the man drew level with the van, Seb sprung from it like a panther, the door knocking Maynard into the wall. Banging on the side of the van with his fist, he wasted no time in grabbing Maynard by the scruff of the neck and slamming him against the alleyway.

'Right, cunt,' Seb spat, inches from Maynard's face, his eyes glinting with suppressed rage. 'Time to answer my fucking questions.'

Trying to pull his head into gear from the total and unexpected jump, John Maynard scrambled for the gun in his waistband, but was abruptly stopped by a swift backhand around his nose which threw him off kilter.

'I think not,' Seb muttered, pulling the pistol from Maynard's waistband and throwing it to one side.

Stumbling from the blow, John staggered back, blinking rapidly from the stinging in his nose, his eyes running like taps.

Shit. The Stokers. Seb Stoker, no less. Whilst he had his gun, he stood a chance, but without it, he was little match for this man mountain.

Attempting to weigh up what available options, if any, John's watering eyes darted around the alleyway, even hoping by some miracle that Bedworth might appear to distract them. If this psycho could be distracted for one moment, then there was a miniscule chance he might reach the small knife he kept stashed at his ankle for emergencies.

'What the fuck is this about?' John cried. 'We're supposed to be on the same side, aren't we?'

Seb's eyes glinted in the light from the single lamppost at the mouth of the alleyway. 'That was before you started fucking around. Besides, I've never trusted you.'

Stepping back, Seb stood silently whilst Andrew and Neil made quick work of binding Maynard's hands. 'Get him in the back,' he smiled. 'We need to get out of here.'

'You'll never get away with this!' Maynard yelled as he was dragged towards the double doors of the Transit.

'I just did, didn't I?' Seb grinned. Turning on his heels, he grabbed Maynard's gun from the alleyway floor, jumped back into the cab and fired the engine.

Hearing the compulsory bang from one of his brothers keeping Maynard company in the back of the van, Seb stamped on the accelerator and screeched from the alleyway, narrowly missing a bedraggled drunk who'd appeared at the entrance.

37

Tom hastily made his way back to the Whistling Pig, feeling more sober than when he'd rushed after Maynard in an attempt to placate the situation.

How he wished he'd never bothered.

Sweat poured down his face as he skittered across the road and slammed back through the doors of the pub.

Fuck. Had they seen him? Those bastards had near on run him over at the alleyway, so they must have, but they hadn't stopped... And if they hadn't stopped, they didn't know who he was, which was good at least.

'Another Jack Daniel's,' Tom barked at the barman. 'A large one.'

They couldn't have seen him. It was okay. And he was glad about that because he knew who *they* were.

That was a Stoker driving that van. A fucking *Stoker*. Although it was dusk and Tom had been initially more concerned by not becoming roadkill, he'd got enough of a glance through the driver's window to recognise those eyes which he'd spotted a mile off. It was a Stoker and they'd got Maynard.

Slugging the double whisky down his throat in one go, Tom

immediately handed his glass back to the barman. 'Same again,' he muttered.

He was in the shit, pure and simple.

Fucked. Finito.

Well, that was it then. Now it was only a matter of time before they came for him. *Bollocks.*

Sweat drenched the collar of Tom's grubby polo shirt. He'd been so close to pulling everything off. *So close.*

Wait! Being as Maynard had been lifted rather than him, then Stoker must think *he* was the one behind everything?

A grin slid across Tom's raddled face. It was plausible, so there was still a chance.

He frowned. Or should he leg it? He could leg it right now before they caught up with him.

Nodding his thanks to the barman for the refill, Tom pulled a fiver from his pocket and chucked it on the bar, double-checking his little stash wasn't caught in the crumpled bank note. That would be the final insult. The way things were going, he'd need all of his gear tonight.

He stumbled back to his table, brushing off the girls' attention. 'Fuck off a minute, will you?' he hissed. 'I need to think.'

Sitting on the rickety stool, Tom glared at the bloke still playing something hideous on the Bontempi. So, should he go? Disappear back up to Macclesfield?

Tom frowned. *No.* He'd already jumped ship once and wasn't doing it again. If he couldn't get what he was owed, then he may as well throw himself off a cliff for all the good it would do him otherwise. He wasn't upping and leaving Birmingham for the second time because of *them*, the Reynolds and John Maynard. The next time he left this city would be of his own choosing, not anyone else's.

Think logically, Tom, he thought, reminding himself that it wasn't him in the back of the Stokers' van.

For the time being, the best thing he could do was to sit tight, keep his head down and wait. As long as Maynard kept his trap shut, it would be okay. But would he keep his trap shut?

It was doubtful, the piece of shit, but being as for now at least, the Stokers believed it was Maynard and Maynard alone behind the trouble, then with any luck they'd finish him without hearing a word he'd got to say.

If Maynard failed to show up over the next couple of days, then it looked like his prayers had been answered. Tom grinned and chucked his fresh drink into his mouth. In the meantime, it was business as usual.

Turning to the two young girls, he made a point of staring at their chests, rather than their faces. 'Fancy another drink, girls? Then we'll discuss what night you're going to start working at my club.'

Watching the girls nodding eagerly, Tom pushed himself to his feet. He'd get these two little sluts another couple of half lagers and then go and treat himself to one of these nice rocks in the bogs. Life was too short for unnecessary worry.

John struggled as much as possible as he was manhandled out of the back of the van, but it was to no avail. Trussed by the wrist and ankles, he could do little to protect himself as his head bounced off the tailgate, then thumped onto the concrete of the floor below.

Determined not to give these bastards the satisfaction of hearing him cry out in pain or even as much as wince, he stoically kept his face impassively blank, refusing to show the pain when the skin ripped from his knees and elbows as he was dragged face down and deposited in front of the metal doors of the building.

John's eyes darted around in the dark night, seeing the cavernous bulk of a warehouse looming out of the shadows before him. He knew he was finished, but whatever happened, he would not make this easy for them.

'Come on, wanker,' Andrew growled, kicking Maynard in the ribs. Between him and Neil, they hefted the man to his feet and dragged him through the heavy doors Seb had just unlocked. *This was the fun bit.*

Flicking on one of the fluorescent overhead lights, Seb dragged a rickety looking chair into the centre of the cold space. 'Secure him to this.'

'You think this bullshit will help, you bunch of overgrown wasters?' John spat.

Swinging around, Seb delivered a meaty right hook to John's face. 'Shut it, Maynard!'

Spitting out a tooth and a gob full of blood, John sneered. 'Thought you wanted answers?'

Seb's adrenaline pumped wildly. He'd love nothing more than to batter this prick to the other side of morning, but he had to wait. He'd promised himself he'd give Sam the chance to hear this and he was a man of his word.

He glanced at Andrew and Neil, now finished securing Maynard's wrists and ankles to the chair with heavy-duty cable ties.

Andrew rolled his sleeves up and cracked his knuckles impatiently. 'Right, can I get started? The first thing I want to know is why he killed our Gary.'

'Yeah,' Neil agreed, pushing himself into Maynard's face. 'Why did you kill our brother, you cunt?'

Seb watched Maynard's bloodied face break into a grin – possibly the first time he'd ever seen the man smile.

'Oh, your brother now, is it? And there was the rest of the world thinking you didn't believe he had anything to do with you!' Maynard's eyes twinkled maliciously. 'That's certainly what he thought the last time I spoke to him.' He looked from Andrew to Neil slowly. 'Quite happy to spill the shit about what a bunch of cunts you lot are.'

Neil's eyes narrowed as his fist smashed into Maynard's cheek, knocking the chair with the man still attached onto its back. 'You pointless fu...'

'Enough!' Seb yelled, unceremoniously dragging the chair and Maynard upright. 'There'll be no more questions tonight.'

'You what?' Andrew cried, spinning around to face Seb. He wanted more than anything to release some of his devastating guilt, even it was only a small percentage of what weighed heavily.

'Oh, look!' Maynard laughed, overriding the grinding pain of his smashed cheek bone. 'You'd best all get off home to eat your din-dins with Mummy.'

'We need to kill this twat, Seb,' Neil growled through clenched teeth.

'I hate to disappoint you, boys, but I didn't kill your little brother,' John added.

'Fuck off,' Andrew spat. 'It was you.' His head twisted to face Seb. 'I'm doing him. I want the truth.' He lurched towards Maynard.

'We'll get the truth,' Seb said calmly, even though the urge to rip Maynard limb from limb was overwhelming. Pulling Andrew's arm, he moved in front and faced Maynard. He scanned the man's already half-smashed face, imagining how he'd look once he was finished tomorrow. That alone brought a giddy sense of satisfaction.

Putting his hands in his jeans pockets, he took a casual laidback stance as he walked around Maynard. 'You might think you're clever,' Seb said slowly. 'But you're not. Not really...'

Seb pulled a long piece of cloth from his pocket and from behind, took Maynard unawares, effortlessly winding the material around his face, pushing it into his mouth.

Ignoring Maynard's muffled protests, Seb tied the cloth tighter than needed around the back of the man's head, making sure as much hair got snagged within the knot as possible for added irritation.

Standing back in front of Maynard once more, Seb grinned easily, his bright smile in utter contrast with the bottomless hate and disdain harboured in his crystal-clear green eyes. 'That's better, isn't it?'

He glowed internally, witnessing the inner rage and impotent frustration Maynard's eyes screamed, his muffled rantings pointless. 'See, bruvs? We no longer need to listen to his bullshit.'

Seb grinned at Andrew and Neil who stood primed, watching with interest. 'Mr Maynard here requires a slightly different approach than our standard way of interrogation.' He pulled a small packet from his pocket, within it a tiny bottle with a dropper. 'We won't waste any more energy on our "friend" here until he's had a long, hard think about how beneficial it will be to tell us the truth about his dealings and what he's done.'

He bent level with Maynard's face, ignoring the rabid hate in the man's eyes. 'And by that, I mean *everything*.' He turned to his brothers once again. 'And what better way to do that but to help him look at things in an in-depth way?'

Clapping his hands together, Seb turned to Neil. 'Come and hold his eyes open.'

For the first time since being grabbed, slung into the van and trussed up in a warehouse did Maynard exhibit any hint of fear. He jerked the chair left to right, his gaze darting around the room.

Seb relished the panic loud and clear in Maynard's eyes as he unscrewed the small glass bottle in front of his face and released the dropper. 'Yes, this will aid Mr Maynard plenty,' he said, stepping forward.

'Nnnn!' Maynard squawked, thrashing his head from side to side.

Seb jerked his head in Andrew's direction, who gleefully grabbed Maynard's head, holding it perfectly still.

'Tilt it back,' Seb muttered, inspecting the amount of liquid in the glass dropper. He glanced to Neil. 'Eyelids?'

With Maynard's head tilted back, held firmly by Andrew's massive hands, his eyes bulged as Neil pulled his eyelids open. His panicked gaze darted between the men. He knew what this was and it would fuck his head over big time.

'NNNN!' he wailed once more but could do nothing as Seb squirted the liquid from the dropper in one eye and then the other.

Feeling the liquid LSD burn his eyeballs to be quickly absorbed into his blood vessels, John realised with mounting dread that all he could do was somehow get through the long waking nightmare that would rapidly follow.

38

Sam picked at her pasta ready-meal and stared aimlessly at the blank television screen, her mind turning like a roundabout. Sitting here doing nothing was getting her nowhere, but then pacing aimlessly around the Orchid had got her nowhere either.

She'd tried unsuccessfully to get hold of Seb. *Twice*. According to the Peacock's receptionist, he wasn't in tonight.

Sam picked at her fingernails, worry sparking harder. Had Seb even been seen since removing Gary's body? She didn't know but could hardly ask.

She could and probably *should* have remained at the Orchid. What if Seb was trying to reach her there? But all she'd been doing was pacing around her office achieving nothing, short of working herself into a frenzy. She didn't want to bump into Liam or John either, having seen neither of them since earlier, so she'd left for the night.

Sam pulled her hair away from her neck into a makeshift pony-tail and glanced at the clock. Nearly midnight. *God, this was frustrating*. She could do nothing but wait.

Contemplating whether to just throw the towel in and go to bed, she instead got up and moved to the cabinet, pouring herself a larger than average vodka. Raising the glass to her lips, she froze with the buzzing of the intercom.

Hurriedly placing the glass down, she rushed to the intercom and with shaking fingers, pressed the button, hoping to God it wasn't Liam. Or John. 'Yes?'

'Sam? It's Seb.'

A wave of combined relief and apprehension flooded her as she pressed the door release button. 'Come up.'

In the few moments she had spare before Seb appeared at her front door, Sam found herself smoothing her hair down, then checking her reflection in the hallway mirror. Before she could analyse her confusing actions, Seb tapped on her door.

'Sorry it's so late,' Seb panted, having loped up the stairs. 'I need to speak to you.'

Sam took in Seb's appearance. His standard black suit and white shirt were replaced with a tight black polo neck and jeans. He looked different to usual, but still as handsome as ever. 'I've been going out of my mind,' she cried, pushing the thumping of her heart to the back of her mind. 'Why has it taken you so long? You need to tell me what happened with Gary. I'm having to lie for you, so you could at least tell me the det...'

'You're lying for *me*? I didn't kill my brother and I thought you knew that or have you changed your mind again?' Seb barked, doing exactly what he'd done the last time he was here – striding past Sam into the lounge and helping himself to a drink.

Pouring himself a large Scotch, he frowned. He wasn't here to argue, but this woman infuriated him. He'd insisted on not going any further with interrogating Maynard against his brothers' wishes so Sam could witness what came out of his mouth, yet she was already on his back?

Sam followed Seb to the drinks cabinet and found herself

placing her hand on his arm. 'I'm sorry. I didn't mean it that way. I've just been so worried.' She picked up her own drink. 'When I didn't hear from you I thought you might have been arrested.'

Seb stared at Sam's hand on his bare forearm and then at her. 'Shit, Sam! What's happened? You almost sounded like you cared for a minute then!'

Sam indignantly pulled her hand from Seb's arm. 'It's not funny! Your mother's been on the phone to mine asking about Gary and I didn't know what to say. On top of that I've been worried sick! What did you do with him?'

Seb stared at his whisky, before locking his eyes with Sam, not wishing to recount the less than acceptable way he'd been forced to store his brother's body. 'All you need to know is that it's sorted for now. I owe you a van, though.'

'But...'

'Don't ask me, Sam,' Seb said, his green eyes cold, yet holding a hint of desperation. '*Please!*'

Sam swallowed uncomfortably and nodded. She wanted to ask Seb how he felt about it all but sensed that would only make things worse. 'The other thing is John Maynard,' she said quietly.

Seeing Seb's head snap up at the mention of Maynard's name, Sam continued. 'He's lying. I spoke to him earlier. You're right about him being behind everything. The problem is, I don't know where to go from here... He's family.'

Seb stared at Sam, the alien feeling of the sudden urge to protect this woman from the unsavoury things surrounding her intensifying. He took her elbow, distracting himself from the need to press her against the wall with his body. 'That's why I'm here. Come and sit down.'

Sam tensed and shook away Seb's hand, the succinct tinge of impending dread flooding her. 'I don't want to sit down,' she snapped. 'I want to know what's happening.'

Seb took a deep breath, then tipped the remains of the whisky into his mouth. 'We've lifted Maynard.' He watched Sam's eyes widen. 'Tonight. Not long ago. We're holding him.'

Sam swayed and steadied herself against the wall. 'What have y...?'

'I haven't hurt him... Much...' Seb interjected, his eyes narrowing. 'Not yet anyway, but I'm planning to.'

Sam nodded. She'd half-expected this to be on the cards. Questioning John was something she understood had to be done, but despite being on the cusp of suggesting it herself, John was still her blood and that wasn't a comfortable situation. 'Where...?'

'Maynard's being held in one of my lock-ups,' Seb said, taking the impetus to top up Sam's drink as well as his own. 'My brothers are with him.' He handed her the glass. 'It's imperative you witness what he has to say.' A ghost of a smile crossed his mouth. 'My brothers weren't too pleased. They're used to getting straight on with it.'

Sam's eyes locked onto the small smile on Seb's full lips, the heat of his body radiating towards her despite him standing over a yard away. 'You're waiting for me?'

'Don't get me wrong, Sam. I know the cunt is behind everything. I also believe he killed my brother, but I understand he's your family and I, more than most, know how important that is.' A lopsided smile slid across his face. 'Contrary to popular opinion, I'm a fair man and feel you need to hear what he has to say yourself. You were good to me with the Gary business, so I figured I owe you the same courtesy.'

Scarcely able to believe Seb had gone against his own plan of vengeance, as well as his brothers', for her, Sam slammed her glass down. 'Then let's go. Let's go now.' Her eyes narrowed. 'If it turns out this is right, then I'd rather know the definitive truth sooner rather than later.'

She rushed up the hall, grabbing her jacket on the way. 'If John is going to be killed,' she glanced over her shoulder, 'and I know you'll end up killing him, then I'd prefer get it over with.'

Seb stared after Sam with ever-growing admiration. He couldn't have been more incorrect in his initial assumption of her if he'd tried. She was more level-headed and centred than most of the men he knew.

His longing for her burned brighter than ever before as he followed her up the hallway. 'It won't be happening tonight,' he said, catching hold of Sam's arm.

Sam spun around, her eyes wide. 'Why not? I need to hear the truth!'

Seb nodded. 'I realise that, but it can wait. Maynard's been dosed up and letting him think about what he's going to say is a good idea. We'll deal with it fully tomorrow.'

'But I...'

'This is the way it's happening, Sam. No arguments!' Seb's hand moved to Sam's face, his finger tracing down her left cheek, stopping at her lips. Gently, he ran his thumb across her over her bottom lip. 'Get yourself some rest. I'll be back to collect you tomorrow.'

Her skin burning from where Seb's fingers had touched, Sam watched him walk to the door. 'Seb?'

He turned around.

'Thank you,' she whispered.

Nodding, Seb turned back towards the door.

'Oh, and Seb?' she whispered, moving to stand in front of him, longing to reach for him.

'Yes, Samantha.' Seb's eyes were focused only on Sam's slightly parted lips.

'Good night.'

Shutting the door behind him, Seb raced down the stairs and

through the main door of the apartment complex. Grateful to be in the cool evening air, he leant against the wall and pulled much-needed air into his lungs, knowing his growing feelings for this extraordinary woman were a *lot* more than base desire.

* * *

The whirlwind of colours rushed from the back and then to the front of John's mind as the LSD continued its drawn-out torture of every thought and sense he'd ever had. In desperation, he grasped onto the infrequent blips of logic and rational thought before his conscience swirled back down the looping, kaleidoscopic and fluctuating tunnels of weirdness.

He'd loved this stuff many years ago, but that was long before he'd become involved in all of this – the quest for what he deserved. What had been promised. What had become all-consuming. And the times he'd enjoyed the effect of this drug coincided when he wasn't in a situation guaranteed to give even a serious acid-head the worst trip ever.

John's heart lurched as his eyes fixed on the blood pumping along the veins in his forearm. His stinging eyes watched in terror as his blood vessels grew and expanded. Grew and expanded. Over and over.

He could even hear his blood moving along, the whooshing noise getting fainter as it branched out into the tiny capillaries across his skin.

Was he leaking? Was his blood leaking? Fuck. FUCK.

He could hear a sound like an injured dog whimpering and yelping. He glanced around the gloomy space. *Where was it?* He didn't dare look up. It was too cavernous and no one knew what might be hiding in the shadows.

Suddenly, he realised the sound was coming from himself.

Entering another lucid loop, John fought to gain control of his mind. He needed to concentrate while he could.

His eyes darted to the two ghouls watching him intently from the corner. They'd been there all night – staring, laughing, trying to steal his soul...

It was okay. He'd got this. He knew what he would do. It all made sense and was the best way. They'd never win. He'd leave a legacy that would haunt that bitch for years. It would finish all of them.

John started chuckling then abruptly stopped, hearing something creaking loudly from within his head. He could hear the floor moving. He could actually *hear* it.

Bending his head forward as much as possible, he searched for evidence of millions of marching ants, before realising he'd turned to stone. He hadn't moved his feet or arms for ages. Probably months. *Why was he in this chair again?*

Clawing to keep the fast-disappearing wave of logic before realising it was pointless, he gritted his teeth and waited for the next band to spin into position so that he could continue to plan.

39

Taking a swig from his cup of tea, Mal tucked into his bacon and eggs, pretending to be enjoying his breakfast. He wasn't remotely hungry, but it was the least he could do considering Judith had put the effort in to make it.

Despite Seb's promise to put scouts out to look for his brother, nothing had yet come back from that – unless there was something he hadn't been told. Two days since Gary had been last seen and still no word.

Mal ran his hand across his freshly shaved chin and frowned. He risked a glance at his wife. Despite her going through the motions, he knew she was torn up inside and her festering worry grew bigger with every minute that passed.

Judith would be even more unnerved if she knew the rest of her sons had been unlocatable when he'd called the Peacock last night to double-check on progress.

One of them not being on site wasn't unusual. With the many facets of the business there were lots of things requiring action on a regular basis, but for *all* the boys to unavailable at the same time? *That* wasn't the norm.

Despite not wanting to go down that road, Mal had the sneaking suspicion something wasn't quite as it should be. He didn't know what that something was, but whatever it was, it didn't bode well.

Thankfully, Judith hadn't made any more noise about registering Gary as a missing person with the police. He'd successfully talked her into leaving the boys to do their digging before bringing the Old Bill into it. However, there was only so long she'd swallow that.

Mal necked a large mouthful of tea in a bid to rid his mouth of the horrible taste the prospect of involving the police becoming a reality brought.

The firm might have several Old Bill in their pocket, which offered a good amount of protection, but a missing person investigation was completely different and would involve departments not necessarily on the firm's payroll.

All it would take would be one overzealous copper unaware of their long-standing arrangement and all manner of nasties could be unearthed. And the mere thought of that made Mal's blood pressure rise almost as much as the gnawing worry over Gary.

'You're still taking those every morning, aren't you?' Judith asked, eyeing Mal as he reached for his pills.

'Yes, yes, of course,' Mal said. *Although he might have forgotten the odd one or two recently.*

'I don't need anything else to worry about,' Judith sniffed, standing to clear the plates away.

Mal smiled. 'You don't have to worry about me. I know what I'm doing. Hey, do you fancy going for a drive today? We could go out of town? Maybe grab a bite to eat in a country pub or something?'

Judith shook her head. 'No. You go out if you like, but one of us should be here in case Gary or one of the other boys rings.' She quickly left the room, taking the plates with her.

In the kitchen, she stacked them in the sink. She'd deal with those later. First of all, she'd go upstairs and use the phone in the bedroom to call Gloria. She should have had chance to get hold of Samantha by now and might have some news.

* * *

Hands trembling, Gloria replaced the handset and stared at it sadly. She wished she'd had better news to give Judith, or at least *some* news, but all she'd been able to say was reiterate what Sam said about Gary yesterday, which was of no help at all.

The plain truth was that however much she wanted to bury her head in the sand on this subject, she couldn't allow it to continue. She'd heard the angst in Judith's voice; sensed the blinding desolation on hearing there was nothing to report.

Gloria sighed. How she wished Len were here. He'd know what to do. He *always* knew what to do.

She stared at her tired and washed-out reflection in her dressing table mirror. *Exhausted.*

The trembling in her fingers spread rapidly to the rest of her body, increasing and growing in intensity. It was no good. What would she do if the Stoker boy really had killed himself because of those vicious rumours? Rumours that *she* had the power to stop?

She wouldn't be able to bear the guilt, that's what.

She couldn't allow that poor boy to take the brunt of this. She would have to put this right, but to do that would mean everything would become public. And what would that do to Sam?

Gloria put her head in her hands and sobbed. There was no right or acceptable way around this. Going ahead would blow her daughter's life to pieces and, at the same time, shatter her own heart into a thousand little fragments, but there was no other way.

Picking up the phone, her shaking fingers dialled the number for Sam's apartment. With rising nausea, she listened to it ringing out for what seemed like years before hanging up.

Frowning, she glanced at the clock. *Stupid*. It was already mid-morning, so Sam would be at the Orchid by now.

Gloria wiped a hand across her brow. She was all over the place. The hours and days rolled into one and she hardly knew whether she was coming or going any more.

Stabbing in the digits for Sam's direct line at the Orchid – the digits she knew off by heart because they had once belonged to Len, Gloria bit back the tears that threatened again.

Her heart lurched when the call connected, only to crash on hearing an unknown voice. 'Erm, can I speak to Samantha Reynold, please? It's Gloria,' she muttered.

'Oh, good morning, Mrs Reynold,' the overbright voice chirped. 'Miss Reynold is out at the moment. She's diverted her calls to reception.'

Gloria's stomach sunk. *Out? Out where?* 'When will she be back?' she heard herself say, her voice sounding as brittle and robotic as she felt.

'I'm sorry, Mrs Reynold, she didn't say,' the happy voice wittered. 'Can I take a message?'

'Yes. Please tell her I called and to call me back as soon as she can. It's urgent,' Gloria said, quickly ending the call.

After staring at the wall for a couple of minutes, not knowing what to do or think, she found herself opening the top drawer of her chest of drawers and pulling out the letter – the one that had arrived nearly two weeks ago, and the one which had played on her mind, plaguing her thoughts ever since.

So, it was done. The ball was in play and now she would have to deal with the consequences.

* * *

'Got to warn you, honey, this ain't going to be pleasant.' Seb glanced at Sam in the passenger seat as he picked his way through the heavy traffic towards Erdington.

Sam's heart was already racing at a pace she didn't believe humanly possible and was too on edge to give a second thought to whether there was any hidden meaning behind Seb calling her 'honey'.

Although, since he'd left last night, the small stretches of sleep she'd managed to steal were peppered with vivid dreams concerning him – dreams she was too embarrassed to even *think* about, along with nightmares concerning John Maynard.

She swallowed painfully, her mouth dry, wishing she'd bought something to drink. She'd even contemplated having a couple of vodkas in a bid to calm herself down but decided against it. Aside from not wanting a habit of drinking in the morning, she needed to be stone cold sober to witness what she knew she would see. And she had a fairly clear notion of what the upshot of that would be.

Sam looked at Seb, his strong, angled face concentrating on the road ahead, his mind already in the zone, and she knew she needed to get herself into some kind of mindset too.

'You're going to kill him, aren't you?' she heard herself say.

Seb only hesitated for a moment. 'I am.'

'I know,' Sam said sadly. 'And I expect it. I also know it won't be pretty. Well, I don't... I mean, it's not like I've ever been party to anything like this before...' *And now she was. The baptism of fire into a life she'd never imagined.*

Her stomach lurched when Seb turned into a large industrial estate, driving through mazes of large factories and warehouses until he turned up a gravel path leading to a single detached warehouse.

Pulling on the handbrake, he switched off the engine and

squeezed Sam's hand. 'It'll be okay. We'll get to the bottom of this and then all of this grief will be over.'

Sam didn't pull away from his strong warm hand, even knowing what those hands were about to do to her cousin. John couldn't be allowed to ruin the firm her father had built and if this was the only way to achieve that, then she'd have to live with it.

'I'm ready,' she said, reaching for the door handle.

40

'Right!' Seb clapped his hands together, making sure he wasn't standing in the spreading pool of urine radiating out from underneath the chair. He ripped the gag from Maynard's mouth. 'Let's get started.'

'Ah, the Golden Child,' Maynard said, his eyes narrowing as he looked past Seb to Sam. 'I'm glad you're here, bitch. I've waited years to tell you what you really are.'

Seb backhanded Maynard. 'Don't speak to her like that. You'll answer *my* questions, cunt, so don't get clever.'

Sam stiffened as she studied Maynard. 'What's the matter with him?' she hissed to Andrew. As well as the beating John had obviously received, he looked manic, wild-eyed. *Deranged.*

'Just a bit of stuff to make him chirpier,' Andrew grunted. 'The vast majority has worn off now, but all night he's been completely fucked up. Doing my head in, he was.'

'Which questions do you want answering, hard man?' Maynard sneered. 'That I killed your brother, that wasn't your brother... or who *she* is, or what?'

Seb's jaw clenched, aware it would be difficult not to total this twat from the off, but he couldn't. Not until he'd got the truth.

'I didn't kill him,' Maynard continued. 'I've already told you that.'

'Then who did?' Neil stepped forward, only to be restrained by Seb.

Maynard raised his eyebrows. 'I can't tell you that,' he smiled. 'Well, I could, but I won't... Actually, come to think of it, it might have been me...'

'He's playing with us,' Neil growled, chomping at the bit to lay into Maynard.

'Irritating you already, am I? That's good to know.' A sneer twisted Maynard's face, the dried blood on his cheeks pinching his skin, making him look even worse.

'John,' Sam said, moving forward. 'What's got into you? Why are you being like this?'

'Why am *I* being like this? Ask your trained fucking monkeys. They've kept me trussed to a chair all night and fed me with shit.' Maynard's eyes rested on Seb. 'And for what?' His eyes narrowed. 'They'll never get what they want. And neither will you!'

Sam didn't like this. John had always been controlled and methodical, but now he was acting strange. *Crazy.* 'Look, if you'd ju...'

'Fuck off, whore,' Maynard screamed. 'This is all your fault if you ha...'

Slamming his fist into the side of Maynard's head, Seb knocked the chair and the man over, the back of the chair snapping in two on the concrete. 'I told you not to speak to her like that, didn't I?' he roared, delivering several more punches to the man's face.

'Seb!' Sam yelled, pulling at his arm. 'We want him to talk. We need answers.'

Gritting his teeth, Seb reluctantly dragged Maynard up from the floor by his hair. 'Thanks to her, you'll get the opportunity to explain yourself properly. If it were up to me, I'd...'

'You'd *what*?' Maynard spat, his right eye already swelling. 'You want me to tell you what you want to know?' He laughed again – a strange gurgling sound. 'Well, you'll have a long wait! I'd rather die than give you *or* her any answers.'

'I'm fucking sick of this!' Neil spat, pushing forward. 'Let's just get on with it.'

'NO!' Sam moved forward once again. *She had to try things her way first. She had to make sense of this.* Squatting down in front of Maynard's broken chair, she forced herself to look into his battered face, but wished she hadn't. His eyes were scarily wrong.

'Why have you been working against me? Against *all* of us? Why would you do that?' Sam stared into Maynard's manic eyes. 'Did you kill Gary Stoker, John? Please tell me.'

Saying nothing, Maynard enjoyed the silence. He knew these bastard Stokers were waiting for him to admit it and then they'd kill him. But if he didn't admit it, they'd kill him anyway. He could tell them it was Bedworth, sure, but where was the fun in that? He was finished either way, so why give them the answers?

During the drawn-out night he'd had a long time for his scattered mind to work overtime and he'd come up with the goods. The best and only way forward. *And this was it.*

Maynard's face crunched into a sickly looking grin. It didn't matter that it hurt. It would rile the Stokers no end and that was all that mattered.

'John?' Samantha pushed, aware the continuing silence would only last so long before the men standing behind her reacted. She could feel Seb's anger growing exponentially with every second that passed. 'Listen, I don't believe it was you who killed Gary, but were you behind it? Something to do with it? Or know who was?'

Maynard began humming 'A Whiter Shade of Pale', the sound echoing through the large space.

'Let me try things *my* way.' Andrew pulled out a machete.

'NO!' Sam cried, seeing the large blade glinting in Andrew's hand. She looked at Seb, her eyes pleading and gratefully watched him give his brother the nod to stand down.

She turned back to Maynard. 'I can only help you so much, but if you tell me what's really going on, then we can go from there. We're family and you need to re...'

'*FAMILY*?' Maynard screeched with such venom it almost made Sam topple. 'We're not family! You've *never* been family!' Hawking, he spat a ball of phlegm into Sam's face.

Yelping with disgust and shock, Sam scrambled to her feet, her hand hastily scraping the green filth off her face.

'You disgusting bastard!' Seb roared, dragging Maynard over to the nearest workbench with one hand. 'Give me that!' he yelled, snatching the machete from Andrew.

Sam's eyes widened. 'No, Seb, don't!'

Ignoring Sam's protests, Seb slit the binding around Maynard's wrists. Knowing he worked faster than the man could think, he whacked one of the Maynard's hands down flat on the wooden countertop, then effortlessly lopped off four of the fingers from his right hand.

Watching with satisfaction as Maynard howled like an animal, Seb smiled. 'Perhaps now you'll stop jerking everyone around and treat your cousin with the respect she deserves. Answer the fucking questions!'

Sam stared in horror at the bleeding stumps remaining on Maynard's hand. Feeling vomit rise, she forced herself to stay in control.

Grabbing Maynard's hair, Seb yanked his head around to face Sam. 'Apologise for what you just did, you bastard,' he spat. 'Apologise to her! Do you hear me? Sam's your cousin and families don't turn on each other.'

'She's not my cousin!' Maynard roared, the one eye that wasn't swollen shut staring malevolently at Sam. 'She's fuck all to do with me!' He glanced dismissively at his missing fingers and then looked at Seb. 'This cunt, this *slag* is fuck all to do with me or my family!'

Maynard's head jerked back to Sam as she stared at him in confusion. 'That's right, bitch! *You're* the usurper here, not anyone else!' He nodded to the Stoker brothers. 'You lot were the ones stupid enough to take that bullshit rumour to be aimed at *your* family.' His head jerked at Sam. 'But it's *her*! She's stolen my inheritance. I'm the only one with a blood tie to Len Reynold.'

His strange high-pitched laughter filled the cavernous space, echoing off the walls. 'You're the adopted kid, Samantha. The fake. The fucking *phoney*. The Orchid should be mine. It always should have been mine.'

Sam's heart pounded as she digested what was coming out of her cousin's mouth. *Adopted? She was adopted? No. It wasn't possible. This couldn't be right.*

Seb watched Sam's reaction, could see she was contemplating whether this was feasible. 'Don't fall for it. He's playing you.' His jaw clenched. 'I've had enough of this.'

Maynard laughed once again, knowing he'd gained control, if only for a split second. 'Yeah, Samantha-perfect-Reynold. What a joke! My father was the only one who knew anything of this. Even *I* wasn't supposed to know, but I overheard him and Len and it was that which spawned my plan.' His eyes glinted. 'All of this stems back to you, Samantha. You're the one to blame.'

His face twisted further. 'Do you not want to know who your *real* parents are, Samantha? Do you not want to know why Len and Gloria never told you the truth?'

His eyes rolled in his head, enjoying the suspicion and fear behind Sam's eyes. 'Because your real parents *sold* you, Samantha. The oh-so-perfect daddy who gave you the Orchid, instead of me, *bought* you!' Maynard's lips split into a wide smile. 'Like a dog...'

'I've heard enough of this utter shite,' Seb snapped, giving Andrew and Neil the nod. 'You killed our brother and so now we're go...'

'I should have had control of the firm, not her!' Maynard screeched, unperturbed. 'That's why I offloaded my own father!' He laughed shrilly. 'Yes, I did that! I killed my own father on your birthday, Samantha. Remember? Because it meant that I could step into his shoes and be in place for when Len went the same way.'

Sam couldn't process this. *Was John being serious?* He'd killed his own father to get closer to gaining control of the Orchid? He'd killed her Uncle Jimmy?

Fear escalated. Her father died in a car... Was John saying he'd killed her father too? That the accident with the tree had been down to him?

Sam staggered slightly, light-headed, her blood rushing from her head to her toes. 'Did you... Were you the one who...'

'Did I kill Len?' Maynard's eyes sparkled with malice, witnessing Sam's growing realisation. *Oh, this was good. Far better than he'd hoped.* 'And did I kill Gary? Did I kill everyone? Oh, so many questions, so little time.'

He could see the Stoker boys were about to pounce. It was almost over. He hadn't got long and he knew it, but they wouldn't have the last word. They would not have the last word at all. *It was perfect.*

'Just answer the fucking questions, you wanker!' Seb barked, going in for the kill.

With surprising speed, Maynard's remaining hand reached down to his ankle for his knife. He only just made it and the pain almost crippled him, but he had to get in first. *Had* to get in first.

The thick fuckers may have taken his gun, but they hadn't bothered looking for this. *Stupid, stupid.* 'Fuck you!' he screamed.

Emitting a piercing scream that didn't sound like anything Sam had heard herself make before, she darted forward, her hands scrabbling towards the blade in Maynard's hand in what seemed like strange, staccato time-lapse bursts.

'NO!' Seb swiped Sam out of the way and lurched forward to knock the knife from Maynard's grip. But he was too late and watched as Maynard drove the blade deep into his own chest.

With hands slipping on the blood-soaked handle of the knife, Seb frantically pulled the blade from Maynard's heart, the blood spurted in a gushing arc into his face. *He wasn't having this. He was finishing Maynard. He would not let him finish himself.*

A euphoric grimace froze over Maynard's face and with gnashing teeth, Seb could do nothing but stare in abject horror and frustration as the remaining life behind the man's eyes rapidly diminished.

'You bastard!' Seb roared, smashing Maynard over and over in the face with his fists, the splintering of bone excessively loud in the stunned silence of the warehouse. 'You fucking coward!' He continued driving his fist into what had once been Maynard's face, but was now little more than pulp.

Sam remained paralysed in shock at the unrecognisable body of her cousin as the extent of the situation seeped slowly into her frozen brain. *John had killed himself rather than give the answers to the questions?*

Her eyes darted to Andrew and Neil, also standing in stunned silence watching the spectacle unfold. Seb's face was a paroxysm of manic frenzy as he scrambled to his feet, raised his boot and brought his entire weight down on Maynard's skull, the cracking of the bones sickeningly loud in the quiet space.

'Jesus Christ,' Andrew muttered, moving towards Seb. 'Leave it, for fuck's sake!'

Neil followed his brother's lead and, with difficulty, together they pulled Seb away from the mangled body of John Maynard, glistening glutinous chunks of brain tissue scattered around the floor.

Seb, wild-eyed and panting, eyed the mess surrounding him. 'The bastard,' he muttered to no one in particular.

Sam leant on a workbench the other side of the lock-up. Taking in great gulps of air, she fought to stop the rising bile from spewing from her mouth. She couldn't look at this any more.

Slowly coming to his senses, Seb looked at Sam's pale face, then turned to his brothers. 'Take her home. I'll sort this out.'

Andrew shook his head. 'No, *we'll* sort it. You take her and get yourself cleaned up.'

Sam was glad Seb was driving. She didn't think she'd have been able to keep her legs still enough to operate the pedals had she been the one behind the wheel. Not that she had a car at the moment and hadn't needed one since moving to the city centre.

Even though she'd wanted to immediately make the journey to her mother's after leaving the warehouse, she'd known it wasn't possible. In her trance-like state, Seb had led her to his car, leaving his brothers behind to clear up.

Aside from the state of Seb's clothes, she herself was in no fit state to have the conversation needed, but now they were finally on their way to Edgbaston, the rush of dread as to what she might hear from her mother assaulted her once again.

Sam gazed blankly out of the passenger window, the well-known sights of Broad Street gradually morphing into those of the Hagley Road.

She knew Seb kept glancing at her, but she couldn't face turning her head to look at him. She was glad he'd insisted she accompany him to his apartment, though. If she'd been left alone, she would have screamed and screamed and screamed until her voice box melted.

Of course, it would have achieved nothing. She couldn't relax until she'd heard the refutation straight from her mother's mouth and even then, not much, if anything, would erase what she'd seen in that warehouse.

Despite already having showered that morning, when she'd stepped into Seb's place and caught a glimpse of herself in the tall mirror in his hallway, she'd experienced the uncontrollable urge to shower again. There wasn't a speck of John Maynard's blood on her, but his death and lies had seeped into every single pore and fibre of her body.

Seb had insisted she shower first, even though he was the one caked in that... that *filth*, but she was grateful by taking him up on his offer she'd no longer had to look at the glutinous residue on his trousers, the splashes on his forearms, or the lumps in his hair. Her heart thundered. She hadn't wanted to see it again, that mess on his clothes, knowing where it had come from.

The hot jet of water in Seb's shower might have cleansed her body, but it hadn't cleansed her mind.

The car came to a halt behind a double-decker bus and Sam absentmindedly watched people disembark – their movements playing in slow motion, like she was part of a film showing at reduced speed.

She glanced in the vanity mirror of the sun visor. The reflection was the same as what she'd seen staring at herself in the brightly illuminated mirror of Seb's bathroom. *Was any of what John said true?*

She kept telling herself it couldn't be, but there was only one way to find out. *And this was it...*

Sam glanced down at her black skirt. Spotless, just as it had been before, but having no other clothes to wear, she'd had to put the same ones back on – the ones she was sure were impregnated with the memory of death.

She slapped the button for the electric window, needing some air – anything to deflect from her racing heart – and listened for a hint from the ether which would explain things. She may outwardly appear controlled, but inside her brain churned.

'I'm not quite sure I understand why you want to do this.'

Seb's low voice threw Sam off kilter. For a moment she'd completely forgotten where she was and who she was with. She pulled her stare away from the window and risked a glance at Seb, his green gaze on the heavy traffic and wondered, not for the first time, how he had reverted back to normal from the rabid, possessed lunatic she'd witnessed thrashing the corpse of her cousin.

'You know Maynard was talking shite, don't you?' Seb continued. 'Deflecting even though it was obvious he was responsible for everything.'

Sam nodded, more to herself than to Seb. 'I know, but I...'

'You need to hear it from her,' Seb interjected. 'I understand, but what will you say? How will you explain the questions?'

Sam stared at Seb's hand on the steering wheel. It looked like a normal hand, with clean nails. It looked like the hand that had touched her face so gently when he'd left her apartment the other night, not the hand that battered the life out of people. Not the hand that killed.

'Your mother will surely want to know why and where you've got these absurd questions from?' Seb pushed.

'I don't know what I'll say yet,' Sam muttered. And she didn't. All she knew was that she had to ask. She had to hear her mother tell her what John had said was untrue, otherwise there would always be a tiny little glimmer of *'what if...'*?

Sam's nerves fluttered anew as Seb turned the car into the road she knew so well. The road where she'd lived for the first nineteen years of her life. She took a deep breath, preparing herself to offend her mother in the worst way possible.

41

At the sound of the doorbell, Gloria wrung her hands with mounting dread. Moving towards the front door, she hoped beyond all measure this wasn't Judith. She didn't think she could bear seeing the woman's distraught face again as she spoke about the escalating unrest between her sons, knowing *she* could do something to quieten the rumours ripping the Stoker family apart.

Her heart suddenly brightened. Maybe Gary had returned and everything had sorted itself out? Perhaps she wouldn't need to break the code of silence she and Len had promised each other after all?

Reaching the door, Gloria peered through the inset spyhole and her heart plummeted further. *Samantha? And Sebastian Stoker?*

'Samantha!' she exclaimed on opening the door, praying she looked brighter than she felt. 'You got my message?' Standing to one side, she gestured for them to enter. 'Hello, Sebastian.'

'Mrs Reynold,' Seb smiled, ushering Sam over the threshold.

Gloria followed Sam and Seb up the hallway into the lounge. 'It's a lovely day, isn't it?' she babbled. 'Can I get you both something to dri...'

'You left me a message?' Sam interrupted, sitting down awkwardly in an armchair. 'I didn't get a message.'

'Oh!' Gloria waved her hand dismissively. 'I left a message for you at the Orchid.' Now Sam was here, her plan of telling her daughter the truth had gone out the window. She couldn't go into those details with Sebastian Stoker present.

Gesturing for Seb to also take a seat, Gloria sat opposite. It was only then that she fully took in her daughter's strained, pale face. 'Samantha? Whatever is the matter? You look like you've seen a ghost!' Her eyes darted to Seb. 'Is it Gary? Have you news on Gary?' Her hands flew to her mouth. 'Oh, please tell me he's okay? I don't think I could bear it if...'

'There's no news on Gary, Mrs Reynold,' Seb said, his voice low. *No news he could possibly tell Gloria Reynold, anyway.* That he could not breathe of until he'd told his own parents.

Relief washed over Gloria, only to be replaced with the initial worry. 'Then what's wrong? Don't tell me nothing, because I can see that the...'

'I need to ask you something, Mum,' Sam said. *This was it.* Suddenly feeling ridiculous with the need to voice the question, her eyes darted to Seb, who nodded, pushing her to continue. He was right. Regardless how stupid it might seem, she still needed to hear it.

Gloria watched her daughter exchange glances with the Stoker man and fear pulsed. *Had something happened to the Orchid?* Perspiration beaded. 'Samantha?'

Taking a deep breath, Sam looked into her mother's eyes. 'These rumours about Gary... I was told earlier today that it concerns *me*, not him...'

Gloria blinked, her mind scrambling. 'You? What do you mean?'

'That I'm not your daughter. Or Len's daughter,' Sam said, her voice brittle, strained.

Gloria's nails dug into the armrest of the chair. 'Who said that? Why d...'

'Mum,' Samantha interrupted. 'Tell me it's not true.'

Gloria's mouth opened, but no words came out.

Sam's face paled further. She glanced at Seb, his eyes trained on Gloria. Clamouring rang loudly in her head. That her mother hadn't immediately denied it told her nothing, yet *everything* at the same time and, at that precise moment, her world folded in on itself.

* * *

Gloria heard her daughter's voice, heard the questions, but they were muffled. Her brain shut out everything short of her own speeding thoughts.

No one knew. Len had *promised* her no one knew. More to the point, they had both agreed that whatever happened, Samantha was never to find out. But Samantha *had* found out, and not from her. How?

Her eyes mechanically moved to Samantha, who was reading the letter she'd handed her – the letter that had been received around the time Len died.

A trace of a sad smile passed across Gloria's face. She knew she might once have been the envy of her friends but it was her who had envied *them*. They might not have had the big house, fancy cars or successful husband, but they had the one thing she wanted and the one thing she was unable to manage. The one thing money couldn't buy...

Children...

She'd tried not to become disillusioned. After all, it had taken a couple of her friends a year a so, but when five years passed and then ten, the problem had become all-consuming.

Len could have left her, she knew that. He could have left her for a woman who would provide him with children, or even got himself a mistress on the side to give him kids, but he hadn't. Instead, he'd promised her that one day *they'd* have a child. But by the age of thirty-nine, she'd sadly accepted this was unlikely.

When it was finally confirmed by a private gynaecologist that it was 'impossible for her to conceive', Gloria's world had shattered.

That was until Len had come home one night with news.

She hadn't taken him seriously at first, he'd had a few too many drinks, but when he'd repeated the same thing the next morning, a glimmer of possibility flickered.

Gloria hadn't been able to relax – not entirely, but Len was adamant it would work. He'd said it was all above board and that no one would ever know the child wasn't naturally theirs. After all, she rarely went out and it was true that no one had seen her for the last few months, so it was feasible...

Still, it had been almost too good to be true until the day it actually happened. That day thirty years ago when he'd arrived home with what he'd always promised.

The minute Len had handed her the tiny, two-day-old bundle, Gloria realised more than ever there was nothing he couldn't achieve and her heart had melted into molten lava.

She had a daughter. *They* had a daughter and her life was complete.

* * *

'Were you ever going to tell me?' Sam whispered, her shaking hands passing the letter to Seb.

Pulling herself away from her thoughts, Gloria looked up, then averted her eyes, unable to bear the betrayal on Samantha's face. 'We, your father and I, always agreed that whatever happened, you were not to find out, but... but that's why I left a message... I knew it was time to tell you...'

As the two women talked, Seb's eyes scanned the typewritten letter Sam had passed to him:

Dear Mr and Mrs Reynold,

I respectfully request payment for the gift of my child. Many years have passed and unless I am fairly and adequately reimbursed, I will ensure everybody knows what you gained at my expense.

I will be in touch.

Seb glared at Gloria, not only for the pain he could taste radiating from Sam, but from what he'd just realised. 'I get it... You only decided to tell her because you knew our family was being wrongly targeted, yet it was you all along! That's why you've been so interested in Gary. I'm right, aren't I? You felt guilty!'

Tears rolled down Gloria's cheeks as she nodded. 'Yes and I'm sorry. I couldn't allow it any longer for you boys to think that your brother wasn't y...'

'But they *sold* me?' Sam cried, her voice strangulated. 'And you *paid* for me?' Her head swirled with the impact. She'd expected her mother to instantly deny it. She hadn't expected *this*...

Gloria dabbed her face. 'I – I don't know the exact details. I know your father gave some mo...'

'He's not my father though, is he?' Sam raged, jumping up from the chair.

'Of course he is, sweetheart,' Gloria exclaimed. 'Len loved you more than anything, as do I and...'

'But who am I?' Sam screeched. 'Who am I *really*?'

Reaching up, Seb placed his hand on Sam's arm. 'You need to keep calm.'

'Oh, shut up!' Sam snapped, batting Seb's hand away. 'I have a right to know.'

With trembling hands, Gloria pulled a small age-worn canvas bag from the side of her chair. The one she'd dug out especially when deciding she had to tell Samantha everything. *It had gone wrong. It wasn't supposed to be like this.* 'This was all that came with you,' she whispered, handing Sam the bag.

Sam stared at the bag in her mother's outstretched hand like it was poisonous before gingerly taking it. Sitting back down in the armchair, she opened it, seeing a handful of tiny unwashed baby clothes. *These were hers?*

Shaking her head in disbelief and a torrent of confusing emotions, Sam was about to throw the bag on the floor in disgust or horror – she couldn't decide which, when she saw it.

Along with the clothes, there was a scrawled note. Her shaking hand pulled it from the bag:

Her name is Violet.

Feeling she might drown in her own tears, Gloria watched Sam staring at the note. She knew exactly what it said. It was all the woman who had given birth to this treasure had written. Nothing else. Just *that.*

When she'd shown Len that piece of crumpled paper, he'd been almost as surprised as she was and they'd both agreed the baby girl was destined to be theirs.

What were the chances of the child being called Violet – the very name he'd given to his successful casino years before? It had been fate, he'd said.

'My real name is Violet?' Sam muttered, her tone devoid of feeling and life.

'We'd already decided you were to be called Samantha, but your father promised to honour the note that accompanied you by giving you a violet orchid every year.' Gloria watched the realisation sinking into Sam's brain. 'It was the least we could do as a silent and anonymous thank you to the woman who gave us the greatest gift of all, as well as gratitude for the prosperous existence the casino provided.'

'Have you any idea what you sound like?' Sam roared. 'Spouting about honouring this and honouring that, yet you *paid* for me? Where did you find me? The black market?'

Gloria shook her head vividly. 'It wasn't like that.' She glanced at Seb embarrassed. 'I couldn't have children... My brother knew of a man whose girlfriend was pregnant and so...'

'Who else knew? Anyone else apart from Jimmy?' Seb questioned, his mind working ten to the dozen. *And, of course, John Maynard.*

'No one,' Gloria whispered.

'Who are they? My real parents?' Sam spat. She had to know. *Had to.*

Gloria looked down sadly. 'I – I don't know...'

Sam gasped in amazement. 'You don't know? Was I even legally adopted? I have a birth certificate. I've seen it! You and Dad are named on it!' She spat the word 'Dad'.

Gloria held her hands up. 'Your father arranged everything, so I don't know how and I – I didn't ask. I'm sorry... All I cared about was that I'd got you. My darling girl. The daughter I thought I'd never have. You made our lives complete.'

Sam stared with resentment at the woman she'd always believed to be her mother. 'But you lied to me...'

42

'That's good to know,' Seb said, his voice business-like as Andrew informed him the warehouse was now clear. He frowned at Andrew's next question. 'No, I won't be back in today.' He glanced at Sam, sitting motionless in a chair. 'I'll bring you up to speed as soon as, but let's just say something has come to light.'

He never went into details over the phone anyway, but certainly had no wish to outline the shocking revelations whilst Sam was in earshot. She was shell-shocked enough as it was, and he couldn't say he blamed her. 'Oh, and Andrew, before you go. Do me a favour and pay the Orchid a fleeting visit. Make sure it's all ticking over nicely... Yes, I will. Okay.'

Sam watched Seb replace the receiver, her eyes staring at him coldly. 'You don't need to handhold me because of this,' she said sharply. 'Regardless of what's happened, I'm quite capable of running my club.'

She glanced dismissively at the scrap of paper which had accompanied the baby clothes. 'Contrary to popular belief, the last couple of weeks have taught me that despite what life throws at you, there isn't room for sentiment.'

Seb moved to sit next to Sam. Since walking out of her parents' house and getting back to her own apartment, she hadn't said a word. *Until now.* 'Stop being a martyr. You don't need to do that on my account.'

She may have surprised him with the unexpected way she'd dealt with what had crashed into both of their lives lately, but she wasn't made of stone.

Seb found himself experiencing a strange and unnatural concept. He *wanted* to be there for her. *Wanted* to help her make sense of it. And he wouldn't let her deal with this alone, despite what she said.

Sam pulled her eyes away from the piece of paper that her real mother had written in her own hand, like it meant nothing. Fury and bewilderment raged. She wanted to hold onto the only piece of her true identity that she had, but at the same time, she wanted it as far away from her as possible.

She couldn't give Seb Stoker any reason to say she was weak or incapable. She could feel his power emanating from him. He didn't need to touch her to be aware of his sheer presence, magnetism and strength. This man scared the living daylights out of her. Not just because of what he did and what he was capable of, but his ability to draw her in. It gave him an advantage which weakened her resolve.

It made her want him. *Badly.* There was a lot more to him than brutal violence and extortion. A *lot* more and she wanted to be part of it. But despite how much her body yearned to reach out and touch him, to feel his skin and prove he was real, she couldn't. It was too dangerous. But she wanted to...

Shaking her head to rid herself of the unwanted thoughts, her lips pursed. 'I take it by the veiled reference to whichever brother you were just speaking to, they've got rid of John Maynard?'

Seb was unable to stop his face from breaking into a smile at the sudden change of subject. 'There's no flies on you, are there?'

'No, there aren't. Sorry if that disappoints you,' Sam snapped, knowing she was being aggressive and unreasonable, but she *felt* aggressive and unreasonable. She wanted to lash out and take the frustration, betrayal and pain raging through her veins out on him. Or someone. *Anyone.*

'And for the record, Samantha, you don't disappoint me. Far from it...' Seb murmured, his fingers brushed a lock of hair from her forehead.

Heating, Sam moved away. *He'd done it again.* Knocked her off kilter. She pulled her eyes from Seb's face, his mouth. 'At least one positive to come from this is there will be no more trouble.'

Seb nodded. 'If the skanky twat was right about overhearing Len and Jimmy, and I think it was, then yes – it's over.'

The weight of everything suddenly bore down on Sam. 'I still can't believe John betrayed everyone! He'd planned this for years.' Her gaze drifted far away. 'He killed his own father and then killed mine... Then he killed Gary and also must have been the one behind that blackmail letter.'

Unable to help it, her bottom lip trembled thinking of her father; the man she'd loved and trusted above all others – the man who wasn't her father at all. Her eyes drew back to the scrap of paper.

Seb watched Sam fighting the internal battle to stay in control of her emotions. 'By the way, Samantha suits you better than Violet,' he said, raising an eyebrow.

Despite herself, Sam found herself smiling. 'It does, doesn't it?'

'You'll find a way to work this out in your head, I promise,' Seb said, his eyes running across Sam's face – so sad, yet so, *so* beautiful.

Sam sighed resignedly. 'I'm trying to be rational about it, but...'

'It's one hell of a mind fuck!' Seb finished the sentence. 'What are you going to do about your mother?'

Sam frowned, remaining silent. *As in Gloria or her real one?* She'd walked out of Gloria's home, leaving her sobbing in the chair. She needed time. Time to let all of this sink in before she could speak to her about this again.

'Don't be too hard on her. She loves you,' Seb said softly, his hand moving to Sam's face again, before stopping himself.

'I need to know who they are.' Sam whispered. She hadn't meant to say it. She'd thought it but had dismissed the idea. Why should she want to know anything about the people who'd happily given her up? Who had *sold* her? She began to tremble. The truth was, no matter how much she fought against it, she needed to know who they were. 'My real parents...'

'I'll help you,' Seb found himself saying. He tilted Sam's head up, seeing her eyes fill with the first unshed tears. 'I'll help you find these people and then you can choose what to do about it. I'll also help you run the Orchid, okay? No strings attached.'

Sam knew the dam was about to burst. The tears were about to fall. *Don't. Don't cry.* 'Thank you, but I...'

'Stop fighting me, Sam,' Seb said. 'You don't have to be on your own.' He pulled Sam into his arms. The dam burst and Sam sobbed against his chest. For once in his life, he felt something other than revenge or absolution. And he didn't want to let that go. *For anyone.*

After soaking the front of Seb's shirt with her tears, Sam was past feeling stupid. Finally allowing herself to cry was cathartic, but more than anything, it had accentuated what she knew she would do. What she should have done before now. Pressing her nose against his chest, she inhaled his scent, giving her the confidence and resolve needed. *She wanted this man like no other...*

Scraping the back of her hand across her eyes, she pulled

herself away and knelt on the sofa. Without giving herself time to analyse what she was about to do, she pressed her lips to his.

As Seb pulled her over him, his hand wrapping in her hair, his mouth greedily searching hers, Sam fumbled to undo his belt, knowing she had just made a decision that would mean a vast difference to her life.

EPILOGUE

The young girl pulled her mother's sheer polyester robe around her naked body. It might be itchy and a bit big, but she looked, and more to the point, *felt* the part.

Her mother had been spot on when she'd said if she and her sister played nice with this bloke, he'd snap them up like a shot. *And he had.* Both her and Stella were now well in here and would make tons of money. She smiled widely at the prospect.

Watching the man roll out of bed to pull his trousers on, Tina frowned. 'You're not leaving, are you?'

Tom playfully slapped the girl's buttocks. As much as he'd love to continue sampling her young flesh, he couldn't hang around any longer. 'Get yourself downstairs now, Sugar Tits,' he grinned. 'It's time you got going with real punters rather than just me.'

Tina pouted, her overly made-up face making her look even younger than her actual years. 'But I've been enjoying myself here with just you,' she whined.

Actually, she hadn't. The man was a wizened old goat and stank of stale beer and fags, but he always had plenty of powder and, being the gaffer of this place, she'd hoped that by impressing him good and proper, he might decide to keep her for himself.

Tom's chest puffed out with the compliment. *Some things never change*, he thought. He'd always been a winner with the girls.

Cutting himself a quick line on the bedside table, he pushed Tina away as she sidled closer. The silly tart was clearly angling for another free snort, but she'd caned plenty of his stash over the last couple of days and enough was enough. It had been a decent way to pass the time, rather than worrying about what was going on in the outside world, but it was time to put the next part of his plan into action.

'I've got things to do and people to see.' Wiping the powder residue from under his nose, Tom turned to Tina, his face losing the expression of contentment. 'Don't take the piss, sweetheart. You've got punters downstairs looking forward to their slot with you, so don't let me down, eh? Otherwise, I might regret taking you and your sister on.'

Fear flooded Tina. 'Oh, no, you won't regret it, I promise you that!'

Tom smiled once again, glad he'd got the message across. He picked up his holdall from the floor. 'I'll be off, then.'

Tina rushed to the bedroom door after Tom. 'When will you be back?'

Tom glanced over his shoulder. 'Dunno, but any problems, speak to Lee. Apart from that, your mother will answer any questions you and your sister may have.'

Continuing down the rickety stairs, he nodded to Lee. 'You know what to do. Anyone comes asking for me, say nowt, but let me know ASAP by leaving a message *here*.' He handed Lee a scrap of paper containing a scrawled telephone number. 'I'll be back when I'm back.'

Quickly letting himself out of the back door of the Aurora, Tom glanced around the car park before stepping into the gloomy light from the lamp post opposite. *All clear.*

Crossing the car park, he slung his holdall in the boot of his car and then fired the engine, breathing a sigh of relief as he pulled away from the building.

It was only a slight sigh of relief because he didn't really want to leave, but it was the sensible thing to do. He just needed a few more days to ascertain whether he was correct in his assumptions. To do that without risk, he needed to be away from the place.

Tom continued down the Hagley Road in the opposite direction of the city centre. The opposite direction from the Stokers and the Reynolds.

It certainly did seem his prayers had been answered. It couldn't have worked out any better than if he'd meticulously orchestrated it himself. Yet he'd planned nothing and still everything had come together in the best way possible.

An utter and unexpected bonus.

Two whole days had passed since he'd seen Maynard. Two whole days since the man had been pulled off the streets by Stoker himself.

And two whole days without a word from either of them.

A wide grin slithered across Tom's face as he pulled a cigarette from his top pocket. Sparking it up, he was surprised the lighter in this crummy car worked, but it did. Everything was on the up.

Things worked in mysterious ways and unless he was very much mistaken, it looked like Maynard had finally levelled his debt from ballsing up the original plan back in the day.

The Stokers must have offed him, and not a word had been mentioned, or more likely, there had been no *time* to for his name to be uttered before Maynard's brains were splattered over a floor somewhere.

Tom shrugged dismissively. Not his problem. And being as no

one was sniffing around, it looked unlikely to become his problem either.

He'd have rubbed his hands together with glee had he not needed to keep at least one of them on the steering wheel. He didn't want to screw up by totalling this car, did he?

Chuckling at his own good fortune, Tom continued. Yes, he could have hung around, but it was best all round to make himself scarce. Of course, in addition to that, he needed to get the next part of this expert plan into motion. The part that hadn't even been embryonic until yesterday when the wonderful realisation dawned upon him.

As the time lengthened without Maynard or anyone else turning up, Tom had realised that as far as everyone else was concerned, it had been him – Maynard – behind *everything*. How cracking was that? And it could only mean one thing.

No one suspected *him*. Those fuckers didn't even know who he was.

Maynard had taken the rap for Reynold's death, the rumours and the sad demise of the Stoker boy too. *Shame.*

Tom's face felt like it might split in two, courtesy of his beaming smile. It meant something else too – Reynold's widow would think it was over as well. She'd think there would be no more blackmail; no more accidents; no more anything...

How wrong she was...

And if she thought that, she'd also not have bothered divulging her secret to anyone, meaning the ability to get money out of her would soon be even easier.

But he had also another idea. Oh, yes, he'd seen his daughter the other night. Yeah, *his* daughter. He'd bumped into her the night of the wake. *Literally.*

He knew it was her without a doubt, because he'd seen the photo in the paper when her pseudo-father celebrated her birthday. Plus, she was now the owner of the Orchid... How convenient...

But fuck me, Tom thought, she was a fine looker. He'd make a mint if he got her to work for him. She'd obviously inherited her mother's good looks, so at least Linda had been good for one thing, despite being shit in the sack.

Tom pressed his foot further down on the accelerator. He'd never thought he'd be doing this. Never thought he'd ever choose to seek out that miserable bitch, Linda Matthews, again, but things changed. Not only did he need somewhere to lie low for a while and was fairly sure Linda would still be around her old haunts, but as well as that, her old cunt of a father would be long dead by now, so there would be no hassle.

Besides, word on the vine that he'd kept his ear close to during his long absence was that Linda hadn't been quite the ticket since he'd left. She'd always had a thing for him, so he was sure she'd welcome his return, especially when he offered her the chance to get to know her long-lost daughter.

And if Linda played her cards right and did what he wanted, then he'd make it so that happened.

He just had to find Linda and put his magic to work.

'Oh, Tom, my old son,' he muttered as he continued down the A38 towards Selly Oak. 'You really are fucking good.'

And he'd only just begun. *Life was good.*

ACKNOWLEDGMENTS

Firstly, I would like to thank Boldwood Books for believing in my writing and for making this latest series possible. Extra special thanks go to my lovely editor, Emily Ruston, whose energy and enthusiasm make it both a privilege and a pleasure to work with her.

I would also like to thank my family, who have long since put up with me sitting in the corner, scribbling and muttering about new ways to torture people!

There are also three wonderful ladies, who I may have only known for a handful of years, but their friendship and unwavering support mean the world to me. Jess Richardson, Sue John and Caz Finlay – thank you!

A special mention as well for Martina Cole and Kimberley Chambers. Reading their books since time began not only instilled in me an interest in the gangland genre, but gave me the incentive to write my own books too, so thank you, ladies.

Lastly, and certainly not least – thanks to all the readers. You give me the passion to keep writing and I hope you enjoy this book.

MORE FROM EDIE BAYLIS

We hope you enjoyed reading *Takeover*. If you did, please leave a review.

If you'd like to gift a copy, this book is also available as an ebook, digital audio download and audiobook CD.

Sign up to Edie Baylis's mailing list for news, competitions and updates on future books.

https://bit.ly/EdieBaylisnews

ABOUT THE AUTHOR

Edie Baylis is a successful self-published author of dark gritty thrillers with violent background settings. She lives in Worcestershire, has a history of owning daft cars and several motorbikes and is licensed to run a pub.

Visit Edie's website: http://www.ediebaylis.co.uk/

Follow Edie on social media:

 twitter.com/ediebaylis
 facebook.com/downfallseries
instagram.com/ediebaylis

ABOUT BOLDWOOD BOOKS

Boldwood Books is a fiction publishing company seeking out the best stories from around the world.

Find out more at www.boldwoodbooks.com

Sign up to the Book and Tonic newsletter for news, offers and competitions from Boldwood Books!

http://www.bit.ly/bookandtonic

We'd love to hear from you, follow us on social media:

facebook.com/BookandTonic

twitter.com/BoldwoodBooks

instagram.com/BookandTonic

Lightning Source UK Ltd.
Milton Keynes UK
UKHW040650020222
398065UK00001B/228